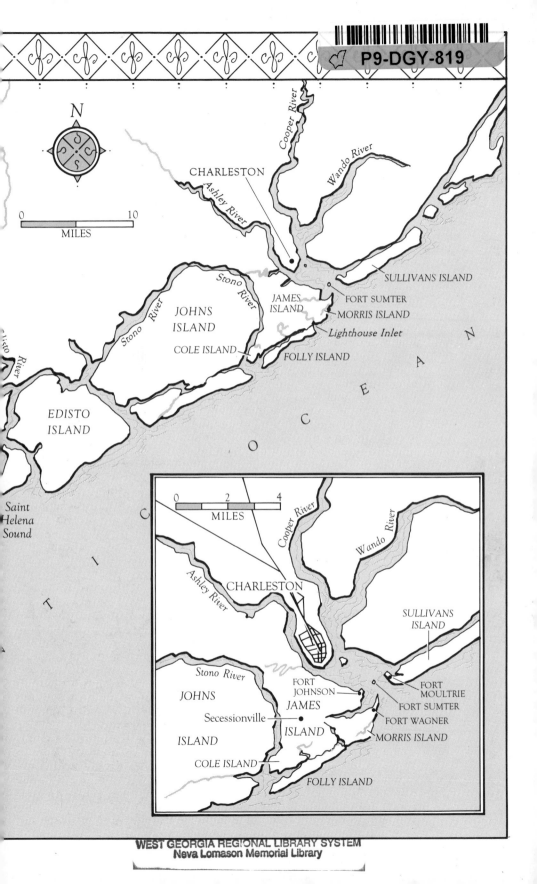

N

0   10
MILES

CHARLESTON

Cooper River

Wando River

Ashley River

Stono River

JOHNS ISLAND

Stono River

JAMES ISLAND

SULLIVANS ISLAND

FORT SUMTER

MORRIS ISLAND

Lighthouse Inlet

COLE ISLAND

FOLLY ISLAND

EDISTO ISLAND

Saint Helena Sound

A T L A N T I C   O C E A N

0   2   4
MILES

Cooper River

Wando River

Ashley River

CHARLESTON

SULLIVANS ISLAND

Stono River

FORT JOHNSON

JOHNS ISLAND

Secessionville

JAMES ISLAND

FORT MOULTRIE

FORT SUMTER

FORT WAGNER

MORRIS ISLAND

COLE ISLAND

FOLLY ISLAND

Fragments
of the
Ark

Other Books by Louise Meriwether

NOVEL

Daddy Was a Number Runner

CHILDREN'S BOOKS

The Freedom Ship of Robert Smalls
The Heart Man: The Story of Dr. Daniel Hale Williams
Don't Take the Bus on Monday: The Rosa Parks Story

Fragments of the Ark

Louise Meriwether

POCKET BOOKS

New York   London   Toronto   Sydney   Tokyo   Singapore

"I vision God . . ." (page 19) from "God" by E. C. L. Adams in *Nigger to Nigger,* with the permission of Stephen B. Adams and Adaline H. Adams.

"Oh, Lord, our deceased brother . . ." (page 20) from "Jeff's Funeral Sermon" by E. C. L. Adams, in *Congaree Sketches,* with the permission of Stephen B. Adams and Adaline H. Adams.

"Out of the Womb, Crying" by Samuel Allen, from *Every Round and Other Poems,* copyright © 1987, Lotus Press.

"A Course in Miracles: Manual for Teachers," copyright © 1975, Foundation for Inner Peace, Inc., Glen Ellen, CA. Used by permission.

Excerpts from this novel have appeared as short stories in a slightly different form in the following publications: *Freedomways Quarterly*, Vol. 25, No. 2, Summer 1985, New York, NY; *Essence* magazine, Feb. 1986, New York, NY; *The Harbor Review*, Nos. 5–6, 1986, University of Massachusetts, Boston, MA; and *The Black Scholar*, Vol. 19, Nos. 4 & 5, July–Oct. 1988, San Francisco, CA.

This book is a work of fiction. Many of the names, characters, places, and incidents are either products of the author's imagination or are used fictitiously.

POCKET BOOKS, a division of Simon & Schuster Inc.
1230 Avenue of the Americas, New York, NY 10020

Copyright © 1994 by Louise Meriwether
Endpaper map by GDS/Jeffrey L. Ward

Meriwether, Louise.
    Fragments of the ark / Louise Meriwether.
        p.   cm.
    ISBN: 0-671-79947-9
    1. South Carolina—History—Civil War, 1861–1865—Fiction.
    2. Afro-American men—South Carolina—Fiction.   3. Slaves—South
Carolina—Fiction.   I. Title.
PS3563.E788F73   1994
813'.54—dc20   93-29504
                                                                                  CIP

First Pocket Books hardcover printing February 1994

10   9   8   7   6   5   4   3   2   1

POCKET and colophon are registered trademarks
of Simon & Schuster Inc.

Printed in the U.S.A.

This one is for my brothers Kenneth and Edward Jenkins, for my niece, Eugenia; and for Joan Sandler and Rosa Guy whose loving friendship nurtures me.

Author's Note

I must give thanks to Robert Smalls, the Sea Island slave whose life was the inspiration for this work. More than twenty years ago I wrote a biography of him for little children and have been bugged ever since to do a fuller work. So I sat by his grave in Beaufort, took off my shoes, wiggled my toes in the grass, and begged his assistance. "I'm in over my head," I moaned. "For God's sake, help me." He did. The historical research that underpins this story was massive and is faithfully recorded. And although most of my characters are based on historical figures, their personal relationships—the words uttered by them when they made love or interacted with others beyond the interests of recorded history—have been developed by me.

I would like to acknowledge my lifeline, the research books I clung to as though demented, but they are too numerous. However, I must mention *A Brave Black Regiment* by Luis Emilio, which gave me an eyewitness account of the bloody war; *Rehearsal for Reconstruction* by Willie Lee Rose; and Dorothy Sterling's *Captain of the Planter*. Her thorough bibliography was a gold mine. And so were the stacks at Columbia University libraries and the librarian at the South Street Seaport Museum, whose brain I picked over the telephone. Talking about gold, let me not forget fellowships from the New York Foundation for the Arts and the Mellon Foundation.

Kind friends nurtured me during this stint: Temma Kaplan, Eileen Lottman, Connie Sutton, Antonio Laria, and Bill Ford—gone to his rest—and all my other darlings, including my Charleston cousins, Edna Robinson and Robert Birch. When I was desperate for refuge, Curtis Harnack always welcomed me warmly at Yaddo, as did the Virginia Center for the Creative Arts. I bless my agent, Ellen Levine, for keeping the faith. And my editor, Molly Allen, for her perceptive, gentle persuasion. I love you all.

Contents

Book One
In the
Beginning

Ladybug, ladybug, fly away home,
Your house is on fire
and your children will burn.

—NURSERY RHYME

1

Charleston, South Carolina
November 10, 1861

He had to go. The *Swanee* was delivering a company of artillerymen to Fort Beauregard in the morning before dawn. The bells of St. Michael's had already chimed curfew but still Peter hesitated, reluctant to leave without making peace. He stood in the kitchen facing Rain, his hand on the doorknob. Her hand held a bar of lye soap, her unbraided hair wild and tangled making her small face appear smaller.

"I is got to go," he said, not moving.

She nodded, not looking at him, her eyes sad, eyes you could drown in, Peter thought, and not know what swamped you because when you felt you knew Rain she was across the room or out the door, any place but where you expected her to be.

A wound had opened up between them, freshly cut, still bleeding, and he didn't know how it had happened. Rain could rush into a wall of silence so swiftly that her skirts rustled. Or else she spoke in tongues. Might as well be a foreign language for all he understood. She would mumble to herself, a low incomprehensible murmur, and when he inquired what she was talking about her answer was "Nothing." Aggravating. Nothing.

Peter reached out now to pat her shoulder, a gesture of reconciliation, but she backed away, angering him.

"What's wrong with you?" he yelled. "Suddenly I is poison? Talk to me, woman."

His raised voice startled their child who woke up crying.

"Hush," Rain said to them both.

She went into the front room separated from the kitchen by a sliding door that no longer worked. As she bent over the bed her distended belly looked as though it was about to drop between her knees. Awkwardly, she pulled the two-year-old girl into her arms.

"Hush, Glory. You daddy ain't hollering at you."

"I ain't hollering at nobody," Peter hollered. He stepped away from the door and attempting to be calm lowered his voice. "Just tell me why you is acting so daft."

Defiantly Rain retorted, "It gon be just another noose 'round your neck."

"I done told you, another chile ain't no noose."

Rain sucked her teeth, a sound of disgust to intimate that he was a liar. She had accused him of overlooking the first signs, the swelling of her belly, the heaviness in her small breasts, because he didn't want to see them. But why, he had countered, had she taken so long to tell him? He had yet to receive a reply.

Rain put Glory down and the child ran to hug her daddy's legs. He had been looking fierce, his craggy face made more rough-hewn by a short, bristly beard, his bushy eyebrows colliding in a frown. But the fierceness fell apart when he gathered Glory into his arms, his sunshine child, born in these two rooms he had secured by shoveling horseshit. Born in the only bed he had ever slept in, obtained for a suckling pig. Their table had cost him a bucket of shrimp, their stove a peck of corn. He was a bartering man with an eye for quality junk.

Before the war in order to earn extra money, since his regular wages went to his slavemaster, Peter had sold produce to a regular string of customers, produce he bought from slaves on James Island. And he had secured these two rooms in exchange for keeping the stable below clean and the horse groomed for his landlord. For her part, Rain brought home leftover food from her chambermaid's job and did sewing. For two years they had pinched every penny until it cried, watching their savings multiply to make good their plan, *his* plan that he had wrenched into existence. They had been bone weary but happy until things went amiss and Rain started talking in tongues. Such nonsense. A baby being a noose around his neck.

Glory bounced around in his arms and Peter kissed her, staring at his wife who was too pretty and tiny, he felt, to be so aggravating. Her face was a burnished brown as if the sun had set behind it and left its light in her eyes. They were a startling auburn color and her thick hair was a dark brown cloud. So naturally Peter had attempted to call her Brownie, which Rain said she hated. "Sounds like you is calling you dog." "No," he had whispered, kissing her, "you ain't no dog. You is my brown buttercup baby." She was also his honeybunch, his sweet li'l bits and his baby cakes. He couldn't seem to find enough cuddly names for her. Sometimes, smiling shyly which made her more adorable, she called him sugarfoot. And when had she last said that to him? Not since revealing with downcast eyes, as though ashamed, that they were going to have another child.

Peter walked toward the door. "I has to go," he repeated.

"Don't get youself hurt," Rain whispered.

That was better than speaking in tongues, he decided, grateful for small favors. He eased his daughter out of his arms.

"I is gone."

The *Swanee* was a whore, the fastest paddlewheel steamer sailing the inland waterways who had sold herself body and soul to the Confederates. A 24-pound howitzer mounted on her fantail and a 32-pounder on her bow had converted her from a trading vessel carting rice and cotton down Wappoo Creek into a military lady capable of transporting a thousand troops. Peter loved the steamer, whore though she was, but he despised working for the Confederates. Slaveowners were required to support the war effort by contributing laborers, and his master had loaned him to the navy.

On schedule, the *Swanee* had deposited the artillerymen at Fort Beauregard. On the other side of Port Royal Sound was Fort Walker and together the two ramparts guarded its entrance. At the moment fifteen Yankee gunboats in the harbor were blasting away at both fortifications with every piece of artillery on their decks. A returning fusillade of grape and shell burst against the hulls of the ships, exploding the sea into volcanic eruptions. The cataclysmic roar shook the little cove the *Swanee* was scurrying into for safety to allow her officers and seven-man slave crew a chance to watch the battle before sailing back to Charleston.

In the pilothouse Captain Regan was grim at the helm. "Peter," he yelled over the booming gunfire, "take the wheel."

"Aye, aye, suh."

He moved past the storage bench to grab the wheel as the captain relinquished it and they brushed past each other, both of them short, muscular, and barrel-chested, innate river men whose sturdy sea legs seemed to have been a deliberate act of God. But there the similarity ended. The stamp of Africa was on Peter, in the brownness of his face, the fullness of his lips and the curl of his hair. There was also a fullness around his jaw that promised jowls if he lived long enough.

Captain Regan was older and ruddy-cheeked, his signature the broad-brimmed hat he always wore aboard ship tilted at a rakish angle, his hair falling beneath it to his shoulders. He looked like what he was, a rough riverboat captain proud to be dressed in Confederate gray.

He picked up his field glasses from his writing desk and stared at the battle scene through the window. "Hold 'er steady, Peter," he yelled over his shoulder.

"Aye, aye, Captain." And steady he held her, telling himself to look as though he was about to cry. This ain't no time to be smiling, nigger, look like the officer yonder.

Standing at the rail outside the pilothouse Officer Malloy indeed appeared grief-stricken, his beliefs crumbling that they were invincible, that the Yankee scum wouldn't fight, the very Yankees who were shelling the guts out of the two Rebel forts.

Watching the action as best he could while steering the steamer toward shore, Peter was entranced. The harbor entrance, two and a half miles wide, was the battleground. The main Yankee squadron of ten boats ranged in a line ahead of the flanking squadron which bore north. Passing midway between the forts the main squadron turned southwest to train all of its guns on Fort Walker in an enfilading fire. The vessels of the line were head to tide and, when abreast of the fort, they passed by in slow succession to

6

avoid becoming a fixed target. Then the ships turned northeast to shell Walker with the port battery nearer than when first encountered. The bold maneuver, which was repeated, allowed the gunboats to concentrate their artillery first on Walker, the stronger of the two forts, and then on Fort Beauregard.

The warships were part of a massive armada of fifty-one vessels anchored outside the harbor, an invasion force of twelve thousand Yankee troops. Surf boats to land them were lashed to the sides of the ships which carried a cargo of several hundred horses, tons of anthracite coal, cement blocks, medical supplies, field ambulances and all manner of necessities required to dig in and set up house.

Peter steered the *Swanee* toward a shoreline which was cut into irregular patches of marsh and swamp. The steamer's chimney trailed cloudbursts of smoke as her paddlewheels sucked in the water, churned it into foam and spat it back into the river, the boat bouncing high as though responding to the thunderous gunfire in the bay. The engines were shut down and the *Swanee* drifted in with the tide. A flock of sea gulls hovering over a rice field beckoned the sailors to land.

Captain Regan had joined Officer Malloy at the rail outside the pilothouse and swept the bay with his naked eyes before seeking refuge again behind his field glasses. The Mate bounced up on the deck on his bandy legs, yelling for July to move his lazy ass forward and drop the anchor.

"Damn you, July. Forward, I say."

It wasn't July but Aaron who materialized from the fo'c'sle and moved toward the davit. "I got it, boss," he grinned, showing his rotten teeth.

At the wheel Peter winced, his usual reaction to Aaron who had a cast in one eye and looking like an idiot acted like one, rushing into every situation with an ingratiating smile.

July finally appeared. There was something about him that always provoked the Mate. Perhaps it was his beauty—chiseled features in a sculptured face—or the way he walked, lithe and sinuous like a black panther. The beast was caged but smoldering and refused to be hurried which now pushed the Mate beyond endurance, already incensed by enemy warships in his backyard.

"You lazy whoreson," he yelled. "You expect the anchor to

lower its goddamn self into this goddamn river?" An explosion of gunfire in the harbor answered the Mate slyly. Infuriated, he pulled out his pistol and slammed the butt of it against July's head. "You black baboon. Move your lazy ass."

July jumped backward and fell into a crouch. Peter, watching from the wheelhouse, was fearful his friend was going to finally jump the Mate and get himself killed in the bargain.

The Mate waved his pistol. "Move, nigger, or I'll blast all the jungle rot out of you."

July stiffened. Not now, Peter breathed silently. As though hearing him, July slowly straightened up. He sidled toward Aaron who had been watching him bug-eyed. Together they swung out the davits, and the anchor and chain clanked down the side of the boat. The captain and his officer had remained unperturbed, accustomed to the Mate's temper tantrums. He joined them at the rail to watch the battle.

Surreptitiously, the slave crew also watched while shamming doing their chores, the firemen in the boiler room, the deckhands keeping out of sight. Peter had discovered that the kerosene lamp in its gimbals needed cleaning. He removed the shade to wipe it clean and propped his back against the wheel, affording himself a panoramic sweep of the bay.

It was the most awesome sight he had ever seen. The Rebel forts were invisible beneath a haze of exploding shells and the ships themselves were ghostly phantoms. But when the smoke thinned and drifted he could make them out, steamers with their chimneys puffing, four-masted sloops with billowing sails, and the magnificent gunboats, their cannons all blasting. But most formidable of all was the forty-four-gun flagship leading the fleet—the *Wabash*—her heavy artillery firing about sixty shells a minute. She was pure majesty to Peter, a steam frigate with lofty rigging built for speed.

He had first glimpsed her earlier that morning while listening to the troops singing as they readied themselves for battle. They had sung in the Confederate forts while inspecting their rifles, then stuck them through the loopholes and aimed them out to sea. In the bellies of the Yankee ships free black men, who had volunteered for the labor battalion, sang while shoveling coal into the furnaces. Above them officers strode on the decks, their swords clanking against their thighs as they listened to the fifers lead the

8

sailors in song. At 8:30 A.M., Commander Du Pont aboard the *Wabash* gave the order to hoist anchor from the sea bottom. Sea gulls dipped their wings and followed the boats. Buzzards squatting in the pine trees on shore soared into the sky. The fleet moved slowly. The music preceded them, danced across the waves, and met the Rebel songs in midair.

The Union gunboats had been met by a Confederate flotilla led by Flag Officer Tattnal, an Annapolis man, who had quit the U.S. Navy when Georgia seceded. Peter identified his flagship as a river steamer and the other six boats as converted tugs. The flanking squadron engaged the flotilla to prevent them from raking the rear ships of the main line. Peter breathed easier when a shell ripped into Captain Tattnal's wheelhouse and the mosquito fleet beat a hasty retreat.

Now the Rebels no longer sang. Their blood was staining the ground in the forts and seeping into the sandbags the powder monkeys had piled high on the decks of the ships. The prize was Port Royal harbor itself. Control of it would cut communications between Savannah and Charleston and strengthen the Union blockade. No longer would it be so simple for British clippers to smuggle in supplies and ammunition to the Confederates. If the forts fell, the larger South Carolina Sea Islands and their plantations—one of the richest sections of the state—would come under Union control together with a long stretch of coastline from Georgetown to Florida. Only Charleston would still be Sesesh.

Peter watched the battle for what seemed like hours wondering if Rain, hearing these booming cannons, was thinking about him. His mother probably was. She lived with their owners in Beaufort, ten miles beyond Port Royal harbor, and was probably scared to death by all this commotion. The *Swanee* often stopped to refuel at Beaufort, and with a few minutes to spare Peter was able sometimes to race to the house to surprise her. Before the war he had seen her only a few times at Christmas. He had been eleven when taken from her.

That was the year their master, Roland Caine, pressured for cash, had sold several field hands, then cast an eye on him, his favorite, the boy he took on hunting trips and to his plantation to help distribute clothes to his slaves. Massa Roland was quality and that made Peter quality also, he felt, proud to be a houseboy living in Beaufort instead of a pickaninny field hand. When he mentioned that once to his mother she blistered his behind with her hickory switch, reminding him that she had been a pickaninny field hand herself. They all had to obey Massa so Peter had no call to be uppity and think he was special. He continued to believe otherwise until his owner considered selling him.

Fear of separation had been a longtime terror ever since he had seen his friend, Amen, when they were both six, chained to a long line of Negroes being led out of town, Amen not sucking his thumb as usual but howling, terrified. His daddy was howling, too, "Loose my son," and grabbing at the boy's chains even after the trader knocked him on the head with a pistol and one of his eyes filled with blood. Amen's daddy kept on running and shouting until two black men knocked him down and sat on him, both of them crying, too, and the trader threatening to shoot them all as the coffle shuffled down the road, their chains clanging.

Terrified, Peter ran home and heard Amen's screams all night long, even after his mother flung out an arm and pulled him into the warm curve of her back. The next day he told his friend Ellsworth, who was seven and Massa's son, the terrible fate of Amen and they both wept. Then they dug up some worms and dropped them into the lily pond in the garden because that seemed a fitting thing to do under the circumstances. A few years later Amen's fate became Peter's. Separation. But Mamma persuaded their owner not to sell her child but to let him hire out his time in Charleston. Massa Roland found him a lamplighting job there and left him with his sister-in-law.

Peter almost dropped the lampshade forgotten in his hand as a series of explosions in the harbor chased each other with a tremendous roar. Bilious black smoke, shot through with bursting rockets of flame, was devouring the sky above Fort Walker.

"Slimy bastards musta hit the ammo dump," the Mate yelled. Impotent with rage he seemed about to hurl his stubby self into the water and swim to the fort's defense.

Captain Regan swung his binoculars in a gradual arc. "The whole goddamn fort's on fire," he moaned.

Good, Peter silently gloated. He was familiar with the terrain of both forts. The *Swanee* had ferried slave labor to them, the masons and carpenters who had dug the exterior ditches and constructed

10

the slats on the seacoast side from palmetto logs with loopholes for sharpshooters. He stared at the exploding fort as if his vision could penetrate the smoke screen and identify the debris being catapulted into space—uprooted trees, the stock end of a cannon, the abbreviated torso of a man traveling in one direction, his left leg in another.

"The forts are gonna fall," Officer Malloy agonized. "Oh, my God."

Let them fall, Peter prayed. Below him on deck July had ceased all pretense of work, traumatized by the shriek of exploding shells. Slowly he turned as if Peter's gaze was a magnet and their eyes met, a secret glance which whispered that maybe, just maybe, the Yankees were kicking the shit out of the Sesesh.

"Aaaiiieeee."

The bloodcurdling Rebel yell startled Peter who this time dropped the lampshade.

"The *Wabash* is on fire," Captain Regan crowed. "She's been hit."

"The lead ship?" Officer Malloy asked, surprised.

With demonic glee the Mate leaped straight up into the air. "Sink, you seamy-eyed bitch."

"The *Susquehanna*'s in trouble, too," the captain gloated. "A fire's raging on her starboard side."

The fire had been too long with the *Susquehanna* and she limped out of the circle. Peter kept his eyes on the lead ship, feeling betrayed. He had not deliberately put his trust in the *Wabash*, but the sight of her, so grand in battle spitting destruction across the waves, had demanded faith.

The crowing of the three white men at the rail offended him. He pasted them together back to back as if they were cardboard figures and dumped them overboard—the captain who trusted him with his boat, the hateful Mate, and the officer who was a cross between the two, leaning whichever way the wind blew. They were no longer separate creatures that Peter liked, disliked, and tolerated, but extensions of that power which forced him to retreat inside himself murmuring, "Yes, suh, I is coming, suh," while he bided his time. Waiting.

"Goddamn," the Mate prophesied, "the forts ain't finished yet."

"Lord, have mercy," a deckhand cried out.

Peter recognized Stretch's voice before he saw him standing aft, casting a long, thin shadow. "Mercy, Lord, mercy," Stretch cried, praying for the ships.

Officer Malloy, misunderstanding and a good Baptist himself, shouted as though at a revival meeting. "Yes, Lord. Have mercy. The forts ain't finished yet."

You is a lie, Peter mumbled to himself.

"Weigh anchor," Captain Regan shouted. He was leaving while there was still a slight possibility of victory for his side.

Peter steered the *Swanee* through the inland waterways, a back alley of narrow, treacherous channels. Abundant tropical foliage, still green, imparted a balmy softness to the landscape. As they approached Charleston, elbows of chimneys and tilted roofs peeked out from between the trees, the tall spire of St. Michael's Church rising above it all. In every direction, other steeples poked themselves into God's eye, offering a place of worship to Anabaptists, French Huguenots, Presbyterians, Catholics, Jews, Quakers. There had once been an African Methodist Episcopal church but the city fathers had run its founder out of town and closed it down. But like Jesus Christ it would rise again.

Before the war Charleston harbor had been a bustling seaport, the city's heartbeat, but now there were only a few lonesome boats anchored in the slips at the wharf. The coastline was dotted with marshes and swamps and tidal streams that cut off the Sea Islands from the mainland. The closest one, James Island, was visible in the bay bristling with fortifications to protect the city. Visible too was the massive wall of Fort Sumter, the vanguard of the forts, built on a sand spit near the entrance to the harbor.

Charleston itself was like a sensuous woman lying in the arms of the Ashley River on the south and the Cooper River on the north, the harbor formed by their juncture. Seven and a half miles out the rivers merged into the Atlantic and beyond the bar sailed the blockading Union fleet.

"Five bells," the Mate growled as the *Swanee*'s crew disembarked, "and the nigger that's late will be flogged."

Peter walked down the gangplank flanked by his buddies, Brother Man, a brawny fireman, and July and Stretch. Behind

12

them came Turno, the other fireman, and the two deckhands he bullied into jellyfish, cross-eyed Aaron and Bite.

Turno, a hulking giant of a man, mumbled, "The Mate try to flog me I'll throw his ass overboard." He was as bellicose as the Mate and they studiously avoided each other. It was as if the fires Turno stoked burned on in his veins, keeping him inflamed and his black face wrapped around a snarl. There was bad blood between him and Peter. Turno resented a Negro wheelsman functioning as a pilot. Only the whites were called pilots.

The sound of gunfire had long ago ceased and the city seemed hushed, its docks ghostly with bales of cotton rotting on the piers.

"Wish we could find somebody what knows how the battle went at the forts," Stretch said. Loping alongside Peter, he came honestly by his nickname. Everything about him was elongated, his neck, his body, his skinny legs. And he was awkward, his joints meeting each other at odd angles.

Usually some Negro lurking around the telegraph station would get the news and pass it along the colored grapevine, but this evening no one was in sight.

July said with his usual pessimism, "Guess we'll find out the bad news soon enough."

"Why you say that?" Peter snapped. "The Yankees done won." His irritation stemmed from his own anxiety.

Brother Man made no comment. He was as hulking as Turno but gentler, and older than his mates. At Tradd Street, Turno and his two buckaroos, Aaron and Bite, parted company from the others.

"Wait for me," Brother Man said and joined them.

Peter called out. "Captain Regan say we gon sink torpedoes in the bay tomorrow morning. Five bells, you all."

"Nigger, I ain't deaf," Turno grumbled. "I heard the Mate."

Brother Man smiled fleetingly at Peter. "I'll be on time," he promised.

To Peter's surprise the two giants were friendly although radically different, one a mean-spirited bully and the other sweet-tempered. Turno never tried to ride roughshod over Brother Man though, perhaps sensing that beneath his quiet demeanor his rage was murderous when aroused. Once he came close to strangling his master who had accepted eight hundred dollars from him as agreed upon to buy his freedom but sold him instead. Brother Man had earned the money cutting and hauling logs in the dismal swamp for five years. It was his owner's sister who talked him out of killing her scoundrel brother, promising to take him to court herself which she did. But the judge ruled that a slave could not enter into a binding contract and that the money rightfully belonged to Brother Man's master.

"Turno is one evil nigger," Stretch said, when the firemen were out of earshot. "Why don't you punch him in his snout one day, Peter."

"Why don't you shut up for once," July snapped.

"And why is *you* so evil?" Stretch grinned at his friend. "You ain't gon see Mariah tonight? Is that's what's making you cranky? I hear tell her missy don't like you none, pretty though you be."

"You is as gossipy as an old woman," July complained.

"You ain't answer my question."

"How's about if I punch you in *your* snout?"

"Betcha I'm right. Betcha you gal's missy done told you to stop hunting pussy 'round there."

"Shut up, Stretch," Peter said mildly.

"Awright," he responded with good humor. He was silent for a few seconds and then began a running commentary on the defects of the Mate.

An impish smile turned up the corners of Peter's lips. "You is a goober head," he informed his friend. Telling Stretch to shut up, he thought, was like telling the sun not to rise. Mistuh Stringbean seemed scared that if he wasn't babbling like a brook he might dry up and blow away.

They continued up East Bay passing several warehouses and parted at the next intersection, Stretch and July repairing to their owners' premises where they lived.

Automatically Peter reminded them, "Five bells, mates."

"Hello," he said, pushing open his door. "I is home."

A whirlwind streaked across the front room, into the kitchen and into his arms. "Daddy!"

He picked up Glory and hugged her, his eyes on Rain. She was sewing lace on a garment for one of the ladies at the inn, and started to rise as he came across the room, then, as if restrained

14

by invisible bars, she sank back into her seat and bit her lips, punishing them for having whispered his name. Peter saw it all, the stifled cry of welcome, the way she pulled the sewing over her belly as though to shield their unborn child from his view. He ignored it, pretended that he was blind.

"We just got back from Fort Beauregard," he said, praying for normalcy. "You all heard the guns?"

Rain nodded. "Couldn't help but hear."

"We weren't in it, honeybunch," he said gently, realizing she had been worried. He sat down at the table, holding Glory on his lap. She curled up happily against him.

Their quarters were cramped and crude with nails hammered in the walls to hold their clothes. The bed, jammed in a corner, served as a couch in the daytime. Baskets of clothes waiting to be washed or ironed were lined up under a shelf in the kitchen which held Peter's charts and tools and the odds and ends he picked up to be bartered.

Rain kept her head bent, sewing assiduously. "Is you hungry? I brought some fish stew home from the inn."

"Not yet." Peter told her about the warships attacking the two Confederate batteries. "White folks 'round here must be half crazy with fear."

Rain nodded. "They scared we gon be attacked next. They was evil as satan at work today. You don't know nasty till white folks be vexed. You Uncle Hiram stop by like he often do to leave you word 'bout a Brotherhood meeting. He were only there a minute, mind you, but our manager had a fit. He holler at Uncle Hiram to get out 'fore he lash him heself."

"My God," Peter said, "he didn't . . . ?"

"Naw. You know you uncle. He bowed real low and walked away. He were walking mighty fast though. It were almost a trot."

Peter burst out laughing and Rain, too. It chased away his gloom, his unease, hearing her tinkling laughter.

"I knew 'bout the meeting, Rain. Maybe I'll mosey over to Uncle Hiram's house to find out what's what."

Hiram Jenkins was not really his uncle but an old friend of his mother's. She had made Peter promise when he left Beaufort a boy of eleven to look up Hiram who would befriend him.

Rain frowned, always worried when Peter was out after curfew, particularly now with everybody's teeth on edge.

"You don't have to go, does you?" Her voice was pleading.

Peter, wanting nothing more than to hold her safely in his arms forever, said huskily, "Naw, I don't has to."

Rain commenced sewing again and they fell into a companionable silence. Glory had fallen asleep and Peter rested his chin on the top of her head. Feeling a surge of sweetness he decided to explore it.

"Remember last year 'fore the war started when white folks was foaming at the mouth? Talking 'bout getting the slave trade started again so every piece of poor white trash could own heself a nigger? And saying they was gon pass a law to make free Negroes slaves?"

Rain nodded. "I does remember."

Colored folks had left the city in droves. In one day alone over three hundred freedmen had departed, headed for New York, Montreal, Haiti, selling their property for whatever little they could obtain. In the confusion slaves had also disappeared, most of them later apprehended.

"When things be shaky like now," Peter continued, feeling reckless, "that may be the time to make our move. To make a run for it."

Rain gave a little yelp and clutched her stomach.

"You awright?" Peter cried. "Is the baby . . ."

She shook her head.

"Something hurt? What's the matter?"

"Nothing." Rain sucked in a huge breath.

"Nothing? How you sound. It is so something. Tell me."

"How I gon make a run for it seven months along? How *you* sound." Her voice was a whiplash intended to remind him that unborn babies could be a noose.

"Rain, I is sorry, I didn't——"

"Don't say nothing to me."

She struggled to her feet and went into the kitchen. Minutes later Rain plucked the sleeping child from her husband's arms and slapped a bowl of stew down in front of him. Feeling miserable, Peter tried to eat and choked on a fishbone.

2

Charleston

1856

Peter and Rain met at a funeral. It was held on a Sunday in order to attract a crowd. Old Esau's funeral. At ninety-two he had been the oldest member of the Brotherhood and Uncle Hiram had promised to put him away in style.

Two white horses were pulling the lorry carrying the pine coffin. Lined up behind it were the Brotherhood men wearing jaunty red scarves to signify their social ties. They were Old Esau's family, his wife was long dead and his children sold away years ago. The musicians were next in line, quietly carrying their instruments, followed by church members, friends, and total strangers. In his coffin the old man was rather cramped but not complaining, wearing a moth-eaten suit he had saved thirty years for his burying.

It was a raggedy procession because folks waiting on the side-lines kept jumping into it. Two women in long rustling skirts were suddenly marching next to Peter, one of them tiny and pretty, wearing a green head wrap.

"Hello," he said, and made himself known. "I is Peter Mango. And what might you name be?"

"Rain."

17

"So how long you knowed Old Esau?" he asked, making conversation.

"Who?"

"The fellow we is burying."

"Didn't know him at all, but I wants to pay my respects."

It seemed as if the entire colored population of Charleston had come to pay their respects and do Old Esau proud. The pine box fascinated Peter and he stared at it speculatively. Would he be cramped in it? Could he breathe? With a few well-placed holes could a living body hide in it and be driven safely to Philadelphia, maybe? He stole a look at Rain, caught her eye and smiled.

When the procession reached the outskirts of town, the trumpet player raised his horn to his lips. Let the music begin. The drummer came in on the downbeat and then the fiddler. A woman's soprano soared over the treetops.

> . . . Joshua fit the battle of Jericho
> and the walls came tumbling down . . .

They were all singing, the drumbeat lending wings to their feet, banishing weariness. In his coffin Old Esau tapped his foot in time with the music. He had always loved that song, imagining himself to be like Joshua, tumbling down the walls.

At the colored cemetery the weeping willows kneeled to the ground and the few headstones that existed leaned sideways away from the wind. The pine box was laid beside an open grave and the mourners faced Preacher Thomas Large who would deliver the sermon, although it was against the law. In fact, the entire procession was against the law, black people forbidden to congregate in groups of five or more without a white person present. But colored funerals were such protracted affairs that no white minister wanted to be so bothered.

Preacher Large was famous for his spellbinding sermons delivered in praise houses situated deep in the woods which slaves had to sometimes attend surreptitiously. Lanky and dark-skinned, he wore a black sombrero, his pants tucked inside his boots western style like a man used to moving at lightning speed with never a backward glance.

Hiram handed each Brotherhood member a single rose which

his fat wife, Helen, had picked earlier. Peter positioned himself next to Rain who was stealing glances at him, at the way he stood flat-footed, his calves curved backward like a scythe. In time she would come to love the way his calves poked out like that against his trousers—and when he pulled them off and his muscular legs pinned her willingly down. But at the moment she was just looking.

The testimonials for Esau began, interspersed with singing. Hiram spoke for the Brotherhood, extolling the virtues of the dear departed. The porters were heard from next, a long eulogy: the old man had once worked with them. A teary woman spoke for the church choir, and on and on the tributes went. Finally, Preacher Large delivered his sermon looking down at the pine box with his fierce, raking eyes which had seen hellfire and the coming of the Lord. He spoke about the trials and tribulations of Esau who, by the time he had hired himself out and saved enough to buy his freedom, was already an old man. But he had not deserted them, just gone ahead to prepare a place for them on high. The preacher chanted:

> I vision God standing on the heights of heaven
> Throwing the devil like a burning torch
> Over the gulf into the valleys of hell,
> His eye the lightning's flash
> His voice the thunder's roll.
> With one hand he snatched the sun from its socket
> And the other he clapped across the moon.

The congregation moaned, "Our God is mighty."
"Preach, Brother Large."

> Yes, our God is mighty
> And we are poor pilgrims
> Poor pilgrims of sorrow
> Sometimes we don't know where to roam
> But we've heard of a city called Heaven
> And are trying to make it our home.

"Yes, we is."

19

"Jesus. Bless thy holy name."

> Oh Lord, our deceased brother was born in sin
> And he died in Christ.
> He sold his lot in Egypt
> And he bought a lot in Paradise.

Ashes to ashes . . .

The Brotherhood flung their roses on top of the coffin. The mourners were in a frenzy, possessed by the spirit, praying they would be liberated from this vale of tears in the sweet by-and-by if not sooner. They stamped their feet, their undulating bodies praising God. Praise His holy name. Hiram's wife threw up her hands, tucked her head under, and executed several fast steps which suspiciously resembled dancing. "I'm gon shout my way to heaven," she cried. "I'm gon sell my lot in Egypt." Tears rolled down her cheeks.

Rain was suddenly screaming, a high piercing sound that curdled Peter's blood. "Mamma," she cried. "Tonk. Alfred. Jamie."

Each name was punctuated by a wail as she flung wide her arms to embrace the invisible. Then she was trembling and would have fallen had Peter not caught her. She sobbed uncontrollably against his chest, so tiny, so stricken, while he dabbed at her tears with his red scarf, touched by her grief.

The procession left the cemetery to the beat of the drums, singing the old songs on their way home, Rain clinging to Peter's hand. They passed a stream and Hiram performed the last ritual. He dropped a white hibiscus into the water and the mourners, knowing its destination, watched it swirl and eddy then right itself and head downstream.

Inside the pine box there was stillness. Old Esau's soul had finally fled. It was curled inside the flower, floating toward the river that emptied into the Atlantic Ocean and would carry him back to the motherland, home to Africa.

Rain was the property of Kenneth Rodman, a banker. Usually on Sundays he allowed her to take the ferry to James Island to visit her daughter and sister on a nursery farm. Peter, acutely smitten, was distressed upon learning that Rain was a mother but naturally anybody so pretty would be taken and he was a donkey's ass for not having realized that.

"Is you baby's daddy here in Charleston?" he asked.

"He ain't in it," Rain replied. "I'm all that Zee's got."

They often met on the ferry come Sunday when they were both returning from James Island. Peter was loaded down with vegetables and fruit toted in a large basket on his head, bought from Sea Island slaves who were allowed to cultivate little plots on their own. He was finding it difficult to court Rain.

"I cain't go out walking with no man," she told him, refusing his request to accompany her home. "You best get them cabbages to your customers 'fore that big basket puts a knot on your head."

In time his persistence prevailed and they did go out walking, Peter falling desperately in love. Kenneth Rodman had brought Rain to Charleston three years ago and made her accompany him to church every Sunday where he was a deacon sitting downstairs and she upstairs in the gallery. Afterward, with the rest of the day off, she scooted over to James Island. Peter kept questioning her about Zee's daddy but Rain was as closemouthed as she was pretty.

"Why you keep pestering me?" she protested, her burnished eyes flashing, her bottom lip poked out.

" 'Cause I is a jealous man."

"Well you ain't got no cause so stop you hounding."

He persisted and she disappeared into a fortress of silence. To coax her out he talked about himself.

"Does you know 'bout the Citadel, Rain? That it was on account of a black man they built it?"

Her eyes widened with surprise. It was a Sunday afternoon and they had been walking. Silently. At Marion Square they paused to look at the massive stone fortress behind it, the Citadel, four stories high with thick impregnable walls and several cannons in the wide courtyard. Peter related the story to Rain as it had been told to him by Uncle Hiram and he also told her about Delia.

It had all occurred when he first came to Charleston, a boy of eleven, Mamma left behind in Beaufort. He finally looked up her friend, Hiram Jenkins, not so much because he had promised his mother to do so but because the slaves he lived with in a room above the carriage house were so hateful.

First off Stubby, the coachman, informed him, "Massa Pope don't like pickaninnies so I don't know why he letting you live here."

Stubby's ferocious look indicated that the boy's tenure in the slave quarters would be short and miserable, which seemed to be exactly what Delia, the cook, had in mind. The pickaninnies that Cuthbert Pope could not abide had been her children, all four of them, which he had sold as soon as they could toddle. The youngest one, Nooky, Delia had been led to believe she could keep because he had reached the age of ten before she woke up one morning to find him gone. Sold. And his daddy, too. And now they had given her this stump from Beaufort to feed?

It was more than a body could bear, she grumbled, and boxed Peter's ears because he was still a boy but smelled like a man. "Haul that tub out to the yard, Mistuh Stink, and wash youself." Or she didn't like the corner where he had left his pallet and would kick it elsewhere and then complain. "I is got to fall over you mess every time I come into this room? You is trying to maim me?" She was a short, dumpy woman but her arms were long enough to slap him up beside his head a couple of times a day. The other servants who shared their quarters complained that it had been crowded enough before Peter had been stuck in there.

In exchange for his board he was required to help Stubby keep the stables clean, the horses groomed, and run errands for Loretta Pope. She wasn't as nice as her sister, Peter's mistress in Beaufort, a gentle woman who had never struck him. Missy Loretta had no such sentiments and boxed his ears. She was considered a beauteous southern belle, with smoky gray eyes, a cinched-in waist and the hauteur of a queen. During Charleston's social season she hosted huge parties and pressed Peter into service, dressing him up in red velvet britches. He disliked those evenings intensely, standing at the sideboard motionless until beckoned. When her husband, Cuthbert, complained that she spent money like water, Loretta bitterly reminded him of her station. She had not come to him penniless but with a substantial dowry including a plantation, but he was reducing her to a beggar. He drank heavily and they quarreled often.

Cuthbert Pope did not flog Peter, who was not his property, but used his fists instead. A fist could blacken a boy's eye, bloody his clothes, and scramble his brains so that he fell out from dizziness. Peter fled from home to find Hiram Jenkins. "Tell him," Mamma had said, "that you is Lily Mango's boy."

Peter liked Hiram instantly. He was a heavyset dark-skinned man, his height and breadth commanding but also so comforting that Peter was ready to hold his hand and be led anywhere. It was a trait Hiram had honed, leading people around so effortlessly they barely noticed it. His fleshy face was hairless and so was his head almost, only a few lonesome gray knots growing on it like cactus in a desert.

They became a fixture walking about town, the balding plum-black man and the chubby boy. At the Battery wall staring at the sea-green water, Hiram showed him the spot where the Cooper and Ashley rivers merged. Then they strolled in White Point Gardens admiring the elegant mansions on South Battery.

At Meeting and Broad streets Hiram told him, "This here intersection is the white folks' heart." On each corner were massive colonnaded buildings, their pillars holding up the City Hall, the County Courthouse, the Guard House, and St. Michael's Episcopal Church whose bells tolled the hour and warned Negroes at sundown to get their black selves home.

The grandeur of the city impressed Peter, but best of all were the people patting his head and exclaiming, "Lily Mango's boy from Beaufort? Ain't that nice." Said it whether they knew Lily Mango or not, which most of them didn't. Hiram knew them all, the street vendors pulling their carts and singsonging their wares, the Negro craftsmen who owned their little shops, and the colored folks who hawked produce in the stalls on Market Street behind a portico which was a roost for buzzards, the city's scavengers.

But Peter closed his eyes when passing the slave mart, refusing to look at a young girl on the auction block, naked to the waist, being sold to the highest bidder. Or coming across a black man's severed head stuck on a pike outside of town, flies buzzing in his eye sockets and in his blood-caked mouth.

"Open your eyes, boy," Uncle Hiram would growl, walking alongside of him. "How can you remember if you don't see the shit they're throwing in your face? Smell it and eat it, if need be, with your eyes wide open. They may blind you but don't blind yourself." Stubbornly, the boy kept his eyes closed.

Hiram's favorite spot in the city was the Citadel. "They built it on account of a black man thirty some years ago," he told Peter one day and whispered the name as though it might still get him hung. "Denmark Vesey."

"He was a free man by then, bought himself after winning an East Bay lottery. At the time I'm telling you about he owned about eight thousand dollars' worth of property. But his children were all slaves because their mammas were and that riled him. I think he had seven wives and maybe more than one at a time." Uncle Hiram chuckled. "Denmark was a genius, not just with women but in organizing men."

According to witnesses at the trials, about nine thousand slaves from the surrounding countryside had been involved in the insurrection plotted by Denmark Vesey. He justified their right to exterminate their oppressors by quoting from his authority, the Bible. "Behold, the day of the Lord cometh," Hiram quoted, "and thy spoils shall be divided in the midst of thee. For I will gather all nations against Jerusalem to battle, and the city shall be taken and the houses rifled, and the women ravished and half of the city shall go forth into captivity."

Peter was spellbound. "That's in the Bible, Uncle? Those very words?"

"Zechariah, chapter fourteen." Briefly he outlined the insurrectionary plot. Denmark carefully picked for his lieutenants slaves who were so trusted by their masters they had freedom of movement, including three servants of the governor. The slaves were organized into blocks, each with its leader, and commissioned to make bayonets, pike heads, musket balls and to steal powder and combustible fuses from the arsenal. Sites were duly noted where weapons could be obtained at the appointed hour. Each lieutenant was given a specific assignment, and they were to strike simultaneously at several locations, kill every white person they met, and any black who stood in their way. "He that is not with me is against me," Hiram stated. "Luke, chapter eleven, verse twenty-three."

The plan was to take over a ship in the harbor and sail to Haiti where slaves had successfully revolted and were free. Peter's excitement mounted. He was riding with Denmark, a dagger in one hand, a musket in the other, his thighs pressed tightly against his horse.

"The insurrection was betrayed," Hiram said, his face stony, "by a house slave who was invited to join it."

"Betrayed?" Peter repeated, crestfallen.

Betrayal meant the hangman's noose for Denmark Vesey who refused to confess and went to the gallows unrepentant with four of his lieutenants. It meant bloody reprisals throughout the Southland and the arrest of hundreds of slaves. To save themselves—to be banished rather than hung—many pointed a shaky finger at their neighbors. The gallows accepted them, one by one, and stretched their necks into the next world.

"But white folks were still terrified, Peter, ever fearful of having their pale throats slit while they slept. They considered what Denmark had been. A free man. A Bible class leader in the African Methodist Episcopal church. And a sailor who had traveled with his master, who was a slave trader, to the West Indies and Africa. So they passed laws to hinder all those things, strangling us free Negroes with more restrictions as if we didn't have enough already. The A.M.E. church, built and owned by us, had always been raided, accused of being abolitionist. This time they closed it down entirely and banished our founder. And they jailed all black seamen entering our ports until their boats left. Didn't want them to contaminate us with notions of freedom. That caused an uproar in foreign countries, jailing their folks like that. And finally, Peter, they built that there Citadel, a fortress where white folks could be assembled to protect them from black folks with freedom on their minds."

"Tell me again," Peter begged, "what Denmark Vesey said 'bout slavery."

"That it's an abomination."

"I mean from the Scriptures, 'bout killing we enemies."

"And they utterly destroyed all that was in the city, both man and woman, young and old, and ox and sheep and ass with the edge of the sword."

"You didn't tell me that one before."

"Well I'm telling you now."

"You sure it's in the Bible? Just like that?"

"Joshua, chapter six, verse twenty-one."

"Was you in it, Uncle? Was you one of them riding with——"

Infuriated, Hiram grabbed Peter by his neck and lifted him clean off the ground. "Are you an unreconstructed fool? Don't let your tongue rattle around loose in your head like that."

"I is sorry."

But Peter was certain Uncle Hiram had been among the chosen. And he had to read those Bible passages his own self. That was a certainty also.

In time he did. Uncle Hiram bought him a primer and began teaching him to read at odd moments, secretly, of course, since it was against the law, an edict constantly bent out of joint. Hiram had been educated in a Negro church school for free children which slave children also ingenuously attended. Supposedly they were delivering laundry or coal or were there on some other pretext, their schoolbooks hidden in their clothing.

Peter, happily obsessed, took to wearing a floppy hat in sunshine and rain, his primer tucked beneath it so he could study at any spare moment. Dodging a backhanded slap from Delia one afternoon, his schoolbook fell to the floor. Pouncing on it like a vulture, she took it to her mistress. Outraged, Loretta Pope beat Peter over the head with a stick until his nose bled.

When Peter's master visited Charleston he was apprised of the boy's sins and angrily threatened to sell him. Peter was duly frightened. Sell him? At one of the slave auctions held every week at Ryan's jail? He was to be chained in a coffle, marched to Georgia and disappear forever? Never to see Mamma again? Or Uncle Hiram and his friends? Terrified, he dug a hole under the pecan tree next to the carriage house and buried his primer.

Delia's turn came next. She burned the roast for a party, insisted it was an accident, but Cuthbert Pope roared that she had been insolent in front of his guests and he intended to whip all the sass out of her. So saying he tied her hands to a beam in the stable and flogged her with his whip until she was bloody. Peter was a horrified witness as was Missy Loretta, who attempted to stop her husband after the first few lashes and Delia screaming, "Mercy, Massa. Oh God. Somebody. Have mercy."

"That's enough, Cuthbert. Cut her down." Loretta didn't think highly of colored people but there were exceptions and Delia was one of them.

But Cuthbert Pope seemed possessed with the whipping, his face crimson with anger. "Bloody bitch," he shouted and Peter didn't know whether he was cursing poor Delia or Missy who was struggling with him, trying to grab hold of the whip.

"You want to kill her?" she cried. "Stop it."

Violently Cuthbert flung his wife away from him, sending her crashing into the wall.

"It's me you really want to whip," she screamed and ran crying from the stable.

He whipped Delia until a bone protruded from her bloody back and he was exhausted. She was unconscious when Stubby and another servant cut her down, and Peter helped them carry her to the carriage house. He ran to fetch water in an earthen jug and watched Stubby attempting to staunch the flow of blood, tears in the old man's eyes. They took turns sitting by Delia's pallet all night, trying to keep her fevered brow cool with some evil-smelling herbs in a gunnysack.

It was around midnight when she came to herself and stared at the shadow squatting beside her. "Boy," she whispered. "That you?" She never called Peter anything but boy. "Is that you, Nooky?"

Peter thought a lie might comfort her. "Yes, ma'am."

But Delia, though pain-ridden and delirious, knew her own child from an impostor. With the strength of a madman she rose up and screamed, "Liar," and hurled the water jug at his head. He ducked and it cracked open on the floor.

Weeks later, when she was somewhat recovered, Peter moved out of their room to a corner of the stable. He found the horses preferable to Delia.

"She's a bitter pill," Uncle Hiram said. "Poor thing. She never got over her husband being sold, too, after all of their children. He was a man that could gentle her down." She was a woman, Peter felt, who needed plenty of gentling.

Then came the day they took Delia away, threw her into an isolated hole in the workhouse to await her trial. It was brief, the charges read and the prisoner found guilty of attempted murder, of feeding her master daily a minute quantity of poison in his turtle soup, his chicken broth, his lamb stew. Cuthbert Pope did not die from Delia's ministrations only because she used a touch too much one evening, perhaps her hands shook, and his stomach rebelled. A doctor hastily called—who had been involved in a similar case—uncovered the foul play.

Peter stood outside the workhouse the day the verdict was rendered. The judge ruled Delia was to be hung promptly and without fanfare. There would be no glaring headlines to nourish another trusted cook into becoming a would-be assassin.

Delia emerged from the workhouse in chains between two guards, half carried, half dragged to a coach for her trip to the gallows two miles outside of Charleston. She stumbled, almost fell, and as she was hauled to her feet she saw Peter.

"Boy," she mumbled.

"Yes, ma'am."

"Peter?" It was the first time she had ever called him by his name. "Peter," she repeated more firmly and nodded to herself. Her eyes were not glazed, not crazy, but her lips had parted to curl at the corners.

Was she in pain? Peter wondered. Were her chains too tight? Or had Delia smiled at him?

The next day he dug up his speller from under the pecan tree.

"Poor Delia," Rain groaned, when Peter told her about the cook. "It's so hard for a mother to lose her chile."

Peter said, "It be hard for a father, too," remembering Amen's daddy. "Maybe your daughter's daddy misses——"

"No," Rain interrupted, agitated. "He . . . he don't know her." Peter appeared puzzled and she explained. "He went away."

"With his master?"

She nodded.

"Did you love him?"

"No," Rain whispered sadly.

On those Sunday afternoons not spent with Rain, and after delivering his produce, Peter attended meetings of the benevolent society founded by Hiram, the Brotherhood for Justice and Equality for People of African Descent. He paid his dues which went into a burial and pension fund and listened to the articles Hiram read aloud which could get them all jailed. Periodically Negro seamen from the North smuggled abolitionist pamphlets to Hiram, bypassing the postmaster's zeal for consigning such seditious material to his regular bonfires. Consigned to flames as well were the homes of "nigger lovers," critics of slavery, sometimes with the critic inside being charred to a crisp. This naturally created a steady exodus of liberal white folks to safer ground.

This Sunday afternoon the meeting was well under way in the storage room of Trinity Methodist Church when Peter arrived. The room was filled with old files, dusty boxes, and spiders spinning cobwebs in the corners. Hiram sat at a rickety table amid the clutter, a kerosene lamp at his elbow, and a large open Bible in front of him. The Bible was his shield. Beads of perspiration danced on his balding head, the room was hot and windowless. A dozen or so Brotherhood members faced him perched on stools.

Peter eased into a seat next to Gimpy, the glazier. The men were discussing the financial problems of Widow Johnson and her five children. The little pension she received from the Brotherhood— her husband had been a member—was proving woefully inadequate. Samuel, the ironworker, offered to hire her oldest boy in response to Hiram's request for help.

"Good. I'm sure Widow Johnson will be most grateful." Hiram leaned over the table, blessing Samuel with a warm smile of appreciation, his head slightly tilted to one side, a habit of his, especially when he was listening to someone's troubles, completely absorbed. He opened the table drawer that was lined with a cardboard picture of Jesus Christ and extracting from under it a newspaper, waved it in the air.

"Here's a little something which swam down to us from Boston."

The Brothers chuckled. Peter sat up straighter. He hoped it was his favorite, the *North Star,* written by Frederick Douglass, a runaway slave who was now a fiery abolitionist. Or Lloyd Garrison's paper, *The Liberator.* That man hated slavery so fiercely it was sometimes hard to remember he wasn't a darky.

"You all remember that article that was in the *Mercury* a few weeks back?" Uncle Hiram asked. "About an abolitionist name of John Brown? I read it to you."

The Brothers did indeed remember. The *Charleston Mercury* had called John Brown the scum of the earth, castigating him and his band of cutthroats for murdering five settlers in cold blood on the banks of the Pottawatomie River in Kansas.

Peter understood that the bloodletting in Kansas was about land. And about them. Colored folks. Slaves. Uncle Hiram had spelled it out fully at earlier meetings. It was a question of economics and political power. For nearly forty years whenever a new state applied to join the Union the North and South quarreled ferociously, South Carolina constantly threatening to secede and drag the rest of the South along with her. They demanded that the new states be slave while the North demanded that they be free. Congress always pried the belligerents apart with compromises but blood was spilled in Kansas. Both the Pro-Slavers and Free Soilers rushed settlers into the area to decide the matter by vote and in the process raid farms, stuff ballot boxes, and shoot each other's brains out. But being against slavery in the territory did not mean Free Soilers necessarily welcomed competition with freedmen. Most of them wanted the land for white men only.

"This article sheds more light on John Brown's raid than the *Mercury* reported," Uncle Hiram said.

"Uh huh," the Brothers grunted, suspicious of whatever the *Charleston Mercury* printed. The newspaper was edited by one of the Rhetts, a powerful slaveholding family that for years had advocated secession.

Hiram quickly read the piece which reported that a band of Pro-Slavers on horseback had ridden into Lawrence, a Free Soil settlement, and sacked it, killing the livestock and burning the place to the ground. In retaliation, John Brown and his followers rode to the Pottawatomie and killed five of the marauders. Brown, a fervent abolitionist and former Underground Railroad conductor, declared that he was an instrument of God.

Peter felt a thrill of excitement. The killings were terrible but also grand. *Behold, the day of the Lord cometh . . . and the city shall be taken and the houses rifled, and the women ravished . . .*

As if reading his mind, Gimpy, the glazier, shook his head, his double chins trembling. "Vengeance is mine sayeth the Lord," he intoned solemnly.

Hiram suddenly stiffened, his head cocked toward the door and the Brothers also became a listening post. A floorboard had creaked outside the storage room, a deliberately weakened floorboard. Footsteps were approaching. Hiram opened the table drawer and slipped the newspaper under the cardboard picture of Jesus Christ, a sanctuary for the seditious.

Their minister, Reverend Damon, stuck his head through the door followed by his pot belly, his presence legitimizing the meeting. He was a huge man with a booming voice to cast out devils and make his flock tremble in fear at the wrath of God. And he was also Hiram's guardian—a requirement for every free Negro—and had bailed him out of jail more than once for conducting illegal meetings at his house.

After the A.M.E. Church had been shut down following the Denmark Vesey affair, the benevolent societies which had used its facilities went underground and for years their meetings were raided and their leaders jailed. Reverend Damon was among those who protested that it was ridiculous to forbid blacks to meet to pool their money and bury their dead. Since they intended to congregate anyway despite laws to the contrary, common sense dictated that their meetings should be conducted openly under watchful eyes. He joined those pressuring the Methodists to allow Negroes to have a separate church again, but this time under a white minister, himself, instead of a colored rabble-rouser who might preach insurrection.

"Am I interrupting your meeting?" he asked.

"We were just about to finish with a reading from the Bible, suh." Hiram glanced down, read several lines from First Corinthians, chapter 1, then closed the good book with a flourish.

"Amen," Peter intoned along with the Brothers, nodding his head piously.

He noticed how sweetly Reverend Damon smiled at Uncle Hiram, their Bible class leader. The two were fond of each other within the boundaries allowed, one man duty-bound to vigilance, the other man duty-bound to subvert it. Having done his duty by putting in an appearance, Reverend Damon led the Brothers upstairs into the light.

Left behind in the table drawer, Jesus Christ finished reading the Boston newspaper.

Peter was making progress with Rain, gaining her affection. He kept on talking, trying to draw her out, but naturally kept some of his business to himself about other women—specifically about that time when he was fifteen and with his master's permission was working on the docks unloading the vessels that sailed into Charleston harbor from every port in the world. Their crews were human flotsam who had set out to sea to avoid debtor's prison, the hangman's noose, two or three wives, or their offspring. Men with hooks for hands, wooden pegs for legs, and many a black patch over a missing eye. They were a swaggering, dangerous lot and Peter was intrigued. Whatever else they were, the mates were free in a way no landlubber was, or so it seemed to him, as they cursed lustily, pissed in the wind, and indulged in the eternal hunt for cunt.

A Jamaican cook on a British frigate proudly displayed a cutlass scar on his back to Peter. His feet had failed him, he explained, not leaping quickly enough out of the wench's bed when her husband burst in upon them. But it was worth it, he grinned, licking his lips and pulling Peter along to a whorehouse.

Peter was all eyes and a clinical curiosity until his insides exploded under the girl's practiced hand. And she was a girl, as young as himself and a black beauty. A few days later, in love but penniless, Peter returned to the brothel alone. His beloved slammed the door in his face, but not before he saw sprawled on her cot a white sailor. Hurt and angry, Peter backed away, his whoring days ended.

The following year he was seriously infatuated with Saralee who was quick-witted and pretty with a mind of her own. One Sunday afternoon while Peter was waiting for her in their usual trysting place, Saralee's master appeared in her stead, a broad-shouldered lumberjack carrying an axe. He pinned Peter up against a wall.

"Boy," he said, his voice calm but the pulse in his temple twitching, "if you even smell Saralee's pussy I'll chop off your prick." And with that threat he strode away.

Peter had not smelled her pussy, although he had tried. But her master, that swine, had more than smelled it? He had wiped himself on sweet Saralee? Peter yearned to kill him deader than a bloated fish floating belly up in the river. But he was also scared. No doubt about that. Nonetheless he dared to see Saralee again.

"You is one stubborn nigger," she told him, not without a smidgen of admiration. "Massa's gon buy me a loom and set me up in business. What you gon get me?"

He realized Saralee knew the answer before posing the question, that she could depend upon him for a lifetime of slavery and perhaps widow's weeds. Saralee acquired her loom and in time two mulatto children and Peter's undying enmity.

At the time he met Rain, Peter was working at a shipyard as a rigger and sailmaker. He had become adept at steering the cutters and sloops they repaired through the treacherous marshes without cracking them up. At ebb tide the creeks and coastal rivers emptied themselves into the ocean, leaving boats grounded on the sandbars. At flood tide the waters rushed in again to float the vessels free. Peter learned the location of the shoals and reefs and how to race a vessel with the tide.

His favorite task when he was not delivering a boat was working high up on the riggings attaching new sails to the masts, with the harbor spread out like a fan below him. Vessels sailing to and fro spanked the water into foam, their sails glistening in the sun. Squat-nose tugs towed in the ocean-going ships which had been waiting beyond the bar for a swelling tide. Which one should he stow away on, Peter often wondered. Which vessel would not return him to bondage if he were caught or toss him overboard to the sharks?

Delivering a yacht up the Stono River once to its owner in St. Paul's Parish, Peter studied the site of the Stono Rebellion which Uncle Hiram had told him about. Here, almost eighty years ago, black men shouting liberty had raided a shop and armed themselves with guns and ammunition, killing the two shopkeepers and every white person they met. By the time the insurrectionists were captured, or became outlaws, twenty white men and forty Negroes were corpses. And a few years later, in a similar attempt to escape from bondage, a hundred or so slaves plotted to break into the Charleston arsenal and take over the city. Their plot was betrayed, fifty slaves were ambushed and hung at the rate of ten a day.

As a boy Peter had closed his eyes, refusing to witness sights which had terrified him. As a man he nourished himself on revolts of the past, thwarted though they may have been.

*   *   *

Once a month on payday, before trudging to his quarters in the carriage house, Peter delivered his wages to Loretta Pope to hold for his master. This afternoon she was not in. He left the money with the cook and was heading for the back door when someone called his name.

"Peter. Is that you?"

He turned around. Young master Ellsworth Caine, his former playmate, Massa's son, was walking toward him from the vestibule. They had met infrequently down through the years, more so recently since Ellsworth was attending Charleston College. He looked bloated to Peter, all soft baby fat which his father complained was foppish, although it was he who insisted that his son remember his station in life. Ellsworth interpreted that to mean to live like an Arabian prince.

"How is you, suh?" Peter addressed him respectfully.

"A bit under the weather, I'm afraid. Too much Irish whiskey last night."

Their boyhood friendship was a thing of the past, a relic which Peter sometimes dusted off but not too often since Ellsworth seemed to have forgotten it entirely. They had been inseparable until the tutor had arrived and insisted that his charge stop rolling around in the mud with underlings and learn the responsibilities of being a gentleman, a position Roland Caine reinforced. Ellsworth had remained defiant for months until finally he capitulated and informed Peter one day about their changed relationship. "I'm the master, you're my slave and must do whatever I say or I'll have you flogged."

Peter laughed until his mother threatened to cure his obstinacy by snatching all the black off his behind herself. The next day Ellsworth invited him to climb up on his pony behind him as in days of old. Stubbornly Peter declined. "I is too busy, *Massa.*" Ellsworth did not order him to comply but spurred his mount viciously and galloped away. They never rode together again, the chasm between them daily widening. And yet, when Lily pleaded for Charleston instead of the auction block, Ellsworth had backed her up, begging his father not to sell Peter.

"My father's going to disown me for sure this time," the young master said cheerfully, his face flushed. "I've been booted out of school again."

"He won't do that," Peter murmured while recalling the complaints of Ellsworth's tutors as they resigned, that the boy was a nasty, spoiled brat. Ellsworth had shoved one teacher down a flight of stairs and bloodied another's nose. When he was thrown out of his academy for stabbing a fellow student with a kitchen knife, Massa had roared that gentlemen didn't behave like common ruffians but settled their differences dueling with pistols. He then dispatched Ellsworth to Charleston College equipped with two slaves, a horse, and a handsome allowance, which his son speedily squandered on liquor and bawdy women.

"I'm going to Beaufort tomorrow and take my medicine like a man," he told Peter breezily, "and then ask for an advance on my allowance."

"Good luck, suh," Peter said, knowing Ellsworth would receive his allowance after a nasty quarrel with his father.

Peter learned nothing more about Rain's past until the Sunday she failed to appear on the ferry. After delivering his produce he went to find her, rapping on the back door of her owner's brick house on Broad Street.

A haggard Rain opened the door, her face caved in on itself, her eyes puffy from crying. Her thick hair was standing up on end as though she had been trying to pull it out at the roots. She flung herself forward and darted past Peter, a tiny wild woman running she knew not where. He caught Rain before she reached the wrought-iron gate and she fell against him sobbing.

"They is gone and I is got to find them."

She strained against Peter, trying to escape from the band of his arms but he held her fast.

"Rain, what's wrong?"

It took a while for her sobs to subside, for the words to come in snatches. That morning after church as she had prepared to leave for the ferry Massa Rodman had told her the news.

"He didn't know Massa Slater were gon do it. That they——"

"Who he?" Peter interrupted. "Who's Massa Slater?"

"He own my Zee and Petunia. He put them on that nursery

farm." Rain looked at Peter piteously and asked, "How this happen? Not again. Why, Lord? Why?"

"Rain. Please. Tell me what . . ."

"My baby and li'l sister's gone. Sold to a slave trader. Gone to Georgia."

Peter's heart flipped over and the earth stood still. The birds forgot to sing and the wind refused to whistle. The only sound was Rain moaning.

"My babies is gone. Gone."

She was crying again and he didn't know what to do. Choke her to stop that infernal wailing which was hammering nails into his flesh? It's Amen all over again, he thought, but there was no place to run to, no place to hide.

"Gone," Rain shrieked again.

Her heartbreak resounded down the long tunnel of Peter's years and found him lacking. He reached out to hold her, feeling useless, but Rain pushed him away.

"I has to go 'fore Massa comes looking for me."

Peter watched her trudge inside. Motionless, he stood straddle-legged, his misery unbearable because there was nothing that a grown man, a black man, a slave could do. Except kill somebody.

In the weeks that followed, Peter glued the story together, the little pieces that Rain reluctantly revealed, rooted as they were in pain. She had lived with her mother, Elizabeth, and her five brothers on a plantation near the Combahee River. After her child and sister were born, Rain's family was sold, scattered like seeds in the wind. She didn't know where any of them were, except for the babies placed on the nursery farm.

"Every time I went there they cried when I left," Rain mourned. "My poor darlings. God, where is they?"

It took months for her to recover. Peter held her in his arms when she was forlorn and when she was demented.

Rain told him once, "I loves you 'cause you is strong but gentle." She whispered it shyly, a slave woman not accustomed to gentleness.

The following year, in the autumn when the leaves were the burnished color of Rain's eyes, their owners gave them permission to marry.

1859

Glory was born the year they hung John Brown and Peter went berserk.

Brown had attacked the federal arsenal at Harpers Ferry to obtain ammunition for a slave uprising. Despite the shadow of the noose, his unrepentant defense that slavery was an immoral act offensive to God swayed many who had never been swayed before into supporting abolition. Brown's hanging, along with two of the black men who had ridden with him, depressed Peter who had been feeling a nudge of lunacy ever since his daughter's birth. Twice he had approached Rain's owner offering to buy Glory's freedom and had been abruptly dismissed.

Peter's nudge became a shove one moonless night and he raced to Kenneth Rodman's house babbling like a madman that he would kill his child if Massa didn't sell her and Rain to him. Kill his daughter because she had no rights. That's what the judge had said denying poor Dred Scott his freedom.

"My Glory ain't got no rights," Peter yelled, bruised anew. "Any white man can beat my chile. Rape her. Kill her." His bushy hair was standing on end, his eyes gone mad in their sockets.

Kenneth Rodman, startled out of his sleep by this Negro banging on his door before dawn, fumed, "I've never beaten Rain nor intend to rape her child." Stringy and asthmatic, he blew his nose, honking like a goose.

"I'll kill them both," Peter raved, adding Rain to his list of victims. "And didn't Isaiah say in the Bible, is such a fast I have chosen to loose the bands of wickedness, to undo the heavy burdens, to let the oppressed go free and break every yoke."

The white man blinked, looking quite fragile with his thin silver hair framing his gaunt face. "Don't lecture me, you black ape. I've searched my soul and find it free of guilt."

They were standing in the foyer, Kenneth Rodman in his nightdress, having been summoned to the door by a frightened servant.

"But you ain't search my soul," Peter lamented. "And I ain't gon let it kill me slowly watching my baby grow up a slave. If you don't let me buy——"

"Stop threatening me. Do you honestly believe you can frighten me? A deacon in the church and a man of God? I've done nothing to Rain except try to instill a sense of virtue in her so she wouldn't turn into a slut like her mother."

Peter was surprised, knowing nothing about the supposed sluttishness of his wife's mother. "Rain ain't no slut."

"At least I've been successful in that regard."

Peter felt his madness slipping into despair. God, help me, he prayed. Massa Rodman was looking at him warily and their eyes met, interlocking as though connected by an axle that had dragged them from birth to this decisive moment.

"Before God," Peter ranted, "I'll——"

Rodman interrupted, his voice wheezy, "Everybody calls upon God." He started to cough, choking, his face flushed. He tried to speak but was unable to and beckoned for Peter to accompany him.

Peter followed him down a carpeted hall to a room where a fire was already burning in the grate. Kenneth Rodman staggered to his desk, sat down, and stopped choking. He regarded Peter with resentment and finally sighed.

"You're a Christian," he said, "and persistent. That's in your favor. I have discovered that persistence usually pays off."

It certainly had paid off for him, a wealthy man by dint of three plantations he had gained by foreclosing on their owners. He started to cough again, picked up a pen and his seizure ceased. Shaking his head and muttering to himself about the mysterious ways of God, Kenneth Rodman slowly wrote a note on a scrap of paper and handed it to Peter.

"Now get out of my house," he ordered, "before I change my mind."

Rain greeted Peter with relief when he arrived at home, aware that he had been acting peculiar.

"Honeybunch, listen." Slowly he read the note to her, stumbling over the words. "Being of sound mind and body I hereby agree to free my slaves Rain and Glory Mango upon receipt of eight hundred dollars. Kenneth Rodman."

"For me?" Rain asked, her eyes wide with disbelief, her bottom lip quivering.

Peter nodded, almost too filled with joy to speak.

"For me and our baby? Oh, sugarfoot." Tears were streaming down her face.

"Massa Rodman said you ain't no slut like you mother." Peter wiped a teardrop off Rain's cheek with a forefinger.

"My mamma a slut?" She shook her head. "Massa Rodman didn't know her. All she wanted was for her children be free. Like I is gon be, Peter? Me and Glory?"

"Yes," he whispered and kissed her.

3

Charleston
November 12, 1861

Peter dressed hurriedly. It was still dark outside and he was anxious to be on his way and learn the outcome of the battle at the Confederate forts. He had slept badly and so had Rain, twisting and turning away from each other all night. Now he felt her eyes burning a hole in his back.

"Baby cakes, we is laying torpedoes in the harbor this morning." He touched her forehead, which felt hot and dry. "Is you all right?"

She didn't flinch from his touch but nodded. Glancing at the mound of her belly he felt guilty.

"Rain."

"Yes?"

"I is sorry I vexed you so last night."

Silently, she pulled his head down and kissed him.

He closed his eyes, desire stirring in his groin, but it was a brief kiss, a peck, not a prelude to love. Still he murmured hopefully with his impish grin, "I has time. I ain't greedy but needy."

Once, greedy herself, Rain would have giggled as they smothered their mirth against each other's flesh so as not to wake up Glory. So delicious, making sweet love before day in the morning. But now she turned away, avoiding his eyes.

"No. I has to get up and do some ironing 'fore I goes to work."

Disappointed, Peter slapped his cap on his head, mumbled good-bye and sprinted down the stairs. Why was he such a fool? Lapping at her like a hound dog.

It was still dark outside and chilly. He hunched down in his pea jacket and hurried along East Bay Street. The house where they lived was attached to a row of other pastel dwellings—pink and sea green and yellow—three stories rising above a ground-floor stable. When the sun was shining it was a cheerful, colorful street but in this morning's grayness it appeared gloomy to Peter. Against the gray sky, the riggings of a clipper anchored at the wharf one block over rose up skeletal and lonely above the flat rooftops. It was probably a blockade runner, Peter decided moodily.

When he arrived at the *Swanee*, the firemen, Brother Man and Turno, were already aboard and told him the good news. The naval bombardment had forced the Sesesh to abandon both of their forts. Yankee troops were marching on Beaufort.

Turno, who was usually brusque with Peter, blessed him with a broad smile. "Ain't this a grand way to begin the day? You is from Beaufort, ain't you?"

"Yeh." Peter's elation was tempered with anxiety. What was happening to his mother and their owners? Were they safe, please God?

The loss of their fortifications made the *Swanee*'s officers ill-tempered. The Mate threatened to hang cross-eyed Aaron from the poop deck and any other nigger who was shirking his duty. And when Peter wasn't nimble enough in responding to an order to suit Captain Regan, he waved his pistol at him and roared, "I'll blast a hole in your black ass so big we can float this steamer through it."

"Yes, suh."

The *Swanee* pulled away from the dock, her deck top heavy with torpedoes. While the Yankee fleet patrolled beyond the bar, Peter piloted the steamer down the channel where they dropped mines in strategic locations. The torpedoes had been strung together by demolition experts using cast-iron lager beer barrels. The explosives had a fuse primer and a charge of gunpowder which had to come in contact with the bottom of a boat to explode.

Peter despised it, as did his mates, sinking torpedoes to blow up

Yankee vessels, and they were expected to be cheerful while doing it. The first mines they had planted, made of tin, had caved in under the pressure of eight feet of water. These iron barrels were being submerged to twenty-four feet, coated with resin and coal tar to render them leakproof. The channel seethed with obstructions including floating mines controlled from shore and heavy booms with dangling ropes to foul a boat's propellers.

Peter thought about Rain ironing this morning. Still ironing. That was the extra work she had taken on to make good their plan to buy her and Glory's freedom, saving every penny they could. Sailors had touched shore with knapsacks full of dirty drawers which Rain had converted into cash. Washing at night. Ironing in the morning. Taking the laundry to the inn with her where the sailors had picked it up. As for himself, he had taken on extra work also, repairing boats for Negro fishermen and piloting the ferry to James Island part-time. At times he had been so weary he couldn't remember which job he was rushing to, only that he had to be somewhere in a hurry.

And it had all been for naught, all that scraping and saving. A few months ago he had approached Massa Rodman with the news that they had saved almost all the money, only to discover his note wasn't worth a fart. Rodman said the authorities weren't signing any manumission papers. No slaves were to be freed. All hands were needed for the war effort.

"All hands," Rain repeated, looking forlorn when Peter told her. "Me and our baby. All hands." She didn't cry but shrugged as though she had known all along that such good fortune was not for her.

Now Peter was worried about his mother. Was she safe? He had heard tell that some Yankee soldiers were mighty hateful. But Mamma could take care of herself. At this very moment she was probably worrying about him.

He was right.

4

Beaufort, South Carolina
November 12, 1861

Benjie was at the back door calling for Lily.

"What does he want?" Joanne Caine asked, on edge.

She was standing in the middle of chaos, a soft, flabby woman whose body would have sagged beneath the weight of this day were it not for her tightly laced corsets. Miserable and perspiring with all of this exertion, she looked at the clutter on the floor—silver serving pieces in a velvet-lined box, an Italian vase, her mother's tea service—all snatched from the buffet and then dropped, for where in the world could she put them? She could not take it all with her, not the crystal chandelier over her head nor the spinet in the parlor. Beaufort had turned this corner too abruptly and since it was not possible to pack up her whole life in a scant few hours she snapped at Lily instead.

"Dispose of that wretched boy in two minutes flat and march yourself right back in here."

"Yes, ma'am."

Lily hurried outside as fast as her rheumatism would allow. Benjie, sinewy and slender, was waiting for her in the driveway, a huge carton balanced on his head. Behind him the street was crammed with buggies and wagons and cursing coachmen. Negroes carrying bundles on their heads jockeyed for space with the carriages which were hurtling over the cobblestones with a frightening clatter.

Benjie had been at the pier yesterday when the *Swanee* refueled on its way back to Charleston and he had a message from Peter. "They warn't in the fighting, Aunty. Peter say to tell you he all right."

Lily sagged with relief. All night she had lain awake worrying about him, praying he hadn't been in the gunshoot. "Thank you, Benjie. I 'preciates you dropping by."

He grinned. "All of we massas running with they tail 'twixt they legs like wounded hound dogs."

"Hush that talk," she snapped. "These is dangerous times and don't you act like no fool."

They were dangerous, all right, he admitted. His master, Luke Lucas, had threatened to whip him ten times already this morning. Benjie continued to grin like the little boy Lily remembered playing with Peter under the front house. He shifted the carton on his head and they both turned to stare at the vehicles on the road. Pale, frightened faces peered out of carriage windows, women and children huddled together in tight-lipped confusion, abandoning their homes with little more than the clothing on their backs. Destination: Charleston. Yesterday the war had come home to Beaufort.

Lily watched Benjie, limping slightly, join the bedlam on the road, the limp a souvenir of a shooting accident when his master mistook him for a deer. There was so much commotion in the air that she stood motionless to collect herself, a wiry woman as dark as a charred peanut. Her skin was pulled taut across the planes of her face and her gray hair was contained in four stubby braids. It was the only thing about Lily that was contained. In her mind she was hurtling toward the approaching Yankees, sniffing like a dog trying to catch their scent in the wind. Was this the day she had been waiting for all of her sixty-odd years? Was freedom at hand? Hurry Mistuh Lincoln's soldiers. Please hurry.

She walked along the brick wall covered with honeysuckle vines to the front, the clamor of the rattling carriages a din in her ears. Facing her across the street was Edmund Rhett's opulent house which Lily regarded with her usual suspicion. Twelve pillars held up a double portico above a series of arches. Massa Roland said the articles of secession as it was called—white folks quitting the Union like it was the plague—had been plotted there and that Massa Edmund was one of those hot-blooded Rhetts like his uncle, the senator. Place seemed vacant now. Like Benjie said, she thought, they done tucked they tails between they legs and beat all of us out of town.

Most of the Caines' influential neighbors had summer homes in Beaufort, town houses in Charleston, and cotton or rice plantations on the barrier islands. The Sea Islands, scattered for a hundred fifty miles between Charleston and Savannah, formed a land of fevers and malaria, but its long-fiber cotton was prized the world over. The more isolated islands, accessible only by boat, were populated mainly by slaves and their overseers. Cut off from contact with the mainland, the slaves spoke a patois so distinctive it was given a name. Gullah. Lily's speech still held traces of its Gullah origin.

Shading her eyes against the winter sunlight, she stared at the carriages hurtling out of town, nary a Yankee soldier in sight. Mindful that she had been gone too long, Lily made her way back inside the house and went upstairs.

In the high-ceilinged master bedroom the velvet curtains were drawn, the room in shadows as though bright sunshine today was too cruel a joke. A full-length gilt mirror reflected confusion, clothes tumbling out of the wardrobe, bureau drawers half-emptied, and Missy Joanne sprawled across the canopied bed crying piteously. Lily rushed to her.

"It's all so dreadful," Joanne Caine gasped. Gradually her weeping subsided and she sat up, her eyes swollen, strands of hair clinging to her wet face. She had undone her corset to free her pendulous breasts which were flopping loosely. Sniffing, Joanne stared at a crumpled dress on the floor, thrown there in the throes of indecision.

"It's going to be a long, cold ride," she said, shivering in anticipation.

"Maybe you brown suit and coat with that nice fur collar will keep you warm and toasty," Lily suggested.

"You think so?"

"Yes'm." Said gently because Missy was close to hysterics and there was a bond between them, a mutual reliance. The mistress had supplied medicines and salves, bandages for a boy's skinned knee, burnt needles to remove splinters, warm clothing barely worn, casseroles of leftover delicacies and an assortment of odds and ends. The slave had supplied her presence at births, washed away the blood, patted the mother's forehead dry. At deaths she cried for the departed, consoled the living, and kept the children quiet. At all times she hovered in the background, materializing at a whisper.

"We're leaving all of this behind," Joanne said.

Struggling to her feet she walked to the settee and touched its green tapestry which was as emerald fresh as it had been when Roland had bought it for her on their wedding day. The little sofa had withstood the stress of time better than its blowsy mistress. What she had possessed as a bride besides a generous dowry was the bloom of youth, a spark fanned by the breath of love before that same breath blew it out.

"Lily, pick up these clothes, please, and pack them in the portmanteau. I no longer care what's left behind. I wonder what's keeping your master so long?" He had rushed off to an emergency Grange meeting.

"I 'spect he be back directly, Missy."

That was Lily's hope as she moved around the room gathering up the clothes Missy shouldn't have snatched from the wardrobe anyway before deciding what was what.

"My babies," Joanne cried out suddenly. "How can I leave my babies behind? Who's going to pull up the weeds?"

"Don't you go to fretting now," Lily pleaded, thinking as she had for years that the dead could take care of their own self. But no, Missy had to trot over to the church cemetery every few days to place fresh flowers on the graves and make the slave gardener pull up the weeds. Massa let her act so because it kept her out of his business, not that the rumors didn't fly about the way he carried on.

Hoping to get Missy's mind off the graveyard, she said, "Thank God young Massa is safe in Charleston."

"Yes," Joanne agreed. "If for nothing else we can be thankful for that."

That was the last thing any of them needed today, Lily felt.

Ellsworth's disturbing presence. She had raised him from a pup and his daddy too, and watched them both drive poor Missy to distraction with their devilish ways.

"Do you remember when he was born, Lily?"

"Yes'm. How could I forget. It was after you came home from Rolling Acres."

Joanne had fled to the upcountry plantation that had been part of her dowry when her husband refused to sell his slave concubine as she finally demanded. But after three months, and his insistence that her place was with him, she returned. Their reconciliation produced Ellsworth, Joanne convinced she had finally become a mother through divine intervention. God had blessed her with a child not stillborn like her other four babies because she had had the good sense to come home.

Still, down through the years she kept puttering around in the graveyard as the slave concubine was replaced by other women of various complexions, Joanne accepting defeat since success so seldom came her way.

"Lily."

"Yes, ma'am?"

"I think I *will* wear my brown suit and coat with the fur collar."

Her grooming was almost complete when Roland Caine returned home and with a heavy tread came upstairs. He was dressed meticulously even at this hour of doom in striped trousers, carrying his silver-handled cane as though it was a weapon. He sat down on the settee.

"Lily. Fetch me a glass of branch water."

"Yes, Massa."

She hurried downstairs and returned with it in minutes.

Roland never imbibed spirits. He had peptic ulcers and was as lean as a greyhound with winter in his face, his graying beard frosty. Despite his sparseness he was a handsome, prepossessing figure.

Massa was some vexed, Lily thought, his mouth a tight, straight line, the look he had when about to chop off somebody's head. A slave. A merchant. His son. She knew his moods. He had been her baby, the one she had to mind, and how could you not love the little tyke watching him grow. He used to wrap his arms around her neck to ask, "Lily, who you love best?" And because he was the youngest and a lonely little boy, she would unloose his arms and say, "You been bad? That's why I has got to love you best?" Waiting now to hear the word, she shifted from one foot to the other, her calves aching.

"We voted to set fire to the cotton in the warehouses," Roland Caine finally said. "Our cotton is what the damn Yankees are after."

His voice cracked and he looked miserable enough to set fire to himself as well. Without his cotton and the slaves who hoed it and ginned it, the cotton which fed them all, he was bankrupt. And it pained him to abandon them also, his two hundred plantation slaves who relied upon him for the clothes on their backs, the food they ate, and the mates with whom they fornicated. Relied upon him to dose them with homeopathic remedies trying to cure their predilection to sicken and die before their time.

He rewarded the faithful at Christmas with an extra peck of corn, a bottle of whiskey and other little gifts, and methodically meted out punishment to instill fear in their woolly heads. An ear cut off a runaway buck could subdue an entire plantation. That was the lesson his father had implanted in him. How to be a gentleman planter.

Absently, Roland rubbed his left shoulder which itched, the spot grazed by a bullet during a duel he had fought with loathing and despair. Had he not fought it with one of his best friends over a trifling matter his father would have disowned him. *The world must understand, my son, that a Southern gentleman will defend his honor with his life. Discipline yourself. No one, nothing should challenge your control and live.*

Joanne was staring at her husband, dismayed. "All the cotton has to be burned? Can't some way be found to ship it to England?"

"Why do you persist in asking ridiculous questions?" he retorted. "No other solution exists. It was one of those blasted Rhetts who suggested that we set fire to the warehouses."

It was no secret that Roland had little love for the Rhetts, often complaining that there were too many of their bloody tribe owning property all over the place. It was in Edmund's house across the street that the endless discussions on tariffs, the price of cotton, and the fight to install slavery in the territories had all come to a fateful climax.

Roland had argued that the South was safer in the Union than out of it, that they could not have retained slavery all these years without the nation's complicity. But Robert Barnwell Rhett, who for thirty years, in and out of the Senate, had tried to ram secession down their throats, finally succeeded. Before Abraham Lincoln took office, the South confiscated all federal property in their states—arsenals, forts, custom houses, and even the mint in New Orleans. The only garrison left in Union possession in Charleston had been Fort Sumter. When the Confederates fired upon it, forcing its surrender, President Lincoln declared that the nation was at war.

At the hour of decision, Roland loyally remained with his region. He had often boasted with pride that his grandmother had purchased the Sea Islands from the Indians with her life. The Yamasee Indians had been routed from this area first by the Spanish and then by the French and British. The Indians retaliated once by attacking Beaufort and scalping its inhabitants. Roland's grandfather, returning home from the mainland after the uprising, found his house in ashes, bodies scattered about and his wife missing. She was never found and he became a relentless Indian headhunter.

Consulting his vest pocket watch, Roland stood up now to announce that they would be leaving for Charleston in exactly one hour.

"I have to leave my babies behind in the churchyard?" Joanne wailed.

"Well, we most certainly can't take them with us," Roland replied coldly.

Lily, ever the mediator, said, "I was telling Missy thank God Massa Ellsworth is safe in Charleston."

Her master nodded. "That's the sensible way to look at it."

"Sensible?" Joanne cried out, stung. "You're the one who is never sensible. You pamper Ellsworth with one hand and crucify him with the other. He can do nothing to please you and has stopped trying. Sometimes I feel you want to keep him dependent upon you."

The blood rushed into Caine's face. "Are you out of your mind

49

finally? I've done everything to encourage that boy to stand on his own two feet."

"You refuse to let him manage Rolling Acres. How many times have I begged you——"

"So he could bankrupt it? You know nothing about business matters so——"

"I admit that but . . ."

"So stop parading your ignorance."

"There's no need for you to shout."

"You're right. You're too miserably endowed with brains to understand anything." He turned to Lily. "You and Selena will ride inside the coach with your mistress and me. Go pack your belongings. We will be leaving shortly."

"Yes, Massa."

Lily closed the door behind her, shutting out the sound of Missy's sobbing.

Selena and her husband, Jethro, were at the tail end of an argument in the little shack behind the garden that they shared with Lily. Selena was staring at him belligerently, her hands on her broad hips.

"I ain't deaf, man," she shouted.

Lily moved to neutral territory, to the other side of the scarred table which stood in the center of the room. There was bad blood between her and the young couple. Their constant bickering irritated her and they in turn considered her a nosy busybody.

"You is worse than deaf," Jethro yelled. "You is a donkey's hind parts."

His sour glance included Lily. He stormed out, wearing an old pair of his master's trousers, slamming the door so hard it shook the little window next to it.

"That nigger," Selena mumbled, stuffing an iron skillet and other odds and ends into a gunnysack. When she swung the pack over her shoulder, she barely bent beneath its weight. Her fierce eyes raked over Lily as if looking for a vulnerable spot to strike a last blow but when she spoke her voice was shaky.

"Massa say if the Yankees catch us they gon rape we women. They gon sell we men to Cuba."

That's what the couple had been arguing about, Lily realized, and felt a chill. Where did the lie end and the truth begin? "Everything Massa say, Selena, ain't the word of God." Her voice was a sharp rebuke.

"Don't I know that. I were just passing on what I heard so don't get uppity with me." She too stomped out of the room, slamming the door behind her.

Lily moved to the table and sat down. Her chill turned into a fever. She raised a palsied hand to her forehead to wipe it dry and felt a strange foreboding. Rape? By Mistuh Lincoln's soldiers? Massa had told Selena that, and Lily directed her anger toward him and his father, Jonathan Caine. They had not raped her but had committed other grievous injuries. Separation. A forcible wrenching apart. Not once but over and over again.

The first time she had been a bony girl of eleven, a quarter hand on Caine's Landing, Massa Jonathan's plantation on St. Helena Island. She had been naughty on that fateful day, not turning back when her mother called her.

"Lily? Where you be, chile?"

Her child was sneaking through the brush after grinding their corn at the mill. It was spring and she was turning somersaults, feeling frisky, the wild grass snapping at her heels.

"Li——ly."

Her mother's voice had an anxious quality to it, like when she was showing her how to split kindling without chopping off her foot. Ignoring Mamma's anxiety, she kept on skipping along. Skipping past the glade of live oaks to the river that dipped in close before widening downstream and not noticing the menfolks until she was almost upon them.

At the water's edge a boat was being unloaded. Massa Bailey, the overseer, and his black driver, Jake, were directing the slave crew who were wading back and forth to shore carrying supplies for the plantation. The overseer caught sight of Lily before she could turn and run back to the protective shadows of the glade.

"That you, gal?" he said. "The one that ain't afraid to speak up?"

She had spoken up that morning, working in the field, dropping cotton seeds into the drill, her first time at this task. Ordinarily in the overseer's presence she tried to blend into the landscape, to become invisible, but this morning when he reined in his horse beside her, she didn't cower but threw the seeds with abandon, liking the way they plopped into the ridge neatly where she wanted them to fall. He asked if she was a quarter hand and she replied, yes, suh. Then, looking into his faded blue eyes, she added, "But I works hard enough to be a half hand 'cause they gets more rations and my mamma is always complaining 'bout that." Today, her mother was working in another section. Chuckling, the overseer had ridden off.

Now, framed against the small boat being unloaded, he said, "Come here, gal."

Massa Bailey seemed suddenly sinister and she couldn't move. Her feet had grown roots to the spot.

"Your master said fetch him a spunky one," Bailey told Jake. "Go get her."

Lily moved then. Jake's touch galvanized her into a sudden fury. She darted away from him, but he grabbed her. She lashed out with her puny strength. Kneed him in the groin. Her unexpected ferocity caught Jake off guard and she was free, skittering on her thin black legs like a gazelle trapped between the sinking sun and the horizon.

"You li'l black bitch. Come back here." Jake's outraged voice. Jake's bullwhip slicing the flesh from her bones. She crashed headlong into a tree and fell to the ground, her cry bleeding into it before darkness snatched her. "Mamma!"

She woke up in the black hold of the boat, lying on a wooden plank, heaving with the boat's motion, her nostrils filled with the rank odor of sweating men. The slave oarsmen were rowing silently, the sinking sun blurred behind them. Rowing away from St. Helena Island. Rowing her away from home.

In Beaufort Lily cried night and day, surrounded by whiteness, never loosened from its grasp. She cried cleaning up the nursery. Bathing the baby. Dusting the banisters. Helping Maybelle in the kitchen. Cutting up the chicken. Polishing the silver. Washing the dishes. Putting the children to bed. At night her sleep was broken by their childish singsong. Lily, fetch the potty. Lily, I need another blanket. Lily, I want some water. Lily, I done peed in my drawers.

She cried to the cook, who said, "Stole you, chile?" sounding like Mamma. But Mamma didn't have a slight mustache and wasn't a fat cook. "But Massa Jonathan wouldn't do a thing like that. He be ornery, but stole you? I best go talk to him."

Massa Jonathan said he was sorry it happened like that but he couldn't send her home, so stop crying all the livelong day. He said when his infant son, Roland, who she had to care for, was older he might let her visit her mother at Christmas. He did allow her to go home a few times, a reward for good behavior withheld if she had been considered impudent or he was feeling bilious. After her mother died Lily did not return to St. Helena again.

It was time to go, to step into the carriage and be whisked away one step ahead of the Yankee soldiers. Lily could hear Jethro outside tying boxes on top of the coach. And Missy Joanne calling her. "Lily? We're almost ready."

She sat stiffly in her chair paralyzed by memory, remembering her lovers and their early departures. They had slipped away during the interval it took to inhale a breath and let it out. A slave woman had to grasp what she could. On the run. Barely had time to lie down and haul up her skirts before Missy was calling her to come fetch her corset.

The most bittersweet memory was falling into the sunshine of Hiram's smile in Charleston that summer Missy Joanne had taken her there. He was so independent, so manly. A wheelmaker. And he was free. Lying against his naked black chest she wondered if that accounted for her consuming passion—the intoxicating fact that he was free.

"I really got to go, Hiram, darlin'." Reluctant words. Stolen moments when Missy was at the dressmaker's or attending the horse races with her sister, Loretta. Whenever Lily showed up unexpectedly, borrowing time, stealing it, they would race into Hiram's little house in front of his little shop, tear off their clothes and aim for the middle of his bed. Once their aim was bad due to haste and they wound up entangled in each other's arms on the floor, laughing.

Strolling around the city, Hiram proudly pointed to the handiwork of black craftsmen in evidence everywhere. They fired the bricks. Glazed the glass. Planed the wood. Ground the stone. Mixed the stucco. Forged the iron. "Africans brought that iron-making skill here with them," he said. "We built this city." He smiled down at her. She laughed up at him. That was part of the beauty. He always made her laugh, joining in with his deep-throated chuckle so that she wanted to hear it starting inside of him, to be lying beneath him, his sweat slick on her belly.

"Hiram, darlin', I must go. Missy be going wild looking for me." Nighttime was impossible. She had to sleep in a corner within hollering distance of Missy. And there was the Negro curfew. But during the day she schemed and carved out a few paltry hours to be with Hiram.

"I is in love," she told Missy Joanne. "I wants to marry up with him."

Roland Caine came to fetch them home and was consulted. Marriage was fine, he approved of the stability of slaves marrying, but no, Lily could not hire out her time in Charleston. Mistress needed her in Beaufort. Her young man would have to move there.

But Hiram said no. Sitting in the middle of his bed there was no laughter left in him. "I cain't do it, Lily. I love you but I cain't put myself under your master's say-so, getting his permission to visit you. And the day he flogs you is the day I die for killing him. I marry you and my children will be slaves. I marry you and I become half a slave myself." She couldn't convince him that Massa had never whipped her, his nanny, and Hiram refused to budge.

Back home in Beaufort she prayed to at least have his baby, desperately craving some part of him, but God was not listening. Her child came later after years of numbing loneliness, then a brief encounter with a slave visiting with his master and a baby born finally. Peter. The child of her middle years.

And then he too was taken from her and she had to be grateful and tell him, "Son, Charleston be better than the auction block." And him crying, "Mamma, I don't wanna leave you, I ain't goin to Charleston."

He ran away, broke curfew, and they slammed his behind in jail, a chunky boy of eleven. Massa Roland had to pay a fine to get him out and was some mad, saying maybe he couldn't trust Peter to hire out his time after all and she wringing her hands and crying, "Trust him. Please, suh." Charleston was better than the auction block.

She asked Peter when they were alone why he had defied the curfew he had obeyed all his life. "Because it only ring for we," he replied, "not for white folks." He had yearned to know how it felt to be like them.

And didn't she understand that? It wasn't a rudeness, but himself demanding to be, like when she sneaked a fluffy biscuit out of the basket before taking them into the dining room. The servants could eat whatever was left over, but to deprive Massa and Missy of the biggest, fluffiest biscuit felt good. That was the part of her they didn't own, that said "no" instead of "yes" and stole their biscuits. It was like that time on the plantation when the slaves stole so many yams out of the ground the overseer had to give up planting them as a cash crop. The slaves won out that time. But Peter wasn't content with eating stolen biscuits and that was scary because he was only eleven.

So she shook him, screaming, "Boy, I ain't raise you to bury you. Them patrollers could kill you. Or you want Massa to sell you away so's I'll never see you no more? You is got to stay alive and you is got to have a plan. Does you understand me, boy. A plan. You cain't go out walking just 'cause you gets the notion. And shut up saying what you ain't gon do and take off them clothes so's I can wash them. I ain't sending you to Charleston in no dirty drawers."

"Lily." This time it was her master calling from outside, his voice harsh. "Jethro, see if that fool woman is still in there. We're ready to go."

Jethro stepped into their room and closed the door, his face sullen. "Lily, you suddenly deaf? You ain't hear Massa calling you? We is ready to——"

She cut him off with an agonized whisper. "No."

Stumbling up from her chair she backed away, shaking her head violently, her body turned into a coil ready to spring. To fly. She confronted Jethro wordlessly, her heart hammering. There was a look of amazement on his face and then a sudden flash of anger. His eyes burned into hers for a moment before he turned around and went out the door. Trembling, she walked toward it. They would have to kill her. Kill her.

She heard Jethro tell their master, "Lily ain't inside, suh. I don't know where she be."

Surprise almost toppled her. Carefully she peeked out the window. Missy had her foot on the step of the carriage, about to enter, but had twisted around to her husband.

"Lily's not in the house? Not upstairs in the bedroom?"

"No, I just came down from there. Get in the carriage."

"But we can't leave Lily behind. I need her."

She stepped away from the carriage as though to commence the search herself. Massa Roland grabbed her arm, swung her around. "I said get in the carriage."

"No." She spat the defiant word in his face. "I'm not leaving without——"

"Goddamnit." He half dragged her to the carriage door. "Get hold of yourself, madame, or do I have to throw you inside bodily?"

Missy jerked her arm free and, with all the dignity she could muster, climbed into the carriage. Selena got in last and peered out the window. It seemed to Lily, peeping out of her window, that Selena was looking directly at her and smiling.

Jethro lashed the horse's flank. "Giddap." The carriage rattled down the driveway and was gone.

Gone? It seemed incomprehensible to Lily. That space seething a moment ago with invisible chains was now nothing but air? Stumbling to the door she pushed it open and hesitantly stepped outside. The town had not yet emptied. She could hear its groans. It pulled her into the street. Dazed, she turned to look back at the house, at its long windows which opened onto ironwork balconies. Its breadth and grandeur—the high-ceilinged rooms, the lavish garden and duck pond—had always made her feel small, insignificant, like the one-room shack where she lived. But now with Massa and Missy gone it was just a house and she no longer was chained to it.

Something beat inside her head like wings. Lord, I is free? She had to test it and started across the street but pulled back as a coach rumbled past almost knocking her down. It passed and she walked on, seeing the town with heightened senses, its neat streets lined with shade trees and palmettos, windswept by sea breezes, scented with jasmine, and sparkling as if God himself had dipped the place in the Beaufort River and hung it out to dry.

Lily walked to Bay Street, which so prettily followed the curve of the Beaufort River. She walked into bedlam. A horde of people fleeing to Charleston was taking the water route. The ferry was in its berth, anxious faces peering over its sides desperate to be gone. Children howled as they were hauled up the gangplank, their hysterical mothers hollering at the black nannies to keep the youngsters quiet. Other folks were hurriedly boarding their private vessels.

Lily saw Luke Lucas standing at the prow of his twelve-oared boat, his black cape billowing in the wind, his face florid as he directed his slave rowers to their positions. His wife and children were already seated in the collapsible cabin in the stern which had berth room for his large family. Amidships were seats for the oarsmen, six on each side. Lily looked for Benjie but he wasn't there, his spot unmanned.

And then she saw him on the dock, slipping through the crowd. But he had made his move too late. Luke Lucas, one oarsman short, had also seen him.

"Benjie," he yelled, "come back here."

With more agility than Lily knew he possessed, for Massa Luke was past his prime, he leaped from his boat to the dock.

"You black bastard," he yelled. "Stop."

Handicapped by his limp, Benjie was running as fast as he could. Lily saw the pistol in his owner's hand. Someone screamed. People scrambled out of the way.

"Run, Benjie," Lily whispered.

But he could not outrun the bullet. It found its mark, slammed into his spine. For a moment Benjie seemed suspended in the air, caught in mid-stride, then slowly he crumpled to the ground. His owner strode forward and bent over him. Benjie's eyes stared past him at the impenetrable sky.

"He's dead," Luke Lucas said.

Terrified, Lily backed away. Benjie was dead? But death was too sudden. Too rude. It dawned upon her that she was not safe either, that Massa Luke or any white person could drag her back into slavery. Inching back, she put distance between herself and the dock, trying not to look like a frightened black woman running away, afraid to return home for fear Massa Roland might double back looking for her.

She ducked into doorways whenever shadows moved. And finally, coming to a gully overgrown with high weeds, Lily crawled into it, burrowing like a mole into the hard, cold ground.

5

Charleston
November 15, 1861

The *Swanee's* crew had been away for three days mining the harbor and when they returned the city was swollen fair to bursting with the influx of Sea Island inhabitants. Hotels and inns were hastily converting hallways into makeshift rooms. Carriages clogged the roads which were already overflowing with hysterical pedestrians in flight from the rumors that were stomping around in hip boots.

Yankee ground troops are marching on the city.

The railroad station has been blown up, cutting off that avenue of escape.

Rebellious slaves are burning Charleston Neck to the ground.

The rumors were terrifying even after proven untrue since the possibilities remained.

Peter, worried about his mother and the Caines, hurried to Loretta Pope's house to inquire about them, hoping they were there. Stubby opened the side entrance door.

"Peter, I is happy to see you," he said, not looking happy at all but old and decrepit.

"How you be, Stubby. Is my master here?"

They had been there and gone, he was told, leaving the day before for Rolling Acres, which was considerably inland.

Peter sighed with relief. "Did my mother leave a message for me?"

The old man looked at him perplexed. "You don't know 'bout her?"

"Know what?" Peter held his breath, afraid to exhale.

"You massa's coachman told me she hid herself so they left without her. He knowed where she was hiding but didn't let on."

Peter stared at Stubby with disbelief. "But where is she? What's happened to her?"

"How is I 'spose to know? But you massa was mighty vexed, I can tell you that."

Bewildered, Peter raced inside the house. Missy Loretta was in the sun room giving the cook instructions about supper. Dismissing the servant, she glared at him balefully. He was always surprised that she had aged so little, still slender and shapely, looking the same to him as when he had been a boy.

"Have you heard from your mother?" she asked without preamble.

Mystified, Peter shook his head.

"Don't pretend ignorance. Your nigra grapevine usually beats our telegraph. Your mother had a bad habit of disappearing when she was here once and she's done it again, and my sister crying that she can't live without her. She thinks Lily might have fainted and is lying half-dead in the house somewhere. I told her nigras don't faint, the wench probably ran away. Your master tends to agree with me although he didn't expect such treachery from his nanny. But you people can't be trusted and that's the bitter truth. They should send the stinking lot of you back to Africa."

Backing away from her tirade, Peter fled from the house. He was frenzied. At home Rain tried to soothe him but to no avail. He could not stop imagining the worst. His mother hurt. Or killed in some brutal fashion.

Peter sought solace from Uncle Hiram but he was not in his shop. Peter went to his house and Helen, Hiram's wife, opened the door, glaring at Peter evilly. That was her usual stance. Furious with her husband, she was jealous of his friends, declaring that he liked them all better than her. Hiram usually had another woman across town—they succeeded one another—and Helen always found out about them, screaming that if he didn't stop bringing their stench into her house she would leave him. It was an idle threat. The other women remained and Helen became obese. She always eyed Peter with suspicion, and he had never been comfortable around her.

"Hiram ain't here," she said and slammed the door, adding to Peter's misery.

The next day a rumor spread that the Negroes in Beaufort had gone on a rampage and torn the little town apart.

Beaufort

The rumor was true. When Lily emerged from the gully that night, cramped and aching and as timid as a fawn, she discovered that the shadows were stepping right smartly along with her. They were servants who had not accompanied their masters. Or runaways like herself who had hidden under porches or bolted into the woods.

A stout, exceedingly black man approached her. The tailor Maceo, a man she had never liked, considering him too sly. But now Lily grabbed hold of his hand, overjoyed at seeing him.

"Maceo. My God. I is glad to find somebody I knows. I run away from my master and . . ."

The tailor grinned. "Me, too."

Lily felt an overwhelming affection for him and blessed him with her gap-toothed smile. "But where all these folks come from?"

"Some of them from around here, Lily. Others rowing in from they plantations on the islands."

The streets were fast becoming populated with strangers as well as a few servants Lily knew.

"My God," Maceo cried out, pointing. "Look yonder."

Dr. Agnew Travis's house loomed up before them gleaming whitely in the moonlight. Negroes were emerging from it toting overflowing baskets on their heads. A young woman was struggling with a feather mattress, dragging it down the veranda steps. Other folks had broken into the smokehouse and were carting off slabs of bacon and whole hams.

"Let's hurry 'fore all the good stuff is gone," Maceo said, and headed toward the smokehouse on the run.

Lily sucked her teeth. The tailor was still a sly old fox. She continued toward the house almost bumping into a man loping down the veranda steps lugging a basket filled with silverware.

"From now on," he said, "I is gon eat like the gentry with a knife and fork."

"Mind you don't stab you fool self," a woman retorted to hilarious laughter.

We is having us a party, Lily thought, and went inside. She knew Dr. Travis. He was the Caineses' physician and would die a thousand deaths if he could witness what was happening. A dozen or more slaves were systematically dismantling his house, carting chairs and couches and anything else they fancied out the side door. Lily stood to one side, a spectator.

Suddenly an agitated man with a purple scar on his cheek burst into the room with such force he almost knocked her down. From his roughspun clothes she surmised he was a field hand.

"Our massas burned the cotton," he shouted. "We plant she and pick she but massa burn the cotton." The muscles in his face bulged with rage.

"I be damn," a voice exclaimed. "They burn the cotton?"

It was a question, it was the answer, passed along until it became a shout of condemnation. The scarred man picked up a chair and hurled it with the force of Hercules into the fireplace. There was a startled hush, then the direction given, the mood of the Negroes changed.

"Our massas done burn the goddamn cotton."

"I saw the fires but didn't know . . ."

"Whoresons."

A black hand wielding an axe splintered a mahogany table, then swung around to chop a wing chair into firewood.

"What you all doin'?" Lily cried out in alarm. A young woman carrying a baby on her hip swept the buffet clean of its cut crystal.

"But you cain't . . ." Lily protested, running from the axeman to the young mother but too late to stop them. Still she tried, grabbing the arm of the man whose axe was hovering over the piano. Roughly he pushed her aside.

Other folks came streaming through the door having heard the news. "Massa done burned the cotton," they screamed. The noise was deafening. The cotton, Lily's mind questioned? She froze seeing Maceo, lately arrived, attack the silver-plated mirror with a sledgehammer. It was more than cotton that had invaded this house, Lily realized, looking at her fellow slaves wreaking destruction. Their faces were snarling, demonic, but behind each pair of eyes gone suddenly insane there was a personal horror.

With surprise Lily heard herself moan, "Massa burn the cotton." She picked up a fire iron and slashed at a portrait on the wall, a gray-eyed man with a long beard. Dr. Travis. Repeatedly the iron tore through the canvas, ripping the face into unequal parts. An unblinking eye fell at Lily's feet. It was maddening the way it insisted upon looking at her. She beat it with the fire tong until the eye was battered and in threads. She stared at it for a dazed moment, then with renewed outrage stomped on it, sobbing. "You friend shot Benjie dead."

Yankee troops arrived in Beaufort the next day bringing a message from President Lincoln that no harm was intended toward the residents and their institution of slavery, but the white folks had all fled except for the town drunk. The soldiers were shocked by the destruction. Senseless, they moaned. Unbelievable savagery.

The slaves greeting them were jubilant. And they kept on coming, deserting the plantations on the outlying islands, fording the river on rafts and barges, on flatboats and canoes. On one day alone six thousand arrived, sneaking through Confederate lines, journeying to meet the Yankee soldiers, journeying to freedom.

Mothers waded ashore with babies tied to their waists. Men carried their sons piggyback. They crowded the beaches, a host of shining black faces, the river clinging to their hipbones, their thighs, their breasts. We have come, they declared, to cook your food, wash your clothes, plant your corn and your yams. We will swill your pigs and be your harness makers, your ironworkers and silversmiths. We will build your bridges and your forts. We will be your eyes. Your ears. Your spies. We will put down the hoe, pick up the gun, and fight alongside of you.

The river was black on black as they continued to tumble out of it, singing in their strong Gullah voices:

> *Been in the storm so long, Lord*
> *Been in the storm so long.*

Charleston
November 25, 1861

On the waterfront a tugboat sailor Peter knew brought him news finally about his mother. The sailor had been told by a slave whose owner had sneaked back to Beaufort to kidnap him that Lily was a free woman working for a Yankee colonel.

"She be safe?" Peter crowed. "And free?" He snatched the sailor off the ground and hugged him.

"Nigger, put me down."

"I knew my mamma could take care of sheself." Laughing as he released the sailor, Peter had to restrain himself from dancing a jig with the man. Instead he vaulted home on winged feet, his blood singing. His mother was free.

He raced up the stairs and pushed open his door intending to whirl his honeybunch off the floor but stopped dead in his tracks. Rain was not alone. It wasn't his daughter curled up under the table sound asleep and sucking her thumb that irritated him but Bettina. Of all people. The hussy was sitting at the table beside Rain, both of them talking and snapping string beans. They looked up when the door opened and automatically ceased their chatter.

Rain greeted him, unperturbed, her thick hair peeping out from beneath her head wrap. "I got home early and Bettina came along with me."

"How you doing, Peter?" His nemesis smiled at him.

He frowned and shrugged, making no attempt to be polite to the woman who unfortunately reminded him of his first and only whore, and also of Saralee whose pussy he didn't get to smell. He lumped them all together as trash, Negro women who bedded down with their white masters, Bettina heading the list.

She stood up to leave. "I has to go pick up my chil'ren."

At least the wench hadn't brought them along, he thought, as she disappeared through the door. Her mulatto offspring had fueled a terrible argument between him and Rain one night when he complained that Bettina was little better than a whore and instead of mingling with decent folks should confine herself to Madame Bouchard's establishment where mulattoes and qua-

63

droons were reserved for high-class white gentlemen. But on second thought Bettina was probably too black and ugly.

Rain had jumped furiously into his face to scream that he was blind to what women had to put up with, what they were forced to do. Peter insisted force was not what he was talking about. Every time a gal like Bettina gave birth to a mulatto baby didn't mean she had been forced. He was talking about liking to lie down with white men. Being pleasured. In love with them.

Love? Rain had walked around the word, puzzling it out. Then, her voice reasonable, she remarked that there was love and there was cow dung and some peculiar things in between. Their masters had all the say-so and sometimes that power was a kind of love.

That's what made those women and Bettina trash, Peter had countered. Rain then hit him with a sledgehammer by asking if his mamma was trash, since he didn't know what she might have done willingly or been forced to do. He howled like a wounded animal that she had never slept with white men.

When Rain asked if he could swear to that, Peter retorted he could swear to slapping the shit out of her if she insulted his mother again. They had remained angry with each other for days, Peter continuing to attack Bettina and Rain to defend her. He failed to see why she couldn't understand that a mulatto baby the color of sick shit was a mule's kick in his groin. An eternal pain. But no, she was an aggravating, hardheaded woman.

"Why you always so rude to my friend?" Rain asked him now.

Peter sat down and reached for a string bean. Snap. Pop. "You know I don't want Bettina up here."

"I ain't paying you no never mind."

"So I notice."

Silently they glared at each other, the only sound between them the snapping of beans.

Finally Rain asked, "You hungry?"

"No," he barked.

"You too stubborn to eat? You gon starve you fool self?"

He shrugged and peeked at his daughter still asleep under the table. "Maybe I should put Glory to bed."

"She's plumb wore out," Rain said. "It was some busy at the inn today, what with all the folks moving in and she following me all over the place. I ain't never made up so many beds and emptied so many chamber pots."

She gathered up the string beans and took them into the kitchen. "I brought some roast pork home and some corn bread. They'll go good with these here beans."

"Don't cook them yet. Come sit down for a minute. I has something to tell you."

Rain returned to the table, moving slowly and with effort, her body weary at being seven months along. Peter forgot about Bettina, tenderness overwhelming him.

"Honeybunch, listen. What I is gon tell you is gon knock you out." Elation glowed on Peter's face. "My mother is in Beaufort working for the Yankees. She be free."

He stood up laughing, expecting Rain to leap with joy into his arms and be danced around the room. But she remained seated, as wooden as a dead tree.

"I is glad you mother is safe," she said, her voice gloomy.

"Well, you ain't acting glad." He was baffled.

Rain avoided his gaze, looking straight ahead as though she were in a narrow tunnel which cut off all side vision. "You is you mother's chile," she said. "I guess you be joining her soon."

A warning bell sounded in Peter's head. "What nonsense is you talking now?"

"You mamma run off and so will you."

Dumbfounded, he stared at her. Rain was trembling. "No," he said and reached for her hand.

She snatched it back but too late. His touch opened the floodgates. The fears she had swallowed these many months crowded in her throat, forcing out the words which finally had to be voiced.

"You remember Daisy? The cook on my job and her husband, Elmo, what both went off to Maryland with they massa? And how Elmo sneak off one midnight and she insane with grief not knowing if the bloodhounds got him till she receive word he safe in Canada? Well, Daisy was glad he were safe 'cause she did love that man but she come back here still a slave with they baby. From that day to this she been dying with grief."

Peter felt sick. "What's that got to do with us?"

"I knows you, Peter. You is a man what's got to have a plan. So we working hard, saving we money and everything's fine. Then my massa say he ain't selling on account of the war. And now I is making another slave baby you has to buy. Another noose. Before long you has to have another plan. How long 'fore you run off by youself? Like Elmo."

Peter rose to his feet shouting, "I ain't Elmo." He had to shout to still that inner voice which was always cunningly suggesting ways for him to escape.

Rain said, "I does feel guilty 'cause you ain't a selfish man. You did think of me and our chile first but now that plan's done fell through. And I knows how it is. When that feeling comes that you has to be free or die, man or woman you is got to run. That's what's been hounding me. You take off for work and I think, maybe this be the day. I ain't never gon see Peter no more. If you ain't in my sight I is too scared to pee."

She was crying. "All I could study 'bout was that you might leave me. Specially since I is making another baby. I felt you sliding away from me. I saw it in you eyes. Felt it in you touch. So I told myself, don't get mixed up with him, keep you distance, then when he gone it won't kill you. And now you mamma done showed you the way."

God, help me, Peter prayed, utterly dumbfounded and desperate to make Rain understand. "Listen," he pleaded, "I ain't gon lie. I does study 'bout being free. But mostly it's just idling, like a cart that ain't got no mule. The cart cain't go nowhere without some muscle to pull or push it. And you is my muscle." He grabbed Rain by the shoulders. "Look at me. Look at this man what loves you. Every day I is so thankful that you is mine. Life don't make sense without you. I ain't never gon leave you, honeybunch. I'd be a dead man looking for a place to lie down." He shook her gently. "I is sorry you been so scared. But leave you? Never."

Rain stared at him, her face wet with tears. "I want to believe you," she cried brokenly.

"You has to believe me. Judgment day will come 'fore I ever leave you."

She closed her eyes, tears squeezing from under her lashes. And then she was in his arms and he was holding her as tightly as a man could hold his woman.

"Daddy," a tiny voice said from under the table, but not too persistently since Daddy was kissing Mamma and everything seemed all right.

They bestirred themselves to put Glory to bed and after she fell asleep, they made love until their skin was bruised and inflamed. Peter felt purged of all despair. His mother's flight to freedom had brought him and Rain together again and he was indeed her son.

"Honeybunch," he whispered looking deeply into his wife's eyes, "I is gon dream us up another plan."

6

Cole Island
May 1862

Peter put his shoulder against the back of the cannon and pushed. His body felt the shock, the resistance of tons of iron cemented in crusted mud. On the other side Brother Man was also pushing, veins popped up like worms on his forehead. They guided the gun toward the jetty avoiding each other's eyes, fearful of any secret glance that the Mate trotting alongside of them might interpret. Behind them the Confederate fort had become a ghost town, the guns removed and the soldiers gone, their cooking fires stamped into ashes. A deer came out of the woods and stood poised for a moment with its head cocked, scenting danger, then sensibly it darted back into the thick underbrush.

Peter kept his eyes on the gun's long nozzle, his stomach muscles tensed with anxiety. This was the last piece of heavy armament to be removed from Cole Island. They reached the jetty where cross-eyed Aaron and Stretch were operating the lifting fork, the rest of the crew securing the armament already on deck.

"Easy there," the Mate yelled, striding up and down on his bandy legs. "If that cannon falls into the river your black asses will follow."

Peter grunted. Their black asses had already been in the river.

Stretch had managed to stumble over the hawser and flip himself overboard. The crew as one had dived over the rail to rescue him although the dumb ox could swim like a fish as the Mate had angrily pointed out to the other dumb oxen before sending them below to change their dripping clothes. Peter was proud of them. All day they had deliberately worked at a snail's pace. July had slammed a hammer down on his thumb which had turned them all into amateur doctors standing around giving advice. A screw came loose from the rail and the tool box was hunted for half an hour before it was found. Infuriated, the Mate had threatened to hang them all.

The last cannon was finally secured on the deck. In the pilot-house Captain Regan, disgusted and weary, ordered Peter to head for home. It was too late to deliver this artillery now. The frown on Peter's craggy face implied that he too regretted the lost hours which had been part of his plan. The Sesesh were abandoning Cole Island and transferring their artillery to another fort.

"Tomorrow we're casting off at four bells, Peter. Is that understood?"

"Yes, Cap'n. The crew'll be ready."

"They better be. Any more foot-dragging like we had today and somebody's going to be flogged. Is *that* understood?"

"Yes, suh. Anything further, Cap'n?"

Peter was anxious to know the procedure they would follow upon reaching Charleston. Weeks ago, due to her light draft and ability to maneuver in the inlets, the *Swanee* had been assigned to a high-ranking Confederate officer. On their tour of duty they had surveyed Charleston's harbor forts and transported Rebel troops and ammunition from the outer Sea Islands farther inland. They had also relocated for safety planter families from upper Edisto and Johns Island. Several planters had also sent their slaves farther inland but the majority of them had been left behind.

Captain Regan was scrutinizing Peter, his eyes cold and unblinking beneath his big black hat. The seconds ticked by in an uneasy silence. A pulse in Peter's temple throbbed. He resisted the impulse to snatch the coveted hat off the captain's head. Why was the man staring at him? Did he suspect anything?

"Four bells," Regan repeated. "That's all." He left the wheelhouse.

It was dusk when they reached Charleston. Peter eased the steamer into its berth and waited for the captain to emerge from his cabin and seal their fate. The city fanned out before him, blocks of it in charred ruins as devastated as if it had been bombed. The destruction had not been caused by a feared Yankee attack but by another dread, a Negro with a match in his hand. Sea Island slaves encamped on the grounds of Russell's factory on Hassell Street had built a small cooking fire one night which flared up out of control. The flames hurdled East Bay, roared down Market and State streets then jumped to Meeting Street. In panic, people ran screaming from their burning homes. Down through the years slaves had set many suspicious fires, and for their efforts a goodly number of them had been hanged.

Staring at the ruins while anxiously awaiting Captain Regan, Peter realized that the crew was undergoing a similar strain. They went about their work quickly, throwing out the lines, jumping onto the pier to wrap the hawser around a thick, rotting stump. No laggards now. Routinely, despite recent orders for all officers of light draft steamers to remain aboard while at dock, Captain Regan and his men often went home leaving Peter in charge. He prayed that tonight would be no different.

The captain finally appeared and Peter almost collapsed with relief. On top of Regan's curly head was his shore hat, the one with purple plumes. He was disembarking as were the Mate and Officer Malloy. Peter raced down to the gangplank to receive his orders.

"The crew will remain on board tonight, Peter. I'll be at home if you need me."

"Aye, aye, suh." This was the sweet news he had been waiting all evening to hear.

Smoothing the plumes of his hat, Captain Regan preceded his two aides down the gangplank.

One A.M. Peter and July broke into the captain's cabin. The curtain was pulled across the berth, a heavy blue cambric which also covered the porthole, shutting out the sun when the captain wanted to sleep. Tentatively Peter pulled back the curtain, possessed by the wild notion that Captain Regan was hiding in his bunk and would leap up and choke him. The berth was empty, of course. In the hanging locker he found what they were looking for—the wide-brimmed black hat, a pistol and a smooth-bore gun. Peter threw the musket to July and shoved the pistol into his waistband. Then he picked up the hat, his hands shaking. Suppose it didn't fit? Suppose it was too big and fell down over his eyes blinding him? Suppose you put it on, nigger. He slammed the hat on his head and after a surprised moment laughed out loud.

"What's so funny?" July asked, a frown on his handsome face at the absurdity of anything being funny on this menacing day.

"The captain's hat. She's a perfect fit."

"Naturally. You both fatheads."

Peter grinned. "Let's get on back———"

Brother Man interrupted him, sticking his big head through the door. "You better hurry up on deck, Peter. Turno's about to kill Aaron."

With an oath Peter hurried topside. The burly fireman had cross-eyed Aaron backed up against the rail, choking him. The crew was hollering, "Let him go," but making no move to interfere except for Stretch.

"For God's sake, man," Stretch yelled, grabbing Turno's arm.

The fireman snatched it free and socked him. The blow dropped Stretch to his knees. Turno lifted Aaron off his feet while squeezing his neck, the deckhand's eyes rolling around like loose pebbles in his head.

"You half-blind turd," Turno shouted. "You is going with us dead or alive." Since Aaron's tongue was hanging limply out of his mouth it appeared as though he would accompany them dead.

"Loose him," Peter yelled running forward. He snatched the pistol from his waistband and reaching the fireman jabbed it into his side. "I ain't fooling, Turno. Let him go."

"This bastard's done changed his mind," the fireman protested. "If he babbles we is all dead men."

"Let him go," Peter ordered, "or you'll be the first dead nigger."

He itched to pull the trigger then turn the gun on Aaron and rid himself of them both. All winter while they had hatched their plans he had worried about these two, the coward and the bully. Peter jammed the pistol deeper into Turno's flesh. All he needed was an excuse to shoot the bastard.

Turno released Aaron so suddenly that the man stumbled and

71

fell. Kneeling on the ground and rubbing his neck he blubbered, "He were gon kill me, Peter."

The fireman stared at him with contempt. "You is a lie. I was gonna toss you overboard only half dead and let the sharks finish you off." He turned toward Peter. "So what you gon do with me? Put me in irons?"

"You ain't gon do us no good in the brig."

"Well, it's me or him so you better start shooting."

"You ain't gon do us no good dead either."

On a sudden impulse, Peter shoved the pistol back into his waistband. He stared sternly at Turno who kept opening and closing his hands as though flexing them to strangle somebody.

"I is sorry, Peter," Aaron whimpered still hugging the floor. "I wants to go with you all but I cain't. Ain't no way we can best massa. They gon set fire to you like they did my daddy. They gon——"

"Shut up," Peter yelled. He should have let Turno strangle the idiot.

The crew had become restless, clearing their throats, waiting for an excuse to panic and he wheeled around to face them. He knew they all shared the same desperate urge to be free but were fearful for their lives. And he felt it too, the danger, the back of his neck prickling.

"What we agreed on still stands," he said, his voice steely, belying the tightness in his belly. "Everybody's free to make up they own mind 'cause if we gets caught we gon scuttle the boat and go down with her. Aaron's got the right to stay behind. It's his life. Anybody else done change they mind speak you piece now."

Brother Man and July declared they were in it all the way. Stretch, who had struggled to his feet, said likewise. Bite, the other deckhand, hesitated, looking furtively at Turno who glared at him. Finally he mumbled something incoherent.

"Speak up," Peter said impatiently. "What you say?"

Bite was another unknown quantity. He was not as hangdog as Aaron but almost, Peter felt, jumping whenever Turno growled. Bite was married to a gal Peter had never met, but rumor had it that she could whip her husband in a fair fight and often did. Bite grinned nervously, exposing brown, rutted teeth, and mumbled that he had not changed his mind.

72

"Awright," Peter said. "And you, Turno?" He stilled his hand from reaching for the pistol.

"I'd like to see the bastard what thinks he can shut me outta this deal," Turno bellowed.

"I'd like to see that bastard, too," Peter replied.

Relieved, the men guffawed. Peter hauled Aaron to his feet. "We gon leave you off by the *Rover* and you stay in they hole till tomorrow or before God I'll be back to strangle you myself."

"Thank you, Peter. God bless you." Aaron grabbed his hand and seemed about to kiss it before Peter snatched it back.

"Stay outta my sight, you yellow-bellied toad," Turno growled. "I still think we oughta feed your black ass to the sharks."

Two A.M. It was time. Gripping the wheel hard, Peter gave the order to weigh anchor.

The logbook was open in its little niche on the shelf. July had been assigned the task of officially recording their journey and slowly in his almost illegible hand he penned, "Two A.M. We casts off." Other black hands hauled up the anchor, shoveled coal into the furnaces, checked the steam gauges. Black eyes searched the sky to find the north star, guiding light throughout the ages. Please do not wink us into oblivion.

The city slept fitfully, nerve ends twitching. A sentry on shore found nothing alarming at the sight of the *Swanee* chugging downstream in the middle of the night. She had made such trips before. Peter steamed toward the *Rover,* a commercial ship moored at its berth at low tide. Upon reaching it he wondered with a pounding heart if Rain had followed his instructions. He trusted her but if anything went wrong . . .

July read his mind. "I hope they is all——"

"We'll soon find out," Peter interrupted. "Tell Stretch to take Aaron along."

The crew worked swiftly, stealthily, and within minutes the two men were ashore. Peter watched them disappear into the darkness. He kept his eyes on the *Rover.* Saw movement. Shadows walking. Stretch and Aaron clambering aboard? Or white men with nooses to tighten around their necks? The crew was also watching, paralyzed with anxiety. How long did it take to collect them? Hurry.

Suddenly the moonlight seemed too bright. A floodlight. Where were the shit-brained storm clouds? Where was God?

A clump moved out of the darkness into the light. There they were. Figures outlined in silhouette. Peter squeezed his eyes shut and reopened them quickly. No, it was not a dying man's vision. Stretch was leading them up the *Swanee*'s gangplank.

The seamen rushed forward to help their families aboard. Was Turno crying, Peter wondered, seeing the big man's shoulders quake as he picked up his small son. Then came Brother Man's fat sister followed by Bite's wife, holding their infant son. Glory appeared next, stumbling, frightened, and then Rain who was clutching the baby to her breast. She reached out a hand to pull the little girl to her then looked toward the pilothouse.

Peter steeled himself to remain at the wheel. It was an effort not to rush down and sweep her and their babies into his arms. She was holding on to them for dear life. Or a watery grave. He had never loved her more than at this moment.

As Stretch led them below deck, July reported that everyone was accounted for. Hunched over the logbook he wrote: "We leves Charleston at haf pas three."

The floating torpedoes in the harbor did not alarm Peter. He knew their location and could avoid detonating them. The danger was the major forts ringing the bay to protect Charleston. Castle Pinckney came first, three fourths of a mile from Charleston, built on a low-lying island. It was a brick fort with a two-man staff. Peter had anticipated no difficulty in passing the castle and he was right. The guard waved them by. Fort Johnson on James Island would be their first mammoth test. The high arching shells of its mortars could explode the *Swanee* into fragments.

It loomed up suddenly through the mists, the shadowy outline of the earth emplacement. A sentry was on guard. Let him be half-blind, Peter prayed. He tugged on the whistle, gave the proper signal and held his breath. And so did the crew, the steamer as hushed as a cathedral.

The yawning sentry on the gun turret waved, apparently recognizing Captain Regan's black hat which Peter was wearing. The steamer sailed by.

"Awright," Peter breathed out loud.

"Amen," July seconded, scribbling in the logbook.

They became silent, the slurp of the paddlewheels and the whine of the engines sound enough for both of them as they anticipated the next hurdle. The Goliath of the harbor fortifications. Fort Sumter. Its pentagon walls were sixty feet high, built on a two-and-a-half acre sand spit squatting in the middle of the passageway to the sea. All ship channels and the entire shoreline were within the range of its artillery as well as the city of Charleston itself.

Stretch came loping into the wheelhouse with his awkward gait, testing the heft of the Mate's pistol in the palm of his hand.

"Sumter ain't never look so scary," he groaned.

July agreed. "She's a killer."

"We's on the fastest paddlewheel steamer hereabouts," Stretch said. "Maybe we should——"

"No," Peter cut him off. "We ain't gon make a run for it. The *Swanee* cain't outrun Sumter's guns. We gon sail by nice and easy like we been doing. And stop playing with that gun lessen you plans to use it on me."

"Damn, Peter. Why you say a thing like that?" Pained, Stretch and his firearm departed.

The minutes ticked by slowly. Lazily. Time did not choose sides and, to prove it, refused to race but crawled. Goliath loomed larger, its high walls dwarfing the paddlewheel steamer.

"July. Take the wheel." Peter was surprised that his voice sounded natural, that it wasn't an agonized shriek.

He stationed himself at the window as he had seen Captain Regan do a thousand times, carefully tilting his face so it was hidden under the broad-brimmed hat. Now. He pulled the whistle chord. It gave the signal. Screamed for him. *Don't crave no special talk tonight. Don't hanker to see the captain face to face.* There was a moment of ominous silence. He knew that the sentry was reporting to the corporal of the guard that the *Swanee* was requesting permission to pass. Time tick-tocked ridiculously slow again. Peter remained at the window, his hand on the pistol. It was cocked. Ready.

The answering signal came. "Pass the *Swanee*."

"Jesus," July breathed, relieved.

Cautiously, with a casualness he did not feel, Peter backed away from the window and took over the wheel. Stumbling, July reached for the logbook.

Standing between them now and the open sea was Fort Moultrie on Sullivans Island. But surely, Peter felt, having negotiated past Sumter they would not be stopped now. Fate could not be so cruel. He squinted as the high sand dunes appeared. The brick walls. The guns in their barbettes facing the open sea. Peter steeled himself, adjusted the captain's hat on his head. His hand reached for the whistle. The signal was two long pulls and a jerk. He felt the cord between his fingers and pulled it as he had done so many times before at night going out on patrol duty. *Sentry, please. There ain't nothing different this time.*

The guard on duty waved nonchalantly. Slowly Peter let out his breath.

"We done it," July whispered. "We done it."

Peter turned around for a last look at Charleston, its outline blurred by mists. The only person he had told about their plans to escape had been Uncle Hiram, who had listened gravely, his head cocked slightly to one side. He did not interrupt but finally nodded. "Sounds like a good plan," he said but refused the offer to accompany them, stating that he could not leave the men in the Brotherhood.

"Charleston," Peter whispered aloud, still looking at the shrouded city. There he had come to manhood, the sea a lullaby and a mournful lament. Now the sound of the sea was repeating inside his head: *It ain't over yet. It ain't over.* He kept to his course for the time he had prescribed, then swung the boat around, by-passing Morris Island, heading straight out to sea through the Swash Channel.

The change of direction was duly noted by Fort Sumter's guard and the sentry on Morris Island. Frantically they signaled each other. Lights flashed and flickered. What in the devil was going on? The answer was irrelevant since the *Swanee* had passed beyond the range of their firepower, her destination freedom a scant three miles away.

The seamen streamed onto the deck, followed by their families, the women hushing the children who were fretful at all the commotion disturbing their sleep. *Hush now. Hush. And look yonder.* The wondrous sight choked them into silence. The tall masts of a fully rigged warship loomed before them on the waves. The *Onward.* Foremost ship of the Union fleet blockading Charleston harbor. Was there ever a sight more glorious to behold?

"Hoist the white flag." Peter's voice was hoarse.

Down came the Confederate flag and a white sheet ran up the flagpole. The night was calm, windless, and the flag of truce hung limply on the flagstaff. Peter steered the steamer directly toward the *Onward* and heard emanating from it a bugle calling the men to their battle stations.

"My God," July shouted, terrified. "They think we's a blockade runner. They gon blow us to hell and gone."

"Wind where you be?" Peter yelled.

Viciously he wrenched the wheel around. The boat shuddered. The inert white flag felt the ripple of a breeze. Slowly it billowed. The flag of truce waved at the captain of the *Onward*, stilling his order to fire a second before it spilled from his lips.

A bullhorn amplified his voice. "Ahoy. Who goes there?"

Peter sucked in his breath and bellowed: "Runaway slaves, suh. Come to deliver a Sesesh gunboat to the Union fleet."

Silence. Then the surprised retort. "Slaves? On a Confederate gunboat?"

"Yes, suh. We stole she."

The voice over the bullhorn warned: "Anybody who moves toward those cannons will be shot. Can you hear me?"

"Yes, suh."

"Proceed alongside and drop anchor."

"Gladly, suh."

Peter's hands were sweaty gripping the wheel. He stared at them. Were they the calloused hands of a free man? July was writing in the logbook that they had reached the blockade, his eyes glassy with tears.

Slaves stealing a gunboat?

Yes, suh.

Peter gave the *Onward*'s captain a full account, reporting that they also had on board four cannons earmarked for Middle Ground Battery but they had successfully delayed their delivery in order to hand them over to Uncle Sam.

By noon Peter was back on the *Swanee*, now flying the Stars and Stripes, with officers and seamen from the Union gunboat aboard.

At ten forty-five that night the *Swanee* docked at Hilton Head in the Sea Islands, Union headquarters, and Peter was hustled ashore. He barely had time to marvel at the new wharf refugee slaves had built for the Yankees before he was being rowed to the *Wabash* for further questioning by the commander of the South Atlantic Blockading Squadron.

Commander Samuel Du Pont had already been briefed and greeted him cordially in his stateroom. Peter was impressed by its spaciousness. It boasted two curtained portholes. And a desk. And a settee. And a rug on the floor as well as a wide double berth.

"Mr. Mango. How good of you to indulge me with your presence. You have to be exhausted but if you will submit to a few more questions?" The commander's voice was as deep as the sound in a conch shell. Pleasant and persuasive.

"Of course, suh."

Peter stood at attention, awed at being in the presence of the man whose strategy had destroyed Fort Walker and Fort Beauregard. He yearned to blurt out that he had seen the *Wabash* on the day of the gunshoot and liked to die when he thought it was on fire, but he held his tongue. The commander was portly, broad in the shoulders and in the beam. Dressed in navy blue with epaulets on the shoulders and beribboned medals on his chest, he seemed like spanking perfection to Peter.

"Let's proceed to the heart of the matter," Du Pont said, "so you can get some rest. You can read charts, Mr. Mango?"

"Yes, suh."

"Excellent."

With a firm hand under Peter's elbow, he guided him across the stateroom to a large chart hanging on the bulkhead. "Here we are," he said, picking up a long pointer and indicating their location on the map. "Hilton Head."

It was the largest chart Peter had ever seen. He stared at the irregular coastline, the waterways interspersed with inlets and the chain of barrier islands, its magnitude condensed so it could be absorbed by the human eye. His palms were sweating, the excitement of the past few hours crystallizing now into a state of nervous shock. Hilton Head, he told himself. That's what the captain's pointing at. The lines ran dizzily together around the pointer in a maze he could not decipher. He dropped his eyes, focused on the toe of his boots.

"You told my officers, Mr. Mango, that the Confederates were changing their lines of defense?"

Peter nodded. "They has moved they big guns from Cole Island and Battery Island to the James Island side of the Stono River. Sesesh been shortening they lines ever since the gunshoot in Port Royal harbor."

"Can you show me on the map where this has occurred?" Du Pont handed him the pointer.

Peter swallowed his panic and raised his eyes. He knew the inland waterways like the back of his hand and he could read charts. He stared at the maze, felt himself being pulled into it, slapped flat like the chart itself. And suddenly it was all right. There was the Stono River. And Cole Island. And to the left . . .

"After they forts fell, Sesesh pull back from here," he said, tracing a path from Edisto Island to Johns Island lying to the south of Charleston. "They move out the planters but plenty of slaves was left behind."

Du Pont nodded. The naval expeditions had enlarged their beachhead beyond the islands initially seized, overrunning the lower part of Edisto Island and making raids down the coast. They were now in possession of seacoast towns in Georgia and Florida.

"What about their forts, Mr. Mango? I understand you are quite knowledgeable about them."

The *Swanee* had done a survey of all the harbor forts and Peter now related in detail the kind of armament each possessed and the relative strength of their troops.

"And they done abandon they fort on Cole Island, like I said. We was supposed to take them cannons to Middle Ground Battery but thought you all could use them instead."

"Good thinking," the commander said, staring intensely at the chart. "With those batteries removed our naval force boats could command the Stono River."

"She the back door to Charleston," Peter averred, "like them English sailors knowed."

Du Pont looked at him surprised. The same strategy the Confederates were employing now, fortifying their harbor forts to protect Charleston, had backfired during the revolutionary war when the

British had sailed up the Stono River to capture the city. Du Pont pointed to Stono Inlet.

"Can our navy boats get through to land men here?"

Peter shook his head. "They defense strong thereabouts 'cause the bar so shallow and shifting she dangerous. Big boats cain't get through. But the *Swanee* with she shallow draft been in there many a time."

"The back door to Charleston," the commander mused.

Peter was excited. "You gon attack she, suh? A quick surprise blow?" He figured that when the city fell, the war would soon be over.

Du Pont smiled at Peter's excitement which matched his own. "We have to check out the batteries on Cole Island first. General Blenham who's in charge of ground troops here will probably want to see you."

"I be glad to talk with him but . . ." Peter hesitated. The most important aspect of his journey had yet to be broached. "Can I ask you a question, suh?"

"Of course."

"What we be? The crew and our families. We ain't slaves no more, is we?"

The question took Commander Du Pont by surprise. "I assumed that somebody had already told you . . . Please forgive this unpardonable oversight. The Union does not traffic in slavery. You are no longer slaves."

Actually, Samuel Du Pont had been given specific orders by the War Department before the invasion not to interfere with the South's institutions. His men were to use force if necessary to repel runaway slaves and return them to their masters. That official policy of President Lincoln had been ground to dust by the actions of the slaves themselves, turning up by the hundreds at every camp and bivouac where the Union established its lines. Some marched in boldly to offer their services. Others, fearing inhuman treatment, which they often received, camped outside attempting to elude the slave catchers pursuing them.

"You and your little band are contrabands," the commander said.

Peter let the unknown word roll off his tongue. "Contrabands, suh?"

Du Pont smiled. "We have to thank General Butler for coming up with that concept. When his camp in Virginia was besieged by hundreds of runaways he declared that they were contrabands of war, subject to confiscation because they had performed useful service for our enemies, building their bridges and fortifications. He employed them in his camp and paid them."

That had become the policy in many camps that no longer allowed slaveowners, waving a white flag of truce, to enter the premises to retrieve their human chattel.

"My plan, Mr. Mango, is to send the crew and their families to Beaufort where they'll be well cared for and safe. But I would appreciate it if you would remain here at Hilton Head. We can use your services."

Peter was overwhelmed. He was no longer a slave. A journey begun before he had been born was ending on this Yankee frigate. He breathed a prayer of thanks, mentally falling to his knees to give God the glory. Looking at Commander Du Pont, Peter offered himself up gladly.

"Please, Cap'n," he said, his craggy face somber, "use me."

After Peter left, Du Pont sat at his desk and wrote a long letter to the secretary of the navy reporting the abduction of the *Swanee* by its slave crew, a most remarkable achievement. Due to her light draft, the paddlewheel steamer would be a valuable addition to his squadron and he was requesting that the dusky pirates be awarded the usual prize money for her capture. The pilot was quite intelligent and knowledgeable. The information he willingly divulged was of the utmost importance and would be put to good use immediately.

The crew and the women saw Peter approaching in the rowboat and anxiously awaited him on deck. The children were asleep below.

"What the big cap'n say?"

"Is I free at last?"

Hands reached out to help Peter clamber aboard. Rain was standing at the rail with Brother Man and his sister. Peter moved toward them and touched Rain's cheek. He wanted to laugh, he wanted to cry, melting with bliss.

"We is contrabands," he said. "We ain't slaves no more."

Slaves no more. The words gathered momentum, reverberated out to sea with a roar and bounced off of continents. The men and women laughed, tears streaming down their faces. They wept and embraced one another. Peter explained what contraband meant to the best of his knowledge and they nodded, understanding the substance of the thing. A slave no more.

Finally the others drifted away and Peter and Rain were alone for the first time since their runaway journey began. He was remaining here at headquarters, he told her, to lead an expedition down the Stono. The crew was being taken to Beaufort and she was to live there with his mother.

"You ain't coming with us?" Rain had not planned on this contingency. Her eyes widened with fear, she bit her lip. "Peter, I don't know 'bout this. I thought we'd be together."

"We will be, honeybunch. Soon's the war's over. And that gon be maybe day after tomorrow." He laughed, exuberant, and pulled her into his arms. "Now don't you fret youself. Everything's gon be all right."

Rain wrapped her arms around his neck to chain him to her. Looking into her flooding eyes Peter pleaded, "Please, don't cry," and kissed her.

Hungrily their lips clung together, bodies pressed close, straining to meet. Desperate, famished, they ran below deck holding hands looking for a place to lie down.

Book Two
Home
on the
Sea Islands

And so I have come back where phantoms play
And from the past the silent guardians stand
But there is something yet within that frets
                              it will not stay
It cries into the night for its lost alien land.

— SAMUEL ALLEN,
       "Out of the Womb, Crying"

7

May 1862

The water was calm, a slight breeze at their back as the *Swanee* coasted up the Beaufort River. Black smoke belched from her chimneys and the crew felt strange at having been relieved of their duties by the Yankee sailors. In fact, they were no longer her crew but had been set adrift, their nervous excitement not untinged with anxiety. It was sobering, freedom dreamed about for a lifetime was now a reality.

July and Rain were standing aft on the main deck watching the foaming wake, the paddlewheels slapping the water with a gurgling sound. Rain untied the bandanna wrapped around her head and scratched her scalp in between the cornrows that trailed down the nape of her neck.

"And why is *you* so sad?" she asked July, after revealing her worries about leaving Peter behind.

"I was thinking 'bout Mariah." Trying to relieve Rain's fears had underscored his own miserable condition.

"The girl what was supposed to come with you?"

"Yeh."

She did not want to die. That's what Mariah had told him. He glanced at Rain and then away as if the sight of her was painful, someone else's woman who had not wanted to die either.

"She change her mind at the last minute?"

A muscle in July's jaw twitched. "Said she warn't coming 'cause she was too scared. Said our massas wouldn't let us get away, they had bloodhounds. She had seen a man chewed to death once. Hounds went after his gullet. I told her dogs cain't track you on water. She said, they got boats bigger than yourn with bigger guns and ain't gon let us get away. I said, don't you wanna be free? She said, I don't wanna be dead."

July remembered the moment and how she had looked, her mouth trembling, her eyes round with fright. *I don't wanna be dead.* She had no faith in him. And how could he blame her? She had a roof over her head, a blanket to keep her warm and a mistress who was kind. And what was he offering her? A chance to drown if they were caught. A promise to hold her in his arms as they sank. Mariah had pleaded with him not to go, not to leave her, and he had almost caved in. Knowing that if he touched her he would melt, he had bolted away from his beloved.

"I shoulda flung that skinny gal in a croaker sack and brought her aboard," he said.

"Yeh," Rain agreed, not knowing what else to say. She peeped at July from beneath her lashes, at the symmetry of his black, brooding face. "It's a misery being separated from somebody you loves," she said, her eyes misty.

"Now don't you go to worrying 'bout Peter again."

"I was thinking 'bout my family."

To distract Rain and plunge the knife deeper into his own flesh, July pulled from his trouser pocket a little wooden figure he was carving. It rested in the palm of his hand, an unfinished but clearly discernible young woman's head, her hair in braids, her neck long and slender.

"Mariah?" Rain asked, her fingers skimming over the figurine.

"Mariah," he repeated, his voice breaking.

Then, half-ashamed that he had babbled too much, July shoved the carving back in his pocket. Turning away from Rain, he studied the approaching coastline, a long stretch of shore bordered by woods, blurred by a mist that had rolled in from the sea. He leaned into the mist, trying to see through it.

Chilled suddenly, Rain replaced her head wrap, tying the ends in a little bow. She had been keeping an eye on Glory, playing under the cannon with Bryant, Turno the fireman's little boy. The imp was trying to climb its barrel, Glory at his heels.

"You chil'ren come away from there," Rain said and bid July good-bye. She quit the rail thinking that Mariah was a fool, not running away from slavery with such a good-looking man.

Bryant straightened up as Rain approached him and smiled innocently, his pointed face so beguiling she had to smile.

"You is a little devil," she said. "Does you know that?"

"Yes, ma'am."

Rain grabbed him and Glory by the hand and pulled them along. She found the others starboard lined up along the rail. Bryant ran to his father who swung the boy up onto his shoulder. Sister, standing next to Brother Man, was holding Peewee in the crook of her arm.

"He wet yet?" Rain felt the infant's bottom.

Sister shook her head, loathe to give the baby up. She and her brother looked alike despite the fact that he was well over six feet and she just barely five. There was an Oriental cast to their flat moon faces, Brother Man's skin leathery and Sister's silky smooth, girded as it was with a layer of fat.

She was a mute but not born that way. Twenty years ago she found refuge in silence after being rented out to a farmer when she was nine. Supposedly, she was to learn how to use a loom. The farmer locked her up in his barn and visited her day and night, returning Sister to her master bruised and bloodied. She never spoke another word. When questioned she had seizures and foamed at the mouth. After a few such unproductive sessions the questions ceased. But Brother Man, ten years her senior, saw the welts on her back, the teeth marks on her thighs, and wept.

The steamer's whistle tooted. The low sandy shore bordered by trees loomed up ahead. Rain felt her heart quicken.

"Hand me the baby please, Sister."

Holding Peewee in the crook of her arm, Rain pulled Glory to her side. They had arrived in Beaufort.

"The soldiers showed we niggers how to really thief," Lily told them. "All over the islands they snatched missy's featherbeds and silverware till the big general made them stop for pure shame. Then along come the cotton agents and they were the grandest thieves of all. The furniture get up and walk. The chandeliers and china closets and pianos. Colored folks wrecked the cotton gins after the gunshoot and relieved massa of some of he furniture. I borrowed some myself. But there was plenty good stuff left what the cotton agents sent north by the boatload.''

Lily, holding Peewee on her lap, had declared at the outset that he was the spitting image of his daddy. Glory was leaning against Rain who was looking around at her future home with curiosity. Lily had moved from her former quarters. This shack had been partitioned into two rooms and was unlike any slave quarters Rain had ever before seen. It was filled with furniture from the large front house, not tatty hand-me-downs but real nice tables and chairs and this pretty sofa she was sitting on and in the other room a bed and commode and more chairs and such. There was scarcely space to move about. Such lovely things, Rain thought, what had gotten up and walked.

She saw Stretch easing his long-legged self toward the door followed by July, and she yearned to tell them, please not yet. I ain't ready for you all to go. They were returning to the inn. Upon landing, the navy chaplain had turned the families over to the care of a Reverend Archibald Ferdinand who had secured temporary quarters for them at the Sandy Cove Inn. He then dispatched Rain and the children to her mother-in-law's house in a hired coach, Stretch and July accompanying her.

Lily had listened avidly to every detail of their escape, grinning her gap-toothed smile and squeezing her grandson until he peed on her. Still she would not relinquish him, telling Rain she had been peed on before so please let her hold this precious child.

"I ain't never seen so many colored folks since I been born," Lily said, continuing to relate what had happened after the gunshoot. "They came here running and died like sand flies. I hear tell they is ten thousand on we islands now and still coming. It were a hard winter. Field hands didn't get they winter clothes 'fore massa up and left them in rags. They was barefoot, freezing and starving, too, 'cause the soldiers grab all the food to feed theyself. But it's some better now. Colored folks is spread out all over working on the plantations. And they done send down a whole passel of white folks from up north to help. They calls it the Project, running the plantations, and everybody gets paid. And

we can keep we wages for our own sweet self. Ain't that grand?"
Lily laughed at this surprising state of affairs. She had been hired
as a housekeeper for a colonel.

"So they's work here for us?" Stretch asked.

"Plenty. On all the islands hereabouts. And that ain't all. Them
nice northern ladies set up schools for we chil'ren. Glory, you can
go. And you, too, Peewee, soon's you stop peeing on you granny."

July and Stretch had reached the door.

"You all ain't gon forget where I is," Rain pleaded, standing up,
a note of panic in her voice.

"Soon's we get located we'll be back," July said, his face grave
to impress upon her that he would keep his word.

"I is mighty happy to be here," Stretch told Lily. "First thing I
said to myself, we has to go see Peter's mammy. I been so longing
to meet you."

He would have elaborated on his longing endlessly had not July
impatiently yanked him out the door. Having no relatives of his
own, Stretch was fond of appropriating other people's kin.

In the silence following their leavetaking, Rain felt a jolting
loneliness. Her feet were on dry land for the first time in days and
like seagoing sailors she suddenly longed for the roll of the boat
beneath her. That at least meant being close to Peter instead of
being inspected so frankly by his mother.

"That's a right nice name," Lily said finally. "Rain. You was
born during a storm?"

"No, ma'am. It was so hot my mamma prayed for a drop of
rain."

She laughed. Lily smiled. It was a nervous laugh and a tentative
smile, both of them willing to be congenial. But in the months to
come, the two children would be the glue that held them together.

"Glad you're back," Turno said gruffly when July and Stretch
bounced into the inn. The fireman was holding his sleeping son
in his arms. "Thought you all mighta got lost."

July was surprised by his apparent concern. During their flight
on the *Swanee*, dependent upon each other for survival, all dis-
agreements had been submerged but he expected them to resurface
at any moment.

Turno was seated with Bite and the others at a large round

table covered with a red checkered tablecloth, all of them drinking molasses and water. It was a homey little place and their group seemed tired but at ease. Reverend Ferdinand, talking to the proprietor in his little cubbyhole, emerged to greet the new arrivals. At the moment, except for them, the inn was deserted.

"Welcome back," the minister said with a broad smile. "I trust you had no difficulties?"

"We went there straight away," Stretch replied, returning the minister's smile. "Miss Lily real nice. I was so glad to meet her." He bobbed his head up and down at the wonder of it.

"We are grateful," the minister intoned "for this glorious day of liberation. I was waiting for the safe return of you gentlemen before I departed. Shall we offer up a prayer of thanksgiving for one journey safely ended and another glorious one about to begin?" He looked at his charges tenderly.

Sister and Brother Man nodded, and Stretch appeared favorable also to prayer. Bite was noncommittal, his wife engaged in the baby nursing at her breast. Only Turno was heard to grumble. He was reverting back to form, July thought. He himself had little use for ministers of any persuasion but at least he had the good grace to keep quiet. Glumly, he sat down at the table.

Standing tall, Reverend Archibald Ferdinand flung out his arms to invoke the grace of God, looking like a bat in his black greatcoat and broad-brimmed hat. He was a squarely built man, his clean-shaven face scarred with acne. His prayer was lengthy as was his wont, damning the evils of slavery and its perpetrators, an offense in the sight of almighty God.

He was among the fifty volunteers in the Port Royal Project under the authority of Treasury Secretary Salmon Chase, an abolitionist. The volunteers had responded to the call of Northern anti-slavery societies to journey south to assist the contrabands in their transition from bondage to freedom, to teach them order and industry and self-reliance, as Secretary Chase advised, and to elevate them in the scale of humanity by inspiring them with self-respect. In short, civilize the Negroes and they in turn could help the Union win the war.

Reverend Ferdinand, like most of the volunteers, had come of age protesting and battling the Fugitive Slave Law which attempted to make them accomplices in tracking down runaway slaves in their Northern communities. They refused to cooperate as many a free Negro was scooped up and dragged below the Mason-Dixon Line into slavery. The protesters organized support groups, broke into jails and courthouses to rescue the runaways and spirit them to safety in Canada. In the process the reverend had been fined several times and once sentenced to jail.

". . . I commit these black brethren into your merciful care as they labor in thy vineyards," he prayed. "You have led them out of their dark dungeons of bondage and for this we give thanks, praying for those still in captivity, praying that our enemies will be smitten and the bondsmen shall go free. Humbly we beseech thy blessings in the name of the Father, the Son and the Holy Ghost. Amen."

"Amen," Stretch echoed as the minister opened his eyes, lowered his arms and beamed a saintly smile at the contrabands.

"I imagine that you are all weary," he said, "and rightfully so. It's been a long, strenuous day."

Turno inquired, "When we gon meet some of these mens you been telling us 'bout what can offer us jobs?"

"In the morning I will round up whoever's in town," the reverend replied smoothly. "I have secured quarters for you all upstairs and if you're ready to repair to your rooms now I will be leaving."

July scrambled to his feet, leading the way. It had been a long, eventful day.

In the morning they were all seated at a table, breakfast barely finished, when Reverend Ferdinand appeared with two white men in tow.

"We are in luck," he said beaming his ministerial smile, "I want you to meet Mr. Youngblood and Mr. Simon, two Project superintendents who came into Beaufort this morning to pick up supplies and their mail."

"And a brace of mules," Mr. Youngblood amended, walking forward to briskly shake the hands of the former crewmen. "I came in on the ferry from St. Helena and the first thing I heard on the docks was about you black pirates. Congratulations on your bold dash to freedom."

The other superintendent, a slender man wearing hip boots

caked with mud, echoed Youngblood's sentiments and shook hands also.

"I was telling these gentlemen," Reverend Ferdinand said, "that you folks are interested in finding work. God is good. I could not have found two people more inclined to be helpful. Mr. Youngblood manages seven plantations for our government on St. Helena, which is the largest island hereabout, and Mr. Simon supervises a plantation on Edisto Island."

Mr. Youngblood, shrewdly studying the Negroes, stated that he could offer them all jobs. July was likewise studying him. Their eyes met and the superintendent smiled as though acknowledging a friend. July merely nodded, not yet certain he liked this hairy man. Reddish blond hair covered most of his freckled face—bushy sideburns, drooping mustache and full beard all running together. When he spoke his ruby lips were barely visible.

"Your wages will be paid by the government," he said. "By our Uncle Sam."

He neglected to add that their Uncle Sam was notoriously late in that regard. Or that they would be cheated out of some of their wages by the cotton agents who had arrived on the islands first, before the volunteers, to confiscate all the cotton they could locate and bale with Negro labor. The crop the fleeing planters had left standing man-high in the fields had to be harvested and a new one planted immediately or next year's yield would be minimal. Sea Island cotton, prized as the finest in the world, would fuel northern factories and replenish the Union's almost depleted treasury. When the superintendents and teachers arrived, the cotton agents viewed them as usurping their authority.

"You want us to chop cotton?" Turno asked bluntly.

Youngblood replied that cultivating cotton was their main resource. He had jumped at the opportunity to volunteer for this project, taking leave from his lucrative law practice. In Cambridge he had been secretary of the local antislavery society and had written articles published in northern journals contending that black labor was more economical than slave labor and that the demise of the plantocracy did not mean the demise of cotton. The volunteers were paid twenty-five dollars a month by the northern societies that had recruited them and received their lodging and board from the government. Youngblood's enthusiasm had overflowed to the point where he donated his first year's salary to the Project.

"You can look forward to receiving an honest day's salary for an honest day's labor," he told Turno. "For years you people have worked without pay but that time fortunately has come to an end."

"How much pay, suh?" July asked.

"Fifty cents an hour. The Union needs your labor, men, and you women also."

"Fifty cents," Stretch murmured, his eyes widening with appreciation.

"I ain't chopping no cotton," Turno said belligerently. "I didn't come——"

Reverend Ferdinand interrupted, "Son, you're free here to do as you please. What is your pleasure?"

His voice was so husky with kindness it took Turno unawares and made Dexter Youngblood frown. It was no secret that the minister's deference to Negroes, always hugging them and their squalling babies, irritated the superintendent. In his opinion, which he didn't hesitate to voice, the Negroes did not need pampering but discipline to develop the self-reliance that would offset the deleterious effects of slavery. By virtue of their centuries-long isolation, Sea Island blacks were considered the most ignorant and backward in captivity. If the Project succeeded in training them to become self-sufficient and productive, its tactics could be employed elsewhere to reconstruct the South.

"I think I'll stay here in Beaufort," Turno said, squaring his bulky shoulders. "Find meself a boat and see how the shrimps be running."

"That's a grand idea," Bite said. "I ain't crazy 'bout picking cotton either."

His wife, Mattie, looked at him sourly, burped their baby, and nodded. They would remain in Beaufort with Turno.

Youngblood eyed the two men suspiciously. "There's other work available on the plantations I manage besides being a field hand. Where I live at Caine's Landing there's——"

Stretch sat bolt upright. "Caine's Landing? That's what you said? It owned by Roland Caine?"

"I believe that is the gentleman's name."

Excited, Stretch punched July's shoulder. "Ain't this sump'n. Yesterday we was with Peter's mother and now this? His owner's plantation. Peter talked 'bout him plenty. And didn't I meet him once myself with Peter?" Stretch laughed, tickled by the connection which bound him to them all. "I don't have to throw no bones to know we's spose to work for Massa Youngblood here."

"*Mister* Youngblood," the superintendent corrected with a smile.

July temporized, "Well, I don't know . . ."

But Stretch was certain. He touched the asafetida bag he wore on a string around his neck. His good luck charm. "July, ain't nothing bad can happen to us on St. Helena. I say let's go."

"Maybe." July was willing to be persuaded.

But not Brother Man. Sister seemed to have taken an instant dislike to Dexter Youngblood who apparently reminded her of someone she would rather forget. Whenever she glanced at his hairy face she shuddered.

Brother Man, ever sensitive to her, asked the other superintendent, "What you say 'bout you place?"

Mr. Simon reported that the Edisto contrabands welcomed newcomers with a helping hand. There was plenty of work and good pay and the climate was healthier than on the other barrier islands.

Sister nodded. Brother Man said Edisto was for them.

"Well now," Reverend Ferdinand glowed, "everybody's settled." He would make arrangements for Turno and his group to be quartered close to town and inquire about obtaining a small boat.

And so the crew of the *Swanee* came to the parting of the ways but not before being treated to a pleasant surprise. A contingent of soldiers was marching by outside on the double, eyes straight ahead, muskets slung across their shoulders.

"My God!" July exclaimed, peering at them through the window, "is I seeing aright?" The soldiers were black.

"They're General Hunter's pet project," Reverend Ferdinand explained, smiling. "He's always scandalizing us with his boldness."

An abolitionist, General David Hunter was head of the Department of the South which encompassed South Carolina, Georgia and Florida.

"It may be too soon to attempt to make soldiers of Negroes,"

Dexter Youngblood murmured. "Perhaps we should allow them a little time to adjust to their new situation."

General Hunter obviously did not agree with such criticism, which was widespread and included Mr. Lincoln, who voiced his fears that weapons entrusted to Negroes would soon be in the hands of the Confederates. And he rescinded a decree issued by General Hunter freeing all slaves in his department with the reprimand that only he, the President, had such authority. The Negroes took it all in stride, considering themselves already free since their owners had departed. General Hunter was still pursuing official sanction for his black regiment.

"Now ain't that a sight to behold," Turno enthused with a raucous burst of laughter.

"A glorious sight," the reverend intoned. "A credit to their race."

Stretch and July grinned at each other. It was glorious, no doubt about that, uniformed black men proudly carrying their weapons, marching in cadence down the street.

St. Helena

Tall evergreen trees on either side of the dirt road cast lacy shadows on the wagon as it rattled along with a string of mules tethered behind it. Young Tanner Weaver, another volunteer and Youngblood's assistant, had met them at the ferry and was seated beside his boss driving the wagon. July and Stretch were in the back leaning against sacks of salt and talking to Absalom, the field hand Youngblood had elevated to foreman. Absalom was in his forties but still robust. Youngblood had wisely not availed himself of the services of the slave driver whom the contrabands universally detested.

Absalom had immediately endeared himself to Stretch by embracing him. "Doggone but I cain't believe I is meeting the bold nigras what stole the Sesesh's gunboat." He had hugged July, too, who liked him but wasn't as garrulous about it as Stretch who was questioning him interminably.

Absalom was chewing a wad of tobacco which poked out one

of his cheeks. He pushed his shapeless felt hat farther back on his head and said, "Sure I knew Massa Roland. On a pass to Savannah once I were a day late getting back and he made the overseer whip me till I were bloody. Massa were a harsh man if you crossed him just a teensy bit. But with Massa Youngblood there ain't no whippings 'cause we ain't slaves no more. And we does get paid, if slowly." He smiled, revealing spacy, stained teeth. "Things is a heap better now, I can tell you that. The field hands still live in they quarters and I has a place up by the Big House. That's where we boss and Mistuh Tanner and the lady schoolteachers stays, in the overseer's house."

"You don't say," July murmured politely. He was absorbing the landscape.

St. Helena was six miles from Beaufort, the countryside flat and sandy with a wealth of woods. The wagon rolled past a rice plantation which looked like a field of mud to July. Then came a real swamp, the soggy land covered with dense vegetation and interspersed with the thick gnarled trunks of cypress trees kneeling down in the marsh. He had to admit that the steamy site had a kind of wild beauty.

Stretch preferred for beauty the ethereal grove of live oaks they drove through. They could barely see the sky through the intermingling branches laden with shiny green leaves and long strands of silvery moss, a dull silver that did not reflect light. The moss hung almost to the ground forming a mist, and seemed to trap sound, the grove hushed and reverent as though listening to whispers from God.

"We is almost home," Absalom said, a touch of pride in his voice. He leaned over the side of the wagon and let fly with a stream of brown tobacco juice. "Yonder is we cotton fields."

Stretching to the horizon, the fields did not seem spectacular to July. The cotton was not yet in bud or bloom. Clumps of field hands preparing the soil for seed straightened up as the wagon passed and waved.

"There it is," Absalom announced. "Caine's Landing."

An orchard hid the house from the road but a puff of smoke could be seen spiraling from its chimney. They bypassed the shaded lane leading to it and drove past the quarters. The huts were lined up in several rows with wooden planks between them, and the only sound emanating from their murky depths was the crowing of a cock. Beyond the quarters were the cow sheds and the stables.

"Whoa, Betsy." Tanner stood up to brake the wagon.

They had arrived at their destination. The stables. And waiting for them on his sorrel palomino was Lieutenant Stryker, head of the cotton agents, looking like an impatient Cossack. A cavalryman from New Hampshire, he sat erect in the saddle, a purple plumed hat on his head and a silver sword buckled around his tunic.

He eyed the mules with interest as Youngblood eyed him suspiciously, and with good cause. By the time he and the other volunteers arrived on the scene, the agents had confiscated not only cotton but everything else not nailed like Christ to the cross, even shipping north all the books in the Beaufort library. That riled the town's general who complained that reading might have diverted his troops from spending so much time in drunken pursuits. Although Lieutenant Stryker had been aware the volunteers were en route he nonetheless had his men haul away all of the furniture from the overseer's house, including kitchen utensils and bed linen. The two lady teachers were forced to sleep on the floor until Youngblood scoured the area to replenish their barren quarters.

"Mr. Youngblood," the lieutenant said, remaining on his mount, "I've been waiting for you."

"Well, here I am. What's your problem?" Without waiting for an answer Dexter turned to his new employees. "You men help Absalom get those mules into the stable and then unload the supplies."

Absalom had already jumped to the ground, his bowlegs as curved as the staves of a barrel, and was untying the lead mule's rope. Stretch went to his assistance. July lagged behind, sensing trouble.

Lieutenant Stryker said smoothly, "I don't have a problem, Mr. Youngblood, unless you create one. I need about twenty of your men over at the Compton place tomorrow morning. We're sending a hundred or so bales of cotton down to the docks."

"They'll be there."

"Also send along five of these mules. I can use——"

"No mules," Youngblood said, scratching a mosquito bite on his hairy hand.

"You are refusing to accommodate me in my official capacity?" Lieutenant Stryker eyed him coldly.

"If that's the way you want to put it. Yes. You can have the laborers but not one mule. The day has passed when you can waltz in here and steal our equipment and livestock."

"Steal, sir?" Stryker's face flushed. "You had better choose your words with care. I have the authority to confiscate whatever is necessary to discharge my duties."

"But not to wreck our project." Youngblood's voice rose. "And I understand you wrote to Secretary Chase that it would be cheaper to gin the cotton up north."

"It would be efficient to process it near the factories that will be using it. That would supply thousands of jobs for workers and . . ."

". . . and keep the Negroes down here impoverished. It's their cotton and they should have the job of ginning it."

Youngblood's position, which he had made known to Secretary Chase, was that the contrabands should be as productive as possible, operate their own cotton gins, and be encouraged to be self-sufficient instead of depending upon the largesse of others. Both he and the lieutenant constantly wrote letters to Chase complaining about each other.

"You don't know enough about cultivating cotton," Stryker said, "to fill an ant's asshole." His horse was pawing the ground and he jerked its head up sharply. "And you know less about working with Negroes. You can't get an honest day's work out of them. You ordered the wrong seed and wasted time planting it although Absalom tried to tell you better. You don't know salt marsh from cow's dung, so don't tell me anything about ginning."

Dexter Youngblood was the first to admit that he had made countless errors, but he considered himself a fast learner and Lieutenant Stryker a self-serving sonofabitch who had volunteered to be in charge of the ginning operations up north. He would shuttle the business to his manufacturing cronies and they would all grow rich. Stryker had also proposed that the plantations be leased to private concerns who would hire the Negroes at a low wage and provide them with food, clothing and shelter.

The balky mules had been led into the stable and July was standing up in the wagon, slowly handing sacks of salt down to Stretch, both of them paying more attention to the quarreling white men. Mr. Youngblood was walking toward the mounted cotton agent, waving a letter in the air.

"Mr. Chase sent these mules to replace the ones you borrowed and never returned. And with them came this letter stating I don't have to provide you with anything except manpower."

Stryker leaned down from his perch and snatched the letter. As he read it Youngblood delivered his final blow.

"I wrote to Mr. Chase last night telling him that your sutlers are swindling the Negroes, selling them a two-dollar pair of shoes for four dollars and a quarter's worth of molasses for fifty cents."

"Goddamn you," Stryker bellowed.

With one swift move he leaped from his horse and landed on the superintendent, knocking him to the ground. July and Stretch looked on horrified as the lieutenant kicked their boss in his ribs.

"Oh Lord," Absalom wailed, running forward, "please don't kill him, Mistuh Stryker."

Dexter Youngblood, undoubtedly breathing the same prayer, rolled over and came to his knees with a pistol in his hand. Blood was streaming from his nose into his beard. Lieutenant Stryker, whose foot was raised to kick him again, froze as the superintendent struggled to his feet.

"Climb up on that horse," he ordered "and get the devil out of here."

Breathing heavily, the lieutenant backed up. His palomino had skittered away and he caught it. He climbed into the saddle and jerked the reins so hard the horse reared up on its hind legs. Horrified, July thought for a moment that the cotton agent was going to run over his bossman.

But respecting the power of a firearm, Lieutenant Stryker wheeled his horse around. Man and beast remained stationary for a moment, both panting, and it seemed to July watching them that they were breathing in unison.

"You haven't heard the last of this," Stryker shouted as he galloped down the road.

Angrily July turned on Stretch. "You nappy-headed idiot. What has you dragged us into."

8

Hilton Head, Union Headquarters
May 1862

Seated at his desk in one of the recently built row houses, General Henry Blenham chewed on an unlit cigar and continued to question Peter exhaustively about the strength and weaknesses of Charleston's defenses. The general, a plump man with a string of medals marching across his chest, had earned himself a line command by leading the advance guard that had routed the Confederates at the battle of Laurel Hill.

At the end of their hours-long session he said exuberantly, "We've got the bastards, Mr. Mango. If what you say is true and they've abandoned Cole Island, Charleston is ours."

"It's true, suh." Peter was also exuberant. He had been covertly studying the man seated before him and liked his enthusiasm. This was the general who would lead the assault against the Sesesh, taking them by surprise.

"You're the man of the hour," General Blenham said, lighting his cigar. He puffed on it for a contented minute. "And as to be expected, the reporters are waiting to interview you."

Mildly alarmed, Peter fingered his stubby beard. "Reporters, suh?"

"A roomful I'm afraid. If you're ready for some more questioning, poor chap, let's go."

Peter followed the general's broad back to a smoke-filled room across the hall where about a dozen reporters were gathered. Standing about in clusters, they ceased talking abruptly when the door opened. That in itself seemed ominous to Peter as he stared into their curious white faces and felt a rush of anxiety.

"Gentlemen, I apologize for the delay," the general said urbanely. "I know you have deadlines but so do I. Let me introduce you to our bold black pirate, Peter Mango."

The reporters surged forward. To Peter's dismay, General Blenham departed, leaving him alone with the Northern newsmen. Under their questioning he related again sailing the *Swanee* past the Confederate fortifications. As he talked an artist sketched him in his seamen's clothes and a cameraman from *Harper's Weekly* disappeared beneath a black hood to work a contraption on a tripod.

"You and your crew have embarrassed the Confederates no end," a reporter from the *New York Tribune* gloated. "They're having a difficult time explaining how slaves who are supposed to be dumber than horseshit outwitted them."

Another newsman interjected, "They've arrested Captain Regan who's facing a court-martial." He chuckled. "And you, sir, are wanted dead or alive. Preferably dead. They're offering a reward of five thousand dollars for your hide."

Peter was astounded. The Sesesh were crazy. He was worth five thousand dollars to them dead? "But how you all know this?"

"We read their newspapers."

The *Tribune* reporter, blinking behind his glasses, revealed that Horace Greeley was writing an editorial on Peter, ammunition to be used in the great debate.

"The great what?" Peter's bushy eyebrows notched up an inch.

"The great nigger debate," a newsman from the *Herald* replied, wagging his finger at Peter. His newspaper was notoriously unfavorable toward Negroes. "The two questions perplexing the Union are whether Negroes will work without the lash. And will they make good soldiers or are they too cowardly?"

The hair on the back of Peter's neck bristled, but before he could answer, the *Tribune* reporter protested, "You're being unnecessarily rude, Blakely. Free Negroes have petitioned President Lincoln in droves to allow them to enlist and he's turned them down."

"I'm not interviewing you," the reporter replied dryly. "I directed my question to Mr. Mango."

The man was a donkey's ass, Peter thought, and carefully chose his words. "I has seen black farmers what was free hitch theyself to a plow 'cause they didn't own a mule. And fishermen spend all night at sea and all day selling they catch. You has Negro men and women up north. Does they work only if you beat them with rawhide? As for being good soldiers, untie our hands and put a musket in it and we'll fight as bravely as any man." And you is the first sonofabitch I'd shoot, Peter thought, staring at Mr. Blakely.

Untie our hands and put a musket in it . . . the reporters wrote, recording the quotable quote.

The questioning continued. Had his master been abusive?

"He often sent others to the jailer to be whipped but not me."

"But surely he must have tortured you cruelly," Blakely suggested, "since you deserted him. Are there no lacerations on your back? No fingers or toes chopped off? No missing ear?"

"He kept me a slave," Peter replied stiffly. "That was torture enough." It was impossible for him to explain the humiliation within his soul that breathed when he breathed. Finally, to his relief, the questions ended.

From the pilothouse of the U.S.S. *Fortune,* the Confederate camp on Cole Island looked deserted to Lieutenant Robinson Mellon who was scanning the area though his field glasses. Nothing moved except a couple of wild hogs grazing at the edge of the piney woods. The *Fortune,* a frigate with her square-rigged sails unfurled, was heavily armed on both decks. She entered the Stono River shelling the land on either side. Following behind in her wake were two other warships, their guns also methodically raking the shore. The artillery shrieked. The trees trembled in protest as the shells gouged up the earth and frightened birds flew around in circles.

Peter stood next to Lieutenant Mellon, trying not to act like a nervous guide as they sailed slowly down the river inviting the Rebels to return their fire. He had to remind himself that he had abducted their cannons himself but suppose that had been a trap? His trepidations were farfetched, ridiculous, but his imagination would not loose them. Suppose they had let him thief the *Swanee* easy as a baby sucking its mammy's tit. Was he an imbecile leading these Yankees into a sudden explosion of gunfire?

Mellon emerged from behind his field glasses. "Place seems deserted to me. But let's sail downstream a little farther, Mr. Mango."

I hope I don't get us all killed, Peter prayed.

May 22, 1862

To: Captain Ammen, U.S. Steamer *Seneca*

From: Commander Samuel F. Du Pont, South Atlantic Blockading Squadron, Port Royal Harbor

You have probably heard of the achievements of a contraband pilot employed on the Confederate steamer, the *Swanee*. The pilot is quite intelligent and gave some valuable information about the abandonment of Stono. At my insistence Lieutenant Mellon made a reconnaissance and, finding the statement true, crossed the bar on Tuesday last with the gunboats *Fortune*, *Unadilla* and *Ottawa*. I have no doubt the Charlestonians thought their time had come.

May 24, 1862

To: Lieutenant Robinson Mellon, Senior Officer

From: Commander Samuel F. Du Pont, South Atlantic Blockading Squadron, Port Royal Harbor

I had the pleasure to read your signal from inside the bar at Stono, on Tuesday last, informing me that you had possession and that the upper battery off Legareville was abandoned, as well as that on Cole Island. I desire, however, to have control of the whole river, and I wish you to proceed with the gunboats and feel the battery near Wappoo Cut which Peter Mango represents as very ineptly finished at best.

Each morning Peter expected that this was the day Charleston would be attacked and as night fell he was disappointed. The *Swanee* had chugged back from Beaufort to naval headquarters and was assigned to Lieutenant Mellon's squadron. Her acting captain was Alphonse Ewald and Peter was delegated his pilot. As Union forces consolidated their strength along the Stono, the *Swanee* steamed up and down the coast carrying ground troops to Edisto Island and to Rockville on nearby Johns Island. Their squadron engaged in minor skirmishes with the Sesesh but that was all.

One afternoon as the company of cavalrymen the *Swanee* was transporting was about to disembark, a Confederate battery on shore opened fire. A bullet shattered the pilothouse glass, a shard flying like an arrow into Peter's cheek. For a moment, seeing the blood, he feared he had been shot.

The *Fortune*, standing by, delivered a broadside that silenced the enemy guns. Lieutenant Mellon signaled the *Swanee* to come alongside and he boarded the steamer.

"It's only a scratch," Peter assured him. The wound had stopped bleeding.

"You're sure?"

"Yes, suh."

The lieutenant examined the cut minutely. He seemed a giant towering over Peter, so pale with ash blond hair and colorless eyebrows that he was almost an albino. His warmth had dispelled Peter's initial awe for a man his own age who already was the commander of three gunboats, and a Georgian to boot. A surprising fact. Peter had assumed that all Yankee commanders were northerners.

"All right," Mellon finally said, satisfied that Peter's cut was indeed a surface scratch, "let's take her ashore and see what's going on."

As anticipated, the *Swanee* was proving her mettle, able to navigate where the larger warships would have run aground. Peter took her in and when they landed several wagons could be seen disappearing over the horizon in a haze of dust, the fleeing Rebels leaving their tents stuck in the ground and their fires burning.

And so it was that parcels of land passed from the enemy into

Union hands as Peter sailed down Wappoo Creek, pointing out torpedoes he had helped to mine and now assisted in removing.

They became friends, the ex-slave and his commander whose family were slaveholders. One evening as Peter was taking a nap prior to going on his watch, Mellon found him on his bunk. They spoke briefly about the day's activities and then, perhaps because they were alone or the need was urgent to explain himself, the Georgian revealed that his family had disowned him.

"I'm a scalawag," he said, "an affront to my mother's womb, a traitor to my class. That's my family's long-standing opinion of me." His voice was pitched low with no inflection. "My brother was an officer at Fort Beauregard and that was terrible. When we were shelling the fort I couldn't help but wonder if I was killing my own flesh and blood."

Peter sucked in his breath. "That be a terrible thing to have to wonder."

"We used to be friends. When we were boys, but . . ." Mellon shrugged. "Our grandfather left us both a hundred slaves. I took mine to Philadelphia and freed them. My brother sold half of his to buy a farm and kept the other half to run it. When I wrote an article questioning the cruelty and ungodliness of slavery, my house was doused with kerosene and set afire. I barely escaped alive."

Peter groaned and stared with compassion at this pale man speaking so calmly.

"That's the price we Southerners pay for slavery. It makes scum out of otherwise decent men. Turns them into murderers and rapists."

Peter nodded. His eyes met the lieutenant's for an instant, then they both looked away, feeling ashamed for different reasons.

"But we is taking too long," Peter complained a few days later. They were giving the Sesesh time to strengthen their defenses, to rectify their error in abandoning the Stono. He had anticipated a swift and deadly assault upon Charleston but the element of surprise was being dissipated with each passing day.

"A little patience, mate," Lieutenant Mellon counseled with a smile. He had boarded the *Swanee* to give Captain Ewald his orders for the day.

"Guess I ain't never been long on patience," Peter admitted.

A short time later he was alone in the wheelhouse when a rowboat came toward them on the port side. The craft was packed with a handful of black people, their clothes in tatters. As they came nearer the watch called out, "Who goes there?"

A man in the rowboat waved his oar. "Please, suh. Can we come aboard?"

Captain Ewald strolling on the hurricane deck wanted to know what the ruckus was about.

"Fugitive slaves, sir," the sailor reported. "Least that's what they look like. Should we haul them up?"

"No."

Peter contemplated the foolhardy notion of strangling Captain Ewald who was by then shouting down at the Negroes, "Are you runaway slaves?"

"They burnt down our shacks and plowed under our crops," the man replied as if that answer should satisfy even God. "We been hiding in the swamp for days and is starving. Please give us a bite to eat."

Bristling with anger, Lieutenant Mellon strode up to the captain. "No ship I command turns away slaves. Haul them up."

They faced each other, the gray-haired acting captain subject to the orders of a man half his age. The war had catapulted infants from Annapolis into leadership and Ewald smarted under the rebuke.

"I understood we were not to interfere with the property of slaveholders," he said sullenly. He had turned away runaways before, swarming like schools of fish wherever the Stars and Stripes were flying.

"I never subscribed to that policy, Captain. And as long as you're sailing on one of my vessels neither will you. I gave you an order. Haul up these people and feed them."

A ladder was cast over the side. Five men, three women and four children, all resembling scarecrows, scrambled aboard, the youngsters trembling with fright. Within minutes the cook brought forth a platter of cold roast beef and the Negroes ate with their fingers, gobbling the food hurriedly as though afraid it might be snatched away.

A wiry black man, the apparent leader, thanked the commander

106

for his kindness, informing him that they were from the Myers plantation on Edisto Island. Their master and his family had been moved by the Sesesh farther inland for safety.

"Then Massa Willie return one night in a canoe. He sneaked past you all lines to come get some of us. He burn down the shed with the cotton and the grain to keep you all from getting it. Then he took Aunt Sally and she three grown boys with him and say he be back for the rest of us soon. We say, 'Yessuh, Massa,' but plan to run when he return. It ain't him come though but the Sesesh soldiers. They carry everybody off in a wagon and burn down our shacks. We run off and hide and find this boat. But we cain't stay here, suh. Sesesh will be back."

"My pilot will give you directions to Beaufort," Lieutenant Mellon said. "Your people will be safe there."

A coxswain replaced Peter at the helm. He hurried down to the deck and hunkering down described landmarks. The men listened intently. And nodded. And groaned.

"How we gon remember all this?"

"You better," Peter said roughly.

They were to avoid the shoals at that juncture of the Stono River where it curved under a big oak tree. It would be low tide when they reached it and the sandbar visible above water.

Noticing how fragile their little craft was when they climbed back into it, Peter shouted to reassure them and himself, "You all is gon be all right." They were energetic and desperate. He prayed they would make it safely to Beaufort. The men picked up the oars. The women pulled the children close.

Lieutenant Mellon, watching them also, muttered, "Haverstock," as though the runaways had jogged his memory.

Peter glanced at him. They were thinking along the same lines. Last week they had seen a thin column of smoke coming from shore. Fearing it was a Rebel outpost on Edisto, Mellon had boarded the *Swanee* to be taken ashore. As they approached land a group of Negroes could be seen running to the beach to meet them. About thirty were assembled by the time the *Swanee* docked. They were abandoned slaves working the Haverstock plantation on their own, growing corn and yams and other subsistence crops. But they could use some grain and other supplies, a thin man leaning on a shovel remarked. This was their home and they intended to remain there and farm.

Lieutenant Mellon had promised to bring them some supplies, which he had not yet secured. He had also requested Commander Du Pont to send a gunboat to patrol the other side of the river in case Confederate troops were still roaming around.

Now the lieutenant said, "We have some extra bags of grain aboard. I'm sure they can use it until we round up the other supplies."

"The gunboat," Peter said, hoping it had materialized quicker than the supplies. "Did they send——"

"I don't know," Mellon interrupted. "We'll soon find out."

A few hours later they docked at Haverstock Landing. Nobody came running to greet them as Lieutenant Mellon led a small party ashore, Peter in the rear. A hen cackled in the dirt where the Negro quarters had been, two rows of shacks facing each other now burned to the ground. Among the ashes stood several mortars and pestles testifying to the durability of iron. Behind the charred quarters the crops had been yanked out of the ground, their roots, exposed to the sun, were dry and brittle. The imprint of wagon wheels in the dust told the sad tale. Rebel soldiers had herded the Negroes at gunpoint into the wagons and carted them back into slavery.

Except four of them. Buzzards hovering over a gully completed the story. Spying the big birds the seamen went to investigate. The thin man who had spoken up earlier, two other men and a woman were sprawled in a ditch, their backs riddled with bullets, their clothes caked with blood. Apparently they had tried to escape and had been shot down running.

Peter cursed under his breath. Mellon turned a shade whiter. Two of the sailors respectfully jerked off their caps.

The lieutenant pointed at them and two others. "You're the burial detail. Get moving."

Peter felt like crying. The gunboats requested to patrol the other side of the Stono River obviously had never arrived.

9

Beaufort
May 1862

This morning Lily was peckish as she stepped out the door, a bent straw hat sitting askew on her head. She was holding Glory firmly by the hand. In a few minutes Rain followed carrying the baby. She deposited him next door along with Glory for an old aunty to mind. Then Rain and her mother-in-law, both silent and glum, proceeded down the street passing a house where roosters strutted under the porch and three toddlers were playing on the unkempt grass.

At the corner Lily broke their morning's silence. "You is putting me in a terrible fix, Rain. I done told my colonel you was coming to work for him."

She was giving her son's obstinate wife one last chance to be reasonable. Lily had concluded during the past few days that Rain was too tiny and pretty to be anything but trouble. Better if Peter had found himself a full-chested gal with big feet.

For her part, Rain did not want to be under her mother-in-law's thumb the livelong day. She considered Lily too heavy-handed, a know-it-all about child raising and everything else. "I is truly sorry," she said, not looking sorry at all. "Tell you boss I has another job you didn't know 'bout."

Lily protested, "I ain't gon lie. Possum in the pot ain't the one that got away."

"It ain't gon be a lie," Rain insisted. "They is gon hire me." She was applying for a job this morning at the Beaufort schoolhouse.

Lily sucked her teeth. The two women parted, Rain continuing down Craven Street. Focused on her goal, she barely glanced at a group of white soldiers drilling in the courtyard of the Arsenal. Two blocks later she arrived at her destination, the Baptist Tabernacle, a white clapboard church that housed the school. Its tall bell tower rose to a red-roofed steeple and Rain interpreted that as a good omen. Red was a mighty friendly color. With her head held high, she strode inside.

"You're so good with the young ones," Carlotta Flowers told her after the first week. "You've saved my life."

Rain loved it, her job and Mistress Carlotta who was a delightful surprise. She was so elegant in her lace blouses, her curly hair piled on top of her head. So educated and refined. And this was the wonder. Mistress Carlotta was a woman of color. A high-toned lady from Philadelphia, as well turned out as white folks. Rain was proud enough to burst.

Oliver Pittman, one of the first volunteers to arrive in Beaufort, had opened the school in the Tabernacle in January with seven students. There were now over a hundred. At the moment they were in the yard chasing each other and shouting, waiting for the bell to summon them to their classes. Some of them had walked four miles to the Tabernacle but seemed none the worse for it. The bell rang. The teachers herded their charges into the makeshift schoolhouse.

"Sammy. If you don't get on in there . . ." Rain snatched up a boy who was trying to run past her. He was five years old and a handful. She set him on his feet and slapping his buttocks lightly sent him scampering in the right direction.

Finally Carlotta's students were all collected. She had the smallest room inasmuch as she had the youngest children, some of them barely four and still leaky. Like Hank. Dripping wet. His older sister, who had to bring him to school with her, relentlessly pulled him along leaving a wet trail behind them.

"I'll take him," Rain said. Hank bellowed upon being swooped up and carried out of the classroom.

The part of her job Rain loved most was helping Mistress Carlotta who had introduced her to a visitor yesterday. She didn't say this is our housekeeper who cleans up the schoolrooms and runs errands and serves our lunch. Or even, this is our baby-tender who wipes shitty behinds and hushes them when they're crying. No. She had declared, "This is my assistant." Rain had fairly glowed. Ain't that something? I is the teacher's assistant.

She was doing the last of her chores one afternoon, sweeping out the room where the grown-ups would meet later, when Oliver Pittman came in wearing his outlandish costume—a flowing white smock with a polka-dot scarf knotted into a floppy bow around his neck and on his graying head a white beret slanted over one eye. He never tired of telling anyone who would listen that his youngsters had progressed beyond his wildest imagination and had the same capacity for learning as the white children he had taught. And the adults were progressing nicely, too.

"Rain," he said, smiling at her, "you're welcome to come to my afternoon class. It's a wonderful thing to get a little book learning."

"Thank you, suh," she said, backing away from him and the idea. She had never dared to dream . . .

For the next several days she contemplated the notion, studying the sweaty men and women who plodded into the schoolroom after their work day had ended, many of them older than her and surely some were dumber. They had a hunger to learn which she shared, listening to them laugh with delight as they inched along toward deciphering the mystery of the written word. They were washerwomen and cooks. Full hands and ploughmen from nearby plantations. Rain watched them sit down in their makeshift schoolroom and pick up a book. Fumbling, stuttering, their lips parted to form a word. Great God almighty! They were reading. That skinny woman looking like death eating a soda cracker. And that fat one busting out of her skirt.

But no, Rain finally decided. Book learning might be all right for them but for her there was a price to pay for being too bold, too forward, for which she had already suffered damnation. No.

111

Put it out of you mind. Don't tempt fate again. God don't like the greedy.

St. Helena

Neither July nor Stretch had journeyed to Beaufort to see Rain as they had promised. July was too busy and Stretch had fallen in love. Her name was Lucinda—Cindy, and he had seen her his first day at work. They were digging up salt marsh and rolling it in wheelbarrels to fertilize the field. His wheelbarrow almost ran over Cindy which was an odd way to begin a love affair.

"Nigger," she said, "is you blind in one eye and deaf in the other?"

Stretch's heart slid down his long frame to his feet. He was smitten. Cindy was tall like him, her legs almost as long, but where he was bony she had curves. Looking boldly into her almond-shaped eyes, he decided that she was a nice handful.

"I is gon make you my woman," he said. "Unless you is already taken." He had learned from experience that a direct approach was the fastest.

Cindy picked up a shovel and slammed it in his chest. "Did I give you leave to be fresh with me?"

Two weeks later he moved into her shack.

July missed Stretch but such was the way of life, he was always missing somebody. He shared Absalom's quarters in a room behind the kitchen and had plenty of carpentry work to do, often riding with Dexter Youngblood to the other plantations he managed and working there. He had grown to like his boss who worked hard and was fair-minded.

July was waiting for him now, sitting on the veranda steps finishing his carving of Mariah. The branches of a shade tree touched the eaves of the roof and ivy vines in tangled abundance covered a trellis and crept under the stairs. It was a peaceful place and a time that July relished.

He stared at the carved head in his hand. Its shape was right, and the long slender neck. And the braided hair. It was a temptation to sculpt into the wood Mariah's full mouth and round eyes, but he resisted. No. She was not family. Definitely not.

His family had been a large brood. His parents. Two sisters. Three brothers. Their owner, Missy Lady, had continued to manage her farm after the death of her husband. She promised the slaves that as a reward for their loyalty and hard work in making the place prosper, she would free them in her will. But upon her death her son declared that his mother had always been daft. Hadn't she defied the law and taught July to read and write? And when reprimanded by the judge she had scolded him, saying that an educated Negro was of more service than a dunce and to put her in jail if he dared. The judge did not dare. Her son won his case and July's family became his property.

It was at that point that July preserved them in wood. Mammy. Daddy. Rebecca. Jeremiah. Clancy. String. Ruth. He carved their heads in exquisite detail. Flaring nostrils. Kinky hair. A dimpled chin. Their faces had been waiting for him in the wood, waiting to be sculpted before they were all sold never to meet again.

The door behind July opened and Abigail Witherspoon stepped onto the veranda.

"July, how pretty," she said, looking at the figurine. "You certainly are talented with your hands. Have you finished it yet?"

"Just about, ma'am."

He stuffed the piece of wood and his penknife into his pocket and stood up smiling. After his boss he liked this lady teacher best.

She resembled a robin redbreast to him, hopping around from branch to branch with her pointy nose and bosomy chest and thin legs. But she could walk for miles, gulping in deep breaths and carrying a satchel full of remedies which she dispensed cheerfully to the Negroes, and even on occasion performed minor surgery since doctors were scarce. And the Negroes clucking, "Ain't that something? She done come way down here from up north to help we poor niggers." And the poor niggers thanked her and the other kind teachers with baskets of eggs and home-grown vegetables and occasionally a freshly killed chicken.

"But you don't have to give us anything," Miss Abigail constantly protested. "Yes, ma'am," the women agreed and the next time plucked the chicken before proffering it. Miss Abigail was learning to say "Thank you" instead of protesting.

Youngblood and Tanner Weaver emerged from the house followed by the other teacher, Mistress Susanne. She was blond and
pretty with a cinched-in waist and lost no opportunity to cast
her flirtatious eyes upon young Tanner, keeping him in a state of
confusion.

Dexter slapped his panama hat on his head and plucked a mosquito out of his red beard. The insects seemed to have a fondness
for him especially on such a muggy day. He looked up at the
storm clouds and expressed a hope that it wouldn't rain.

"Are you ladies ready?"

Yes, they were. Within minutes they were in the rig being driven
by the Negro handyman who would deposit them at their school
in the nearby church. Initially Dexter Youngblood had questioned
the wisdom of employing female teachers in this swampy, malarial
land, but he had quickly changed his mind. The women were a
boon on all of the plantations where they were deployed, keeping
house for the superintendents, hiring the servants, and traveling
out of their classrooms to offer calcimine to whitewash cabins and
soap to cleanse black flesh. Often they were ferried around to
settle disputes because the Negroes trusted them more than the
male superintendents.

July clambered into the wagon parked behind the rig which
was loaded with supplies to be delivered to the other plantations
Youngblood managed. He himself sat up front with Tanner who
was driving.

The two vehicles took off and were soon surrounded by cotton
fields. Field hands were singing spiritedly as their hoes hit the
ground.

> "Read about Samson from he birth
> Strongest man ever lived on earth
> He lived way back in olden times
> Killed him three thousand Philistines
> He cried
> > If I had my way, Delilah
> > I'd tear this building down.
>
> Delilah were a woman fine and fair
> Pleasant looks and coal-black hair

Delilah changed ole Samson's mind
When he first saw that woman of the Philistines
He cried
   If I had my way, Delilah
   I'd tear this building down."

The rig and the wagon parted at the juncture of Oak and Ridge roads. July, wedged in between the supplies, was frowning as he listened to Tanner Weaver complaining as usual to their boss.

The young man was a divinity student, a pacifist, and had elected to come south instead of going into the army, choosing to serve God by ministering to the needs of the wretched of the earth. The problem was that these Negroes were too wretched to suit him. They were either too docile, too sly, or too irresponsible.

"They're so ungrateful," he whined, pushing his glasses up on the bridge of his nose. "Yesterday I drove out to the Jackson plantation and over to Richlands. I handed out a thousand pounds of bacon, seventy barrels of salt and a hundred sacks of flour. The Negroes thanked me, bowing and scraping, but soon's I turned away they were complaining loud enough to make sure I heard them. A woman whined that she couldn't feed her six children on such a stingy ration. A ploughman grumbled that he worked too hard for such a few crumbs. I get so tired hearing them moan there's no molasses, no shoes, no tobacco."

"Well, that's all true enough," Youngblood said calmly. "But we'll soon iron out some of those kinks."

Tanner groaned. "A gang of women over at the Tyler plantation complained that they were in rags. That the clothing from the North had all been distributed before they got any."

"Well, when the next batch arrives see to it that they're taken care of first."

Dexter Youngblood had his own problems. There were seven hundred Negroes under his jurisdiction, superintendents to instruct, cattle and property to protect, tools to procure, food and clothing to distribute, a payroll to make out and reports to write. He was the Negroes' judge, jury, hangman and priest. He broke up fights between field hands battling each other with pitchforks and ordered an errant husband to stay away from his wife's cabin since that's what he was doing anyway, fathering babies all over

the place. On Sundays he preached against such loose moral behavior. And yes, the Negroes were sly and given to bold-faced
lying, their docility only skin deep. While proving his contention
about the superiority of free labor, he had expected to find here
a malleable mass of humanity but was learning to his discomfort
what lay beneath the mask.

> "Delilah took Samson's head 'pon her knees
> Said tell me where you strength lies, if you please
> He said shave my head clean as you hand
> And I'll be just like a nat'ral man . . .
>   Oh if I had my way, Delilah
>   I'd tear this building down."

The wagon rattled down the road, the singing a balm to Dexter
Youngblood's ears.

Two or three field hands straightened up to wave at the wagon,
an automatic gesture to relieve the monotony. The tyranny of
cotton demanded year-long obeisance. While one gang was baling
it another gang was fertilizing the field with salt marsh for another
immediate planting. The laborers sang lustily, their slave skins
scarred from the whip and chains and the salt rubbed into their
wounds.

In the field Stretch stopped singing to look at Cindy. She smiled
at him and not touching one another they were making love
again.

Absalom, striding about on his bowlegs supervising the hoeing,
was singing, too.

> ". . . Samson called on God and started to pray
> God growed he hair back that very day
> Samson put he hands up against the wall
> Great Godamighty, house started to fall
>   Oh Samson had his way, Delilah
>   And he tore that building down . . ."

The singing lasted for another ten minutes and then petered out.
Mistuh Youngblood was gone. White folks always liked to hear

their nigras making a joyful noise while they worked. It was reassuring. "Why aren't you all singing?" Roland Caine, like his father before him, had often queried. "Come on, strike up a tune." And they did. For massa. For themselves. But slavery time was over.

Crip put down his hoe with deliberation. The toes of his left foot had been chopped off for running away one time too many. "I is goin home to pull the weeds outta my cabbage patch," he announced.

Several other field hands dropped their hoes as Crip limped down the row headed toward the quarters.

"Nigger, come back here," Absalom hollered.

Crip kept on walking. "Tell bossman we all don't want to work in gangs no more but by the task."

"Yeh," other voices chimed in.

"Tell him youself." Absalom, outdone, let fly with a stream of tobacco juice. He had informed Dexter Youngblood of the field hands' preference and had been told that the task system was inefficient. It would allow the hands to work the fields and their own little plots on hours they arranged themselves and be paid by the task, which offended Youngblood's orderly mind. There was little control. No set pattern of neat calculations that gave forth predictable results. It was unsystematic. Chaotic. The field hands, he declared, were idiots. Why couldn't they understand that cultivating cotton was their salvation, proving to the world that they were more profitable as free workers than as slaves.

Papa Seth, who had been standing upright next to Absalom, fell into a crouch as if his bones had suddenly atrophied at the age of forty-five.

"Ouch," he said to Sal, his woman, "I cain't stand up straight. The rheumatism done come down on me again."

"Me too," she replied, suddenly disabled also.

Holding onto each other they hobbled off the field. Angel, the ploughman, announced that he was going fishing.

"You niggers are crazy," Absalom fumed.

"You gon fishing with Angel?" Cindy asked Stretch.

"Naw. I is gon home with you."

"How come?"

"Well, for one thing, I aims to fix that broken chair and take

117

care of another matter or two what craves my attention." His smile was amorous and they too departed.

Why work for the white man when they could work for their own sweet selves? Raise crops in their own little gardens to sell. Dig up clams and lobsters that the soldiers were happy to buy. Slavery time was over. To hell with growing cotton.

Cindy had a small hut to herself which had once been the tool-shed. Squatting on his haunches at the edge of the little vegetable patch where Cindy was working, Stretch was trying to glue a loose spoke in the chair. As usual he was jabbering away, looking at the chair and then over at Cindy. He loved the way her willowy body moved and the exhilaration he felt just being with her.

"You know," she said absently, interrupting him, "I ain't never been offa this here island." Her long face was pensive.

Stretch was surprised. "Not even to Savannah? Or Charleston?"

"I ain't never had nobody to go see. If a body had kin close by they might get a pass come Sunday. A fisherman rowed me 'cross the river once to Ladies Island but it were just like here so I really ain't been nowhere at all."

"I been too many places," Stretch recalled. "Seems like every time I laid my head down it was on a different stone."

He talked on as was his wont but for once he wasn't rambling. His voice was lower, thoughtful, allowing Cindy to peek into his soul.

He started at the beginning with his first recollection, eating slop from a huge earthen bowl. There were other toddlers crawling around on the ground on all fours, dipping their fingers into the gruel and instinctively carrying it to their mouths. A sudden slap. "Leave some for the others, you little pig." A hand jerked him away from the bowl, flung him onto the grass. He howled and peed and made doodoo. Nobody cared. He tasted his shit, spat it out, and crawled away from the mess he made. The other tots were bawling, too, scratching at the ants crawling over their limbs. At sunset a pan of bones was thrown their way.

"I don't know how old I was at that time. I dates myself at two just so's I can be of an age. Two slave women ran that nursery for we babies, two miserable hags what hated chil'ren. And then one day they was gone, or I guess it was me that went. Taken away. I was maybe five? Then seems like I lived on a farm for a while. There was horses and cows, chickens and pigs and fists what knocked me to the ground. White fists what was learning me to milk the cows, open the gate for missy's carriage and throw slop into the pigs' trough. I fell into the trough once 'cause the slop jar was so heavy. I was drowning in it, bumping into the pigs when massa hauled me out and whipped me so bad I limped for a week. Then he was gone. But it was me again being taken away to another farm.

"I never stayed in one place long, just passed from hand to hand. The worst massa I had was a pop-eyed man what looked like a frog. He used to line up his five slaves once a week for a whipping to keep us terrified. 'When you see me coming,' he'd say, 'tremble.' One of the mens had a woman what was big with child and when she couldn't keep up her work massa stuck her in a deep hole in the ground so only her head showed. That's when I decided he would have to kill me fast 'cause I warn't taking no more whippings and die slow. When it came time for me to tremble I was gone. Into the woods. Reckon I stayed in there 'bout three weeks, eating berries and nuts. A friend sneak me a piece of pone one time and another. Then he show up, my friend, and say massa say come home and he won't flog me. I was near 'bout to starve so I stumble outta that forest and sure enough massa ain't lick me. What happen, he lost a nigger gambling on a steamboat and decided that nigger was me."

Stretch squinted at the spoke in his hand. "This wood's too rotten to hold. Guess I have to make another one."

Cindy had quit her gardening and was sitting with crossed legs next to him. "You never knew you mammy or you daddy?"

"I don't recollect them at all." His voice was calm as though it no longer mattered, that void and aching lonesomeness. He stood up and pulled Cindy to her feet. "Let's go inside and lay down a while."

"But it ain't dark yet. Is you daft?"

He laughed. "Anytime is the right time to make love to my woman." He pulled her inside and proved it.

When they were lying side by side resting, he murmured, "You is so tasty." He sucked her nipple into his mouth and then bit it.

Laughing, Cindy pushed him away, her hand against the asafetida bag dangling from a string around his neck. "Nigger, you ain't toothless. That hurt."

She rolled over exposing the raised welts on her back. Silently, gently, for the first time Stretch touched them. The scar tissue spoke of the hell of cowhide, a strip of rawhide tapered to a sharp point, its dry, hard edges drawing blood at every stroke.

"Cotton," Cindy whispered in explanation. She uttered the word with a sigh that was centuries old. Stretch hugged her, his body curved around hers, and she told him how it used to be, a field of snow-white blossoms standing six feet tall. "It were always too pretty a sight I always felt to cause so much misery. Come harvest time we work the fields from sunup to past sundown. Lashed for moving too slow. Lashed for resting. Bullwhip always flying through the air. Some nights we work by moonlight hauling the cotton to the mill to be weighed. Iffen you load's too light you gets whipped. Then we stumble to the stable to feed the mules and pigs. Then we is home splitting kindling to fix supper.

"Stretch, I does remember thinking God don't love me. 'Cause soon's I settle into sleep, my bones one long ache, the horn sounding to hit the fields again. And if I is late, the whip is lashing me." Cindy sat up, too agitated to lie still. "How I did hate that overseer." She was trembling.

Stretch shook her shoulders gently. "Cindy, love. Don't. We ain't slaves no more."

She slumped against him. "Thank God," she whispered.

Early the next morning they were getting dressed when there was a sudden banging on their door.

"Stretch. It's Angel. You in there?"

"What you want with him?"

"Soldiers is rounding up all the young mens. We all is running off to the woods."

Stretch opened the door pulling up his trousers. Angel was backing away holding his axe and Stretch grabbed his arm. The other men, six of them, were a straggly line hightailing it into the woods.

"Angel, what's going on?"

"Soldiers is on they way over here. Leggo of me." He jerked himself free. "And come on. If you goes to the fields they gon carry you off."

"Carry us where? What is you talkin?" Stretch was trembling.

Cindy cried out, "Angel, who told you all this?"

"Crip saw the soldiers marching off the men, saying they is being sent to Hilton Head."

Cindy shoved her fist into her mouth. "They is gon sell you mens to Cuba. Just like Massa Roland say."

"That's what we figure," Angel agreed. "Look, I is got to catch up with the fellows. Come with us or no, but I is gone."

"Stretch, hurry," Cindy urged him.

Panic-stricken, half dressed, he raced after Angel.

10

May 31, 1862

To: Hon. Gideon Welles, Secretary of the Navy,
Washington, D. C.

From: Commander Samuel F. Du Pont, South Atlantic
Blockading Squadron, Port Royal Harbor

I have the honor to inform the dept. that the gunboats have possession of Stono. From information derived chiefly from the contraband pilot Peter Mango, I had reason to believe that the rebels had abandoned their batteries and accordingly directed Lieut. Mellon to make a reconnaissance to ascertain the truth of the report. This was done on the 19th instant; and the information proving correct I ordered the gunboats on the next day to cross the bar. They entered Stono, proceeded up river above Old Fort opposite Legareville. Captured six prisoners. Later *Huron* and *Pawnee* crossed the bar. Drayton says "We are in as complete possession of the River as of Port Royal and can land and protect the army whenever it wishes." Rebels have battery at Wappoo Cut. This important base of operations, the Stono, has thus been secured for further operation by the Army vs. Charleston, of which Genl. Hunter proposes to take advantage. I have put at his disposal, for the transportation of troops, the steamers *Alabama, Bienville, Henry Adams, Hale* and the *Swanee*. The Army is very deficient in vessels for transportation.

Legareville, Johns Island
June 5, 1862

Standing near the gangplank with Lieutenant Mellon, Peter felt churlish watching the soldiers march on board, a company of New York Engineers being ferried from Legareville to James Island. "All we doin is shufflin soldiers around instead of attacking Charleston," he complained.

"You're not running this operation," Mellon retorted sharply. "The generals know what they're doing, Mr. Mango."

Peter was stung by the unexpected reprimand, having felt that his commander was also disgusted with the delay. Now he's telling me I is a nigger what don't know pot likker from piss, he thought.

"I'll be aboard the *Fortune*," Lieutenant Mellon said. "Captain Ewald has already received his instructions."

"Yes, suh."

Moodily Peter watched him thread his way between the soldiers who were trooping up the gangplank. They, too, were out of joint and steamy, having tramped to Legareville in hundred-degree weather. Heat exhaustion had felled quite a few and then the rains came, a heavy torrent sinking them in mud up to their knees.

Groaning, cursing they came aboard to cluster in small groups. Peter watched them for several minutes then headed toward the wheelhouse. A strapping soldier with hair growing out of his ears was sitting on the stairway smoking a cigar, surrounded by his buddies.

" 'Scuse me," Peter said. "I has to get by."

The man did not move but inspected him from stem to stern, focussing on his pea jacket and seaman's cap. "You're in the navy?" he finally asked.

"Yes. I is the——"

"Hey, have you heard this one?" He blew smoke into Peter's face and began to sing.

> "Some say it's a burning shame
> To make the niggers fight
> And that the threat of being kilt

Belongs but to the white
But as for me upon my soul
So liberal are we here
I'll let Sambo be murdered
In place of myself
On every day of the year."

The songbird and his friends burst out laughing. A chuckling voice said, "Jasper, let the man pass."

Grinning derisively, Jasper swung his legs around and Peter brushed past him. Making an effort, he walked up the steps calmly. Slowly. Scummy bastards.

He had reached the pilothouse when a voice below said: "You men are a bunch of assholes."

"And you're a goddamn nigger lover."

Peter slammed his door shut. The contempt of white soldiers was nothing new but it never failed to inflame him. First Lieutenant Mellon and now this. Peter sought an anodyne by staring into the vast arc of the sky. It was serenely blue spotted by fleecy white clouds, little lambs floating, merging, all the way to Beaufort. He conjured up Rain's face. Touched her with a sunbeam. She and their children were safe with his mother and he could endure anything. This loneliness. This pain.

The door opened and a soldier lurched inside, spiky red hair shooting out from under his cap.

"I came up to apologize for those fellas," he said. "They're lunkheads and we don't see eye to eye."

Leaning against the door to steady himself, the engineer belched, his breath reeking of alcohol. " 'Scuse me. My name is Bartholomew. Greg Bartholomew."

"You ain't allowed up here," Peter said gruffly.

The soldier pulled a brandy bottle from under his jacket and waved it triumphantly in the air. "I stole this from one of the medics. We was in this swamp, see, mud up to our necks. What a godforsaken country. I figure if I'm gonna die strangled by mud let me at least be pissy drunk." He smiled happily at the bottle and took a swig. "If it wasn't for this likker I wouldna had the nerve to take on those fellas. I been squirming in silence for weeks listening to them complain. So I told them tonight, 'Lunkheads, we can't save the Union without freeing the slaves. That's what this bloody war's about so you better get used to it.' " He belched again and grinned. "I thought they were gonna toss me overboard."

Peter frowned, craving a lonely space to lick his wounds. This white man hadn't bothered to knock but had barged right in assuming that his intrusion would be welcome.

"You soldiers have the run of the boat, but not up here. You has to leave."

"Jasper's a nasty type," the man said cheerfully, "the worst of the lot. A first-class bastard."

"Mister, you's off limits. Get out of my wheelhouse." The firmness in Peter's voice finally connected. The blood rushed into the soldier's face.

"Off limits? I . . . I didn't realize. I just wanted to palaver a little. You say I'm out of bounds?"

"I been saying it." Peter's bushy eyebrows were bunched together.

Out of his element, the soldier fumbled for the door knob. "I'm sorry."

He sounded forlorn but Peter refused to relent. The man at least should have knocked. Bumping into the door, he finally got it opened and stumbled outside. Stoically Peter watched him leave.

In the morning the engineers disembarked at the southern tip of James Island. Their intent was to camp at the abandoned Thomas Grimball plantation. However, they were uninvited guests and a Rebel brigade in the dense woods fired that message at them wrapped in a barrage of bullets. The gunboats escorting the transports shelled the woods. When there was no answering gunfire, the Confederates driven back, the soldiers safely marched across the field and gained the plantation.

For several days the *Swanee* and other steamers continued to move supplies and troops to James Island. Since the batteries on Cole Island had been removed they were able to sail unmolested up and down the Stono River insuring a safe landing for their troops by shelling the tip end of James Island. It was a concentrated Union buildup and Peter prayed constantly, Attack she today. Charleston ain't gon leave her back door open forever.

Louise Meriwether

June 14, 1862

To: Lieut. Robinson Mellon, Senior Officer, USS *Fortune*

From: Commander Samuel F. Du Pont, South Atlantic Blockading Squadron, Port Royal Harbor

I'm glad that the *Swanee* has proved so useful a transport and that we have again been so materially able to aid the army especially at a critical time when its generals were almost helpless for want of transports . . .

The Yankees now occupied the southwest corner of James Island within six miles of Charleston. The battle plan finally being put into operation was to capture the Rebel breastworks at Secessionville, a narrow peninsula on the river, and then advance on land to Fort Johnson which would give the Union access to the harbor and Charleston.

At headquarters General Hunter requested a reconnaissance of Rebel strength. The report of their considerable buildup stunned him and he ordered General Blenham not to advance without reinforcements. But Blenham decided reinforcements were probably never coming and it was now or never. He ordered his troops to attack.

They are being slaughtered. The 8th Michigan. The 7th Connecticut. The New York Engineers. Three assault columns are committed in waves, one advancing the other retreating. They die abruptly when the Rebel garrison surprises them by opening fire. The Yankees fall on their knees and scramble over the dead and wounded to take cover in the bushes. Another column rushes to the parapet, sabers drawn, fighting hand to hand. Bloodily, they are repulsed.

From their nearby encampment, the Confederate Pee Dee and Charleston battalions charge onto the battlefield. From over the bridge a regiment of Louisiana Troops arrive on the run to finish the slaughter. With their dying breath the Yanks curse their warships anchored in the inlet that are shelling the garrison at long range. Whoresons. Your aim is deadly. You are killing us.

Fragments of the Ark

After two and a half hours, with six hundred dead and a hundred wounded, General Blenham orders a general retreat.

Some of the ambulance crew held handkerchiefs to their noses. Peter didn't have a handkerchief and his skin felt blistered by the stench of rotting flesh mingling with the fetid odor coming from the marshes. Grimball's plantation had become a way station for the dying. Wounded soldiers weakened by dysentery and typhoid fever were giving up the ghost.

"Get these men into that ambulance," a sergeant commanded, indicating five amputees lying on litters under a tent pitched in front of the Big House. The walking wounded were making it down to the waterfront on their own, limping along on crutches or leaning on the arm of a buddy, their gaunt faces grimacing in pain, their ragged uniforms caked with blood.

Peter had volunteered to work with the ambulance crew as a last resort in his search for the red-headed engineer. For days he had been looking and by now had grown desperate. Several times he had spied a shock of red hair and rushed forward only to discover a man who didn't have freckles or was too fat or old. It had become a passion. Find him. Alive. Wounded. But don't be dead.

He picked up one end of a litter and a bearded soldier picked up the other end. They had been silently working together all morning. Lugging the stretcher to the ambulance, they set it down. The face of the amputee was covered with a blanket which he fitfully pushed aside. Peter glanced down. A bandage covered the man's eyes, protecting the onlooker from the horror of staring into empty sockets. Peter nonetheless recognized him. He bent over the stretcher.

"Hello. Is you sleeping?"

The man twisted his head around. "Are you the bastard who's been carrying me? Why are you so goddamn rough?" It was Jasper. The songbird.

"Sorry," Peter apologized. "We tries to be careful."

"Well try a little goddamn harder."

"We will. Does you know the whereabouts of a man in you outfit? Red-headed fella. Greg Bartholomew."

The amputee spat out an oath. "He's dead. I saw him take a

minié ball square in his chest, opened him up like a spring chicken. Hey," he yelled, "who's that standing by my head."

"Corporal Berger," the bearded soldier replied.

"Don't sneak up on me like that," Jasper screamed. "When the doc takes these bandages off my eyes I'm gonna find you and kick your ass."

The sergeant called down from the ambulance, "Shove that litter up here. What the devil's holding up you men?" They lifted the cursing amputee into the ambulance.

All right, Peter told himself. Stop looking. A minié ball got him. A dead man cain't palaver. He felt miserable. All Greg Bartholomew had wanted on that lonely night was to talk. "I is sorry," Peter whispered out loud. Maybe the dead could hear. "I is so sorry."

In the weeks that followed, Union transports evacuated James Island, moving out the soldiers and horses, wagons and ambulances they had so recently moved in, two gunboats covering their retrograde movement. The *Swanee* towed schooners in and out of the inlet, everyone working swiftly before the Confederates realized they were departing and cut off their escape. Word drifted down that General Blenham had been sent home in disgrace and faced a court-martial and possible imprisonment.

It was less than two months since Peter had reported to Commander Du Pont that Charleston's back door was open. She done slam it shut, he mourned. Everything had been too late. An exercise in dying.

11

Beaufort

August 1862

Peter came home to Beaufort confused because he had been notified of his leave so abruptly. An indefinite leave.

"You deserve a rest," Lieutenant Mellon had said, giving him his orders. "Go home."

For the past two months they had been involved in several skirmishes with the Confederates who were overrunning northern Edisto. The *Fortune*'s cannons would blast Rebel outposts and after routing the enemy the *Swanee* would take the men ashore to destroy their camps.

"Home? I is getting shore leave?" Peter had been delighted. "For how long, suh?" Two weeks at least, he hoped. And thirty days wouldn't be bad at all.

His blond giant was looking uncomfortable. "I'll send a message to the Beaufort quartermaster letting you know when to return."

Peter had never heard of such leave and his excitement fizzled. "Has I done something wrong, suh?"

"No. You're one of my best pilots."

"So why I don't get leave like everybody else? Two weeks. Three weeks."

Lieutenant Mellon reprimanded him gently. "It's not customary to question your superior officer. When we have another assignment for you I'll notify the quartermaster."

It's because I'm colored, Peter felt. They didn't know what to do with a nigger pilot. Were he white he'd have command of his own boat and they would pay him. Soldiers were paid. And sailors. And the laborers the quartermaster hired. But they hadn't offered him a cent. Disheartened, he packed up his gear and left.

But he could not remain depressed in Beaufort for long. Peewee belched up sour milk on this man throwing him in the air and catching him, thank God, on the way down, and Glory shrieked, "Daddy, do me, too." Up into the air she went, squealing with laughter, to settle finally on Peter's shoulder, her little feet held firmly in his hands. Secure on her perch she crowed like a rooster.

"That's enough, Glory, don't wear you daddy out," Lily admonished the girl but stared at Rain as though she also had to be restrained, having run lickety-split to Peter when he came through the door, pressing herself against him like a shameless hussy.

Peter set his daughter down. "Mamma," he said and hugged Lily. She had grown more wizened and felt featherweight in his arms. Her hair was grayer in its stubby braids and she seemed to have shrunk. Peter looked around, smiling his impish half-smile. "You has moved, I see. And collected a lot of furniture? You plans to sell some of this stuff?"

"Never, son. And stop you joshing. I got these things one step ahead of the cotton agents and the soldiers." She tilted back her head with pride. "They say we acted like heathens choppin up massa's piano for firewood but them agents was mad 'cause they didn't get they hands on it first. And some of them soldiers bears watching, Son, they is some lowdown. But ain't that a right nice bed?" She beamed. "Big enough for all of us."

Rain murmured, "We don't want to crowd you none, Mamma." Her manner inquired mutely, Ain't you ever been in love and wanted to sleep with you man alone?

She and Peter didn't get that chance until the following morning. They spent his first evening at home gloating over newspaper and magazine accounts of the abduction of the *Swanee*. The articles had been mailed to Beaufort directly as the newsmen had promised.

Lily, seated in a high-back chair in front of the fireplace, grunted with pleasure as Peter slowly eked out the words in Horace Greeley's editorial. The editor praised him as a bold, enterprising example of the capacities of Negroes, all of whom should be emancipated as a war effort.

"The man write true," Lily said, looking with brimming eyes at her son, the child of her middle years.

Peter read the article in *Harper's Weekly* and the other newspaper reports, his likeness in his seaman's cap staring solemnly back at him. It was grand.

Then his mother asked him about Charleston. And Hiram. Was he well? And was his wife, Helen, still as fat as a sow?

"Last time I seen her she was."

"Uh huh. As I recollects, Hiram never did like no fat women." Lily smiled with relish, which went unnoticed by Peter but not his wife.

In the morning Rain decided to remain at home. Would Mamma please take Glory and the baby to Aunty next door? She would get to her job by noon.

"Such foolishness," Lily grumbled as she departed with the children.

Before the door had closed behind her Peter and Rain were jumping into the middle of her featherbed. They spent the rest of the morning making love. As soon as one passionate wave subsided, another rode in on the ebb tide. Finally, scrambling into their clothes, they hurried outside into a pool of sunshine. It was almost noon.

Rain's intention was to go straight down Craven Street to the school, but Peter pulled her in the opposite direction.

"Let's take the long way, baby cakes."

They held hands as he led her past Johnson's Castle situated around a bend in the Beaufort River. The immensity of the castle occupying an entire block had always intimidated Peter and still did. As a boy its windows blinked disapproval of him whichever way he turned—seventy-nine windows set between massive columns which supported a double piazza and a parapet that was five feet tall.

He showed Rain the grove of palm trees huddled together facing the river, his favorite spot as a boy to play in the wild grass and swim. Above them, built in the inlet where the river made a hard angle, was a white clapboard house, its lower story hidden by flowering japonica bushes.

Peter paused. "There used to be a orange tree at the end of that garden. The owner got so tired of we children stealing he oranges he cut it down. They were some sweet."

" 'Cause they were stolen," Rain said smiling, seeing the boy within the man and loving the way he stood with his calves poked out. He chuckled, and she loved that, too, the long sweet curve of his mouth with that half-smile tucked in its corners. It caused a tingling between her thighs. A melting. A hunger.

"That place over there," he pointed to the crumbling foundation of a tavern, "is supposed to be haunted."

Rain shivered, leery of haunts, and hurried to safer ground, back to Craven Street. Her superstitions made Peter smile.

He was struck by the wartime changes in Beaufort. All the white people he had known were gone, replaced by pink-cheeked Union soldiers patrolling the streets. The Beaufort library, once forbidden to Negroes, was now a shelter for homeless contrabands. The auction block had disappeared along with the auctioneer, and black people knew it. Peter read it in their stride as they greeted him on the sun-drenched streets.

Tabernacle Baptist Church, though, looked the same. It was recess time and the children were noisily chasing each other on the lawn. Rain led Peter inside where they found Mistress Carlotta.

"Please meet my husband, ma'am," Rain bubbled with wifely pride. Deliberately she had not told Peter that her adored teacher was a Negro. It was the first of several surprises that were to astound him.

Carlotta was smiling at him. "I understand you were a sailmaker." Peter nodded, struck by her elegance. "And so was my grandfather," she said.

"Now ain't that something." Peter chuckled.

The coincidence was fleeting. Her grandfather, a Philadelphia freedman, owned a sailmaking factory. Reared in abolitionist circles, Carlotta had mastered French, Latin, and German, published poetry and had volunteered for the Project to demonstrate to a hostile world that Negroes were not subhuman.

"I remembers you," Cindy told Peter with a little laugh. "You

132

came to Caine's Landing a couple of times when I was a li'l bitty girl. Once it were Christmas and you was giving us chil'ren an orange. You ain't look at none of us, just put an orange in our hand. 'Thankee kindly' we had to say 'cause Massa Roland were close by handing out winter clothes. Thankee kindly, Massa, for these shoes. Thankee for the calico Mamma gon sew up for my dress. Thankee for this nice orange and this li'l black boy handing them out. He move an inch away from you we gon push him into the pig trough.''

Stretch howled and Peter asked, chuckling, "But what I do?"

It was Sunday and he was sitting in Cindy's cabin in front of the open door enjoying the little breeze filtering into the room at sundown. Outside the crickets were humming loudly.

"You looked too nice. Too cocky and stuck up 'cause you lived in Beaufort with Massa. We wanted to dirty you up a little. But you never stepped far enough away from him for us to say you tripped and fell.''

They all laughed and Peter thought, I like her. "Well now, looka who's coming,'' he said, glancing out the door.

It was July, emerging from the shadows. Peter jumped up to meet him halfway. They punched each other, grinning.

July held his friend at arm's length. "Hey, you look mighty good for a man the Sesesh been shooting at.''

Stretch said, "A fella what escaped being dumped in the pigsty knows how to dodge bullets.''

"Come on in,'' Cindy invited and fetched them all jugs of water sweetened with molasses.

As they sipped it they talked. Briefly Peter told them about the disastrous rout at Secessionville and was amazed to learn about the existence of Negro troops.

"You all is lying.''

"Me and July were in it for a coupla months.''

Stretch related the details of that scarifying day when the soldiers had appeared with drawn bayonets all over the islands, the women screaming hysterically as their husbands and sons were carted away. "Massa Youngblood was some mad, taken by surprise, too. General Hunter din't tell the superintendents his plans till that morning for fear we'd get wind of it and hide. I did run off to the woods." Stretch looked shamefaced. "But they dragged us outta there.

"The soldiers took us to Hilton Head. To they camp there. After a few days the foremen and ploughmen was sent back 'cause the superintendents was screaming the crops needed they care. The rest of us stayed a few weeks training to be soldiers. Then, we was allowed to come home if we wanted to or stay and join the regiment."

July added, "Some mens did but I was too mad at the way we was snatched without a by-your-leave." His voice was strident. He was still angry.

Stretch agreed it had been terrible, grabbed like that, but learning to drill with the soldiers and being in their company wasn't half bad. He glanced sideways at Cindy.

July grunted. "You always was a goober head."

Peter was confused. "But I heard that General Hunter was a abolitionist. How come he do a thing like that?"

"Sometimes," July replied moodily, "a snake in the grass look just like a nice whittling stick."

"What about the rest of our crew?"

"Brother Man and Sister's on a plantation on Edisto Island." Stretch took another sip of molasses. "We ain't seen them since they left. Turno and Bite was doing good selling lobsters and shrimps to the soldiers. They was living on a plantation near Beaufort but the superintendent wanted them to work in the fields and had a run-in with the fellows fishing on they own. Turno said he got tired of being called shiftless and he and his little boy moved. I don't know where they's at now."

"Wherever Turno be there is trouble," July said. "That's his name. Bad Man Trouble. But there's trouble everywhere. You hear what happen over at Daufuskie Island last week?"

Peter shook his head.

"It were some terrible. Sesesh rowed over on a dark night and forced a family at gunpoint into they boat. Kidnapped them back into slavery. So we black mens done form our own patrol. Our boss got us some guns and we intend to blow the damn head off any Sesesh sneaking 'round here."

Peter's eyes met those of his friends. There was no need for words, it was understood. Three months ago they had elected to

134

go down to the bottom of the sea on the *Swanee* if their escape plan failed. They would not be turned back now.

"There were quite a ruckus on our plantation when some of the mens refused to work in gangs," Stretch reported. "Massa Youngblood threatened to fire the lot of them but changed his mind. He allowing us to work by the task now. He a man what knows how to bend with the wind 'fore it breaks him in two."

"But we just now got our pay for work done in May and June," July said glumly. "Guvment slower than molasses sending money. God knows when we gon get paid for last month."

At least they were being paid, Peter thought. He hadn't been concerned about wages until given his indeterminate leave. Pushing that unpleasantness from his mind he said: "I cain't get over it, you two galoots working at Caine's Landing."

"It's 'cause Stretch loves you," July said, "and I'm a damn jackass."

Another surprise. They sent for him. General David Hunter and General Rufus Saxton. A note requested Peter's presence at General Saxton's headquarters at ten o'clock the following morning.

The hierarchy on the islands had changed. The cotton agents were gone, dismissed abruptly when Secretary Chase learned they were cheating the contrabands. The Project had been transferred to the War Department and Rufus Saxton, an abolitionist, appointed military governor in charge of contrabands and abandoned plantations. He had arrived in the islands along with the occupying troops, seemingly the only army officer intensely concerned about the welfare of the contrabands. The troops had been abusive. Their drunken escapades—stealing livestock, beating Negro men and raping women—lessened after General Saxton's appointment.

His headquarters was in the refurbished parlor of a manor, a high-ceilinged room with marble mantels and an elaborate frieze on the ceiling. With a heightened sense of incredulity Peter followed a sentry into the room. Two medal-bedecked officers were present. The younger one, seated behind a huge mahogany desk, Peter assumed was General Saxton. He appeared to be in his early forties, a slightly built handsome man with curly hair and a full chestnut-colored beard. The other man standing in front of the fireplace was gray-haired and scowling.

The sentry saluted. "Peter Mango is here, sir."

General Saxton sprang to his feet and moved forward, smiling affably.

"My dear fellow. It's so good of you to come." He exuded warmth as he clasped Peter's hand and shook it. "We have heard all about your splendid deed relieving our enemy of a worthy vessel. I am pleased to finally meet you. And this is General Hunter, our commander. He's on his way back to headquarters from Florida."

Hunter remained at the fireplace, a round-bellied man in his sixties with a crafty look on his chinless face. Both men were splendidly attired in blue tunics and Peter was glad he was wearing his new black frock coat and string tie at Rain's insistence. "You ain't goin to a fish fry," she had rebuked him, "so put that pea jacket down."

"Yes," General Hunter said perfunctorily, "you have inspired us all with your bravery." He rested a hand on his sword shaft.

The pleasantries dispensed with, General Saxton propelled Peter to a chair and returned to his seat behind his desk.

"As you perhaps know," he said in his gentle manner, "I've been placed in a position to be of some small service to your people. My prime concern is that their future be secure. That they not find themselves destitute after the war, in a position to be exploited. I'm in favor of parceling out land to Negro farming families in lots large enough to provide subsistence for them."

"That sounds just grand," Peter said, wondering what that had to do with him.

"The point is," General Hunter said, "we have to win the war first. Do you agree?" He sounded impatient, his voice rasping.

"Of course, suh."

"Good." He moved a step away from the fireplace. "Mr. Mango, I would like your honest opinion. Do you think Negroes will make good soldiers?"

The question startled Peter coming from the man who had organized a black regiment. Nervously he cleared his throat. "I hear folks say this is a white man's war but we colored has the most to lose if the Sesesh come back. Given the chance, Negroes will fight as well as any man."

General Hunter quit the fireplace and, walking over to Peter, stared at him intensely as though to gauge his reaction.

"I disbanded the First South Carolina Volunteers this morning."

Peter was stunned. Dear God, had they done something disgraceful?

Sensing his turmoil, General Saxton explained, "The regiment has not been paid since they were formed. They were never inducted into the regular army."

At the moment General Hunter was under Congressional scrutiny for raising a black regiment without authorization but he was not at all intimidated.

"I requested permission months ago to raise Negro troops which I did not receive," he said. "But I formed the company anyway to let the men prove their ability which they have done admirably. They're as good as any white troops I've commanded. I honestly felt I could get them mustered into the army and paid but resistance has remained strong. I've disbanded them except for Company A which I'm sending to garrison St. Simons Island off the coast of Georgia."

"Disbanded," Peter repeated, dismayed. "That's terrible."

"It's crass stupidity," General Hunter stated, pacing the floor. "I was ordered to send ten thousand soldiers to bolster General McClellan's forces in Virginia. Ten thousand soldiers, Mr. Mango. That meant shortening our lines and as a result we've lost a fifth of the islands we controlled. The Confederates have overrun Edisto. The contrabands and superintendents living there have been evacuated to a refugee camp here in Beaufort."

It had been a hasty departure. Sixteen hundred Negroes snatched up their children under one arm, their chickens under the other, and boarded flatboats camouflaged with leaves one step ahead of Rebel sharpshooters, leaving behind the cotton and corn they had planted.

Peter's heart was hammering. Brother Man and Sister had moved to Edisto. "Everyone was moved out? A member of my crew . . ." His voice trailed off.

"As far as I know we managed to evacuate all the people from the area under our control. Edisto is now a no-man's-land." General Hunter stopped pacing and bent so low over Peter he could see the gray hairs in his nostrils.

"You black men know these swamps and bayous better than soldiers from the North. If I had ten thousand colored troops from these parts we'd chase the Rebels off these islands forever."

"Mr. Mango," General Saxton said, leaning forward over his desk, his voice solemn, "we are sending a minister to Washington, Reverend Archibald Ferdinand, with letters to President Lincoln and Secretary Stanton asking for authorization to arm five thousand Negroes and——"

General Hunter interjected, "My Negro regiment can be speedily recalled."

" . . . and we are asking you to accompany him."

Peter's bushy eyebrows shot upward. He was as astonished as if God himself had leaned down from heaven to ask for a favor. "Me, suh?" He stared at the two white men who were regarding him gravely. "You want me to go see the President?"

"We do. Reverend Ferdinand is an old hand at Washington politics. He will secure an audience for you both with Mr. Lincoln and Mr. Stanton."

Peter felt like an idiot. "But I ain't a learned man. What can I tell Mistuh Lincoln?"

"Tell him what it feels like to be a slave," General Saxton suggested. "Tell him why you pirated a Confederate steamer and turned it over to his navy. Learned men, white and black, have beseeched him to allow Negroes to enlist. Let him hear it now from you."

General Hunter touched Peter's arm to get his attention. "Horace Greeley has been writing editorials about you in the *New York Tribune.* You represent loyal black men, an untapped source of military might. I'm sure the President, like everybody else, reads Horace Greeley and has heard about you. I know him quite well."

Peter was dumbfounded. "You know who?"

"President Lincoln. I was captain of the guards during his inauguration."

And you is crazy sending me to see him, Peter thought. To his surprise he heard himself asking an impertinent question. "General Hunter, why you send soldiers to snatch colored men and carry them off to you camp in Hilton Head? I heard it cause a lot of misery."

If the general was annoyed by such boldness, he did not reveal it. "I wanted to demonstrate to the men themselves the benefits of the army. Recruitment had slowed down. They were not volunteering, out of ignorance and fear. And the superintendents were a hindrance also. They discouraged the field hands from enlisting, preferring to have them grow cotton. I felt that once exposed to camp life, the rigorous discipline would stand them in good stead for the rest of their lives. We drilled the men for several weeks then allowed those who wished to return to the plantations to do so. A goodly number who liked soldiering left because they had families to support and had not been paid."

Peter stammered, "I . . . I don't rightly know what to say."

General Hunter straightened up. "Say yes," he suggested bluntly.

"We really need your services, Mr. Mango," General Sexton said in his earnest manner. "I pray that we can count on you."

12

⚬⚬

Washington, D.C.
August 15, 1862

Reverend Ferdinand rented a coach and Peter glued himself to
its window as it rattled away from the clamorous waterfront to
less congested streets. He thought Pennsylvania Avenue quite
grand despite the fact that ducks were waddling down the road
and that the heavy traffic and trolley cars rumbling over the cobblestones had created huge mudholes where hogs were rooting.
The avenue was a broad thoroughfare of public buildings and res-
taurants. Strolling ladies carried parasols, gentlemen wore tall silk
hats. And there were soldiers everywhere. On foot. On horseback.
Marching behind a fife and drum. Or riding in open barouches
with lady companions, some of whom looked decidedly bawdy.

Reverend Ferdinand took note and complained in booming ministerial tones that decent women were rightfully outraged by the
scandalous behavior of some servicemen. "Washington is overrun
with harlots. Police raids seem to encourage a greater number to
come trooping in. It's tempting the Lord to smite us down as he
did Sodom and Gomorrah."

In the wake of the army had come the freewheeling adventurers,
the prostitutes and their madames, the gamblers and pickpockets,
the medicine men with their vaunted miraculous cures for syphilis

and gonorrhea. They installed their saloons and bawdy houses in shoddy areas and in fastidious ones as well.

"I know you won't believe this, Peter, but there's a flourishing whorehouse within spitting distance of the President's park."

Peter believed it, impressed by the tenacity of the adventurers.

Black people were also abundant. Hawking their wares on street corners. Pushing little vending carts. Selling newspapers. Washington's slaves had recently been freed by an act of Congress, abolitionists long contending that slavery in the nation's capital was a disgrace.

At Fourteenth Street, the reverend pointed to an immense five-story brick building. "That's the hotel they sneaked Mr. Lincoln into when he came here for his inauguration. Washington was a hotbed of sedition then. Full of Confederate rowdies. The rumor was Mr. Lincoln wouldn't get out of Baltimore alive, so Pinkerton, his private detective, changed his schedule. Then we heard they planned to assassinate him on his way to the ceremony."

Peter was shocked. Such a wicked city.

"I was here for the inauguration," Reverend Ferdinand added, "and so was our General Hunter."

The assassination threats continued after Mr. Lincoln moved into the executive mansion amid new rumors that the Confederates were about to attack and seize the nation's capital. They did burn down the railroad station and severed connections between Washington and Baltimore. The city encircled by hostile Maryland and Virginia, lived in panic for six days. Northern troops being rushed into Washington had to fight their way through mobs in Baltimore but they finally prevailed and rescued the district.

As their coach drove past the Capitol, Peter was awestruck by its sheer magnitude although its marble extensions, spread like wings on either side of the rotunda, were still incomplete, not all of its hundred Corinthian columns yet in place.

"We've been building this city for sixty years and haven't finished it yet," Reverend Ferdinand said with a possessive smile.

The original Capitol dome had been removed, to be replaced by one of cast iron, and a black workman was operating a crane in the huge hole. Men scrambled like ants up and down the network of scaffolding. Work sheds were scattered over the grounds together with piles of lumber, blocks of marble and hills of coal.

The construction and noise pleased Peter. The capital city had a tumultuous heartbeat but was not solidly set in concrete which made him feel welcome.

Part of his excitement was being in the presence of this garrulous minister. During their three-day sail he has regaled Peter with stories about himself and his abolitionist friends. He had been a college teacher in Ohio and had gone on the lecture circuit to help Salmon Chase, who was governor then, raise funds to establish Wilberforce, a college for free Negroes. Both men viewed education as a way out of the deprivations imposed by bondage.

The reverend's wife, Luisa, now deceased, had then been writing inflammatory essays on women's rights, intended to arouse the weaker sex from their passivity and dependence upon men who exploited them. The debate over women's rights split abolitionist ranks down the middle. Two of Luisa's supporters and friends had been Lloyd Garrison and Frederick Douglass. That made her almost a saint in Peter's eyes and by extension her husband, Reverend Ferdinand. At times Peter detected in the minister a savage intensity which suggested that if he couldn't lead you to salvation he'd drag you there by the scruff of the neck.

At the moment he was regarding Peter with affection, a broad smile on his acne-scarred face. "I have secured rooms for us with a Quaker friend," he said. "And tomorrow morning bright and early we'll start on our rounds."

Peter returned the reverend's smile, exhilarated and scared.

The Department of the Army was on Seventeenth Street in a four-story colonnaded building almost a block long and bordered by maple trees. Peter tried to stifle his anxiety as he and the reverend climbed up the steps and entered the building. A provost guard admitted them to the secretary of war's reception room in the rear.

Gingerly Peter stepped inside. Sunlight from the long windows glowed on the pale faces of portraits on the wall, oil paintings of the Founding Fathers who frowned at two semi-nude statues at either end of the room.

A crowd had already gathered, seated in rows of chairs in the order of their arrival, well-dressed gentlemen holding satchels, military officers resplendent in uniforms trimmed in braid. The few women present, the genteel poor, were not so stylishly arrayed but looked well scrubbed for the occasion.

Peter and his mentor took a seat in the fifth row next to a sallow woman who was weeping quietly into her handkerchief. She looked up briefly at their arrival and it seemed to Peter that his black presence made her cry a little harder.

Edwin Stanton, Secretary of War, finally arrived, a man powerfully built but so short he just missed being a dwarf. As he walked to a tall writing desk in the front of the room, the petitioners snapped to attention.

Reverend Ferdinand had already briefed Peter that the secretary was an implacable foe of fraud and corruption and conducted these open hearings to discourage duplicity. He had transformed his graft-ridden department into a model of efficiency, firing idle army officers and readjusting swindling war contracts to save the government millions of dollars. He relished the rumor that he was the most hated man in President Lincoln's cabinet and worked hard to live up to his reputation, dealing harshly with the treasonous and the corrupt. At the top of his traitors' list were the Confederates.

The high desk cut off Mr. Stanton at the neck so that this head and long beard seemed suspended in air, adding to the God Almighty quality he assumed in dispensing judgment. Peter listened amazed as the secretary disposed of the requests of the first four rows of people with dispatch. A young gentlemen seeking a war contract had invented a repeater rifle which only occasionally, he was forced to admit, backfired and knocked the man holding it to the ground. Or shot him in the foot. Then there were merchants anxious to manufacture for their Uncle Sam aprons which never showed dirt, canteens which never ran dry, tents which never collapsed.

The weeping woman next to Peter stumbled to the desk to request mercy for her son who, worried about her being left destitute on their New Jersey farm, had deserted his cavalry unit and been caught. The secretary of war was merciless. The line moved so swiftly because he listened politely for a few minutes and then responded with a stock answer. "Sorry. No. Next."

Too soon for Peter it was their turn to approach the desk. He stumbled to his feet and managed to traverse the distance somehow. Reverend Ferdinand introduced them smoothly and handed the secretary a letter from General Saxton. Peter, who had lost his faculties of speech and locomotion, stood dumbly by. He knew the contents of the letter and watched Mr. Stanton's face as he read it. Peter tried to detect a glimmer of hope but the man was a rock.

General Saxton had written:

> I respectfully but urgently request of you authority to enroll a force not exceeding five thousand able-bodied men from among the contrabands in this department. The men to be uniformed, armed and officered by men detailed from the army. The rebellion would be very greatly weakened by the escape of thousands of slaves with their families from active rebel masters, if they had such additional security against recapture as these men, judiciously posed, would afford.

"Gentlemen," the dwarfish secretary said, inserting the letter back inside its envelope, "President Lincoln has consistently refused to accept Negroes into the armed forces. He insists that the war is to preserve the Union not to emancipate the slaves."

Peter, who expected him to say "Next," was surprised when he didn't.

Reverend Ferdinand was prepared. "I understand the President's rationale," he said. "The patriotism of Northerners has been rallied to fight for the Union. The last thing they want is a mass exodus of ex-slaves to their shores to compete with them for jobs and exacerbate racial tensions. But, Mr. Secretary, our armed forces need replenishing and the Negroes in our area know every inch of that terrain. They would be invaluable. I realize many soldiers feel that the right to defend their country is reserved for white men. But other loyal soldiers are asking why black men are being left safely on the sidelines. The war is dragging on beyond expectations and not proceeding well for us. The question not to be beggared is this. If the war can be won with black soldiers and lost without them, which road should we choose?"

The secretary, who had been listening stoically, turned his harsh gaze on Peter. "You also feel, Mr. Mango, that armed black men

144

will embolden slaves to desert their masters and lessen the Rebels' labor pool?"

Peter swallowed. "Yes, suh. I do."

"And by what reasoning have you come to that conclusion?" Mr. Stanton's voice was unemotional as if it mattered not a damn.

Peter chewed on his bottom lip until finally the words came. "There was nobody what said you all come but thousands of slaves done already stole away. They did it on they own and it were risky, getting pass Sesesh lines. And Union officers sometimes sent them back into slavery. But they came anyway and is still coming. So with a little help from the army, a little protection, thousands more will make they way to the Union side."

Mr. Stanton was regarding him obliquely. "Anything else?"

Peter was surprised to hear himself reply, "Yes, suh. I was a pilot up by the Stono River and seen how the Sesesh does murder my people to keep us slaves. I is heartsick knowing they run us from Edisto 'cause General Hunter had to shorten his lines. Black soldiers could have held the Sesesh back when the other troops was pulled away."

Mr. Stanton grunted. It had been his order that had depleted Hunter's force. At the time General Lee's Confederate troops had pushed General McClellan back to the James River in Virginia. Washington had been panic-stricken fearing invasion and Stanton had rounded up nearby reinforcements to once again save the capital.

Peter added boldly, "I know my people, suh. They craves freedom and will fight hard for it."

"How many contrabands are we talking about?" Mr. Stanton asked.

The reverend estimated ten or eleven thousand and reported that they kept on arriving. "Somehow they manage to escape through enemy lines, taking their own freedom so to speak, not waiting to be liberated."

The secretary could have mentioned that the refugees kept pouring into Washington also, had he been given to idle chatter.

"Gentlemen, your information is interesting. But arming Negroes is against Mr. Lincoln's policy. I suggest that you seek an audience with him. And give my regards to General Hunter and General Saxton. Next."

*   *   *

Their room in the Quaker boarding house had two beds covered with green chintz spreads that matched the curtains at the dormer windows. Sitting on his bed Reverend Ferdinand was thumbing through the *New York Tribune* he had bought from a newsboy. En route home he had noticed Peter's dismay and attempted to cheer him up stating that there was no cause to be discouraged. Mr. Stanton hadn't dismissed them out of hand but had spent time questioning them and that meant something in Washington. All was not lost. Peter was far from convinced, castigating himself for being such a stumbleweed instead of a smooth talker like the reverend.

"Ah, here it is," the minister exclaimed, folding the newspaper to the coveted page. "Horace Greeley's letter to President Lincoln. 'The Pleas of Twenty Millions.' It has all of Washington standing on its head."

Peter perked up, listening to the excerpts the reverend read aloud. The long scolding letter by the radical editor detailed atrocities against fugitive slaves who had sought refuge in army camps and been turned away by army officers and even murdered.

> We are sorely disappointed and deeply pained by the policy you seem to be pursuing with regard to the slaves of Rebels. Men loyal to the Union and willing to shed their blood in her behalf should no longer be held, with the nation's consent, in bondage to persistent, malignant traitors, who for twenty years have been plotting and for sixteen months have been fighting to divide and destroy our country. Why these traitors should be treated with tenderness by you, to the prejudice of the dearest rights of loyal men, we cannot conceive.

Greeley contended that all attempts to put down the rebellion while upholding its inciting cause would prove futile. If the rebellion were crushed tomorrow it would soon be renewed if slavery was left in full vigor. "We must have scouts, guides, spies, cooks, teamsters, diggers and choppers from the blacks of the South or we shall be baffled and repelled . . ."

Reverend Ferdinand's face was flushed with pleasure, but Peter felt pained. Behind the editor's every word stood a bruised slave.

"Can I have it, suh? The newspaper?"

"Of course."

The reverend handed it to him. Peter decided to keep it forever. He trusted Horace Greeley who had written nice things about him and the *Swanee*'s crew. But Abraham Lincoln had long been a muddle in his head, a sad betrayal as the editor had noted.

"Reverend Ferdinand, I is confused 'bout our President. Seems to me he talks with a forked tongue. He say one time slavery be wrong, that it makes thieves out of white people and degrades black people and he seem to be for us. He say another time he's against white folks sitting down with us as equals. He say we is inferior and he favors them staying on top."

The minister bent down to tug off his boot, pull off his stocking and wiggle his cramped toes. "You mean Lincoln's debates with Stephen Douglas," he said slowly. "How do you know about that?"

Peter told him about the Brotherhood meetings. In his newspaper Frederick Douglass had often criticized the President's hypocrisy.

Reverend Ferdinand sighed. "Mr. Lincoln is a very complex man. That bothersome statement about Negro inferiority came at the time he was attacking the expansion of slavery into Kansas and Nebraska. He fought the expansion tooth and nail and went after Stephen Douglas's Senate seat."

Ferdinand tugged off his other boot and stared at it absently. "Mr. Lincoln felt that the bloodshed in Kansas had brought America to the brink. That either the nation would go forward and be the democracy it was intended to be or slide back into the Dark Ages. He believed slavery had to be contained in the South and not expanded into the new states. In their debates, Stephen Douglas played upon the racial fears of the voters. Negroes might be Lincoln's equal and his brother, he said, but they were no kin to *him*. He warned that Lincoln would unleash a horde of stinking blacks rushing north to compete with white workers for jobs and have sex with their daughters.

"It was then that Mr. Lincoln stated that blacks were inferior to whites, should not intermarry with whites nor have the vote and inasmuch as somebody had to be on top let it be the white man. He understood the fears of the Illinois voters and was attempting to reassure them. He lost the Senate race to Stephen Douglas but it was because of his strong stand against slavery that the Republican Party nominated him for president two years later on an antislavery platform."

The reverend had his own problems with the President's vacillating policies toward slavery and often wondered along with his abolitionist friends whether they had put the wrong man in office. From the outset they would have preferred to elect one of their own radicals whom they could trust, someone like Salmon Chase, rather than Abraham Lincoln who considered himself a moderate. The President had envisioned a speedy victory over the South with slavery left intact. He advocated that emancipation should be gradual, slaveholders compensated for the loss of their property, and the Negro problem solved by assisting former slaves to migrate to Haiti, Liberia or South America.

"But we're making Mr. Lincoln into an abolitionist, Peter," the reverend said. "The times and black people themselves. The thousands who've crossed over to our lines are forcing his hand. But we have to remember he's faced with tremendous problems. And two of his sons have died, the last one only a few months ago of typhoid fever. I don't think Mr. Lincoln or his wife have recovered from that tragedy yet."

"I didn't know," Peter said, feeling remorse. "It's a sad thing to bury you chile. I is here on account of my chil'ren. To keep the Sesesh from claiming them as they own."

Carefully he smoothed out the creases in Horace Greeley's newspaper.

In the morning at the executive mansion they discovered a host of seekers hoping to cash in on their Union credentials—factory owners, bankers, railroad men, contractors, land speculators—all there to offer their services for a price. High-ranking military personnel sought commissions. Wives were present to inquire about their husbands missing in action or to request a pension. Two freedmen bearing petitions from their Boston constituents sought permission for Negroes to enlist. The throng overflowed the parlors, huddled in the corridors and sat on the steps of the wide staircase which led to the President's office.

We'll be here forever, Peter thought gratefully, welcoming a breathing space between encounters as he and the minister took their place at the end of the line. When the guards turned them out that first afternoon, they had not even reached the second parlor.

By the third day they had progressed to the waiting room on the second floor. A wooden gate, guarded by a ferocious-looking Negro, separated the executive office and cabinet room from Mr. Lincoln's living quarters. Surely by tomorrow, Peter felt, they would have an audience with the President.

That evening he had a brief diversion, invited to speak at a meeting of the Contraband Relief Committee, founded by Elizabeth Keckley, an ex-slave who had purchased herself and was Mrs. Lincoln's dressmaker and owner of a shop with seven employees. She had founded the committee to raise funds for the poverty-stricken refugees pouring across the Long Bridge into Washington from Virginia.

"Don't fly in the face of God," Reverend Ferdinand told Peter when he protested that he wasn't a public speaker. "He has provided you with this golden opportunity to bring a message to your brethren."

Peter met Elizabeth Keckley, a handsome, light-skinned woman, at the door of the lecture hall. He was stiff with nervousness as she led him to the lectern and introduced him to the sixty or so people in attendance. Peter, who heard nary a word of the introduction, suddenly found himself standing alone, gazing at black and brown faces gazing expectantly at him.

Silence. Embarrassing and protracted. Something had to give. A person in the audience coughed. Silence again. It was Peter's turn. Taking a deep breath, he reared back on his haunches and began.

"I ain't a public speaker so I'll tell you plain 'bout we flight on a Sesesh steamboat. It were a matter of life and death. We crew decided to be free in this life or scuttle our boat and go down with her to the bottom of the sea."

It became progressively easier talking to upturned faces which hung on to his every word, holding their breath when his safety seemed imperiled, smiling with relief when the frightful journey ended.

At the conclusion of his speech they stood up to applaud him, those in the front rows rushing forward to shake his hand. It's because they had been slaves, Peter reasoned, or they still had kinfolks under the Sesesh. That's what was producing this flowing warmth, this feeling that made him want to embrace them all.

Mrs. Keckley smiled at him proudly and Peter smiled back. Rain would like her, he decided, and promised himself to write her in detail about this evening. God how he missed his baby cakes.

Suddenly, Peter was ready to meet Abraham Lincoln.

"Gentlemen, please be seated."

There was nothing elaborate about the President's office, it was surprisingly plain. A map stand was next to the window and a picture of Andrew Jackson framed in gilt hung over the marble fireplace. Several chairs were arranged in a half circle in front of Mr. Lincoln's desk, a massive scarred affair with pigeonholes.

Peter waited until his chair was safely beneath his rump before he dared to look directly at the President of the United States, at his brooding, craggy face and eyes sunk in hollows. He was swarthy and lanky and his neck was scrawny.

"You have come a long way?" Mr. Lincoln asked, his friendly voice inviting them to be at ease.

"From Beaufort, Mr. President." Reverend Ferdinand introduced himself and Peter whose own vocal chords were paralyzed. "You might have heard of Mr. Mango, sir, who together with his crew abducted a Confederate gunboat."

The President smiled at Peter. "I could hardly forget it. Horace Greeley reminds me every chance he gets that you and your race are loyal Americans but that I seem to regard the Rebels more favorably."

Peter's heart was thumping so loud he could hear it.

"You gentlemen have come to add your prayers to Greeley's twenty millions?" Mr. Lincoln asked with dry humor.

"I live on my knees praying that our black brethren will be delivered from bondage," the reverend replied, looking pious enough to drop to his knees forthwith. "But we are here as emissaries of your old friends General Hunter and General Saxton who both send you their warmest regards." He handed over letters from each of them.

Mr. Lincoln absorbed their contents with barely a glance. "Black soldiers," he sighed, looking pensively at Peter. "I'm always receiving deputations of Negroes requesting permission to enlist. The patriotism of your race warms my heart but arming them is a delicate matter. The Border States, you know. There's a rumor making the rounds that as President I'd like to have God on my side but that I must have Kentucky."

Reverend Ferdinand chuckled. The President could be depended upon for his droll sense of humor.

"I hope you gentlemen realize that the slaveholding border states, which have fifty thousand guns aimed at our enemies, must be kept on our side. And they are alarmed by the increased calls for abolition. If Kentucky and Missouri went over to the Rebels, they could establish bases to attack Indiana and Ohio. A Rebel Maryland would cause havoc here in Washington. My plan, as you perhaps know, calls for gradual abolition and compensation to slaveholders loyal to the Union."

It was a plan he had been attempting to implement for months, the voluntary relinquishing of slaves. Reluctantly, Congress had signed a bill to pay such compensation but the Border States remained adamant. No abolition at any price, they insisted, although Mr. Lincoln had warned them that time was running out. The exigencies of war demanded abolition.

"But we are losing ground, Mr. President," Reverend Ferdinand said. They all knew he meant "losing the war." It had been months since the Union had a military victory and Mr. Lincoln was known to complain of being cursed with idiots for generals, all the brilliant strategists having seceded.

"You yourself have said, Mr. President, that our nation's experiment with popular government must not fail. It's the best hope of mankind. But our soldiers need reinforcements. Volunteering is at an all-time low and desertions high."

Mr. Lincoln stood up and walking to the window glanced outside at the fetid canal, once a sewer and still rank. More pleasing to the eye were the banks of the Potomac River and the blue-green mountains of Virginia.

"Mr. Mango," the President said, still gazing out the window, "why did you abduct that Confederate vessel?"

The question startled Peter. "Me?" he asked, his head as empty as a bleached seashell.

Mr. Lincoln returned to his seat, his melancholy face reminding Peter that the man was still mourning the death of his son.

"It were grief, suh," he finally replied. "A hurting what was always there. And when my chil'ren were born that grief turn me into a madman. I plan how they gon be free, my babies and they mother. When one thing don't work I try another. So we crew steal the *Swanee* and put our families aboard. We all agreed. Freedom or drown."

His voice sounded like the croak of a frog and his mind went blank again except for one last thought which he uttered slowly. "I was born a slave, suh, but always felt that I was a man."

Mr. Lincoln nodded. "A man is entitled to the fruits of his own labor." That was one of his oft-stated beliefs, Negroes had such rights that had to be protected. "Gentlemen," he said "thank you and your generals for sharing your views with me. I will take it under advisement but at the moment I am bound by other considerations."

Peter scrambled to his feet. They were being dismissed empty-handed.

"Mr. President," Reverend Ferdinand said, ."even Kentucky must bend to the will of God." His voice was stern, his face unsmiling.

The President, who considered himself a God-fearing man, nodded again. "Perhaps," he suggested, "you might call on Secretary Stanton while you're here."

"We already have."

"Well, another visit might be in order."

Peter groaned to himself. White folks sure knew how to run you around till you collapsed.

As they were leaving, there was a knock on the door which led to the cabinet room. A tall silver-haired man pushed it open when told to come in.

"I'm sorry, Mr. President," he said, "I didn't realize you were busy."

"They were just leaving, Senator Sumner."

Reverend Ferdinand smiled at his friend Charles Sumner and they exchanged greetings. "And this is Mr. Mango," he said, indicating Peter. "One of Admiral Du Pont's pilots." Commander Du Pont had recently been promoted to Admiral.

"My pleasure, sir." Senator Sumner crossed the room to shake Peter's hand.

Mr. Lincoln glanced into the cabinet room and winced. Senators Zachariah Chandler and Ben Wade and Congressman Owen Lovejoy were seated at the table, men who had worked tirelessly for his election and were now pressuring him to emancipate the slaves as a war measure. To do so, they insisted, would hasten the end of the war.

"Am I late for our meeting?" the President asked.

Sumner murmured politely that it had been scheduled for three-thirty and it was now after four.

Mr. Lincoln's smile was disarming. "I'm like that absentminded fellow who put his clothes in the bed and draped himself over the back of a chair."

They all laughed except Peter who was frozen-faced as he followed the minister outside to the corridor. "It were all a waste of time, Reverend," he moaned.

"It was not a waste. We're going back to see Mr. Stanton. As long as we have a tiny opening, Peter, give thanks to God, crawl into it, taste victory in defeat and remember Lazarus. Also remember those gentlemen in the cabinet room who are the most anti-slavery men in Congress after Thaddeus Stevens. His wrath reminds me of Jesus attacking the moneylenders in the temple."

Ferdinand poked Peter in the chest with his forefinger. "A tiny band of people with messianic fury can lead the multitude into righteousness. Please understand that."

"Yes, suh."

The minister spoke rapidly, hardly pausing to take a breath. "Take Charles Sumner, for example, the senator who shook your hand. What a magnificent man and scholar. He believes American slavery is the greatest organized barbarianism in the world and his essays damning it have been read by millions. He's Mr. Lincoln's chief foreign policy adviser and has the President's ear and so does bluff Ben Wade who I hope you noticed. He fairly aches to smash the planter class. That doesn't mean he's tolerant of Negroes, for Ben would solve the race problem by shipping all of you back to Africa. But he did warn the planters that the first blast of civil war would be their death warrant. Their party dominated Congress, the Supreme Court and the White House for years. But instead of respecting that they invited in the winds of change themselves which I pray will blow them into oblivion and enlighten Mr. Lincoln to hear the clarion call of God over the whimpers of Kentucky."

Peter took a step backward, fairly bowled over by the minister's avalanche.

"I hope you noticed how huge Zachariah Chandler is," he continued, "how well preserved. He took up calisthenics and practiced his marksmanship when a South Carolina Congressman whipped poor Charles Sumner almost to death in his Senate chambers. Other chivalry from the South started wielding their bowie knives and pistols in Congress threatening to kill their opponents, but Zachariah Chandler was ready for them. Their kind murdered Owen Lovejoy's brother, burned him up with his crusading printing press and forced thousands of other Southerners sympathetic to Negroes to emigrate to safer ground. I say with Frederick Douglass, 'Down with treason and down with slavery the cause of treason.' "

Trembling and looking fierce, Ferdinand sucked in a huge breath.

"Amen," Peter whispered, mesmerized. He wondered if the reverend's explosion had been caused by his unspoken fear that their mission had failed.

In the morning they sat subdued in the first row of seats in the War Department's reception room. Anxiety had catapulted them there early. Fifteen minutes after Mr. Stanton arrived they were standing in front of his tall writing desk.

"I understand you saw the President yesterday?"

"Yes, Mr. Secretary. And he suggested that we pay another visit to you."

Stanton took off his spectacles and wiped them on a lace handkerchief. His eyes were so pale they seemed sightless, which they almost were. "Tell me everything the President said. Do not leave out even a comma."

He listened without comment until the reverend finished, then nodded vigorously. Throughout the recital Stanton barely looked at Peter but now he favored him with a benign glance.

"Here's a letter for General Saxton." He handed the minister an envelope. "You may read it but outside. Next."

In the corridor Reverend Ferdinand read the essentials to Peter.

" ' . . . You are hereby authorized to organize colored persons of African descent for volunteer laborers . . . not exceeding fifty thousand . . . assign them to the Quartermaster Department.

" ' . . . In order to guard the plantations and settlements occupied by the United States from invasion and protect the inhabitants thereof from captivity and murder by the enemy, you are also authorized to arm, uniform, equip and receive into the service of the United States . . . volunteers of African descent . . . to receive the same pay and rations as are allowed by law to volunteers in the service.

" 'The population of African descent that cultivate the lands and perform the labor of the Rebels constitute a large share of their military strength, and enable the white masters to fill the Rebel armies, and wage a cruel and murderous war against the people of the Northern States. By reducing the laboring strength of the Rebels, their military power will be reduced. You are therefore authorized by every means in your power to withdraw from the enemy their laboring force and population . . .' "

How had this miracle happened, Peter wondered, hallelujahs exploding in his head. It was more than General Saxton had requested. "I don't understand, Reverend. The President said——"

"My dear fellow, that's politicking." In his exuberance, Reverend Ferdinand grabbed Peter and hugged him. "Secretary Stanton is as astute as they come. In Washington you don't kick down the stable door but waltz around it. Where do you think General Hunter got the rifles for his Negro regiment? And their uniforms?"

Peter looked at him blankly and then grinned. "I be damned."

"And saved by the grace of God," the reverend boomed, laughing.

They were en route home aboard a steamer when President Lincoln's answer to Horace Greeley was published in the Washington *Evening Star*. Despite his personal wish that all men everywhere could be free, the President stated, his primary objective was to save the Union and not to either save or destroy slavery. If he could save the Union by freeing all of the slaves, some of them, or none of them that is what he intended to do.

13

Beaufort

September 1862

As the weeks passed Peter's excitement over their success in Washington was replaced by exasperation. He had hoped to find upon his return home a message from Lieutenant Mellon ordering him back to active duty.

"No, sugarfoot," Rain said, "ain't nobody send for you."

The way she said it so cheerfully, not wanting him shot at, maimed or killed, made Peter peevish. "You sure you ain't forgot to tell me, Rain?"

She had been known to suffer such lapses in Charleston. Fearful of his repairing a fisherman's boat after curfew and bumping into a patroller, she often wouldn't relay the message until morning. "It slip my mind," she would apologize while Peter ranted that she had caused a poor fisherman to lose a whole day's pay. Rain would be contrite but now, telling the truth, she was insulted.

"I ain't forgot nothing. Why you keep asking me over and over? Mamma, please tell this nigger ain't nobody send for him."

"Not so far's I know," Lily replied placidly. "But you is forgetful, Rain. And contrary when it's about other people."

"Contrary? Me? It's spiteful of you to say that."

This was something else to irritate Peter. Rain and Mamma

pecking at each other like roosters in a cockfight. His mother was too bossy, Rain complained. And Lily told him, "There's something 'bout that gal what don't set right with me. She's too close-mouthed and cain't accept advice."

The prize money also vexed him when it arrived. The *Swanee* had been appraised by the government at $9,000 instead of the $75,000 she was worth plus her own armament not to mention the other four cannons. The crew was awarded half of the appraised value, Peter as the leader receiving $1500, and the others $600 each. Had the vessel been rightfully appraised they would all have been far more generously rewarded.

"Son, you all didn't steal the boat for the money," Lily reminded him, but he refused to be consoled, raging inwardly. First Lieutenant Mellon had dismissed him abruptly and now this. All because he was a black man not supposed to have enough sense to figure things out.

Brother Man was vexed, too, when Peter located him on St. Helena Island. Evacuated from Edisto, he and Sister had left the crowded refugee camp and, encouraged by Stretch, were now working on one of the plantations Dexter Youngblood managed.

"I'll be glad to get the prize money even so," the big man said, looking weary.

They were sitting on the steps of the shack he and Sister shared with two women field hands whose menfolks were in the Negro regiment. At the moment Sister was at the side of the house at the mortar pounding grain with a pestle. She looked up, caught Peter's eye and smiled, her chubby face bunching into squares and triangles like chunks of chocolate. To Peter she seemed to have grown fatter.

He had reported to Brother Man his activities aboard the *Swanee* around northern Edisto and was listening now to what had happened to him and Sister on the southern part of the island.

"It were real nice working there, Peter. We planted another cotton crop and put down some yams and corn. Me and Sister had us a nice little place. The pay was slow coming but it was ours. Didn't have to turn it over to nobody. Then suddenly Sesesh was everywhere and we woulda been slaves again." Brother Man's face hardened into granite at the memory of their flight.

"The superintendents hopped around night and day to get us

all down to the flatboats. We grabbed whatever we could, covered the boat with twigs and branches so's we'd look like a bog floating down the river. By the time we reached the refugee camp our poor superintendent had worked heself into a fever. He died a few days later. He were a nice man, Peter. Believed in we colored folks. And we had a sweet little place on Edisto, me and Sister, right next to a pecan grove. For the first time we had us a home and figured to spend the rest of our life there. Goddamn Sesesh. When they gon let us be?"

He looked at Peter who hunched his shoulders and said glumly, "I been trying to enlist but General Saxton won't let me."

September 22, 1862

President Lincoln issued a preliminary emancipation proclamation announcing that as of January 1, 1863, slaves in the Rebel States would be forever free. He had finally conceded to abolitionist demands that emancipation be a war aim.

Reverend Ferdinand crowed that while fighting for its own existence the government had been obliged to take slavery by the throat and choke it to death. With tears in his eyes he ecstatically embraced every Negro within arm's reach who did not scramble out of his way. They pretended to be ecstatic, too, but actually felt they had already come out of the wilderness. Freedom meant massa was gone and slavery had departed with him. Contraband or fugitive, whatever it was called, meant that they were free.

Slaves in the Border States loyal to the Union were not affected by the President's decree but it was indeed a catalyst. General Saxton, recruiting laborers for the Quartermaster Department, soon reached his quota. On the heels of the proclamation the number of Negroes in every Union camp in every theater of war increased dramatically. They were used for military labor to build roads and forts and bridges. Familiar with the area, they made excellent teamsters and scouts. The aim was to deprive the enemy of those black hands that grew their foodstuff, harvested it, cooked it and when it turned to shit, emptied the slop jars and cleaned up the outhouses.

But this did not sit well with all Union soldiers. On St. Helena, in an attempt to discourage Negroes from enlisting, white soldiers went on a rampage setting fire to Negro shacks, beating unarmed men and raping their women. General Saxton finally had to restrict the marauders to their barracks.

December 1862

Peter was thinking about buying one of the town houses in Beaufort that the tax commissioners intended to auction off. He had yet to hear from Lieutenant Mellon which he found aggravating. He was not the only one upset and confused.

The three tax commissioners had arrived in Beaufort two months ago, sent by Congress to sell not only the town houses for unpaid taxes but also the plantations. They were to auction that land off in lots not to exceed 320 acres.

General Saxton and most of the Project volunteers were appalled. They were in favor of the land being subdivided into twenty-acre lots and sold to the field hands on installment. That would insure their security and prevent them from being forced to work for subsistence wages after the war.

The Negroes had already proven their mettle, bringing in the bumper cotton crop the planters had abandoned and demonstrating from the corn and potato crops they harvested their ability to feed themselves and supply foodstuff to the army. Some of the proceeds from the cotton harvest the government had returned to the islands in a fund to assist the steady flow of impoverished contrabands coming across their lines. But if the plantations were sold in huge-sized lots, the field hands would be unable to compete with Northern speculators who would flock to the islands to gobble the land up and then hire the Negroes to work for them. Surely, General Saxton and his supporters contended, these laborers who had farmed the land all their lives without recompense should be given a chance to own it.

The tax commissioners did not agree. Their agenda was to sell the land to the highest bidders to benefit the Union treasury.

And then Dexter Youngblood jumped into the dispute, contending that the Negroes, so long unlettered, still needed the guidance of white men, preferably him. He was forming a combine with Boston investors to buy several plantations on St. Helena to be run by himself and his superintendents.

"I'm as interested in the welfare of the Negroes as you are," he told Reverend Ferdinand, his most outspoken critic, who waylaid him in Beaufort one afternoon and invited him into his office. "But I don't believe they're ready yet to own land."

The reverend, agitated by what he deemed Youngblood's mercenary reversal, sat in his chair frowning as he listened to the superintendent. Dexter, refusing a seat, was standing near the door as though ready to bolt out of it if necessary.

"Speculators have no interest in the Negroes beyond making a dollar," Youngblood said, "and could wreck our experiment with free labor which has been successful so far."

It had been a success. Youngblood had shifted his work force from the gang to the task system and his plantations had proven more profitable than those managed by other superintendents who were now adopting his methods.

His combine did not expect to make a profit, he explained. His chief concern was to give free labor a fair trial and avoid the danger of speculators. "People appreciate what they have to struggle to obtain and Negroes are no exception. Do you want to spoil them, Reverend, with handouts? Encourage them to be shiftless and lazy? Working as free laborers they're subject to the laws of supply and demand. That's what will develop their self-reliance and independence."

Reverend Ferdinand's face turned redder than the superintendent's beard. "I'm surprised at you, Dexter. I daresay the field hands have taught you all you know about growing cotton. Now they're supposed to step aside while you buy the land out from under them? And be grateful for the privilege of working it for you? Some of them are mighty upset by that notion, I can tell you that. They want a chance to buy a little piece of the home place they've been slaving on all of their lives. Isn't that being self-reliant?"

Patiently, as if talking to an imbecile, Youngblood stated his position. "Any Negro who can buy a large plantation has my blessing. I'm merely trying to safeguard the rest of them from being exploited by speculators. And whether you realize it or not we're under scrutiny here. Whatever we accomplish with free labor can be a model for the rest of the South. But the blacks have to stand or fall in the marketplace without any special favors."

"The marketplace?" Reverend Ferdinand jumped to his feet. "You dare talk about the marketplace? Up north colored people ask only for the right to work. It's the whites who demand special favors. They want Negroes barred from the trade guilds. Barred from certain occupations. Barred from high-paying jobs and then attacked for daring to show up at work. Last summer in Newark a mob set fire to a tobacco factory where Negro women and children worked. About twenty-five of them were almost trapped in the flames. Your marketplace, sir, is a hellhole."

As the days grew shorter and winter blew its icy breath over the contentious land, the quarrel boiled and bubbled, all sides agreeing that the huge estates had to be broken up. They were the foundation of the enormous political power the planters had wielded, the minority who had ruled the Southland. Reverend Ferdinand sped to Washington to plead General Saxton's proposal to subdivide the land into twenty-acre lots accessible to Negroes. One of the tax commissioners also raced to the capital to defend their position.

"It's all right, Peter," General Saxton assured him when he mentioned the possibility of buying a house but expressed concern over the predicament of the field hands. "Put in your bid as soon as possible. The houses here in Beaufort have nothing to do with our problem on the plantations. I'm hoping that Reverend Ferdinand will return from Washington with good news for us."

In the meantime General Saxton had put in his bid for one of the town houses to which he would take his bride, a schoolteacher he was soon to wed.

He and Peter were conversing after a recruitment meeting held at the Tabernacle following the Sunday service. The general had invited Peter, their local hero, to speak to the men, urging them to volunteer, meanwhile denying Peter's own request to enlist, assuring him that Admiral Du Pont had other plans for him.

The house Peter was eyeing was a two-bedroom cottage that had been rented to the German butcher by Roland Caine. One by one the butcher's three sons had attended a private academy through the good graces of Massa Roland. The apothecary man had been similarly indebted and the tavern owner as well, their enterprises dependent upon the patronage of one planter or another for leasing land or obtaining bank loans or other favors.

When Peter mentioned his tentative plans to Rain she was openly skeptical. "A house you massa owned?" She thought her husband had gone crazy.

"Somebody's massa owned every house around here," Peter retorted and the following Sunday steered her to the little frame cottage that sat far back on a tiny lawn on East Street. The place was vacant, the overgrown weeds waist high. The slanted tile roof possessed of two dormer windows extended itself to overhang the shady porch.

"Let's go inside," Peter said, although by this time he was doubtful if buying it was the smart thing to do. It was complicated. He would have to submit a bid and pay cash.

"Ain't we trespassing?"

"No. We is maybe buyers."

Rain hung back until they were inside and then fell in love with the dining room even though the window was broken and a film of dust made her cough. And she fell in love with the two upstairs bedrooms. And the little alcove. It was the alcove with a cot in it that made her clap her hands, sunny with delight.

"Oh my, this is the cutest house. Just big enough for all of us."

And then her face caved in and she looked forlorn enough to cry. Peter knew she was thinking about the missing children.

She asked him with downcast eyes, "The President say slaves the Sesesh has is free. That means my Zee and Petunia, too? Wherever they be?"

Gently Peter answered, "Only if they can get someplace what's in Union hands."

"They masters ain't gon free them?"

"No."

She shrugged, visibly closing her mind against contemplating the sad riddle further. It was the first time in quite a while she had mentioned the girls, accepting that they were never to be found in this world, gone forever from her. But every so often she retreated into a private place to weep for them and Peter could not reach her. What's the matter, honeybunch, he would ask and she would reply, Nothing. He grew to dislike those times, excommunicated from her. He never mentioned the missing children himself and was grateful that she seldom did either.

Now he followed her downstairs and into the kitchen where she peeped into the cupboards.

"Peter. Ain't this too cute? We is gon buy it?"

"I don't know," he temporized. "I has got to study up on it some."

Rain was petulant, her bottom lip drooping. "How come you drag me over here if you ain't already study up on it some?"

He chuckled. "You is a very funny woman, does you know that?"

Rain knew it and kissed him.

The next day, with the help of Miss Carlotta, Peter put in his bid for the house Roland Caine had rented to the butcherman.

January 1, 1863

July was so tipsy he could barely keep his eyes focused. In the days to come he would forget practically everything about this jamboree except its fateful climax.

General Saxton was throwing this mammoth party to celebrate the Emancipation Proclamation. Five thousand freedmen, their teachers and superintendents, army officers and honored guests were crowded into the oak grove next to Beaufort's army camp. Black people dressed in their Sunday best, in straw hats and turbans, greeted each other with shouts of joy. Soldiers from the 1st South Carolina Regiment, lined up in front of the platform and looking splendid in their dress uniforms, filled July with pride. Another group of black soldiers escorted visitors who had arrived on beribboned steamers.

Nature had cooperated, providing a cloudless sunny day. The great oaks stretched themselves toward the sky, primordial and reverent, a home for the chirping mocking birds that were flitting from branch to branch.

On the platform, crowded with seated dignitaries, the regiment's chaplain invoked the presence of God and solemnly read President Lincoln's proclamation. ". . . On the first day of January in the year of Our Lord, 1863, all persons held as slaves within any state, or designated part of a state, the people wherefor shall then be in rebellion against the United States, shall be then, thenceforward, and forever free . . ."

The military bands played. Black throats pulsated with song.

> "My country t'is of thee
> Sweet land of liberty . . ."

Twelve oxen roasted on spits were sliced and dished out. People crowded around the long wooden tables, happily eating and quenching their thirst with watered molasses.

July was drinking moonshine. He had been unable to find Peter and their friends in the huge crowd and was celebrating without them. Absalom knew a bootlegger who operated an illegal still deep in the woods and had brought along a jug of the stuff. It was sitting under a small table they shared with four other men. More or less surreptitiously, as if the others couldn't smell the potent alcoholic fumes, Absalom would bend down to pour a dollop into his and July's cups.

As he plied July with the liquor, Absalom slyly asked him once again to become his partner.

"For the last time, nigger, no," July replied. He was not that drunk. "How many times is I got to tell you I ain't interested in this swampy land?"

The controversy over subdividing the plantations had made the field hands fractious. They damned the tax commissioners, even those laborers like Stretch and Brother Man who did not intend to buy twenty acres if it became available, but preferred to work for wages for a while "to see which way the wind blows," as Brother Man cautiously put it. But Absalom had a solution if the 320-acre proposition prevailed. Together with two other field hands he intended to buy the land jointly. The only problem was they were a wee bit short of cash and were inviting July, and his prize money, to be a part of their enterprise.

July took a healthy swig of moonshine and burped. A burly chap sitting opposite Absalom looked at them both with suspicion.

"I ain't gon stay in St. Helena," July said. "Soon's the war's over I is heading back to Charleston." His eyes had begun to cross and his tongue to thicken, still he spoke what had long been on his mind. "Absalom, you is talking 'bout owning a whole lot of land, but you just got around to owning youself."

"You don't trust me," his friend said. Openly cradling the crock, forgetting to be sneaky, he poured himself a large shot. "But let me tell you this. I been working cotton since I was knee high to a toad. And I is a man just like Massa Caine what cotton made wealthy. So why not me and my buddies?"

July was not listening but paying attention to the activities on the platform. General Saxton, smiling and handsome, had just introduced Colonel Higginson, a staunch abolitionist and supporter of John Brown who had given up command of a New England regiment in order to accept this post as the new commander of the 1st South Carolina Volunteers. The celebrants gave the colonel a tumultuous round of applause.

General Saxton announced that the 1st South Carolina Regiment has just returned from an expedition raiding the coastline between Georgia and San Fernandino, Florida. "I had two objects in sending them there," he said. "First to prove their fighting abilities in destroying Rebel saltworks and breaking up Rebel picket stations along the coast. Second, to bring away slaves. In every respect the expedition was successful. Our soldiers made thirteen different landings from their transport. The pickets were driven in by their cool bravery, the saltworks destroyed and slave families brought aboard the steamer."

Stamping their feet and voicing approval, the assemblage applauded. July reached under the table for the moonshine.

General Saxton held up his hands for quiet. "Our colored soldiers fought their way out of a Rebel ambush with fierce energy. Their colonel said it would have been madness to attempt with the bravest white troops what was accomplished with black men. They know the countryside and are fighting on the homefront to protect their families. I am convinced that the successful prosecution of this war lies in the unlimited use of black soldiers. Men like Sergeant Prince Rivers, born right here in Beaufort, who I am proud to present to you now on this glorious day of liberation."

A stalwart soldier seated on the platform stood up and strode forward. He was a towering six-footer as erect as a Georgia pine.

"By God, but he looks like we fireman Turno," July claimed, squinting at him and seeing double. " 'Cept this fella is better looking." He laughed.

The sergeant spoke bluntly without preamble. "Our regiment captured Sesesh soldiers and made them our prisoners. Our former masters. And I tell you it can spook a fellow having at his mercy a man what has whipped his mammy, messed over his sister and would make him a slave again."

July stopped smiling.

"But you cain't disgrace your uniform," Prince Rivers boomed. "So you don't smash him in the face with the butt of your gun and break his jaw. You don't put a pistol to his temple and blow out his brains. No. You puts him in the stockade. And what does that prove? Highborn or lowborn he ain't your master no more. You ain't his slave. He is your prisoner."

The audience roared. They shouted hallelujah. They cried.

"My first encounter with the Sesesh was last August when General Hunter sent our company to guard the fort at St. Simons Island off the coast of Georgia. Only black people lived in the little village but the enemy was on the mainland and a band of Sesesh Rebels were hiding in the swamp on St. Simons. Before we got there 'bout twenty-five colored men on they own armed theyselves and went after the Rebels who got away after a pitched battle. So when we arrived we hunted them day and night, mucking about in that blasted swamp. But we didn't find them. Later we learned that a treacherous slave, who had belonged to one of the Rebels, supplied them with a boat and they escaped back to the mainland.

"Our company did picket duty for two months on St. Simons and no more Sesesh came skulking over. Every coupla days one of our scouts sneaked to the mainland to get news from Negroes about Sesesh movements. And our scouts always returned with runaway slaves who would enlist. Slaves who understood that in order to be free we has to beat the enemy on the battlefield. And you know what one of them said? One of them Rebels what escaped from the swamp? He wrote in a letter left behind: 'If you wish to know hell before your time, go to St. Simons and be hunted for ten days by niggers.' "

The exultant revelers burst out laughing. Prince Rivers waited until the last guffaw subsided, then said soberly, "Men, join we regiment and give the Sesesh hell before their time, after their time, all the time."

Wild applause followed him to his seat. July and Absalom regarded each other drunkenly.

"Absalom," July slurred, looking at his friend with one eye closed to avoid seeing double, "I is lucky you is my friend."

Absalom grinned, revealing his spacy, stained teeth. "You is gon come in with us? Be we partner?"

The look on July's face was beatific as if he was hearing angels sing. "No, but I is gon loan you the money. And better'n that, my good buddy, I is gon keep the Sesesh from sneaking across the creek again to snatch your raggedy behind." He was referring to three Confederate guerillas in a skiff who had been captured yesterday by the Negro guards patrolling St. Helena.

"Thank you, July."

"You is welcome, Absalom."

They staggered to their feet, Absalom hitching up his trousers as arm in arm they made their way through the crowd to a long table set up under a spreading oak tree, flanked by the Stars and Stripes waving on two flagpoles. The 1st South Carolina Regiment had completed its roster, July learned. Undaunted he signed on with the 2nd South Carolina, the obliging recruiter holding him up.

"If I were a young fella, July, I'd join up, too," Absalom said, tobacco juice running down his chin.

14

$\diamond\!\!\!\sim\!\!\!\diamond$

March 1863

On the day of the land auction July was aboard a Union gunboat, the *Ben Hur*, sailing up the Combahee River, his army pants tucked into his boots, his tunic belted and a visor cap sitting straight on his head. He had tried tilting it to the left, then to the right, but both ways had seemed too cocky and it had settled itself dead center.

The troops had left Beaufort in the middle of the night and dawn was just now painting a pink streak across the sky, but it was still chilly on deck. Soldiers crowded at the rail were fearfully staring at the algae floating on top of the marsh and the moss-covered bogs which converged to form little islands five and six feet long. Other floating islands, somebody had suggested, were alligators.

"What about that one?" July asked his friend, Archie, standing next to him. He pointed at a suspicious large lump.

"It's got a Georgia 'gator look," Archie replied with an impish grin. He had large buck teeth which his lips didn't quite cover so that he appeared to be always smiling. A refugee from Savannah and barely in his twenties, he was full of spirited high jinks that kept July from becoming too morose.

Shuddering at the prospect of becoming alligator fodder, July turned around, aware of the woman standing on the poop deck above him. Her head was tied in a red bandanna and she looked like somebody's harmless plump grandmother except that she was wearing rough workman's boots and there was a pistol stuck in the broad belt encircling her waist.

Half an hour ago General James Montgomery had addressed his troops and introduced the woman. His command embraced two hundred and fifty Negro soldiers sailing on two other gunboats besides the *Ben Hur*. Standing on the bridge he told the troops that within forty-five minutes they would be disembarking in rowboats and were to follow the detailed instructions of their officers. Their goal was to carry off as many slaves as wished to accompany them.

The general's brisk cold manner did not inspire affection from his troops. A militantly erect man with a wind-bitten face, General Montgomery had ridden with John Brown in Kansas and had a reputation for being outrageous. He introduced his two guides, a Negro man, Sanchez, recently escaped from this area, and the plump woman.

"Harriet Tubman," Montgomery said, "has been mingling down here with the slaves and they trust her. She will assure them that we have come as liberators. I had the pleasure of working with her in Kansas and we are privileged to have her services."

The two other gunboats were being deployed to the mill and the railroad bridge which was to be destroyed. Their goals were identical, to relieve the rice plantations of their black workers.

The name Harriet Tubman meant nothing to July although she was a legend in abolitionist circles. Slave raids were her specialty but without benefit of gunboats or armed soldiers. Alone she had led more than three hundred slave men and women from Maryland to freedom in Canada, outwitting posses with bloodhounds. She had never lost a slave and reputedly threatened to shoot the fainthearted who wanted to turn back. Now she went behind enemy lines to locate supply routes and test the temper of plantation slaves.

On schedule the *Ben Hur* dropped anchor and the soldiers climbed down the ladders to the rowboats. General Montgomery jumped into the first one with his two scouts and a squad of men. The guide had assured him that the Confederates would not attack them as they disembarked. Their picket station was a mile and a half away at the Combahee ferry. He also disclosed that the Rebel soldiers were disorganized which was how he had managed to escape.

July and his squadron were assigned to the last rowboat under the command of a lieutenant. The *Ben Hur*'s gunners were at their stations, covering the disembarking soldiers. In July's craft, everyone's eyes combed the river for signs of danger, the rowers bent over, each black face alert as their oars dipped into the water and the algae and bogs floated harmlessly by.

Sitting midship on a plank next to Archie, July realized that every dip of the oars brought them all closer to jeopardy beyond the perils of normal warfare. The Sesesh had written it into law. Captured Negro soldiers were not to be treated as prisoners but as runaway slaves and returned to bondage.

Suddenly July panicked. It was the steamy land itself which terrified him. It flew into his throat, clogged his nostrils and choked him. Gasping for breath he wondered what madness had made him enlist. Moonshine. And Sergeant Prince Rivers. Damn them both. This was his outfit's first expedition. In a goddamn rowboat on the goddamn Combahee.

Their craft touched bottom. "Quickly," the lieutenant ordered. "Overboard. Push it ashore."

The shock of cold water steadied July somewhat. He was able to move, to follow orders, to help shove the rowboat onto land. All right, he told himself, you is back on slave soil but it don't mean a damn.

He stumbled forward following the soldiers in front of him. They moved away from their beached boats and the detail of men left behind, and marched up a causeway, a raised road over the swamp under the protection of the *Ben Hur*'s guns. On both sides of the causeway were marsh and rice fields and piney woods in the distance. The woods looked impenetrable but July feared they hid Rebel pickets. At any moment shots could ring out cutting him and his buddies down. Instead he heard a whistle blowing.

The lieutenant led his men toward a plantation directly ahead. Another detail of soldiers in front of them had angled down a side path which led to the rice mill. Several minutes later Archie, striding alongside of July, cried out, "Look yonder."

The road ahead of them, which moments ago had been empty,

was suddenly swarming with plantation slaves heeding the word that had spread like brushfire. *Yankee gunboat in the river. You all heard the whistle?* They came a-running, dropping their hoes, picking up their babies. Or a clucking hen. Or a squealing piglet. An enterprising woman had snatched a pot of rice still steaming off the hearth.

Up ahead Harriet Tubman was directing traffic. "You all get on down to the river. Rowboats will ferry you to our warship." The slaves, initially struck dumb by the sight of Negro soldiers as their liberators, speedily recovered. "God bless you," they cried, running toward the river.

A grizzled old man paused to grin at July. "Massa say run to the woods and hide and I 'bout near knock him over coming down here."

"Where's he at now?" July inquired.

"He jump on he horse and gallop lickety-split down the road toward the ferry."

The soldiers guffawed. Archie said, "You best get along, Uncle, and catch up with the others." There were hundreds of them, their black faces shining, hurrying to wade in the water.

By the time the lieutenant and his men reached the plantation the outbuildings were already on fire. General Montgomery had given the order to burn everything to the ground except the slave quarters.

Archie was jubilant. "I is gon piss in the flames," he crooned to July.

The air was acrid with smoke, the noise of the fire deafening as the barn caved in. The soldiers hurried on to the next burning. The master's abode. A handsome two-story frame house with a wraparound veranda situated in a grove of orange trees. With a kerosene can in his hand, July raced through the house with the others dribbling destruction, his eyes smarting.

Then they were outside again being ordered back to the rowboats. July paused to watch fascinated as the house blazed beyond control from the veranda to the gable, a smoking inferno consuming the familiar objects of someone's life which he had glimpsed racing through. Shelves of books. A canopied bed. A child's rocking horse. How strange, he thought, looking at his black hands which had helped set the fire. But it was sanctioned. They weren't going to hang him for it.

"Where's Archie?" a soldier yelled as he ran past July.

"I don't know."

July found him at the other end of the house with spread legs, directing a stream of urine at a flaming timber.

"Archie, come on." July's voice didn't carry over the roar of the fire. Running forward he swung his friend around.

"I did it," Archie laughed, holding his prick.

"Idiot, let's go." July wondered if he had ever been that young and crazy. A burning section of roof almost fell on them. Coughing, sputtering, they turned and ran away from the blazing house.

The plantation hands and most of the soldiers were gathered at the river, the rowboats ferrying them to the gunboat. There was no one else on the road except July and Archie. They had almost reached the causeway when the sound of gunfire stopped them in their tracks. Then they heard hoarse shouts and the shrill scream of women.

"Dear God, what now?" July breathed.

Cautiously he and Archie crept forward. The commotion was on the wide road leading from the mill. About thirty Negroes were trapped on it, wailing hysterically as bullets felled them. Confederate troops in a ditch below the road were shooting at them indiscriminately, herding the slaves back toward the mill. The causeway was protected by the *Ben Hur*'s gunfire, the pathway to it no-man's-land.

Negro soldiers on the causeway fired a barrage of bullets into the ditch. A Rebel's hoarse cry split the air. And in that momentary confusion, the enemy's guns silent, a young woman darted from the side road and ran toward the causeway.

July groaned. The girl was thin and dark. Not Mariah but her double. A sudden blast of gunfire from the ditch and she fell writhing to the ground. With a curse July dashed forward to reach her. Archie tackled him from behind, toppling them both into the mud as a hail of bullets sailed over their heads.

"Is you crazy, July?"

"Let me go, nigger."

"She's dead. You cain't help her. Look."

The girl's body was being riddled with shot. The trapped Negroes on the road, screaming and terrified, turned and fled back to the mill, stumbling over the fallen. Rifle shots from the black soldiers again silenced the Confederate guns in the ditch.

Cursing, July and his friend slithered forward on their bellies toward the causeway. Like worms covered with dirt and brambles they inched along. Finally, they were almost there. Gulping in a deep breath July raised up ready to sprint the last few yards. A single shot rang out from the ditch and found its mark.

"Why you do that?" Archie screamed as July fell face downward in the Combahee mud.

The *Ben Hur* rendezvoused with her sister gunboats as prearranged, their decks overflowing with 670 joyful slaves, a labor force valued by their owners at over two hundred thousand dollars. The pontoon and railroad bridges had been destroyed and tons of rice confiscated from three mills which were then burned down.

Beaufort, already swollen beyond capacity, was ready to welcome the newcomers to their refugee camps. As they streamed down the gangplanks, black recruiters singled out the able-bodied men, urging them to enlist immediately.

"You're free, brother. President Lincoln done declare it. Now what you gonna do for your Uncle Sam who needs you to shoulder a gun?"

Over three hundred suddenly free black men signed up that first day, their palms sweating with the effort to make their mark. Some of them looked up as the ambulances clattered by carrying the wounded and dead soldiers from the *Ben Hur*.

On the day of the auction, unaware that July's regiment had embarked on a slave raid, Peter impatiently awaited the results of the land sale. Congress had not solved the controversy between General Saxton's supporters and the tax commissioners but had postponed it by reserving a major portion of the land in contention to be sold next year. General Saxton felt it would be offered then in twenty-acre lots accessible to the freedmen. The commissioners, prevailing at this time, auctioned off the available plantations in 320-acre lots.

The most startling development occurred on St. Helena Island. About two thousand acres were purchased by Negroes who had pooled their resources, including Absalom and his partners. Northern speculators bought another few thousand acres. But the largest windfall went to Dexter Youngblood and his Boston combine. For a dollar an acre he purchased eleven plantations and leased two more. He now owned one third of St. Helena and had a work force of more than a thousand field hands.

In Beaufort several town houses were sold as expected. General Saxton was among the successful bidders. And the schoolmaster. And Peter. He now owned the butcherman's house. Both he and the house had once been the property of Roland Caine.

Disbelieving their good fortune, Peter and Rain walked through the cottage holding hands, mesmerized.

"It's ours?" she asked, questioning fate. "I ain't gon believe it till we moves in."

It was a dizzying day for Peter. On a routine trip to the quartermaster's office he was informed that his sailing orders had finally come through. He was being put on the payroll at fifty dollars a month and was to report immediately to Lieutenant Mellon at Hilton Head.

"Kiss you father good-bye," Rain told Glory, pushing the child forward. *Remember his face. And how he stands with his legs poked back.* Rain was carving his image in her heart which had turned to stone, stunned by this sudden turn of events. She had relaxed, set aside her fears, and see what had happened? *Lord, don't let them kill him lessen you plans to take me too.*

"Is you wearing you long drawers, son?" Lily asked. "It ain't summer yet. And don't worry 'bout us moving into the new house. Me and Rain'll manage just fine."

Peter bounced Peewee into the air one more time and kissed Rain. "Honeybunch, don't worry 'bout me. Smile now."

She tried, tears forming like pools in her eyes.

Book Three

Hostages
of War

∽◦∽

I have toiled all my life for this failure.

—DEREK WALCOTT,
"Another Life"

15

Union Headquarters, Hilton Head
March 1863

The wharves were crammed with warships and transports, more than seventy vessels at anchor. It was a beautiful kaleidoscope to Peter, the sun gleaming on white sails and smokestacks jammed so closely together it was difficult to tell where one boat ended and another began, all of it mirrored in the gently rippling blue water. He spied the frigate *Wabash*, a grand sight to his eyes, and next to it a strange-looking contraption resembling a box on a raft which was the vessel he was looking for, the *Cayenne*.

Lieutenant Mellon was aboard her talking to another naval officer, both men spic and span in white tunics and gold braid. As Peter approached them the lieutenant stopped talking and, turning toward him, smiled. It was a warm, infectious smile of welcome. Peter saluted smartly, glowing inside, and smiled back at his blond, gray-eyed commander forgiving him for everything, for his abrupt dismissal and the vexatious wait to be recalled. And he thought, with a silent chuckle, fifty dollars a month was more than he had ever earned. Thank you, suh, for that.

"Captain," Mellon said, turning to his companion, "this is my pilot, Peter Mango. He knows Charleston harbor like the palm of his hand."

"Really?" The captain barely glanced at Peter who was staring at the craft fascinated. She was peculiar, sitting low in the water, and appeared to be made of iron. She had two huge turrets, round like a stack of pancakes, and a thick smokestack between them. A stanchion for hauling a small boat was fenced in with a railing.

The lieutenant grinned. "Quite a little monster, isn't it. She's an ironclad. Like the *Monitor*. We're going on an expedition with a fleet of them."

"They're *improved* monitors, or so we've been told," the other man said acidly. "Let us pray that they're considerably improved. I find it hard to forget that on the *Monitor*'s maiden voyage the waves completely submerged the wheelhouse, flowed down the smokestack to douse the fires and suffocate the firemen with gas. Idiots who walked on deck during a strong wind were blown overboard. The crew arrived at their destination more dead than alive."

Lieutenant Mellon said with deceptive calmness, "Our boat has a freeboard of five feet so her deck is safer."

Peter's heart was beating double time. He was going to pilot an ironclad? When the derisive captain departed, Peter was glad to see him go, and Mellon also seemed relieved.

"Do you know anything about ironclads?" he asked. "About the *Monitor* and the *Merrimac*?"

"I read 'bout they fight in the newspaper," Peter said. "They the first two boats made of iron. Sesesh drape they wooden boat, the *Merrimac*, in iron and she attack a Union fleet. She slam into them like a iron monster and they shells cain't pierce her hide. Her gunfire set the Union boats on fire. Then here come the Yankee *Monitor*. Them two iron gunboats rear back and ram each other like bulls. They guns go lickety-split but iron is iron and don't smash up like wood. After a couple of hours the *Merrimac* back away leaking. The *Monitor* done save the Yankee fleet."

Lieutenant Mellon laughed. "That's not exactly in naval jargon but you've got the hang of it." He escorted Peter around the ironclad pointing out its unique features.

Mellon had been aboard a monitor when it attacked a Rebel fort during a trial run. The ironclad had absorbed forty-eight hits within four hours, which would have sunk a wooden ship, but she was not badly damaged. However, although she had sailed quite close to the fort, bombarding it with all of her artillery, she had done little or no damage other than kicking up dust. Nonetheless, Washington officials, in love with ironclads, had rushed a number of them into production. Neither Admiral Du Pont nor Lieutenant Mellon shared their enthusiasm, doubting that the monitors were as formidable against land batteries as Washington believed.

"Mr. Mango," the lieutenant said solemnly, "Admiral Du Pont has assembled a fleet of monitors to attack Fort Sumter. When we disable the fort, our fleet can push into Charleston. Think you can learn to navigate this hunk of iron in a few short weeks?"

Peter nodded, too ecstatic to speak.

He and Rain had been among the crowds thronged in the streets and on the rooftops on that terrible day when the Confederates had fired into Fort Sumter, starting the war. And how anxious he and his crewmates had been when the *Swanee* had approached the fort, their most crucial test when they were escaping. Now he was going to be part of an attack against it? Nothing could please him more.

April 5, 1863

Peter had discovered that the *Cayenne* moved slowly in the water, about seven knots, because she wasn't built for speed but to be a floating battery. She was one hundred sixty feet long, forty feet in beam and drew eight feet. About five inches of iron covered her wood frame. Most of her was under water, only the pilothouse and two turrets sticking out.

He also discovered that an iron boat wasn't too easy to live in. The temperature in the seamen's quarters was over a hundred but the coal heavers and firemen suffered the most. In the boiler room it hit a hundred and fifty and was so fiery that the poor workers had to handle everything with canvas pads. The coal heavers were Negroes, as were the cooks and mess boys and several seamen. White and black took their meals together and shared the same sweaty quarters.

And the pilothouse wasn't too comfortable either, Peter found out. Its circumference was only about eight feet, not much space for Lieutenant Mellon, the helmsman and himself.

But all was forgiven for he fell in love with the turrets, twin beauties to behold. The other monitors had only one but the *Cayenne*, which was an experiment, had two. The turrets resembled little round rooms about nine feet high, all iron plate with holes in the armor for the guns, two 11-inch Dahlgrens mounted on a pivot so that the gunners could fire in a wide arc.

Earlier that day Peter had felt quite proud when Admiral Du Pont chose the *Cayenne* to buoy the harbor and report the water depth. Peter realized his craft wasn't selected because he was her pilot but because she was smaller than the other monitors and had a lighter draft. It was hard to steer the ironclads if they were moving slowly, especially in shoal water. But he felt proud anyhow dropping the buoys. All of the ironclads had arrived and he saw six or seven warships, packed with soldiers waiting for the opportunity to land on Sesesh soil.

Tomorrow, Peter rhapsodized, the monitors would blow up Fort Sumter. Their soldiers would smash through to take Charleston. And the war, thank God, would end.

April 7, 1863

Peter prayed. By eleven A.M., God responded. A northeaster came in strong enough to blow away the haze but not roughen up the sea. Yesterday the ironclads had been unable to execute their plan due to a hazy cloud cover which obscured all landmarks in the channel. Now Admiral Du Pont's signalman sent out the message to weigh anchor and take advantage of the slack water. Slowly the ironclads steamed up the main ship channel toward Fort Sumter. They had been directed not to return the fire of the batteries on Morris Island unless signaled to do so. When Fort Sumter was within easy range, they were to engage its northeast face at a distance of six hundred to eight hundred yards, firing low at the center embrasure.

A fifty-foot-long raft was attached to the bow of the lead monitor, a layer of beveled timbers and iron plates holding chains to which were attached grappling irons with double prongs to sweep up and set off torpedoes. Admiral Du Pont's flagship, the *New Ironsides*, was positioned in the middle of the fleet to facilitate sending signals to the other ironclads and to General Hunter aboard a gunboat. The *Cayenne*, with Peter at its helm, chugged along last in line. A squadron of warships stood by in readiness waiting for Fort Sumter to fall. They would then support the ironclads in the grand sweep toward Charleston, which was heavily fortified by island batteries on all sides of the harbor.

"Stay about three hundred yards behind the monitor in front of you," Lieutenant Mellon ordered Peter.

"Yes, suh." He peered at its stern through the small oval holes, barely more than slits which served as windows. Rollo, the tow-headed helmsman, was at his side. Lieutenant Mellon stood behind them near the door. The pilothouse was compact with barely space to move around. Any sudden jar and the three men bumped into each other.

A signal was received from Admiral Du Pont's flagship. The lead vessel had become entangled with the grapnels of the raft. The other ironclads were to wait until she was free. Peter groaned inwardly. His eyes met Rollo's, equally dismayed. They were both keyed up and now another delay after yesterday's wasteful hours? The lieutenant slammed out of the pilothouse to check on his gunners in the turrets. He had a crew of over a hundred and seemed unusually tense to Peter who had known him to be always decisive but collected under fire. Half an hour later he returned and handed Peter the field glasses.

"The Confederates are hauling guns down the beach on Morris Island. No doubt they've seen our troops signaling from little Folly."

Folly Island was in Union hands but opposite it, across a narrow inlet, was Morris Island and the formidable Rebel battery, Fort Wagner. Peter looked through the glasses and, sure enough, there was the enemy trundling cannons down the beach. He handed the field glasses to Rollo who was not overly talkative but pleasant enough. He and Peter shared quarters with the engineers and were carefully polite to each other.

After another hour's wait the signal came to proceed. Peter gripped the wheel firmly and stared through the window slits. He could see the line of vessels ahead of him steaming forward within range of every Sesesh fort lining the harbor. The channel was narrow, the tide swift, and suddenly the ironclads fell out of line, lurching erratically as though drunk. It started with the lead vessel pushing her unwieldy raft and yawing wildly. The next monitor, turning in the lead ship's wake, forced the ironclad following her to veer sharply to avoid being hit. She lost headway and seemed in danger of being swept ashore.

Oh Lord, Peter gasped, glad they were last in line. He heard a tremendous roar and saw the waters gushing up like a geyser near the lead vessel. A torpedo had exploded almost beneath her. And now she was sending a message. Obstructions in her path. Rows of anchored casks extending across the harbor. Unable to pass them, the lead ship veered to port. The two monitors behind her were forced to turn around. Admiral Du Pont's flagship, having difficulty steering in the narrow channel, collided with another monitor.

Before Peter could react to these new developments, a barrage of cannon shot deadened his eardrums as they exploded against the *Cayenne*. All of the harbor batteries had opened up, the salvo trapping the entire ironclad fleet in the crossfire.

Struck by several mortars below the water line, the *Cayenne* sheered wildly. Peter hung onto the wheel and twisted it starboard to avoid crashing into another monitor. Lieutenant Mellon was shouting instructions through the tube to his gunners and to Rollo checking the steam gauge.

The thunderous roll of gunfire increased. The monitors closest to Fort Sumter were firing their artillery. Looking through his window slits Peter could make out the fiery smoke from their guns. His eyes smarted from the strain of trying to see. He cursed the goddamn little holes that limited his vision.

Lieutenant Mellon shouted down the tube again, "Fire at will."

The monitors had reached the gorge of the channel and were tossing like driftwood in the strong flood tide. And being bombarded by Confederate firepower.

"Admiral Du Pont is sending a signal, sir," Rollo yelled.

The lieutenant interpreted it and shouted at Peter above the roar, "We're on our own. Disregard the order of battle."

Peter nodded, using all of his wits to keep the *Cayenne* from fouling the monitor in front of him.

"Can you get ahead of her?" Lieutenant Mellon shouted.

"Yeh. We can sail in closer to the fort."

"Good. That will give our gunners a crack at it."

A shell exploded on top of the pilothouse, rocking the craft. Peter fell sideways. His hands slipped from the wheel. Rollo, who had also fallen, scrambled forward on his hands and knees. He reached for the spinning wheel but Peter, pulling himself up, grabbed it at the same time.

"I has she."

Rollo yelled, "You all right?"

Peter nodded. Struggling to keep the ironclad on keel, his eyes focused on the brick wall of Fort Sumter, crazily looming closer. The channel was convulsing with exploding shells. The *Cayenne* shuddered, sailing high one moment and sinking in the foam the next.

Peter passed one vessel, then another and finally the entire fleet. Fort Sumter rose up larger. Its sheer brick wall holding up heaven seemed about to swallow the littlest ironclad.

Help us, Lord, Peter prayed, panic rising. Sweat was beaded on his brow. They were trapped in an iron cage. Lieutenant Mellon yelled to the engine room for more power. Bracing himself to keep from being thrown against the wall, Peter could no longer see the monitors. The *Cayenne* had sailed to within nine hundred yards of Fort Sumter. Its eastern face, scarred with craters, filled his vision, as did the flash of flames from the Brooke rifle which was hurling 117-pound iron bolts at them.

"Fire! Fire!" Lieutenant Mellon's voice was hoarse.

It ain't gon do us no good, Peter suddenly realized. He felt the repercussions as the gun in their forward turret lobbed a shell at the fort. Then hell rose up from the deep attempting to suck the *Cayenne* into its embrace. A tremendous explosion rocked the three men off their feet. The impenetrable armor had been pierced by a hundred-pound bomb. The pilothouse tilted, threatening to turn itself upside down. Missiles were flying through the air, iron bolts blasted loose from the armor. En masse they were as deadly as bullets. Peter felt a sharp pain over his left eye. His vision turned hazy with blood. Rollo was rolling around on the heaving floor like a toy, killed instantly. Lieutenant Mellon, wounded, ignored the blood gushing from a hole in his thigh.

Feverishly he cried: "Every Rebel gun in the harbor's shelling us. Let's get out of here."

Peter, who had fallen away from the wheel, crawled back to it. *Lord, help me. Help me.* Wiping the blood from his eye he again cursed the tiny window slits through which he could barely see. *River, I knows you in the dark and it's still daylight. Let us go. Let us through.* He clawed at the wheel. Forced the prow leeward to ride with the tide. The *Cayenne* hesitated for a minute then kicked up foam and ran. Shot and shell followed, exploding with a thunderous roar against the hull and the pilothouse. The guns in both turrets were silent, death a visitor there, too, as the *Cayenne* sailed out of range of the enemy's firepower.

At their anchorage near Morris Island, they pumped and bailed water all night, stuffing the *Cayenne*'s holes with sandbags in an attempt to keep her afloat. The barrage of shells had pierced her hull above and below the water line. There were serious fractures in the bow, two starboard and one port. The forward turret was completely wrecked, pierced by shot, its ironplates warped. In the second turret all of the gunners were wounded or dead, their artillery immobilized.

The other ironclads had also limped away from the battle. The dead and disabled were removed to a tug standing by, then the commanders reported to Admiral Du Pont their considerable damages. Pilothouses and turrets were in danger of collapsing from broken bolts. Gunports were jammed. Five of the monitors were seriously disabled, precluding the possibility of resuming the attack.

The cut over Peter's eye had stopped bleeding. It was a surface wound, and all too clearly he could see the outline of the city in the arms of the Cooper and Ashley rivers. Charleston was laughing, unharmed.

16

〜⤢〜

Folly Island
July 8, 1863

I don't see how we can stick another damn cannon in here,"
Peter told Pegleg, staring at the sand dunes which camouflaged
their artillery.

Yankee soldiers worked at night, covering with branches and
bushes Parrot guns and Coehorn mortars which they secreted between the sand dunes. Since spring, about ten thousand soldiers
had been moved in, together with their big guns and six hundred
engineers. The enemy, almost within spitting distance, was to be
kept in ignorance about this buildup of weaponry.

"But we does hide them nicely," Pegleg replied with a touch of
pride. Like Peter, he was one of the quartermaster's pilots, a former
slave who was quite agile with his wooden leg which he no longer
considered a handicap.

They were en route to the wharf, strolling along Folly Island's
sand dunes. It was a little island, separated from its Confederate
neighbor, Morris Island, by a narrow body of water, Lighthouse
Inlet.

Morris Island was situated at the mouth of Charleston harbor,
host on its northern end to Fort Wagner, which sat on a ribbon
of land so narrow that the fort's guns stretched across its entire

width. Any vessel entering the harbor on the main ship channel and attempting to reach Charleston six miles away had to run past Fort Wagner's guns, which looked seaward and landward.

The Yankee assault against Charleston had moved from sea to land and Peter had moved along with it. Admiral Du Pont and General Hunter had both been replaced, due to the dismal defeat of the ironclads, and Lieutenant Mellon was in a naval hospital recovering from his wounds. Peter, though, had been praised for his expert piloting,

The strategy of the new commanders, General Quincy Gillmore and Admiral John Dahlgren, was to capture Fort Wagner with ground troops. From that base they would then attack Fort Sumter—squatting in the middle of the harbor—immobilize it and take Charleston, the jewel, the prize.

When Peter and Pegleg arrived at the wharf it was swarming with activity. Tugs were towing in supply ships. Soldiers, under the instruction of shouting, cursing sergeants, were unloading ambulances, covered wagons and more artillery. It was a familiar sight to Peter and his friend who grinned at each other and parted company, hastening to their separate assignments.

That afternoon a troop transport ran aground on a reef and the cantankerous captain stared coldly at Peter. "We've been waiting hours to be tugged and they sent *you*?" His double chin quivered with indignation. They had sent him a nigger.

"Transports been coming in like bees," Peter said, "and we pilots trying to keep all of you afloat. I got here soon's I could."

He understood the cranky captain but kept his voice cheerful. Piling your boat up on a reef would make anybody evil. They were in the pilothouse and the helmsman, leaning his back against the wheel, was also glum.

The captain inspected Peter with a jaundiced eye, looking suspiciously at his hip boots and yellow rubber slicker and the shapeless slouch hat flapping around his ears. "I heard that a supply ship sank a little while ago. Were you bringing her in?"

"No. That was Redeye Murdoch." He was aptly named, a bullying Georgia cracker with bleary eyes and a fondness for baiting upstart darkies, as he called them. Although Peter disliked the man heartily, he added in fairness, "But it weren't his fault the boat sank.

186

These waters is some mischievous and he couldn't get her prow into the wind. The accident throwed us all back a spell. But . . ."

The captain threw up his hands. "Spare me the details. We've been marooned here long enough. My crew is standing by to attach your tug. I pray you can get *our* prow into the wind?"

"It's flood tide. I think I can back her off."

"You think? You're not dead certain?"

Peter replied calmly, "She ain't gon be no trouble at all, suh."

Within record time he had the transport off the reef and docked at the pier. Quitting the wheelhouse, Peter joined the soldiers lined up knee deep to disembark, blanket rolls on their backs and muskets strapped to their shoulders. They were Negro troops, the 1st or 2nd South Carolina, he assumed, and felt a sudden warmth being surrounded by black and brown faces even though the men were fidgety.

"If I ever get off this goddamn boat . . ." one of them exclaimed. Somebody else shouted, "Hey, Josh. Stop puking. This tub ain't moving."

There was a burst of laughter, Peter smiling too, as the press of bodies slowly moved to the gangplank.

"God almighty," a familiar voice said, "what took you so long to tow us offa that blasted reef?"

Grinning at Peter was a string bean of a man in an ill-fitting uniform, his long arms dangling from sleeves that were too short. Taken by surprise Peter's mouth became unhinged, to Stretch's delight. They embraced and, laughing boisterously, pounded each other on the back.

"Stretch. Sonofagun. Man, is I glad to see you."

"Didn't you hear me yelling your name when you came aboard?"

"Sounded like a pig squealing. How was I to know that was you?"

They were being pushed and jostled among the soldiers tramping down the gangplank, still they stopped to pummel each other again.

"Get outta the goddamn way," a voice yelled.

"I cain't believe my eyes," Peter exclaimed.

"Can you believe my fist knocking the shit out of you?" the angry voice bellowed.

Grinning, Peter leaped over the gangplank railing to the wharf. Stretch followed suit. There was absolute confusion on the dock, hundreds of soldiers being regrouped behind their colors, strident sergeants contributing profanity to the bedlam.

"I told Rain I'd find you," Stretch shouted above the thunderous clamor of horses pounding down the gangplank. They bucked and pawed, flicking their tails nervously, anointing the wharf with steaming piles of horseshit. "I told her, 'If that nigger's any place nearby I'll find his raggedy behind.' "

Peter chuckled. "So you saw my fam——"

He was interrupted by a Negro sergeant shouting at Stretch. "Fall in, private, or are you deaf as well as being an asshole? Move it."

"Yes, suh."

The sergeant strode away to collar other stragglers. The horses were being saddled by stable boys for the officers, and around them a column of men was being formed. Stretch tried to drag Peter toward them but he pulled back.

"I has another assignment now but I'll find you outfit later. What company you in?"

"Company C."

"This the First South Carolina or the Second?"

Stretch's grin was lopsided. "This here outfit's from the north." He squared his thin shoulders. "You is in the company of the Fifty-fourth Massachusetts Voluntary Infantry."

Peter found the soldiers' bivouac later that evening in an open field about two miles inland. He stood on the outskirts dismayed, looking at a jungle of tents squatting on the matted ground for as far as the eye could see. They dotted the landscape like a new species of growth, sterile and collapsible, spawned by man. On the haphazard paths between the tents, mule teams pulled covered wagons. Tethered horses nibbled on buckets of oats. Soldiers were roasting chunks of pork at scattered bonfires, courtesy of sharp-shooters whose rifles had been quicker than the hooves of the wild hogs. The succulent aroma tantalized Peter's nostrils but what dismayed him was the complexion of the soldiers—an endless field of them, shining their boots, oiling their rifles, hammering stakes into the ground—white men all. Where in the devil was the 54th Massachusetts?

After tramping around for what seemed like hours, he was finally in their midst, their camp similar to the others in every detail down to plodding mule teams and the smell of roasting meat. Peter approached a chubby soldier with a shaven head, who was unhitching a pair of mules from a wagon.

" 'Scuse me, I is looking for Company C."

"You has found it."

"At last. Can you tell me where I can find Stretch Johnson?"

"Who you?" the soldier asked impudently.

"I is his friend. Peter Mango."

"The pilot that brought us in?"

"Yes."

"Well tell me this. You all really stole a Confederate steamer?"

Peter smiled. "Stretch don't always tell the truth but he didn't lie 'bout that."

"Just goes to prove what the white man's always said. Show me a nigger and I'll show you a thief." The soldier burst out laughing, his tubby belly quivering. "Stretch is over there in that third tent. Me and him bunks together. My name's Chicago and I'll see you later."

Upon reaching the tent Peter pushed the flap open. Stretch, grinning, bounced up from a cot where he was oiling his musket. He stepped outside and wrapped his long arms around his friend.

"I told my buddies you be a bloodhound on the trail and find us. They anxious to meet you."

Peter chuckled. "I almost didn't find you company, Mistuh Stringbean. What's happening in Beaufort?"

As they walked back down the path Peter had just traversed, Stretch reported that Rain was as perky as ever and Peter's mother and children were fine.

"And Cindy? How she take to you joining up?"

"She ain't had much to say. You know womenfolks. Now I be thinking I shoulda married up with her 'fore I left, but . . ." Stretch shrugged and changed the subject. "I guess you know July's out of the hospital?"

Peter nodded. "Rain mention it in a letter the schoolteacher wrote for her."

"They were gon amputate his foot but July told them to amputate his head instead and leave his damn foot alone. He cussed them doctors so they fair left him alone. And didn't his foot heal on its own? So he limps but still got his foot. But you know July with his moody self. He don't favor being no cripple."

"I does worry 'bout him," Peter admitted.

They arrived at a bonfire where several soldiers sitting around it were roasting a rabbit on a spit.

"Hey, you all, meet my friend, Peter," Stretch said. "Sandy, I told you he'd find us."

A light-skinned fellow who could have passed for white except that his blond hair was thick and woolly waved at Peter, grinning. "Now that you're here this clown can stop talking 'bout you."

"That's Sandy," Stretch said. "He's a New York undertaker. 'Stead of putting his butt in the ambulance corps they's trying to make a foot soldier of him. Ha, ha."

A soldier older than the others, with curly graying hair and a long, jagged scar running from his eye to his chin, was rubbing two knives together, sharpening them. "Yeh," he said, "every time I fall asleep I pray Sandy don't think I'm dead and bury me."

Sandy laughed good-naturedly as Stretch introduced the others. The man with the knives was Pinch. Next to him was Felix, stringy and frowning, holding a dog-eared little Bible. And seated apart from the others was a soldier wearing a coonskin cap despite the heat, its tail hanging over one ear. The cap was his talisman, his good luck charm. He was conversing with a woman who was writing on a tablet.

"Albert," Sandy called, "I want you to meet my friend Peter. Albert's from Philadelphia. And that's Chloe, our laundry woman. She's so nice she writes letters home for us."

Peter swept off his slouch hat. "I'm pleased to make your acquaintance, Miss Chloe." She seemed rather delicate to him for a laundry woman. They were usually robust and big-breasted, broad in the beam, but Chloe was small-boned and slender.

"Sit down a while, Peter," Pinch said, "and have a piece of rabbit. It's just about done to a turn."

Peter and Stretch sat down. Pinch, who seemed to be the cook, slid the roast off the spit and began cutting it up. The fire crackled and hissed until Sandy complained, "Let's out the damn thing. I'm burning up," and smothered the fire.

Peter slapped Stretch's arm. "So is you gon tell me how you got to Massachusetts to join these fellas?"

"I flew up there like an eagle." Stretch winked at Chloe who, standing up, said she had to get back to her work and departed.

"That nigger ain't flew nowhere," Pinch said. "We found him sucking titty down in Beaufort." The men guffawed, Stretch leading the pack. "None of us is from Massachusetts, except Felix. I was living in Newark but come from Mobile, Alabama, myself."

"And you can guess where I'm from," the chubby fellow Peter had first met said, joining them. "Chicago."

The soldiers chuckled at Peter's perplexity. Stretch started talking, eager to unravel the mystery but Albert said, moving over to the group, "You weren't there, so shut up and let me tell it." He pushed back his coonskin cap and, wiping beads of perspiration off his forehead, reported that Governor Andrew of Massachusetts, a staunch believer in the capabilities of Negro soldiers contrary to popular opinion, didn't have enough coons in the state to make up a regiment. So he sent black recruiters out far and wide to enlist them.

"Not just any old ragtail bunch," Sandy interrupted, his hazel eyes gleaming, "but our black leaders. Martin Delany. William Wells Brown. Frederick Douglass . . ."

Peter sat bolt upright. "Frederick Douglass, you say?"

Sandy nodded. "I went to this meeting in New York just to hear him. And that man does have a way with words. He say the war gives us a chance to prove we ain't dogshit. So what he do? The first two men he enlisted was his own sons."

Peter glanced at Stretch, excited. "They is in this regiment and you knows them?"

His friend looked pained. "Man, there's a thousand soldiers in the Fifty-fourth. You expect me to know them all? They's in a different company."

"I be damned," Peter breathed, impressed with the high quality of the 54th Massachusetts.

Pinch was passing around chunks of the roasted meat, bypassing Chicago who complained, "Hey, why you skipping me?"

"Because, Mistuh Greedy Gut, you ate up almost all the pork and you're lucky I'm letting you even smell this here rabbit."

"That's right," Stretch said. "The less for him, the more for me. I is starving."

"You always is," Peter grinned.

"Mistuh Douglass say the army is the fastest way to overcome prejudice," Sandy continued, "because if a man fights for his country they is got to respect him and give him his goddamn due. He say——"

"He curse like that?" Felix asked, fingering his Bible.

"Well, those ain't his exact words but that's the heart of the thing. Mistuh Douglass is a fine speaker and I is . . ."

"A horse's ass," Chicago suggested.

The men chortled, Sandy laughing along with them. "Anyway, I went home and told my wife I was joining up. They sent me to a camp outside of Boston and when our regiment left for Hilton Head, what a farewell they gave us. The governor and politicians showed up. Everybody. Crowds lined the streets for miles."

Pinch related that it had been a momentous occasion, a victory for Governor Andrew. He had carefully selected for the regiment's officers young men with strong antislavery principles and military experience. Robert Gould Shaw, scion of a prominent abolitionist family, accepted the command of the regiment as an honor. The governor had been in favor of granting a few commissions to qualified Negroes but President Lincoln demurred inasmuch as some of his military had already protested against fighting alongside of Negroes. At the moment, the President argued, it was not politic to push black officers down their throats as well.

"My brother refused to enlist 'cause our officers be white," Albert said. "We argued some 'bout that. Said he warn't gon to die for a country what insulted his manhood."

"I felt the same way," Sandy said, "but Frederick Douglass changed my mind. He said take this little bit so's you can get more. Take this bayonet and free our folks still in bondage." Sandy sighed. "My mamma is still a slave in Richmond."

The soldiers grunted. He had hit a raw nerve that touched them all.

Hazarding a guess, Peter said, "You daddy was you massa and he freed you?"

"Yes."

But not the woman what gave you birth, Peter thought with disgust, wiping grease off his mouth with the back of his hand. White men sleeping with slave women was a bruise within him that never healed.

"Our first stop after leaving Boston," Albert said, "was Hilton Head. And then on to Beaufort."

The 54th's roster was still open when they arrived in Beaufort and Stretch was among the men recruited there. He had enjoyed the camaraderie of camp life when impressed into service. The discipline and drilling had made him feel like a man.

"Next thing I knows," he said, "our regiment is sailing down to Darien, Georgia, and hooking up with General Montgomery's troops, the Second South Carolina."

Peter interrupted. "That's the company July was in?"

"Yeah. I met his buddy, Archie, who saved his hide. When July was shot, he dragged him to safety. Anyhow, we looted everything in sight in Darien. Chandeliers. Furniture. Silverware. Whatever wasn't nailed to the floor left Darien with us piled up on our schooners."

Chicago added, "Then General Montgomery said, Burn the bastard down. Every house. Every lumberyard. Ha, ha."

Felix looked morose. "Our commander didn't think it was funny, burning up people's homes like that. Colonel Shaw was some disgusted. Didn't want us acting like ruffians. But warn't nothing he could do, General Montgomery was in charge."

"Lucky we didn't burn up the people, too," Chicago retorted. " 'Cause what they gon do if they catch us? Make us slaves again. So General Montgomery say, oh yeah? Well we gon make you bastards holler so's you know you is in a real war. We gon make you tremble 'fore the wrath of God, you bloody sonsofbitches."

"Man, why your mouth so filthy?" Felix protested.

"Man, you is always complaining. Why don't you shut up?"

"Who's gonna make me? Your cross-eyed mother?"

Chicago jumped over the ashes with the agility of a cat and landed on Felix's chest. They tumbled into the ashes, punching one another.

In a minute the fracas became general. The others rushing forward to separate the combatants got in a few licks of their own.

Suddenly blows and curses were flying in all directions. Peter was just about to jump into the brawl, feeling that friendly, when a voice yelled: "Attention!"

The freeze was instantaneous. Fists aimed at an inviting belly or a stubborn jaw were stilled in midair. The black sergeant who had been at the wharf was shouting at the men, his pop eyes bulging. Did they all want to end up in the stockade? One more such brazen incident and they'd be swabbing shit out of outhouses for the rest of their lives.

Shamefaced, the soldiers straightened up.

"We was just horsing around, Sergeant Carney," Chicago said. "Ha. Ha."

The sergeant looked suspiciously at Peter.

Stretch introduced him. "This is Peter Mango. The pilot what hauled us off the reef."

"Humph," Sergeant Carney snorted and strode away.

When he was beyond hearing Stretch complained, "That's one high-falutin' nigger I cain't stand."

Peter stood up. "I has to go, you all. I had a grand time." It had been invigorating. "I'll come back tomorrow evening, Stretch."

The soldiers shook his hand, reiterating their pleasure at meeting him.

Walking back through the camp, Peter noticed a young officer on horseback dressed in a light blue tunic with a sword buckled around his waist. As his mare pranced between groups of Negro soldiers they became respectfully quiet until he had passed. He sat erect in his saddle but stiffly, as though riding a horse was not a natural thing for a man to do. There was a wispy quality about him that touched Peter like a gentle breeze—pale hair, pale eyes, a mustache which drooped sadly.

It's him, Peter thought, judging from the deference the man was receiving. It's they commander.

He was right. The pale rider was Colonel Robert Gould Shaw. As they passed each other going in different directions a bugler blew "Taps." The soft, melancholy notes accompanied Peter, floating in the air like a dirge.

The next day was an aggravation. Peter worked around the clock. The *New Ironsides* monitor ran aground. He no sooner had her afloat than a transport piled up on a reef and had to be towed off. At flood tide a man-of-war exploded with a tremendous roar in the middle of the inlet. Ammunition stowed on her hurricane deck had accidentally been ignited, the fire roaring out of control. Peter helped to transfer her crew onto barges minutes before the boat sank. When he finally fell exhausted into his tent that night he slept like a dead man.

The following evening to his dismay he discovered that Company C had been sent on a diversionary maneuver to James Island along with brigades from Pennsylvania, New York and Connecticut. The diversion was intended to draw troops and attention away from Morris Island to defend a supposed attack upon Charleston. Simultaneously, covered by naval gunboats, Yankee infantrymen would cross over from Folly to Morris Island, establish a toehold and attack Fort Wagner.

17

⤢

James Island
July 16, 1863

It was pitch black and raining, not even the fireflies offering a pinprick of light. The 54th walked double file in the mud, Stretch and Sandy side by side, their rifles heavy on their shoulders. Wet branches slapped them in the face, the sting a reminder that they were alive and kicking. Less than a week after landing on James Island, still a Rebel stronghold, the brigade was returning to Folly Island by different routes.

The battle was over. There would be no more sudden bursts of gunfire, Stretch prayed, no more clash of steel against steel and a bayonet slashing Felix's jugular vein. How strange that when breath departed, the corpse that remained was frightening and obscene. Stretch was still shaken. To die so suddenly. So completely. Felix had been most irritating with his Bible and strict ways, but now that he was dead, killed in battle, Stretch felt guilty.

Their excursion with the brigade had accomplished its goal, diverted Confederate soldiers into engaging them while Yankee ground troops crossed over stealthily at night from Folly to Morris Island and attacked Fort Wagner. Although they had been bloodily repulsed with heavy losses, the Yankees had gained a toehold. They were now moving their heavy artillery to the little strip of land on Morris Island that they controlled and were erecting a battery.

In the pelting rain, the 54th marched all night to reach a crowded beach opposite Folly Island, a loading arena for transport boats. Stretch groaned with relief as he collapsed in a heap on the muddy ground.

"I couldn't have gone another step," he confided to Sandy who dropped down beside him.

It was before dawn, on a gray soggy morning. The company quartermaster, an aggressive young man, was scurrying around in search of food but to no avail. Troops had been arriving and leaving all night, depleting the rations, and even drinking water was scarce.

Chicago found a piece of hardtack in his knapsack and gnawed on it like a hungry rat.

Stretch eyed him slyly. "You gon give me a piece, man?"

"You got a sister you gon give me in return?"

"You know one thing, nigger? You is a greedy sonofabitch."

"So I been told."

The soldiers spread themselves out on the beach like locusts, footsore and weary, falling asleep where they dropped. The sun rose, burned through the haze with brilliant harshness casting a glaring light which awakened Stretch. Or had it been that hoarse scream which startled him into bolting upright.

"You assholes. Let me go." A string of curses followed, indicating the command had been ignored.

Stretch struggled to his feet. Shit, what now? He hurried toward the commotion. Chicago and Pinch were already there among a circle of soldiers looking down at Albert, who was wearing his coonskin cap, struggling to free himself as three orderlies attempted to strap him to a litter. The bandages were off his wounded foot which was a raw piece of meat oozing pus. Albert, shiny with sweat, was kicking anyone who got too near his good foot. Finally the orderlies managed to truss him up.

"Sheep fuckers," Albert bellowed. "Untie me."

Two of the 54th medics were there, a mulatto and an Irishman who had bandaged up the wound at the outset, warning Albert that if it turned gangrenous he would be put on a transport and sent to the field hospital. That time had come.

Gently the colored doctor said, "That's the best place for you, son, we've done all we can for you here."

The orderlies raised the litter.

"No," Albert screamed. "I ain't going. They ain't gonna cut on me. Put me down, goddamnit." His voice cracked on a sob.

That the field hospital was a one-way ticket to hell nobody could deny, least of all the medics who practiced radical surgery as a wartime measure. Lacking drugs to fight infection and with little or no anesthetics, amputation was routine, the afflicted limb sawed off, blood splashing on the floor, on the walls and on the doctors who, drenched in it, resembled hog butchers.

The orderlies trudged down the beach with the litter, leaving behind the echo of Albert's cries. His weeping unnerved Stretch. Poor bastard. He needed more than luck to survive the field hospital.

They marched up the beach during a raging thunderstorm that night to embark on a schooner anchored offshore. Soaking wet and shivering, thirty soldiers at a time climbed into a leaky longboat and were paddled to the transport. Colonel Shaw, sopping wet also, was directing the boarding himself instead of retiring to his cabin aboard the schooner. Judging from its snail's pace the embarkation would probably take all night.

"He gon catch his death," Stretch said to nobody in particular. He was sitting on his knapsack in the rain together with Chicago and Pinch, awaiting their turn to embark.

Chicago agreed. "He don't have good sense, leaving his bride to mess around with the likes of us." With one accord they stared at their youthful commander, a bridegroom of scarcely two months. He was so pale that in the downpouring rain he appeared ethereal. He had left a secure post to assume command of the 54th, earning his regiment's loyalty by demanding respect for them. "He treats us like grown men," Felix had once said, "not like boys."

Military brass treated the officers of the 54th with contempt, labeling them nigger lovers, and the men of the regiment had been assigned to more than their share of fatigue duty. They had been left behind on St. Helena to do camp duty when the rest of General Strong's brigade had sailed to Folly Island. Colonel Shaw had written a letter to General Strong suggesting that the 54th was capable of more than guerrilla warfare and the men ached to prove themselves in battle. As a result they had again been attached to Strong's command and dispatched to James Island to prove their mettle.

There was a long queue waiting to board the longboat. Stretch saw Sergeant Carney up front talking to Colonel Shaw.

"I hope Sarge is asking him about our pay," Stretch said. "How come white folks always trying to cheat us?"

Pinch rubbed the scar on his cheek and said, "They're afraid of us."

There were hoots of derision from his buddies. "White folks scared of niggers? Man, is you crazy?"

"Deep down, maybe they is," he insisted.

"I don't care if they is or they ain't," Chicago retorted. "My wife and children need that money I was supposed to send them. First off they didn't give us that bonus when we enlisted like they promised. And now this."

They had been promised at recruitment that they were to receive the same compensation as white privates, thirteen dollars a month plus rations and clothing. But two weeks ago, mustered to receive their wages, the paymaster informed them of a ruling from Washington. Colored troops would be paid ten dollars a month minus three dollars for clothing. Sergeant Carney, whose pay was also being reduced, had snarled, "I won't take a goddamn cent less than was promised. Equal pay or nothing." And that's what the regiment decided. They had not volunteered for the money but to fight for freedom, to prove themselves men. Sergeant Carney, the elected spokesman, delivered their message to Colonel Shaw. "Equal pay or nothing."

The colonel, also incensed, shot off a protesting letter to Governor Andrew. There were other protests from outraged abolitionists. President Lincoln explained to Frederick Douglass that employing Negro troops was a great gain for their race but flew in the face of popular prejudice. White soldiers were insulted at receiving the same pay and this was a necessary temporary concession.

Stretch remained silent listening to his friends grumble, sorry he had reopened the wormy subject of money. He had left the balance of his prize money with Cindy to use as she saw fit. He stood up and moved on down the line, his feet sinking in mud, the rain stinging his cheeks. The longboat gathered up a group of soldiers and departed. Stretch hoped to be included.

Their transport ran down the river and dumped them at Pawnee Landing. Their officers rode up and down the line to keep the men from straggling as they tramped through the woods en route to Lighthouse Inlet. Sandy had found a cheroot and was hoarding it like gold. He would take a few puffs, then tamp out the flame, looking at the butt critically to see how much was left.

"Give me a draw," Chicago implored. "No food. No tobaccy. What kind of stupid army is this?"

"The stupid one you joined." The undertaker blew a gust of smoke into Chicago's face and pocketed the butt.

Stretch was not listening to his friends but thinking about Cindy. She was always tucked away in his mind somewhere and now she emerged to make him forget how clammy he felt in his damp clothes and how hungry. The officers had eaten aboard the schooner with the captain, but there had been no food for the soldiers. Cindy, Stretch murmured. He held her calloused hand which could chop kindling wood and pick a row of cotton as fast as a man. Walking along beside him she laughed, her eyes dancing like when he had taken her to the general store and bought her every piece of clothing that fit. Skirts and dresses and high-necked blouses sent down from the benevolent societies in the North. Shoes that laced up to the ankle and hats that were a bouquet of silk flowers.

She skipped ahead of him now in the woods, teasing him, her smile tantalizing like when she wanted to make love. And why hadn't he married her when Reverend Ferdinand was demanding that folks stop living in sin? That they legalize their union and stop having bastard children. Every Sunday after church service there had been two or three weddings, the brides dressed in hand-me-down finery, the tots, ignorant of their bastardy, playing happily underfoot.

Cindy had asked him point blank once, "Stretch, we getting married?" He answered just as bluntly, "No." And she said, "All right, I ain't mentioning that ever again," putting the weight on him. Why had he been so scared? It wasn't Cindy he didn't trust but himself. Cindy, love, soon's this war's over I is gon marry up with you.

Company C walked past several camps, the last one the 10th Connecticut, which had preceded them here from James Island. As word spread that the 54th Massachusetts was marching by, several white soldiers ran forward to greet them. A red-cheeked corporal grabbed Stretch's hand and shook it. "I'm proud to know you men," he said. "I swore I wouldn't fight with niggers but you boys saved our hides."

"Thanks, Fifty-fourth," rang out from the sidelines. The white men waved. The Negro soldiers waved back.

Sandy and Stretch looked at each other and grinned. Three days ago about two hundred men from their regiment had been sent on advance picket duty to relieve the 10th Connecticut which had received the brunt of a bloody dawn attack by the Rebels. Both sides had fired their weapons in the pitch-black night fighting for possession of the rough terrain. Shoved back by the bayonets of a Rebel cavalry, the black soldiers had retreated, dragging along their wounded. Then they regrouped with reinforcements Colonel Shaw had held in abeyance, and fought their way back to the front, step by step, the air exploding with the screech of enemy shells ricocheting into the trees over their heads. Stretch surprised himself with the swiftness of his own attack when he shot a Rebel in the temple who was about to whack off Captain Emilio's head with his saber. Tenaciously the 54th held the line. The vital time they bought allowed the 10th Connecticut, trapped by the swamp, to escape to safer ground. And it allowed Union gunboats in the Stono River to sail beyond the range of the enemy's artillery and blast them while other Yankee batteries lobbed percussion shells. The Confederates had apparently depended upon the element of surprise at dawn but the stubborn resistance of the 54th had fouled their plans and forced them to retreat.

"Thanks, Fifty-fourth."

"You're welcome, Tenth Connecticut."

The commanding general had sent a message to Colonel Shaw that he was exceedingly pleased with the 54th, with the steadiness and soldierly conduct of their pickets who were on duty at the outposts and had met the brunt of the attack.

The march to the inlet was a six-mile tramp in the mud accompanied by the sound of booming gunfire. Yankee warships lying in the harbor outside the enemy's range had joined the land batteries in shelling Fort Wagner, gouging huge craters in its walls. Shells ruptured the earth, sand shooting high into the air. Fort Sumter in the harbor and the Confederate batteries on the nearby islands answered the fleet's gunfire with a thunderous volley of their own, sending clouds of blackened smoke billowing over land and sea.

The 54th soldiers reached the inlet bone weary and hungry. The place was jammed with troops and no food in sight. Stretch would have been happy to scout up some victuals for himself but the company had been instructed to remain intact until Colonel Shaw returned with their orders from General Strong.

Late in the afternoon the guns of Wagner fell silent giving rise to speculation that the fort was mortally wounded. The Yankee barrage against it continued.

Peter already had his assignments for the day but it dawned upon him suddenly to inquire about his friends and he went back to the quartermaster's office, a dilapidated shack near the waterfront. His friend Pegleg was coming down the path. And bristling.

"That bastard Murdoch just left the office with his nasty self. One day I'm gonna take off my wooden leg and flatten his goddamn head."

Peter smiled. "Not if I get to him first."

Redeye Murdoch couldn't abide colored pilots, and the feeling was mutual. He belonged to a maritime union which excluded Negroes, its members receiving four times the salary Peter was paid.

He proceeded into the office. Clerks were bustling about the cluttered room and he was relieved to see the quartermaster, Lieutenant Schwartzenberg, seated at his desk blinking behind his horn-rimmed glasses. The wall beside him was plastered with notices and boat schedules, an alarming maze, but the lieutenant could put his hand on any document he needed at the moment and was possessed of a phenomenal memory for details.

"I is on my way to check on the buoys, suh," Peter said, "and I was wondering . . . Has you heard anything 'bout the Fifty-fourth Regiment what went to James Island a few days ago?"

Schwartzenberg dropped his eyes to his desk and shoved some papers around routinely. "They're here. About to be ferried to Morris Island." The sound of a tremendous explosion rose above the continuous thunder of gunfire and the lieutenant had to raise his voice to be heard. "Perhaps we've finally blown up that god-damn fort," he said. "Stubborn bastards."

"Can I be they pilot, suh?"

"What?"

"The Fifty-fourth. You said they is . . ."

"I just gave out that assignment. Sorry."

He wasn't as sorry as Peter, who quit the office cursing himself for not having thought of it sooner.

Morris Island
July 18, 1863

Stretch was running, his breath labored, his musket a weight on his shoulder. He ran not with the swiftness of a panther but sinking in water up to his knees. In a goddamn defile. In the darkness. The only light unwelcome, an occasional flash from a mortar sending a death-dealing shell arcing over his head. He stumbled, bumped into Chicago in front of him. An idiot from behind crashed into both of them. Sandy. Breathing hard, too, and cursing. "How they 'spect us to run in the goddamn sea?" But they were. Running forward. A black phalanx of six hundred men and twenty-two officers on foot. Colonel Shaw in the lead pointed his sword dead ahead.

He had received his wish. He had written to his superiors that his regiment had learned the details of camp service as readily as other soldiers who had been under his command. It was his desire that they be relieved from fatigue duty and associated with white troops so other men than their officers could witness their merits. Dispatching them to James Island had been part of that response. Arriving on Morris Island straight from that campaign, and not having been fed, they had been informed by General Strong that the signal honor of leading the assault on Fort Wagner had descended upon them.

"Men," Strong had addressed them mounted on a gray stallion, his hawk's nose blistered, "I'm sorry you're going into battle tired and hungry, but the soldiers in Fort Wagner are tired too. They've been fighting all day. Don't fire a musket on the way up but go in and bayonet them at their guns."

Six hundred black throats grunted. Bayonet them. The enslaving enemy. The day of deliverance was at hand. They had been chosen as the advance column. Black soldiers. Black men.

Gone were hunger and fatigue. The wait had been interminable. Centuries. Support brigades were formed. Regiments from New England. New York. Ohio.

Colonel Shaw, wearing a light blue staff officer's jacket with silver eagles on each shoulder and a silk sash wound around his waist, had then addressed his troops. "The eyes of the nation are upon this night's work. Prove yourselves men. Move in quick time until within a hundred yards of the fort. Then double quick. And charge. We will take Fort Wagner or die there."

He was leading the right wing now. A formation of twenty-two men abreast, a long broad column stretching across the sand like a new species of bush that moved. Stretch was thinking about Cindy again. He wanted to tell her how the sun had fallen suddenly into early night, helped along by smoke and gunpowder, the tear-dimmed stars a reminder that nighttime was made for loving her. My love. Tell Reverend Ferdinand he gon get the chance to marry us.

Colonel Shaw led them into the defile, an unexpected obstacle about two hundred yards short of their goal. The passageway was already narrow, pressed between the sand dunes and the sea. A sudden bend of the creek and its impassable marshes shrank the passageway in half. The regiment had to break rank. The soldiers on the right waded in water. And while they were thus engaged, their formation broken, a tremendous explosion lit up the sky. The water turned red. Bloody. Stretch saw Fort Wagner in front of him change like a mirage. Its shadowy outline became a wall of fire spitting flame. From bastion to bastion its guns were blasting them. It was a signal. The Rebel batteries on the nearby islands and Fort Sumter joined the fray crisscrossing the sky with streaks of lightning. Bullying the air with man-made thunder. The bullets screamed. The shells whined and blew the limbs off suddenly bloodied men.

"On the double," Captain Emilio yelled. An unnecessary order. Stretch and his buddies were running with the swiftness of light, scrambling in and out of craters over the dead and wounded. A shell burst in front of them, the explosion deafening. Stretch zig-zagged followed by Sandy. But the soldier next to them had stopped running, half his face blown away. A bleeding hole remained. No eyes. No nose. He remained upright for half a second surprised that he was dead.

"Stretch," Sandy yelled, "come on. Don't look back."

They ran, Stretch crying, "Jesus Christ. What happened?"

He knew. They all did, the officers and black men rushing out of the defile and into the ditch. Into two feet of brackish water. The last obstacle. They knew. The Sesesh had been playing possum. Deliberately they had stopped shooting their guns to spring a trap. Retreated into their bomb shelters. Let the Yankee bastards think we're all dead. In the dusky twilight they had manned their guns and waited for the enemy to fall out of formation in the narrow defile.

The 54th sloshed in and out of the ditch. On the other side of it was Fort Wagner. Stretch was barely aware of the water. It felt neither warm nor cold. Just wet. Around him men were being mowed down by raking fire from the bastions. They fell singly and in piles, bombs exploding in their midst.

"To the parapet," Captain Emilio yelled.

The men scaled the wall. Found a toehold in the craters which seamed the slope. Stretch seemed to fly up there, not remembering the climb. The Rebels were waiting. Hordes of them. Hurling hand grenades. Advancing with swords and spikes.

Colonel Shaw, in the vanguard of the invaders, stood on the parapet. "Forward, Fifty-fourth," he shouted, his sword held high.

Stretch heard the whirr of bullets. Saw the blood on the breast of the blue jacket. Seconds later the colonel toppled from the parapet. Four or five black men fell with him, among them the flag bearer carrying the national colors. The flag though did not touch the ground. Springing forward, Sergeant Carney grabbed it. A bullet nicked him. He fell to his knees. Jammed the pole into a crevice in the parapet. Another bullet sent him sprawling. Lying flat he grabbed the staff. Held it in place.

"Aiiiiiiiieeeee!"

The Rebel yell was met by a bloodthirsty shout from the throats of black men. They leapt forward to meet the enemy. Bayonet them at their guns had been the order and they tried. Steel clanged. Parried and thrust itself into soft flesh. Stretch felt a terrible rage at the wild-eyed Rebel aiming a pike at his head. His bayonet deflected the blow. Arched downward to stab his would-be-assassin in the belly.

"Sonofablackbitch," the wounded man cried, refusing to die. He lunged forward. Stretch slid his bayonet across the Confederate's throat like a man playing a fiddle. The Rebel fell. Two others took his place wielding sabers.

"Charge," a major shouted, suddenly materializing at Stretch's side. His sword drove one of the men backward. The other man lunged at Stretch. He sidestepped and cracked the butt of his rifle against his enemy's skull. The man fell, impaled on his own blade.

The defenders poured out of the fort, wave after murderous wave. The black troops were being decimated. Outnumbered everywhere, slashing out with their bayonets. On the parapet. In front of the ditch. Several of them jumped or fell inside the embrasure and were slaughtered there.

"Niggers?" the Rebels yelled. "We're fighting a bunch of goddamn coons?" They seemed surprised by this degraded state of affairs. Niggers standing up and fighting like white men? "Aiii-ieeeeee," the Rebels screamed, enraged.

"Where is we support?" Stretch yelled.

"Yes, God," another soldier cried. "Where are the whoresons?"

Stretch saw Sandy on the other side of the parapet. In the fort. Loading ammunition for Captain Emilio who was manning one of the Rebel guns. Suddenly Stretch felt ten feet tall. He was centered deep within himself. He jumped off the parapet and landed in the mêlée below drained of all fear and desire. And with that dissolution the strength of Samson welled up within him. He fought with the instincts of a man with enhanced vision. He could see behind him. And to the sides. His ears detected a pike in the hands of a foe. He wheeled around as it was aimed at his back and ducked. Swinging his bayonet with reckless abandon, he cut down his enemies like a scythe cutting cane.

But the blacks were being pushed back to the ditch. Still they fought valiantly. Cursing. Shouting. Praying for reinforcements. Which arrived for the Rebels. On the run. Reinforcements hurling hand grenades, shoveling destruction on the men backed up to the ditch.

A grenade exploded against Stretch in a burst of flame. Surprised that there was no pain, he looked down at his shattered side. At a widening circle of blood. It grew darker, the circle, inhaling the night, the stars, the sky. He fell into a deep, black hole.

Before dawn, Yankee soldiers were crawling over the ground cautiously listening for bodies that groaned, that proclaimed they were still alive among the corpses cluttering the landscape.

"Water," a parched voice cried.

Thank God. A live one. He was dragged inch by inch to the back where there was a row of litters. It was tedious, dangerous work, a line drawn three hundred yards on the Yankee side of the ditch beyond which the rescuers could not go for fear of being captured. They had handkerchiefs tied over their noses to protect them from the stench as they slithered over the ground bumping into mangled flesh which death had robbed of its spirit and transformed into grotesque lumps.

The 54th had been slaughtered, more than half of them dead or missing. The support brigades also had suffered heavy casualties, committed too late to take advantage of the fierce onslaught of the advance column. In the darkness, a Maine regiment standing on the other side of the ditch had fired their weapons in confusion at their own men until a hoarse voice shouted, "This is the Fifty-fourth Massachusetts, goddamnit. Stop shooting."

Crawling like crabs over the ground littered with bodies, the rescuers dragged the wounded back to their lines.

Stretch came awake in a bed of slime. His head had poked itself into a crevice in the ditch, his body lay in two feet of stinking water. Migod, he cried, remembering, and raised his head to stare at the dead bodies sprawled on the ground in front of him. Migod-migodmigod. He tried to move his legs, to get up and run, which sent a pain so intense through him that he blacked out.

When he came to again and raised his head he saw movement

among the fallen, bodies being dragged by their hands and feet. The Rebels were separating the corpses clad in gray from those in blue, and white men from Negroes. One of them being dragged suddenly cried out in pain.

"Hey, this nigger's alive," a voice proclaimed. A shot rang out. The nigger was dead.

Involuntarily Stretch winced as if his body had received the bullet. He heard another voice. "What in the hell do you men think you're doing? This is the army not a slaughterhouse."

"Yes, sir."

Stretch peeped over the edge of the trench. Three surly soldiers a few feet away were being reprimanded by an officer. Another shot was fired near the parapet and the officer hurried in that direction. A few minutes later Stretch saw a flurry of activity at the southeast bastion. A body was being dragged by its heels by two men.

"Bury him with his niggers," an officer said contemptuously and departed.

Left alone, the three privates quickly searched the remains of Robert Gould Shaw. One of them pocketed his watch and chain. Another pried a ring off his finger. Then they flung the body on top of a pile of Negro corpses.

A driving pain shot through Stretch's shattered side so tormenting that a yelp escaped from between his clenched lips. Too late he clamped his mouth shut. Migodmigodmigod. Where's that officer who didn't believe in killing wounded Negroes?

The three soldiers looked at each other. Slowly, with ominous tread, pistols in hand, they walked toward Stretch lying immobile in the ditch.

18

Folly and Morris Islands
August 1863

A siege, Peter finally came to understand, took its murderous toll week after week. The siege against Fort Wagner. Every night he gave thanks to God that he was still alive, having luckily escaped being blown into bits on several separate occasions. The Yankees' swift assault against the fort had failed and now they were inching forward like worms.

Union batteries increased on Morris Island daily as did the sap the engineers were constructing—parallel trenches devouring the ground between their front line and Fort Wagner. Behind the engineer corps came fatigue details—often the 54th Massachusetts—enlarging the trenches, shoring them up with logs and throwing up protective parapets. They widened the trenches at night by the light of the moon, pressing their shovels into the muddy earth and throwing it over their shoulders.

Experience had dictated working at night to reduce their heavy casualties and limit the visibility of Rebel sharpshooters armed with Whitford rifles with telescopic sights. Without mercy they lay in cover in a rifle pit under a ridge and picked off the New York engineers sweating in the advance trench and the soldiers working behind them. As fast as one parallel was completed, the engineers cut another one in front of it, battling with the mud and rising water. The first one, but 1,350 yards from Fort Wagner, was already a battery mounted with ten mortars and other artillery. The second parallel was 400 yards closer to the fort. Connecting the two parallels were zigzag approaches for the troops. Their goal, first Fort Wagner, then Fort Sumter in the harbor and finally the bloody hand that rocked the bloody cradle—Charleston.

New Negro regiments had arrived—the 55th Massachusetts, the 1st North Carolina and the 3rd U.S. Colored Troops—all of them an enlarged brigade under the command of General James Montgomery along with his own regiment, the 2nd South Carolina.

There also had arrived at Folly Island a grand surprise for Peter. The *Swanee*. He hollered at her, waving his hat and laughing as she sturdily chugged into the inlet, her chimneys smoking. "You has followed me here, you little devil? Is you gon stay?" She whistled at him in reply.

He was often at her helm, assigned there by the quartermaster who was aware of their connection. Her skipper, Captain Doboy, was unfamiliar with the waters and relieved to have a local pilot aboard. The steamer had a light enough draft for Peter to steer her across the inlet without being towed. The new black regiments were quartered on Folly and daily he ferried them to Morris Island.

This morning Peter boarded the *Swanee* and reported to the acting ensign on the main deck who as usual was disagreeable. Kenneth Cherry regarded Peter with inflamed eyes and blew his nose. He had an undefined allergy which he accepted as his cross in life, along with being stuck on this steamboat with niggers. Honking like a goose, he reminded Peter of Rain's former master.

"They sent you again?" The ensign sniffed as though smelling something stink. "You may proceed to the wheelhouse, Mr. Mango. We're casting off at seven bells."

It had not taken Peter long to discover that Ensign Cherry disliked him heartily, a feeling that was mutual. He threaded his way past clumps of soldiers to the companionway. Artillery fire had already commenced and the troops were somber, their black faces gloomy. They were being ferried to hell. Shot and shell would fly through the air as they filled sandbags, hauled logs and ammunition, and dragged heavy Parrott guns on their sling carts through the mud to the Swamp Angel Battery. The three-hundred-pound-

ers weighed a total of twenty-six thousand pounds and were forever breaking down the carts. The Swamp Angel, when completed
in the marsh, would be able to bomb Charleston a scant six miles
away. At night the *Swanee* picked up those soldiers still alive and
ferried them home.

Occasionally in between ferrying troops Peter had an opportu-
nity to spend a few minutes at the 54th's campsite on Morris
Island with one or two of Stretch's friends, usually Sandy and
Chicago or Pinch. Peter had been grief-stricken upon learning that
Stretch was missing.

"I cain't believe he's dead," he had mourned. "Maybe they
taken him prisoner."

"Yeah, maybe," Sandy said but without conviction.

The 54th had suffered the heaviest casualties, three hundred
men dead and missing. Anxiously Peter waited for the arrangements to be completed for an exchange of prisoners taken during
that battle. That day came and with it despair. The Confederates
delivered up white Yankees only, supplying no information about
Negro soldiers, no listed names as was customary for prisoners
remaining in custody.

Bastards, Peter groaned. Slimy Sesesh whoresons. Then came
the news that although his two sons were safe, Frederick Douglass
had quit his post as an army recruiter in disgust, demanding to
know how many black men had to be killed in custody or sold
into slavery before Mr. Lincoln would say, "Hold, enough." The
President finally issued a decree announcing that the Union offered
equal protection to all its soldiers and would punish offenses by
retaliation. For every U.S. soldier killed in captivity or enslaved, a
Confederate prisoner would be executed or placed at hard labor.
Carrying out the proclamation was another matter, but at least,
Peter consoled himself, the President had spoken.

Following that questionable victory came other chilling news
which had taken a little time to reach them from the North. Although the Negro chaplain informed Sandy that his wife and baby
son were safe, not among those strung up on lampposts or beaten
to death in New York, the undertaker was nevertheless weeping
when Peter stopped by his camp.

"Our tenement was burned down, Peter. My family barely escaped alive."

"Jesus," Peter moaned. "White folks is demons."

Earlier that morning the newspapers had arrived on a steamer and he had read the grisly details. For four days in New York City a ragtag mob, of foreign-born Irish mainly, had gone on a murderous rampage angered by the new law which would draft their men into the armed forces. Their fury vented itself on blacks who were competitors for the same low-paying factory jobs, and the visible cause of the war. While the police stood idly by, Negroes were beaten in the streets by mobs, slain in their homes, and the colored orphan asylum and black neighborhoods burned to the ground. Hundreds of Negroes fled for safety to the countryside.

"I is so sorry 'bout you family," Peter told Sandy. He liked the man, mulatto though he be.

Returning to Folly Island Peter reported as usual to the quartermaster's office. The white pilot, Redeye Murdoch, as surly as ever, was standing at the counter when Peter arrived. He never lost an opportunity to needle Negro pilots and today was no exception.

"What we need around here," he said, "is more Black Irish who know how to whip nigger heads to a pulp."

The blood rushed to Peter's nigger head. With a half-smothered oath he slammed his fist against Murdoch's jaw knocking him backward. Redeye was taken by surprise and Peter managed to sock him again before the man threw up his hands to defend himself, howling, "You black baboon."

Four clerks rushed forward to pull them apart followed by Lieutenant Schwartzenberg, the quartermaster, who yelled, "Stop it this goddamn instant."

Peter felt a knee in the small of his back and his arms being held from behind. Redeye was also being restrained, snarling and pushing against the clerks holding him, as anxious to continue the fight as Peter.

"Let them go," the quartermaster ordered, eyeing them furiously from behind his horn-rimmed glasses. The clerks released the two men and stepped back. Peter and Redeye glared at each other but neither made a move toward the other.

"I'm really surprised at you, Mr. Mango," Lieutenant Schwartzenberg said. "I thought you had more self-control."

He did not chastise Redeye, a known troublemaker, but ordered him out of the office.

In the days that followed Peter laboriously read all of the newspapers as they arrived. The New York riots were not an isolated incident. Racial conflict existed in the North. White workers, fearful of Negro competition, often used violence to keep them off job sites. And to fan the hostility when there was a strike by all-white guilds, unemployed Negroes were hired as replacements. In Manhattan where the draft riots had started, the Negroes had been taken by surprise and hit the hardest. Forewarned, black men in Brooklyn armed themselves and patrolled their streets. And in Flushing Village when a rumor spread through the Negro community that a mob was coming, black leaders hastened to advise a Catholic priest of their intention to burn down two Irish houses for every one of theirs torched and kill two Irishmen for every murdered Negro. Flushing was not attacked.

That was balming news to Peter. A small consolation. He kept the newspaper to give to Sandy but found him desolate anew the next time they met, his pale face streaked and grimy.

"Why? Why?" the undertaker groaned, shaking his head.

"Jesus, what's happened now?" Peter cried.

"Last night . . ." Sandy's voice broke. He looked at Peter piteously, trying not to weep. Finally, he managed to get the words out, his eyes glazed as he relived the horror of the previous night.

At the front his company had been working in a parallel trench as usual behind the engineers who were cutting another sap. Steadily they were moving closer to Fort Wagner.

A full-tide moon had filled the trench with two feet of water. Sloshing around, the long line of soldiers cursed the stupidity of trying to shore up the slope with logs and sandbags which kept collapsing into mud. Sandy's face was crusty with mud which did not hinder the sand flies that were adept at burrowing beneath clothes to find a man's most tender parts. Every inch of him itched. Gently he massaged his genitals. Chicago, working beside him, his shaved head slick with sweat, caught the contagion and scratched his balls also.

"How they get in your drawers?" he muttered. "Goddamn varmints."

Pinch grunted, the scar on his cheek outlined by moonlight as he lifted a sandbag and wedged it into place. "Mosquitoes and such never bite me. Guess I is too black for them. Ha. Ha." He was indeed the color of tar.

"Peanut Battery," an armed lookout standing on higher ground screeched.

The 54th men turned to watch a trajectory of flame arching toward them from a Rebel battery. A week earlier they would have all been scrambling out of the trench to dive headlong into another one. Experience had taught them that this shell would hit harmlessly several yards away. It exploded into a crater with a great roar and without another glance Sandy and the others returned to their digging.

It was not yet daylight but the darkness had been diffused with its first pink blush when his shovel pinged as it hit a hard object.

Chicago looked down. "What's that?"

"Let's find out." Sandy dug around it.

Pinch yelled as a human head emerged, its eyes being eaten by a swarm of maggots. Farther down the line, a soldier's shovel uncovered another corpse. Then yet another dead man floated into the trench.

Shouting hoarsely the soldiers scrambled out of the ditch, all but Sandy, and into a fusillade of bullets. Fort Wagner's riflemen were up early under the ridge which afforded cover for their rifle pit.

"Take cover," the captain of the armed guards yelled.

The soldiers dove headlong back into the trench, falling on top of each other and the floating corpses. Their guards fired at the enemy, bullets whizzing past. When there was no answer from the ridge, the Yanks stopped shooting, the air swollen with the moans of the wounded men in the trench.

"Why you men jump out the trench like goddamn idiots?" Sandy screamed.

As an undertaker, the decomposing corpses, apparently the hastily buried victims of the recent battle, had not filled him with panic. Then he saw Pinch, crying, holding Chicago in his arms. Sandy bent over to stare into Chicago's open, sightless eyes. Blood was oozing from a hole in his chest. Enraged, Sandy shook him hard, almost jerking the body out of Pinch's possessive grasp.

"Why you run, Chicago?" he screamed and kicked a floating

corpse viciously. "See? It cain't kick back. The dead cain't hurt you. Only the living."

Sandy stopped talking now to look piteously at Peter. "Why, why?" he moaned.

"Poor Chicago. I is so sorry." Peter patted Sandy's quaking shoulders. "But it's gon end soon. This blasted war will soon be over." Please, God, Peter prayed. Let it end tomorrow.

The huge Parrott gun in the Swamp Angel Battery bombed Charleston for the first time. Peter was in the wheelhouse of the *Swanee* which was tarrying near the marsh. On the deck below him was the crew and the captain and Ensign Cherry. Peter was relieved at being alone. Anxiety gnawed at the pit of his stomach and his eyes were gritty.

There was a tremendous roar. The Parrott had spoken. The *Swanee* lurched and trembled. Marsh and land and sea quaked from the impact, the noise deafening. Smoke billowed and rose. Peter saw the silhouette of a steeple against the sky and then a fiery burst of red. The shell had found its mark, exploding in the city six miles away.

Peter was distraught. It was one thing to march on the city and capture her. And another to blast poor people into their graves. Uncle Hiram, is we killing you and all we friends? I don't want any of you dead. July is crippled. Stretch is missing. Chicago is dead. And is we own Yankee shells killing you, too, Uncle Hiram?

Mainly, poor whites and Negroes were the only ones remaining in Charleston. Prisoners had reported that the gentry had departed, had taken the high road to safer ground.

Another shell was lobbed across the channel, and below Peter on deck Mr. Josephus, the helmsman, was shouting, "I can see the fires. We hit something big. Maybe we've blown up the whole damn city."

That was a hopeful exaggeration, Peter realized. His craggy face turned darker with rage as silently he cursed the Sesesh. It was their fault Charleston was being bombed. General Gillmore had sent a message to the Confederates to surrender Fort Wagner and Fort Sumter or the city would be shelled. General Beauregard had replied, "Take them if you can."

A Confederate battery had been firing mortars ineffectively at the Swamp Angel and now one came dangerously close to the *Swanee,* churning water onto its decks. Wearily the captain trudged into the pilothouse.

"Mr. Mango, can we safely run down the river home?"

"Yes, suh."

"Good. Let's weigh anchor before those Rebel whoresons learn how to shoot."

Peter wrote slowly, his spelling erratic, the paper spotted with ink blots and his tears.

Rain, I got you mesage bout Peewee. I is hartsick. I dint know he were sick or Glory. I cant come home. My boss say we to bisy. That brakes my hart not being with you now. I aint never luv you so hard. Is Glory realy all rite? And Mama? And you? Why he die, Rain? We lil baby boy . . .

Smallpox, a letter from the schoolteacher had informed him. An epidemic. His son had succumbed. Peter's mind had staggered around the word. Succumbed? Peewee was no longer running around on his fat little legs? No longer holding out his arms to be picked up and hugged? Glory had been sick also but had recovered. And Rain had never written him a mumbling word. Probably to keep from worrying him.

He pushed the letter aside and looked dully at the clutter in his tent. His boots and raingear shared space on the floor with two lanterns. An axe. His box of tools. A load of firewood. The sight of it all galled him. Why was he here in this mess instead of home with his family? The rumble of gunfire outside fueled his torment. Every livelong day he could be blown to hell and gone but it was his son safe behind the lines who had died.

During the weeks that followed, every time the mail boat arrived Peter expected a note from Rain. Finally, when he had grown desperate and had written to her twice again it came, written by Miss Carlotta, the schoolteacher. They were all in good health except for his mother's rheumatism. Rain had seen July and Brother Man and Sister who were all as well as could be expected. That was the sum total of the letter after weeks of silence, no details about their son's illness, his death. Nothing personal, not even a forlorn cry. It left Peter feeling lonelier than he had been awaiting word. Rain was hurting, he brooded, realizing her capacity for suffering and overwhelmed with the desire to be with her. Still, the thought nagged him, she could have written him a more feeling letter. He was hurting, too.

Obsessed with thoughts of home he penned three more brief notes to Rain but received no reply. He then sought out Chloe, the laundry women, with the intention of having her write a longer missive to his errant wife. But upon reaching Chloe's tent his desolation turned to anger. Rain was such a hardheaded, aggravating woman. Well he could be just as stubborn and damn if he would write her another word. Instead he asked Chloe if she would do his laundry.

At sunrise every day navy ships steamed in from the bar to shell Fort Wagner. They were soon joined by the land batteries on Folly and the new ones constructed on Morris Island.

To delay the approach of the parallels, the Confederates planted mines in front of the fort. A Yankee engineer tripped on one of them, the force of the explosion ripping off all his clothes and hurling him several yards away.

"God, what is this shit?" an outraged soldier cried, his eye on the man's naked butt as he sailed through the air.

Other engineers suffered a similar fate, stepping on land mines and being blown sky high. Artillery from the nearby Rebel islands strafed the Yankees, impeding but not halting the march of the parallels. As the trenches moved ever closer to Fort Wagner an American flag was placed at their head, a signal for the Union fleet not to fire upon its own troops. But their erratic aim killed thirty-seven men on a single occasion which was not singular.

"This blasted funeral music is driving me crazy," Peter complained to his friend Pegleg. He was thinking about Peewee but spoke for the multitude. The funeral dirges were heard with such depressing regularity all through the day that they were finally banned, the dead buried in silence, music no longer reminding the living that they were clinging to this side of the grave with weak hands.

The fifth parallel armed with howitzers and field pieces was but two hundred yards from Fort Wagner which enabled the Yankees to take the rifle pit behind the sand ridge along with eighty prisoners. While enlarging the sap of the fifth, Sandy and his company discovered a constructive use for the corpses which continued to float into the trench when the water rose. They used the dead bodies along with the sandbags to shore up the sides of the trench.

At the front several huge calcium lights were planted which illuminated every nook and cranny of Fort Wagner. Before they learned better, an entire detail of Rebels firing from the parapet were gunned down. No longer could Confederate sharpshooters man the parapet, aim and fire. Any Sesesh head raised above ground was in danger of being shot off, the soldiers forced to live in their underground bombproofs. Deserters were not infrequent, babbling scarecrows sneaking across the line waving a white flag.

"I been vomiting for two days," one of them complained. "Cain't keep nothing down. Our food and water's contaminated. It's getting damn hard for Fort Sumter to send us supplies and replacements." Rebel soldiers had been rotated regularly every three days along with their Negro laborers, it being understood that was the longest time any man could remain sane living and sleeping in underground shelters with unburied dead men and horses. Many a Rebel had dashed screaming from the bombproof, pushed beyond human endurance, preferring death by a bullet.

The Union generals concluded that their enemies were exhausted and set a date for foot soldiers to take possession of Fort Wagner backed up by the guns of the fleet.

September 7, 1863

For forty-two hours all naval artillery and Union batteries on Folly and Morris islands had been firing steadily at Fort Wagner. The thunderous bombardment deadened Peter's eardrums aboard the ironclad whose gunners were also lobbing shells at the fort. The pilot and helmsman had been killed yesterday and Peter was a temporary replacement, chosen because he was familiar with monitors. He was in the small wheelhouse with the captain who was at the helm, both of them tight-lipped and riddled with anxiety.

It gon be over soon, we siege is ending, Peter kept telling himself, praying that his life wouldn't end with it.

On land the parallels had been prepared for thousands of soldiers to march to the front. In the advance trenches they were waiting for the signal to storm the parapet. The assault was to commence at nine A.M., at low tide, but before that hour arrived a blessed rumor surfaced. A deserter reported that Fort Wagner had been evacuated.

This message was signaled to the fleet and Peter almost collapsed with relief.

"Maybe it's another goddamn trap," the monitor's captain said tersely, deflating Peter.

For another twenty minutes artillery from the vessels and land batteries blasted the fort. Then soldiers from the 39th Illinois volunteered to march forward to substantiate the rumor.

They returned in short order to report booby traps everywhere. Torpedoes half buried in the ground. The ditch in front of the parapet layered with spears and stakes. The heavy guns and howitzers partially spiked, although the fuses laid to explode cannons and magazines were defective and had not worked. And yes, the enemy had fled, leaving behind in their stinking bombproofs unburied dead men and horses partly decomposed.

At sea a gunboat captured two enemy barges containing fifty-five men. The prisoners revealed that General Beauregard had begun evacuating his troops to Charleston two nights ago.

A few hours later Peter was on shore, mingling with the soldiers who were laughing with joy at being unscarred and alive. Jubilantly officers shook hands and later would pen their reports to their superiors. "Probably in no military operations of the war," a major wrote, "have Negro troops done so large a portion, and so important and hazardous fatigue duty, as in the siege operations on the island."

Peter ran across Pegleg, who was hopping around on his wooden foot like a whirling dervish. They hugged each other, laughter spilling from their mouths like wine from a cask.

"Charleston," Peter said, drunk with the sweetness of it, "you is next."

19

Folly and Morris Islands
November 1863

The siege had shifted to Fort Sumter, the Goliath squatting in the channel, and to the city it so zealously guarded. Charleston had gasped but she had not stopped breathing. Fort Sumter was shelled from the vantage point of Fort Wagner and Charleston bombed from batteries in the marsh. But still those enemy bastions held.

Aboard the *Swanee* Peter could observe the flight of Union artillery smashing into the fort. Its seawall was breached, pounded into debris which covered the lower casemates. Four arches on its northern side had been blown away together with their weaponry, and Negro laborers could be seen furiously working at repairs, filling the craters with sandbags. Yet with their heavy guns damaged and inoperable, the Sesesh had bloodily repulsed a naval attack and refused to surrender.

Deserters revealed that the lower part of Charleston was in ruins which prompted Yankee cannoneers to shift their sights from St. Michael's steeple to St. Philip's spire farther inland. Uncle Hiram, Peter continued to moan, has we killed you yet? An unsubstantiated rumor had surfaced that some captured Negro soldiers were imprisoned in Charleston. So maybe, Peter agonized, Stretch was alive and being shelled, too.

Peter moved into the constant thunder of gunfire as most soldiers did, almost oblivious to the air-splitting shrieks, the roar of exploding shells, the earth rupturing, the sea in turmoil—unless caught in the middle of it.

December 1863

The 54th Massachusetts was departing from the area, part of a massive troop movement being deployed to Florida. Chloe, their laundry woman, was remaining behind, transferred to another unit. Peter managed to see Sandy and Pinch to say good-bye and found them disgruntled. Their regiment was still refusing to accept less money than was paid to white soldiers. The governor of Massachusetts had passed a bill to use state funds to make up the difference but the regiment had rejected that offer.

"It ain't the money," Sandy said. "It's hard on my wife not getting a cent from me, but it ain't the money. We works just as hard as the whites and die just as dead. The gov'ment's got to respect that."

The stand of the 54th had spread to other Negro regiments. They, too, were refusing to accept less pay and many a black soldier was becoming surly and mutinous.

Two covered wagons appeared in the woods on Folly Island and the word spread like a brushfire. Ladies. In the wagons. Well, not ladies exactly. Their madame sent out the word that the price was right and democratic to suit everybody's fancy, white girls in one wagon and Negro girls in the other to accommodate both races. As soon as the transports docked everybody was privy to the word. Whores, mates. Down yonder near Blind Man's Creek. There were only a few women on the island. Clara Barton, the nurse. The Negro laundresses. An occasional officer's wife. Now there were two wagonloads of whores? The soldiers and sailors grinned, hiked up their trousers and took the shortcut into the woods.

It was dusk. The evergreen pines were softly blurred by a misty haze that had rolled in from the sea. The haze did not affect Peter's vision as he sat on a sand dune watching the action in front of the canvas-covered wagons.

Half an hour ago Pegleg had waylaid him at the wharf. "Peter," he said, "I hear a line done form in them woods as long as from here to Alabama." He slapped his wooden leg with glee. "You coming?" Avoiding his friend's eyes and feeling like an idiot Peter had muttered that he had to collect some firewood.

Pegleg sucked his teeth in disgust and turned his attention to Boy Whistler who was walking not toward the woods but in the opposite direction. The older man yelled, his voice peremptory, "Boy. Come here."

The lad, not yet fifteen, who could whistle better than he could talk had been snatched into service rather than drafted. Unable to meet their quotas, Northern states sent recruiters south who often resorted to virtual kidnapping. A number of those so shanghaied deserted at the first opportunity but this youth was still around, smooth-faced and big for his age. He hurried over to Pegleg, anxious to be in everybody's favor.

"Boy," the pilot said, sizing him up from head to toe, "it's a disgrace to be in this man's army and not know the difference between a woman's pussy and a sheep's ass. You been diddling sheep, boy?"

Whistler sighed. "I ain't been diddling nothing."

"Well don't cry about it. Come along with me and learn how to make your prick whistle."

"Me?" the boy asked, mesmerized.

"I ain't talking to you mammy."

Grinning, Boy Whistler followed the nimble pilot, who, using his wooden leg as a vault, was hopping ahead of him like a jackrabbit.

Sitting on the sand dune, Peter felt a weird languor which prevented him from stumbling down the incline although the blood was racing in his stiffened joint. His reluctance was an enigma to him. There was still a long line of soldiers in front of the wagons being ushered in by a big-bosomed madame with rouged cheeks. Whites predominated on both lines, colored men restricted to the Negro prostitutes. Peter grunted. White men were such hogs. Why didn't they stick to their own kind? He remembered his first and only prostitute, and Saralee whose axe-toting master had threatened to cut off his prick. They had preferred white men to him because of their money. But you has money now, he told himself, so why you sitting here, dummy? The palmettos at the edge of the forest beckoned to him softly in the mist.

Suddenly, realizing what was bedeviling him, Peter jumped to his feet. Stumbling in his haste, he made tracks to the regimental campsite. His shadow raced along with him to the open field where he bumped into soldiers hurrying toward the woods, anxious men hoping they weren't too late.

Peter paused in front of Chloe's tent to catch his breath. The flap was down but a lamp was glowing inside. "Miss Chloe," he called, his heart pounding, "is you in there?"

She was. Sitting on her cot, oiling a rifle she had taken apart, her head raised to greet her visitor. Peter caught his breath. Chloe was smiling, deep dimples dancing in her cheeks, which was the friendly way she greeted her customers when they came to pick up their laundry.

She rose to her feet, her long skirt settling in folds around her ankles. Peter felt giddy. "Can you shoot straight?" he asked with his teasing smile, "and hit the target?"

Chloe nodded, avoiding his eyes, and put the gun down. "The soldiers taught me. Said it might turn out to be more useful than a flatiron."

There was a sudden boom of cannonfire outside from the direction of the marsh, the gunners were again shelling Charleston. They varied the times of their bombardment to keep the Rebels guessing. Neither Peter nor Chloe responded to the noise which had become commonplace.

She walked to several bundles resting on the floor and bent over them. She had a high butt, a sassy butt, Peter thought, mentally caressing it and feeling the heat rising in his groin.

"I don't think I have anything here for you, do I?" Chloe asked.

"No. I just dropped by to see you." His hardened joint pushed him forward. It had a mind of its own.

Chloe raised her eyes to meet his, which Peter interpreted as encouraging. He put his hands on her shoulders and when she didn't flinch he claimed her lips. It was a brief kiss inasmuch as Chloe banged him in the chest with her fist. He took a step backward.

"Get out of my tent," she shrieked.

"What?" Peter's eyebrows shot upward.

"There's two wagons in the woods with whores in them. How come you ain't out there?" Her eyes flamed with anger.

"For Chrissake," Peter sputtered. "I don't . . ."

"I ain't no substitute for whores. I seen you out there peeking at them. Then you come in here all steamy and hot. Get out!"

"Chloe, I . . ."

"Out."

Feeling like an idiot for the second time that night, Peter backed away, reached for the tent flap and stepped outside. Why was it that a man never knew what the devil a woman was thinking? Chloe was just as exasperating as Rain. From now on, he'd do his own damn laundry.

The next day army brass foreclosed on the rouged madame and her wagons disappeared from the woods.

The *Swanee* was attached to the boat infantry, a dozen vessels under the command of a brigadier general. Their assignment was to chase enemy vessels out of the nearby creeks and marshes. With Peter piloting the *Swanee,* the flotilla swept the prescribed area clean. The boat infantry's work allowed Union squadrons to advance into Rebel territory to blow up bridges and railroads and then retreat while their warships exchanged gunfire with shore batteries and attempted to capture blockade runners. This afternoon, two had been apprehended, a British schooner carrying a cargo of salt and a brig from the Bahamas that was chased and sunk off Rattlesnake Shoals.

When Peter arrived at his tent, his instincts told him somebody was inside. At first he saw only a shadowy form. Then recognized her. Chloe. Sitting on his cot. Nervously twisting her hands in her lap. Dressed in something dark and shapeless but no matter he could still detect her jutting breasts.

"Chloe," he said with a genuine smile. "How happy I is to see you."

She jumped to her feet. "I came by to . . . to find out if you had any dirty laundry. I was just about to leave."

"I got plenty of dirty clothes," he said solemnly. "Every stitch on my back."

Tentatively, she sat back down and lowered her eyes.

Peter strode forward to light the kerosene lamp but changed his mind in mid-stride. Chloe, naked, might be more at ease in the dark, and naked he intended to have her.

"I hope you haven't been waiting long," he said.

"No."

"I has some molasses and water in a jug. Let me get you some."

"Thank you kindly."

She drank it slowly from his tin cup. He took the cup from her to refill it and their fingers touched. Peter held on to her hand and sat down beside her.

"Chloe." Her name on his lips was a soft caress. "You is too sweet and purty. For months I has been longing to touch you."

He brought her hand up to his lips. She trembled but did not pull away. His mouth brushed against her palm, then her eyes and the tip of her nose, all the while he murmured how precious she was, so kind that everyone adored her. Gently, tenderly, Peter kissed her lips.

He took his time and was rewarded. Chloe, aroused, was passionate. It was almost dawn when they disentangled their limbs from one another and arose to get dressed, stopping often in the process to laughingly kiss a dimpled cheek or a bushy eyebrow.

The *Swanee*, the last vessel in the boat infantry, ran into trouble late one afternoon passing through Folly Island Creek, a narrow body of water between high bluffs. The sun was setting, a flaming bowl in the water, and a raw wind blowing hard, but sailing had been smooth until now. Mr. Josephus was at the wheel. Peter, standing next to him, had always felt that the helmsman was in league with Ensign Cherry, who hated him.

Suddenly, there was an explosion on the roof of the pilothouse, followed by a ricochet of bullets. The steamboat sheered sharply, sending both men crashing to the floor.

"Jesus Christ," the helmsman howled, "we've been hit."

Peter crawled to the spinning wheel and pulled himself upright. The boat was listing to port, about to crash into the bank, and with all the strength at his command he tried to reverse its pull. A Confederate battery was on the bluff but the *Swanee* had sneaked through here before. Rebel gunners were sending them a message that their sneaking days were over.

Another volley of gunfire hit the deck, the steamer reeling drunkenly. The door flew open and Ensign Cherry stuck his head inside.

"Captain Doboy's been wounded," he shouted. "His orders are to beach this boat before we're all killed. Mr. Josephus, run up the white flag." The ensign's head disappeared.

"No," Peter yelled at Josephus who was about to follow the officer outside. "We is almost out of they range. We can make a run for it."

"Are you crazy?" The helmsman was outraged. "The captain sent us an order." He pulled open the door just as a bullet came whizzing through it.

Another mortar slammed into the lurching boat. Peter fell sideways but hung on to the wheel. Josephus, on his knees, stared without comprehension at the blood oozing out of his side. Dazed, he mumbled, "The white flag," and grimacing tried to crawl out the door. The effort defeated him and he toppled forward, groaning.

"I ain't gon surrender this boat," Peter yelled. The whites would be swapped for Sesesh prisoners but not the Negroes. They would be killed or enslaved and there was a price on his own head.

He shouted down the tube to the boiler room, "Pile on the steam till she ready to burst."

"You're going to get us all killed," Mr. Josephus howled.

Peter did not need an echo of his innermost fears and yelled, "Shut you mouth." He realized that their gunners were not firing back. The captain was surrendering without a fight. Sucking in his breath, Peter struggled to maneuver the steamer into the middle of the narrow stream to keep her from running aground where she'd be an easy target for Rebel artillery. But she kept lurching to port.

A bullet exploded in the wood above his head. He felt a sharp pain and suddenly his left eye was clouded with blood. He closed it and squinted out of his right eye, praying that he could see. The steamer was still lurching and for the first time in his life Peter cursed her.

"You diseased whore!" he screamed out loud, startling Mr. Josephus who assumed he was talking to him. "You misbegotten hunk of shit."

As if surprised, the vessel trembled and then leaped forward. Mortar shells burst behind her stern blasting a geyser high into the air. The *Swanee* ran down the creek, the distance lengthening between her foamy wake and the bouncing shells. Lurching, she made it safely home.

It was only a surface wound, the shore doctor advised Peter, the cut reopened which he had suffered aboard the *Cayenne*. Thank God, he thought, already in deep trouble. Disobeying orders was insubordination. The captain, in the field hospital along with the helmsman, could press charges. Have him dismissed. Jailed. Depressed and worried, Peter trudged home.

For days he anxiously awaited word from headquarters. What penalty were they cooking up for him? A court-martial? The firing squad? His healthy imagination was making him ill. Routinely he went about his work and when night came found relief in Chloe's arms.

They talked, sweet talk full of cooing and kissing and little lies that stared down the truth because the woman did ask him constantly, "Does you love me?" One evening, watching her break down a gun to clean it, he said with his impish smile, "I is scared to say no 'cause you might shoot me." Chloe did not think that was funny.

Peter hedged. "I is so worried 'bout disobeying my captain I cain't think straight."

Full of sympathy, Chloe filled him with other visions, offered up her Georgia past on a platter, warmed him with her tinkling laughter. She was sweet, he told himself listening to her, not hard to puzzle out like Rain.

"My mistress doted on me when I was a young one," Chloe said, smiling at the memory, her dimples flashing. "She used to let me sleep at the foot of the bed to keep her company. When I was six Missy let me go to Savannah to live with my Granny Rose. I was the youngest of nine children and the others were enough to help out on the farm."

It was Granny Rose who raised Chloe, a freed woman who

immediately captured Peter's heart because she was a bartering lady like he'd been a bartering man.

"She came to see my mother 'bout every three months, arriving in a hired wagon loaded with flour and molasses, tobacco, bacon and sugar. The islanders bought them for cash or with chickens and eggs which she carried back to Savannah to the market. She also did laundry for bachelors and kept their rooms clean, altogether making a tidy living."

Granny Rose also insisted that her granddaughter learn to read and write. It was a clandestine enterprise, Chloe journeying every morning to a kitchen schoolroom with about twenty-five other pupils, all of them arriving one by one. Their schoolmarm was a freed black woman, a widow, who the neighbors assumed was teaching the children how to cook and sew and clean.

After her grandmother died, Chloe returned home to her mistress and married a slave named Miles Harrison. In the early years of the war, together with his brother, Cleveland, they ran away from their owners attempting to reach the Union lines.

"We slept during the day, Peter, and traveled through the swamps at night and were almost there when the slave catchers caught up with us. . . ."

Chloe groaned, still stung by the memory of that night, by the feel of the nettles stinging her skin when Miles shook her awake abruptly, his hand over her mouth to keep her from making a sound. Shh. White men on horseback. Seven or eight of them. Riding hard and whacking the bushes with their rifles. She could hear the brush snapping beneath the horses' hooves. Whispering, Miles suggested that they split up. He would take one path, to divert their pursuers, while she and Cleveland went in the opposite direction and they would meet at the Yankees' camp. Before Chloe could protest he was gone.

His ruse worked too well. The white men gave chase and caught him. Chloe tried to run back to her husband but Cleveland knocked her to the ground and sat on her until the sound of the horses' hooves faded. They made it to safety, Chloe crying all the way and cursing her brother-in-law. Months later she heard from a Georgia contraband that Miles had been killed attempting to escape again.

"I know he would've enlisted 'cause he was that kind of man,"

Chloe said, "so I did it for him. And I didn't want to be around Cleveland. I knew it wasn't fair, the way I felt 'bout him, but I couldn't help it. I'd look at him and ask God why He took the wrong brother. So when the Fifty-fourth came down to St. Simon and needed another laundry woman, I joined up with them. Miles would like you, Peter. So much about you reminds me of him." Chloe lowered her eyes. "I ain't had no other man till you."

Tenderly Peter touched her cheek. His lips trailed down to kiss her neck, her breasts, to explore the delight of her body. "Sweetheart," he whispered and told her the lie she wanted to hear. "I love you."

"Mr. Mango," the quartermaster said, his pop eyes magnified by his glasses. "I've just received a message from headquarters."

Peter sucked in his belly prepared for the worst. Automatically, Lieutenant Schwartzenberg pushed papers around on his cluttered desk.

"It has been decided that on the day in question Captain Doboy's judgment was impaired by virtue of his wounds. When he's released from the hospital he'll be transferred. Headquarters has noted the admirable leadership you displayed in saving the crew and a valuable steamer from falling into enemy hands. Effective immediately, you have been promoted to captain of the *Swanee*."

Peter stared with disbelief at the man who had just delivered a bombshell and was smiling happily at him.

"Along with the promotion goes a raise in pay. Congratulations, *Captain* Mango."

It took several moments for Peter to control the urge to leap over the railing and hug this pop-eyed little Jew. Instead, he saluted him smartly.

"Thank you, suh."

That evening Pegleg stole a bottle of liquor from somewhere and they got gloriously drunk. In his own tent later, still woozy and ecstatic, Peter made love to Chloe the livelong night.

The crowning touch was striding about in the captain's cabin the following morning. Peter swiveled around in the chair screwed to the floor in front of the small desk. He pulled down one of the rolled-up charts stuffed between the overhead beams simply because this was his cabin and he could do as he pleased. Chuckling, he sat on the settee facing the curtained bunk, remembering the night he and July had broken in here. How frightened they all had been but the good Lord had set sail with them.

Outside Peter peeped into the galley then went to inspect the howitzer mounted on the fantail. The crew was doing its housekeeping chores and Ensign Cherry was aft lambasting a seaman for some dereliction of duty. The man scurried away as Peter approached the ensign to relate the glorious news, which he hoped would shock him into lunacy.

But Mr. Cherry abruptly collapsed Peter's sails. "Good morning, *Captain*," the devilish fellow greeted him.

"Well, now," Peter said, sorely disappointed. "Good morning."

The ensign blew his nose. "The quartermaster has instructed me to turn over the crew to you, but I'm a scrupulously honest man and must inform you that I have always doubted the wisdom of enlisting Negroes into the military."

Staring into the rheumy eyes of the man second in command to him, Peter realized the ensign intended to thwart him every step of the way just short of insubordination.

"Mr. Cherry," he barked, "the only wisdom you has to remember is that I'm the captain. The first time you forget it, I is gon feed you dumb ass to the sharks. Understood?"

"Yes, sir."

Never mind the white man's rules, Peter thought, which he hadn't been schooled in anyhow. Let this whoreson understand some plain nigger talk.

Peter often spent one or two nights aboard the *Swanee* on assignment and was grateful to come home to find Chloe there. She had developed the habit of repairing to his tent after finishing her laundry to spend the night, which pleased him, particularly when casualties had bruised him raw. His white gunner was in the field hospital having his left leg amputated. It had been peppered with grape, and two seamen had also been wounded in the same skirmish with the enemy.

"Sweetness," Peter murmured when he arrived home. Quickly he undressed his little laundry woman, his hands roving over her body, threading past her pubic hair to find that warm, moist spot. She opened up to him like a flower and they made love. It was wonderful, but once Peter had to bite his lips to avoid calling the woman in his arms Rain.

The inevitable confrontation with Ensign Cherry occurred when the *Swanee* was returning to Lighthouse Inlet from an expedition into enemy territory along with several other transports. The Yankees had liberated thirty slaves from a rice plantation and took as prisoner twenty Confederate soldiers. The Rebels were in the hold of the *Swanee*.

Repairing to the pilothouse to set sail, Peter revealed their course to Mr. Cherry and the helmsman who was at the wheel. They would not go through the channel but would skirt it in favor of the Stono River.

"Captain, skirting the channel is taking the long way home," the ensign said.

Peter agreed. "But it's low tide and they's not enough water in the channel to spit in. We'd have less than a foot under our bottom and would run aground."

"It's almost an hour before low tide, Captain. We have time to make it through."

"That's for me to decide," Peter snapped.

At this time of year a falling tide occurred quite early, grounding many a vessel in the channel. And while they struggled to get afloat Rebel shore batteries could shell them, inflicting heavy casualties. It was a reckless undertaking for those not familiar with the treacherous channel.

"What should I do, sir?" the helmsman asked, looking not at Peter but the ensign.

Peter yelled, "Didn't I just tell you our course?"

Mr. Cherry nodded almost imperceptibly and the helmsman mumbled, "Yes, sir."

The exchange did not go unnoticed by Peter but he checked his anger. The ensign's disrespectful attitude was drifting down to the crew and Peter decided to throttle it once and for all as soon as this expedition ended. He was not deaf, he had heard the seamen grumble about taking orders from him, and only one voice reminding the others, "He kept our asses from becoming prisoners, mates."

It was dawn, when the transports sailed into the inlet. Peter stood near the gangplank as the Confederate prisoners disembarked. They were a disagreeable bunch, he thought, their hostility plainly evident by the baleful glances they directed toward their guards who were Negroes. Obviously that was an ignominious insult.

"Good morning, Peter," a Rebel said in passing.

Surprised, Peter stared at a gaunt man wearing a black eye patch and then at the back of his head as he shuffled down the gangplank with the other captives. On the wharf they were herded into a covered wagon to be taken to a newly built prison compound.

Was that Ellsworth Caine, Peter wondered, or is I going crazy? He did not have time to pursue the matter at the moment and the disembarkation continued. When the prisoners were all ashore, Peter assembled his crew on the main deck. Sullenly they stood before him—the ensign and the helmsman, the gunners, deckhands and the cook—anxious to finish their chores and be dismissed. Peter himself stood stolidly as though anchored to the deck, a harsh look on his craggy face.

"There's been a lot of mumbling since I took over," he began, his voice loud and clear, "and a slackness in obeying orders. You can mumble till your tongue falls out but you'll obey orders pronto or get offa my boat. I can run this steamer better than any man aboard and if you doubt that, this is you last chance to jump ship. March youself right down that gangplank to the quartermaster and ask for a transfer. Tomorrow will be too late 'cause I'd have thrown you ass into the brig by then."

Peter had hoped that the ensign would speedily depart but instead he was looking around innocently as though wondering who the miscreants were. A white seaman made the first move toward the gangplank. Everyone else stood pat except the Negro cook whose defection was no surprise to Peter. The man had been a prime mumbler, preferring to take orders from a white man.

"Anybody else?" Peter asked gruffly but pleased. He had expected a greater defection. "All right, men. Company dismissed."

The crew went about their duties with more alacrity, but if there was a semblance of harmony more or less aboard the steamer, it did not extend beyond. The white pilots were livid, led by Redeye Murdoch. Frequently and loudly they complained that appointing

a Negro captain was an insult to them and goddamnit they didn't
intend to stomach it.

"I knew you would find me," Ellsworth Caine said.

Peter grunted. "You knew more than I did."

He had been bedeviled for days and finally to put his mind at
ease he had hitched a ride to the prisoner compound, a cluster of
newly built barracks, encountering no difficulty in arranging to
see Ellsworth. "Your former master?" a Negro sergeant had inquired. "They hate to give us up, you know. Think God borned
them to own us."

Armed with a pass, Peter met Ellsworth in a small storeroom
filled with tall barrels.

Former slavemaster and slave stared uncomfortably at one another, Peter shocked by the scarecrow Ellsworth had become. He
was no longer flabby but gaunt, his clothes hanging loosely on his
frame. Peter pointed to the patch covering his eye.

"I hope you ain't gone blind, suh."

Ellsworth's smile was wan. "No. It's healing. I heard on the
boat there was a nigra captain, but I never dreamed it was you."

He hauled himself atop a barrel. Peter followed suit and suddenly everything seemed familiar to him. "Seems like they was
some barrels somewhere like these we used to scramble up on,"
he said.

"That warehouse on Peach Street."

"And one down by the wharf we sneaked into once."

Smiling, they sat side by side, kicking their heels against the
wood as they had done as boys.

"If we could just turn back the clock, Peter, wouldn't that be
nice?"

"No." He stilled his feet. "I was a slave then."

Ellsworth's face turned red. "Of course. I'm a dunce." He
stopped kicking the barrel also and cleared his throat. "What have
you been doing since you became a pirate? Do you know there's
a price on your head?"

"Dead or alive," Peter said grinning.

"My daddy was outraged." Ellsworth laughed, relishing the
memory of his father's discomfit. "Both you and Lily running

away. Such ungrateful niggers. God, but he had a fit, practically foamed at the mouth."

"How is he and Missy?"

"They're living at Rolling Acres outside of Charleston which he would never let me manage. They're raising foodstuff for the army with about forty slaves. I was there for a while, wrestling with Daddy as always. He bought two substitutes for me so I wouldn't have to go in the army. Then it was decided all hands were needed and I was drafted." Ellsworth sighed and changed the subject. "What did you say you've been doing?"

Peter shrugged. "I is married and a daddy and a pilot for the Yankees."

"You always did like boats. And how is Lily? I dearly loved your mother."

"She got a touch of rheumatism but she works for a Yankee colonel in Beaufort."

"Tell her . . . tell her I'm glad she's free." Ellsworth's voice was suddenly choked. "And I'm sorry, Peter, we couldn't . . . didn't remain friends. It's a pity we had to grow up. No. That's not what I mean. You grew up too fast perhaps, and I . . . I . . . It was hateful the way they pulled us apart. We were still children."

Peter refused to look at him. They had different memories about the same events. He said with deliberate slowness, "But it was you who said 'I is the master, you is the slave.' " The words were branded on his heart.

"Because they kept pressing me," Ellsworth protested. "Daddy and the tutor." He sounded petulant and as if realizing that, he sighed and shook his head. "No. I can't blame anybody but myself, can I?"

Peter didn't answer and Ellsworth said wearily, "I hope the Union wins the war. I'm tired of being a slaveholder."

Surprise almost toppled Peter off the barrel. "How long you been feeling like that?"

"I don't know. Maybe always. I only know I want to sit out the war right here. A prisoner. It's safe and I've never been a brave man. But if I am exchanged maybe I'll have enough guts to refuse to fight. Maybe. I don't know. My daddy will really disown me then, his disgraceful turncoat son."

Peter realized for the first time that Ellsworth had been hurting

234

for years. He felt a rush of warmth and heard himself say, "Last year I met a Yankee soldier who cussed out his mates on account of me and wanted to talk. That's all he wanted, but I was feeling evil and shunted him off. A few days later he was killed and I didn't get a chance to say how sorry I was." Peter paused. "I don't know why I is telling you this."

Ellsworth nodded as though it made sense to him. Guilt was guilt. "I think I can do it," he whispered. "If I am exchanged I will defect."

A problem was brewing in Peter's bed. Dimly he noticed that at even the most casual mention of Rain's name Chloe crawled inside her shell refusing to acknowledge that he had another life.

Today a letter had arrived from Rain, the first in weeks, written not by Miss Carlotta who had returned home to Philadelphia after a bout with malaria, but by the schoolmaster. Glory and his mother were fine and all his friends, Rain stated, and she herself missed him dreadfully. It was such a warm letter that Peter decided before going to bed to pen a reply.

Sitting on his cot in his underwear he was laboriously writing when Chloe came in. She sat beside him and kissed his cheek.

"Who you writing to?"

"Rain."

Chloe sprang to her feet as though the bed was on fire. Striding across the room she picked up Peter's shirt from the floor and shoved it into his burlap laundry bag.

"Hey," he protested, "I has only worn that a few times."

"It's filthy," she snapped.

He stood up and pulled on his trousers lest she snatch the very drawers off his behind. "Woman, what's wrong with you?"

Angrily, she stared him down, one hand on her poked-out hip. "When can I visit your boat?"

Peter sat back down, his mind searching for a way out. He had been putting her off for days. It was becoming a major grievance, Chloe's need to move beyond their nighttime lovemaking onto more public ground, to be seen with him in the light of day. At first it had been a wistful request, murmured between caresses. Now it was a demand. He did not fully understand his reluctance to have her aboard his boat other than having made love to his

235

wife there. Why couldn't Chloe be content closeted with him in his tent?

"Sweetheart," he said, "I cain't do it right now. Maybe next month . . ."

She regarded him fiercely. "All right. I'll be in my tent until then." She stormed outside leaving behind his dirty laundry.

Stunned, he walked over to it, pulled out his shirt and put it on. Damn that woman. She could stay in her tent until the devil cut off his tail. Who did Chloe think she was, aggravating him so. She wasn't Rain and he wasn't traipsing after her.

February 17, 1864

A Confederate submarine blew up the *Housatonic*. The Union gunboat was on blockade duty in Charleston harbor when the torpedo struck forward of the mizzenmast in line with the magazine. The stored ammunition exploded with a tremendous roar.

The warship sank fast, seamen desperately clinging to her top mast. Those on the lower riggings were sucked into the sea, bobbing about amidst the debris, holding on to floating spars and planks. They were rescued, those who had not drowned, by two launches from another gunboat on blockade duty. Word of the *Housatonic*'s sinking spread quickly, relayed by signalmen from ship to ship.

Peter heard the news when he stepped ashore from the *Swanee*. A bunch of sailors had collected and the wharf was buzzing. "Enemy engineers have built a goddamn submarine, mate. It travels underwater, then bang. Your goddamn ship's at the bottom of the goddamn sea and you along with it."

The sheer magnitude and horror of it followed Peter home to his lonely tent. He sat down on his cot and pulled off his boots. The mere idea of men propelling a torpedo boat beneath the waves was so daring and terrifying. A submarine could attack anytime, anywhere, sneak out of Charleston harbor and ram a torpedo into the *Swanee. Mate, your goddamn ship's at the bottom of the goddamn sea and you along with it.* So why was he sitting here alone tonight like a donkey's ass? Chloe was surrounded by soldiers who would give their eyeteeth to sleep with her. If one hadn't done so already. Hurriedly Peter put his boots back on and stepped outside into the night. Explosions lit up the sky. Charleston was being shelled again.

It went off without a hitch. The crew was busy with their housekeeping chores and mostly out of sight except for a black gunner.

"Howdy-do, Miss Chloe." The gunner greeted her with a smile.

She nodded at him, her face grave. The man was probably one of her laundry clients, Peter assumed as he led Chloe up the steps to the pilothouse to explain the gear. He let her touch the wheel and pull the whistle cord. He shouted a command through the tube to the boiler room to demonstrate its use and took her to his cabin. Pulling down a chart he showed her where they were. Then they walked around the deck and back to the gangplank.

"Thank you," Chloe said, her eyes adoring him.

She was so grateful, her visit so brief and simple that Peter wondered why he had made it a problem.

"The Philadelphia navy yard will completely overhaul the *Swanee*. New engines. Everything." Lieutenant Schwartzenberg handed Peter his orders. "Be prepared to sail to headquarters in three days. You will have a week's leave at home before departing for Philadelphia. Any questions?"

"No, sir." Peter had realized for quite a while that his steamer was in need of repairs, but Philadelphia? He felt a vague foreboding.

"It's a trap," Pegleg fumed later that evening. "Them white pilots been grumbling up a storm. It's their way of getting rid of you. They don't care if you crack up on the rocks of Cape Hatteras. They is praying that you do."

Wearily, Peter said, "Well, I has to go. There's no way out of it." At least he would finally get rid of Ensign Cherry who undoubtedly would ask for a transfer.

But the ensign made no such request. Philadelphia was his home and he was anxious to visit his family.

"Ain't you afraid," Peter needled, "that I'll send us all to an early grave at the bottom of the ocean?"

Mr. Cherry sneezed. "I have faith in your navigation skills." His cold voice conveyed the message, *But I still don't like you.*

Peter chuckled, not giving a damn whether the asthmatic man liked him or not. "I has heard the rumor," he said, "that Admiral Dahlgren got the submarine's specifications from an engineer what defected and is asking Washington to build him a few."

Excited talk on ship and shore centered on the submarine, producing admiration and revulsion. Mr. Cherry belonged to the latter group. "We should not tamper with God's universe, Captain. He did not intend for man to go plunging beneath the waves like a blasted whale."

"I think it's quite spunky," Peter said cheerfully. The existence of a submarine made him feel bold. If men could navigate beneath the waves then surely he could sail without peril to Philadelphia.

He was overjoyed at the prospect of a week's home leave at Beaufort but uncomfortable about leaving Chloe. But, he reasoned, he had allowed her on his boat and that assuaged his guilt somewhat.

Lying beside him their last night together, she cried, her tears warm against his bare chest.

"I knew this day was coming," she moaned.

"Hush," Peter said gently and kissed her.

But he was already gone, sailing out of the inlet, headed for home. To Rain.

20

Beaufort

March 1864

There was no tombstone. It had been all Rain could manage to
get her son into the cemetery, never mind the embellishments.
Lily had placed the tin cup Peewee had loved on his grave and
that's how they found it. A slight mound in the earth, the grass
withered and brown, the naked limbs of the trees etched harshly
against the gray sky. Rain, still wearing black, seemed a part of
the wintry bleakness to Peter. Silently he stood with bent head
contemplating the peculiar nature of things. I ain't hardly had time
to hold you, son, and now you is gone.

Rain, hollow-eyed, the skin pulled taut across her high cheek-
bones, reiterated for the tenth time, "I didn't write you he were
sick so's not to worry you none. I is sorry."

"Stop blaming youself," Peter told her as he had done last night
and again this morning. Still it hurt, this desire to have seen Peewee alive one more time. Maybe if he had known . . .

Suddenly Rain was crying. "Is they all dead?" She flung out
her arms and threw back her head. "God, why you take them all
from me? I is cursed."

Peter was confused until he realized she was talking about the
other children also, Zee and Petunia. Her eyes widened as she

wheeled around looking from grave to grave. "Glory, where you be?"

Peter grabbed her trembling shoulders. "She's all right."

"Where . . ."

"In the buggy."

They stumbled against the wind back to the path, Rain breaking away from him when their vehicle came into view. She ran awkwardly, holding up her black skirt with both hands. Stumbling inside, she snatched Glory to her breast. Frightened, the girl began to cry.

"Hush," Peter said, scrambling inside to put his arms around them both. "Rain, you is suffocating our chile."

When they were both dry-eyed he nudged the mare home, vowing never again to bring Rain to the cemetery. Next time he would come alone to say good-bye to his son.

Later that night Lily told him, "I don't know why you wife fault sheself. Everything a body could do she done. Kept that boy so clean he squeaked. Sat up all night with him till she was a shadow. I done told her time and again, 'Rain, you ain't got no cause to fault youself.' But she won't listen to me. Maybe now that you is home . . ."

"I is home now, buttercup," Peter murmured against Rain's cheek, pulling her into his arms, or trying to, whenever they were alone.

But his buttercup refused to be held, to be loved, to surrender her vigil. She climbed out of bed in the midnight hours to push clothes around in a tin vat with a stick. Trousers and sheets. Curtains and dresses. Drawers only worn once. Anything her eagle eye fell upon ended up in the washtub. By dawn the clothes were billowing on a line and with pursed lips she would crawl back to bed for a few minutes, then leap up again to help Glory dress for school. Although she looked haggard, her eyes sunk in deep hollows which shuttered their flame, Rain did not appear to need the sleep she missed but went faithfully to work each day. Aching to hold her, Peter kept on trying.

"This house is nice," he told her. "Lovely."

Rain agreed. The parlor was painted pale blue with oak paneling. She had polished the brass vases on the mantel and kept them filled with fresh flowers. Next to them was a figurine of herself that July had carved which she treasured highly. It was her, all right, wearing a head wrap, but her face was featureless.

The butcherman's taste in furniture was plain and sturdy and the dining room chairs all matched, a delight to Peter accustomed as he was to odds and ends. And how pleasant to have a bedroom just for himself and Rain, his mother and Glory in the room down the hall. An alcove formed by the sloping rafters had a cot in it, obviously for a child, but Glory, given a choice, had selected her grandmother's company. Outside there was a garden, and a tall live oak on the front lawn cast its shade over the piazza which could be enclosed with blinds. It was really grand.

Peter sat on the piazza with Rain one afternoon telling her about the bombardment of Charleston and how worried he was about their friends and Uncle Hiram, a concern she shared.

"He and your mamma was close," Rain said.

"Yeh," Peter responded automatically.

"I mean close close."

He didn't get her drift right off and was irritated when it struck him, growling, "What you talking?" Making lewd suggestions about his mother was no light matter.

"Why you getting vexed, Peter? Your mamma was young once. All I got to do is mention you uncle's name and she gets as fidgety as a june bug."

The possibility struck him like the kick of a mule. Uncle Hiram and his mother. And she did get flustered whenever they talked about him. For a fleeting moment he wondered whether Uncle Hiram might be his father but discarded the notion. His mother had not been in Charleston for several years before he was born. Too bad. She had never told him who his daddy was and he had never inquired, considering himself lucky to have her.

In the morning Peter asked Lily, "Mamma, how long you been knowing Uncle Hiram?"

"A long time, son."

"And his wife? Did you . . ."

"That fat sow."

"So you did meet her."

"Never."

"Then how you know she's fat?"

Lily looked at her son as if he were daft. "You told me. Them two or three Christmases when Massa let you come home for a visit. You said she was fat as a sow and getting more so every day. Tee hee. Hiram never did like no fat womans."

"When he tell you that?"

Lily was vexed. "Boy, why you questioning me? Don't be disrespectful. I bet that wife of yours put you up to this like I is somebody common."

"No, ma'am. I . . ."

Lily swept out of the room grumbling, "There's something about that gal I just cain't stand."

He would let it alone for now, Peter decided, and at some other time when Mamma was not so easily riled, he would prick the truth out of her.

Tension was everywhere, inside and outside of his house. "Niggers is some mad on account of the land sales held last month," Rain informed Peter.

Reverend Ferdinand confirmed that when Peter bumped into him one day on the ferry en route to St. Helena. As effusive as ever, the reverend embraced him, a broad smile on his pockmarked face. The ferry was not crowded and they were able to find a seat on a bench, Peter answering the minister's inquiries about the progress of the war on the battlefront.

"We've been having a battle here, too," Reverend Ferdinand said wearily, "a most despicable time and the scoundrels took the day." Defeat was difficult for him to swallow and they had been roundly defeated.

During the last sale of confiscated property the controversy between the tax commissioners and General Saxton's supporters had been openly hostile, fanned by the vacillating attitude of Secretary Chase. First, sixteen thousand acres were set aside for charitable purposes, for Negroes selected upon the basis for their industry and moral propriety. General Saxton sent the reverend to Washington to argue that all of the land offered at this time should be available to Negroes not as charity but as their right.

"Peter, I returned home filled with prayerful thanksgiving and a new set of instructions to the tax commissioners, a preemption plan similar to that used to settle the West."

All the land would be available to persons residing in the area for at least six months, rendering the freedmen and volunteers eligible but eliminating the pesky speculators. Single people could buy twenty acres and families forty at $1.25 an acre. Rallies were held all over the islands exhorting Negroes to stake out their claims before the sun went down.

But the tax commissioners, again concerned with revenue, resisted disposing of the rich Sea Island plantations as though they were the virgin lands of the West. The property was improved, they complained, ignoring the fact that it was the field hands who had improved it. The commissioners were insistent and prevailed upon Secretary Chase to revert to the original mandate.

"That was a dastardly blow, Peter. More than a thousand colored heads of families had staked out their claims and made the down payment, expecting to buy a little piece of the home place, as they termed it. We were so certain that if the Negroes were squatting on the land and cultivating the soil they would not be evicted. But they were. They are so furious now many of them are refusing to work for the new owners."

Peter sucked in his breath sharply. "The speculators got most of the land?"

"Indeed they did. Paid from five to twenty-five dollars an acre at the public sales, an unexpected windfall very gratifying to the tax commissioners. Even Mr. Youngblood was surprised at the high price the land brought. Last year he paid a dollar an acre for his eleven plantations. And proved his point that cotton could be profitably grown with free labor. His profits were so handsome that his superintendents, who came here for twenty-five dollars a month, received as their share from six to seven thousand dollars each. And Mr. Youngblood paid himself a fat salary, about twenty thousand dollars."

Reverend Ferdinand sighed and lowered his eyes as though ashamed. "Your people are learning not to trust any of us and with good cause. We keep making promises we don't keep."

Unhappily Peter agreed. It was a miserable state of affairs. He parted company from the reverend when the ferry docked. Declining a ride with him, Peter rented a buggy and headed down the wide road to Caine's Landing.

It was unseasonably warm. Pretty white puffs of cotton buds were ankle high in the fields and the hands singing as Peter's buggy rattled by. They raised up from their stoop labor to wave at him.

Reluctant to face Cindy and her anxieties about Stretch, Peter had decided to see if he could find July first. But a commotion on the road that deterred him decided otherwise.

Dexter Youngblood, his freckled face flushed beneath his straw hat, was standing up in his buckboard surrounded by about a dozen Negro women who were angrily waving their fists in the air.

"A dollar a task," one of them shouted. "For shame you cheat us so."

It was Cindy. Peter recognized her, taller than the others.

"Mistuh Youngblood," another woman cried out. "Me and my chil'ren made two bales of cotton last year and two bales this year. I is a poor ignorant person but I ain't daft. I knows them two bales fetch good money but not for me. My little bit of money go so fast at the store. Everything so dear, a bit of cloth and such. And the molasses watered down but sky high. My money gone, and my chil'ren is naked. Now those field hands what be planting cotton for theyself make good money. And don't I work just as hard? So I is through with our agreement, suh. A dollar a task."

The other women joined in. "A dollar a task."

Cindy added, "And not a penny less."

Peter was astounded. Last year these women had seemed grateful for whatever they were paid, pleased with the Northerners "who done come down here to help we. God bless they bones." It was obvious that now they would rather break Mr. Youngblood's bones than bless them.

"You won't get any pay whatsoever," he said, his voice rising above the women's cries, "if you plant corn between my cotton rows again."

Shocked voices shouted, "No wages. No work."

Planting corn between the rows of cotton was an old custom and, when ordered by the superintendents to pull up the stalks, the field hands had refused. That galled Youngblood who ranted that they were too stupid to realize that their progress was measured by cultivating cotton. But no, the idiots preferred to grow vegetables and sell the surplus over and above their needs for cash.

Grumbling, the women dispersed, all except two who lagged

244

behind and approached the buckboard, their simmering manner indicating they intended to make a deal. Peter took it all in, marveling at the defiance of the rest of the women, most of whose menfolks were in the army or a labor battalion. Cindy was walking ahead of the others, her long legs taking giant strides.

"You want a ride home?" he called out.

"No," she snapped, angry at the world. She peered curiously into the vehicle keeping pace with her and stopped. "Peter? Sweet Jesus. It be you?"

He bounced to the ground and was hugging her while she was still wide-eyed. "Peter. When you get home?"

"A few days ago."

He helped her into the buggy. As it clattered down the road he asked, "What was that fuss back there 'bout?" Mainly Peter was postponing the inevitable, talking to Cindy about Stretch.

She sucked her teeth. "Massa Youngblood make so much money last year he brag 'bout it. But he think pot likker good enough for the likes of us. Field hands on other plantations does get more pay. And you friend July, since he lame is the boss's right hand. Riding 'round looking for pieces of the cotton gin and threatening folks."

Peter winced. "July?"

"Well he toting threats from Mistuh Youngblood and that's the same thing. He found them pieces and . . ."

"Cindy, what is you talking 'bout?"

After the gunshoot, she explained, after the planters burned the cotton in the warehouses, black folks went wild. They invaded the big houses, broke into the mills, dismantled the cotton gins and hid the pieces. "We does hate planting cotton, Peter. Seems like that's why we was slaves. Sorting cotton by hand be slow work. The gin made it faster. So massa planted more cotton and needed more slaves. Anyway, Mistuh Youngblood got the mills back to running and he ginning all the cotton grown hereabouts."

"And you all wants more pay which is only fitting."

"That's right."

The buggy had stopped in front of Cindy's shack, the horse nibbling on the wild brown grass. "I ain't coming in," Peter said. "I is gon mosey over to the Big House and see if I can find July."

"He done changed," Cindy said sadly. "July warn't like that

'fore he got lame, bedding down with two or three gals at the same time. He even come pussyfooting 'round here once. I threatened to chop off he good foot with my axe."

Dear God, Peter wondered, what's happened to my friend? To add to his dismay Cindy was suddenly crying, her body collapsed against him. "I is sorry," she wailed. "I been trying not to think about it, but tell me Stretch ain't dead."

"He's missing." Awkwardly Peter patted her shoulder and voiced his opinion that Stretch was probably in a prison camp somewhere. That was doubtful but still hope fluttered weakly in his chest. "He talked 'bout you all the time. Said you all was gon get married when he came home."

"For true? Stretch write me that, too. How did he look?"

"Skinny. Always eating. Or looking for something to eat. Or saying he were hungry."

Cindy smiled, remembering, and wiped the tears from her eyes. "I don't want nobody else but him. And he ain't dead 'cause I woulda felt it." Shyly she kissed Peter's cheek, thanked him for dropping by and climbed down from the buggy.

He drove away, glad to put the meeting with Cindy behind him. Several minutes later he arrived at the Big House and took the side road to the rear. An elderly black woman with an unlit corn-cob pipe in her mouth was in the yard wringing the neck of a chicken. Her motion was practiced, the bird's neck broken before its writhing body realized it was dead.

"Aunty," Peter called out, "does you know where I can find July?"

She shook her head. The veranda door opened and Miss Abigail stepped outside. Peter bowed slightly toward her. "Good afternoon, ma'am."

"You're looking for July? When I came home from school a few minutes ago," she said, "he was down by the barn mending the fence."

"Yeh," the colored woman said, swinging the dead chicken by its feet, "we cows keep going down the road."

"Thank you both," Peter said.

At the barn he halted the buggy and jumped down. July was pounding a fence post into the ground and absently glanced up, frowning, holding his hammer aloft. He froze in that position for

246

a moment and Peter's breath caught in his throat. July's left foot lay sideways on the ground, ankle up, making his body tilt, deformed. His face, though, was as strikingly handsome as ever, if more brooding. He lowered the hammer and greeted Peter with an exuberant shout.

They rushed toward each other, July dragging his left foot, which seemed all but dead, behind him. They embraced, pummeling each other's back.

"I was thinking 'bout you just the other day," July said grinning. "And here you are, as black and rusty as ever. And still in one piece. You always was a lucky sonofagun."

A twinge of guilt made Peter wince. Should he mention that he'd almost been blinded in one eye? Instead he punched July's shoulder again. "You old seadog," he said. "You is looking good youself."

"Except for this, huh?" July slapped his left leg. "So tell me how's the war going? Is we gon win the bastard?"

"We better." Briefly Peter related some of his activities, that he was taking the *Swanee* to Philadelphia for repairs and that he had seen Stretch before the battle for Fort Wagner. "You know he's missing?"

July frowned. "Yeh. Cindy told me."

"Well, we don't have to bury him yet, he's just missing."

July nodded without conviction. They both knew full well the plans the Sesesh had for captured Negro soldiers.

"You is the lucky one," July repeated. "You got a nice family and all I has is this dead foot." He hobbled back to the fence.

Peter said jovially, "I hear you got plenty of gals what don't care 'bout you lame foot. That ain't what they's after." He expected his friend to laugh with him and admit his sins.

Instead July said coldly, "They is too loose with they pussy. I cain't even remember they names." He obviously did not want to discuss the matter and reported that Brother Man was pining to get back to Edisto where he had been farming until the Sesesh ran them off.

"Wish I had time to visit him and Sister," Peter said. "They is awright?"

"Yeh."

"And Absalom? I hope he's done paid you back you money."

"Most of it. They gon plant more acres this year and come harvest time hire fifteen or twenty laborers."

Peter whistled. "So they is doing right well." July was looking sour and Peter wondered if he regretted not becoming Absalom's partner.

"Massa Youngblood say it's a risky business even so," July stated. "He say Negroes need more supervision 'fore they can strike out on they own. And a heap of them wants to work for wages they get every month and not have to wait for harvest time for they money."

"Some folks ain't leery 'bout taking a chance," Peter retorted.

"Some folks don't have enough brains to fill a peanut shell," July responded. "Massa Youngblood say——"

"How come you is siding with him?"

" 'Cause he knows how to make a heap of money. And that vexes folks."

Peter frowned. "You is sounding mighty strange. What's wrong with you?"

"Ask me that again," July shouted, suddenly out of control, "and I'll hit you in the head with this hammer." He raised it in a threatening manner.

"Nigger, that's the first time I asked you," Peter said.

They glared at one another, Peter alert for any sudden movement from July who had to be crazy if he thought that with his crippled self he could brain him. But still the idiot might try.

The idiot didn't. He turned and struck a stake a vicious blow. And then another. Without a word Peter climbed into the buggy and took off. He realized that July was banging the stake into the ground as a substitute for him. What he didn't understand was why.

Their bedroom was nice. The furniture matched. The chiffonier and the chest of drawers. And the huge mirror on the wall framed in gilt was pretty. The bed itself had a feather mattress and there was a green rug on the floor, slightly worn, and lace curtains at the window. It should have made Peter content but it didn't. There was a frozen woman in his bed.

His last night at home he rolled off of Rain disgusted with himself for having bothered. Her stony silence had been an order. *Hurry up and finish. Get offa me.*

"You has changed so," he said, hoping to shame her.

"I is sorry," she whispered, sounding miserable. "But I just cain't. I wants to be with you in the old way but then I hears Peewee calling and I has to go to him."

Peter raised up to lean over Rain who was staring straight up at the ceiling, her burnished eyes dull as though covered by a film. She twisted her head away, avoiding him, but he grabbed her chin with his hand.

"Look at me. I is here so don't pretend I ain't. What you mean you has to go to Peewee? Is you crazy, woman?"

She whimpered, "I stayed with him all the time so he couldn't slip away. Long as I was watching him nothing could happen. But one night I was so tired I dozed off. When I woke up he was dead."

"It weren't your fault," Peter muttered wearily. "Whether you fell asleep or no it . . ."

"Long as I kept watch, I knew I could hold onto him."

Peter groaned. "Rain. Please. Stop dragging our dead chile into our bed."

She swallowed a sob. "I is sorry."

"You keep saying that and it's driving me crazy."

He lay back down knowing what would happen next. Rain twisted and turned for several minutes trying to find a comfortable spot. Then sighing, she crept out of bed and padded out the door in search of dirty clothes to wash.

Hilton Head
March 1864

Peter had a day's layover at naval headquarters in Hilton Head when he arrived there to pick up the *Swanee*. Hasty repair work on her boiler to enable her to steam safely up the Atlantic had not yet been completed.

He was seated at the desk in his cabin studying a chart when there was a timid knock on his door and a grinning man entered, exposing a mouthful of rutted teeth.

"Bite," Peter exclaimed, jumping to his feet to greet his ex-crew mate. "If you ain't a blessed sight. Come on in."

He stepped inside tentatively, bundled up in a pea jacket, a woolen scarf wrapped around his neck. "I been waiting for you, Peter. Ever since I seen the *Swanee* moored here. I heard you was her captain and I jumped for joy."

"Is that so?" Since they had never been very friendly, Peter was skeptical about this joyous jumping.

Bite was as jerky as ever, twisting his cap in his hand, his eyes darting furtively around the room. "I ain't never been in a captain's cabin before. It's nice."

"Have a seat," Peter invited, returning to his desk.

Bite eased himself down to a chair. "I been a laborer in the quartermaster corps for the last coupla years and has a favor——"

"You and Turno?" Peter interrupted. "I haven't seen him since we stole the *Swanee.*"

"He's a sergeant in the army. The Thirty-eighth U.S. Colored Regiment."

Peter grunted. A sergeant. That figured, Turno being paid to be a bully. "So the draft finally got him."

"Naw. He enlisted."

Peter grunted again. "We talking 'bout the same rusty nigger? Last I heard he was making good money catching shrimps and lobsters."

"The Sesesh kidnapped his little boy, Bryant," Bite said quietly.

The back of Peter's neck prickled. "My God, man, when that happen?"

"Bryant was with a gal Turno was sweet on. She lived on the Birney plantation and he paid her good money to look after the boy while he sailed around selling he catch. Well, them Birney men with they guns come sneaking back to the plantation one night in a canoe and grab all the folks what had been they slaves. A fella what hid and didn't get took overheard them men cursing out the Negroes, saying they was living high off the hog while they ole missy was doing poorly far from home. So come along damnit and take care of her."

Peter was infuriated. When was this shit going to end? "I heard something 'bout that on St. Helena. That's when July and them started patrolling the place theyself."

"This was on Daufuskie Island."

Peter and Bite looked at each other and then glanced away, the fear of being enslaved again alive between them.

"Turno must've gone crazy."

"He were a lunatic ready to kill every white man what crossed his path. So I told him, join the army. They'll give you a gun and a saber. Who you don't shoot you can stab to death. That's what he did. Joined up. And to make him madder still, he ain't got paid yet. He refuse to accept less than what was promised saying white soldiers don't deserve more than him."

"Jesus Christ," Peter breathed. "I was on Morris Island with the Fifty-fourth Massachusetts when they refused reduced pay. It done spread to other outfits."

Still, it was hard to believe Turno would turn down a cent for any reason. The thought made Peter ashamed. The man's son was back in slavery and his woman, and here he was thinking that Turno had always been mean-spirited.

Bite coughed delicately. "Peter, I was looking for you 'cause I is hankering to ship out again."

"What?" Peter's mind was still on Turno.

"I want to ship out with you."

Peter looked speculatively at Bite who avoided his eyes. "You in some kind of trouble here?"

"No. Why you think that? I done ask the quartermaster for a transfer and he say if it's awright with you I is your new cook."

"I is gon be eating burnt grits all the way to Philadelphia?"

Bite stood up, looking hopeful. "I is a good cook. You ever taste my she-crab soup?"

Why, Peter wondered, was this runt so anxious to leave Hilton Head? "How is you wife?"

Bite glanced down at his feet. "We ain't together no more. Ain't been for quite a while."

She left him, Peter thought. Bite looked so hangdog, so forlorn, that Peter decided, why not? "The first time you scorch my rice," he said, "I'm gon toss you black ass overboard."

Bite looked up and smiled. "You sound just like Turno."

* * *

Turno turned up the next morning. An ebony giant clumping up the gangplank, sergeant's stripes on his blue uniform which was bursting at the seams. He crashed into the captain's cabin without knocking, catching Peter off guard. He was at his desk, rolling up the charts he had been reviewing since daybreak.

"Sergeant Turno," he said smiling, "how——"

"That pussy," the big man roared, the veins in his thick neck bulging. "Why you taking him with you to Philadelphia?" He stood straddle-legged in front of the doorway, blocking the light.

Peter walked around him and closed the door. "I ain't seen you in years and this is how you talk to me?"

"I ast you a question, nigger."

"Stop hollering, Turno, 'cause that ain't gon get you nowhere." They eyed each other as of old when they had been slaves on this selfsame boat, despising their condition and each other. "I was sorry to hear 'bout you boy," Peter said.

Turno relaxed his stance and took a few steps forward. "You remember Bryant?"

"Course I do." Peter had seen the child for the first and last time on the *Swanee* when they had been escaping. He resumed rolling up his chart but kept an eye on Turno.

"I is gon kill the sonofabitch what kidnapped him. The army say shoot to kill and that's what I is doing. I been trying to get Bite to enlist, too, but he's a piss-poor nigger. You know why he want to get up north? So he can run off to Canada. His ass is scared."

So that's it, Peter thought. "Bite didn't mention Canada to me."

" 'Cause he's a sly weasel. Now that you know, leave him here. I intend to kick his balls into jelly and make him join up."

Peter frowned, his bushy eyebrows meeting. Ever since he had known them Bite had jumped when Turno just belched, but now he was standing up to him? "If Bite wants to ship out on the *Swanee*, it's awright with me."

The sergeant exploded. He had a sailor's stockpile of profanity which he dipped into liberally. Peter was dipshit, a mule-brained asshole, a whore-mongering bastard.

"Get out of my cabin," Peter said with deadly calm, "or do I have to shoot you?"

"You don't have the guts."

"Don't tempt me." He pulled open his desk drawer and took out his pistol.

Turno took a step forward to show his mettle and spat out between clenched teeth, "The next time we meet it's your balls I'm gon kick into jelly." He turned around and stormed out of the cabin.

Peter slammed the gun back into the drawer, the sound of Turno's voice still ringing in his ears. It was a fitting climax to his week's leave. He was on terrible terms with his wife and July and now this. He was glad to be leaving the islands.

A low narrow sandbar stretched along the South Carolina coast interspersed with shallow beaches. Twice a day the tide swelled the lagoons, damning up the freshwater streams which flooded the cypress swamps. Heavy interior rains swelled the rivers, depositing on the coasts of the sandy islands organic residue from the mountains and the forests through which they flowed, enriching the soil.

Peter sailed beyond the sandbar but hugged the coastline as closely as he dared. The weather was perfect, a balmy westerly breeze and a smooth sea. With no difficulty he navigated past the graveyard of Cape Hatteras and steamed up the Atlantic coast.

Book Four

The End
Begins Again

∾

Your brother calls to you . . .
and no trace remains of dreams
of spite in which you dance
to death's thin melody.

—A COURSE IN MIRACLES

21

Philadelphia

September 1864

Why was it taking so long for the blockheads to overhaul the *Swanee?* After his gratitude that his poor steamer hadn't sunk en route, she was that decrepit, Peter fussed and fumed that he could have calked ten hulls while the workmen were dawdling six months over one. Never mind that her boilers and engines had to be replaced as well as the pumps and hydrometers and that several parts in short supply had to be ordered from the Brooklyn navy yard. And in the name of God how long did it take them to replank the deck and put up new rails? Were they imbeciles?

It was also aggravating to have that selfsame question addressed to him.

"Mr. Mango. Are you an imbecile?"

Julian Breed rapped Peter lightly across the knuckles with his ruler. They were seated at the table in Mr. Breed's well-appointed dining room and Peter felt like pummeling the man who every day he promised himself to fire. Why was he paying good money to this donkey's ass to insult him? A man who acted white though he was as black as himself and his hair just as nappy. Julian Breed was a teacher at a private boys' academy and an elegant man in every sense of the word, Peter was forced to admit. He had a handsome face and a manly build—a broad chest straddled by a watch chain, and a full head of graying hair. He was always impeccably dressed, and arrogant. Peter rubbed his knuckles which throbbed more from indignation than pain.

"I heard you speak at Concert Hall last night and was livid with shame," the tutor said, his mustache quivering with disdain. "Don't tell anybody that I am your teacher and disgrace me. Why can't you remember the simple rules of diction I've been trying to drum into your head. Imbecile."

He raised the ruler again and Peter quickly removed his hands from the table. "You was there?" he asked surprised.

"Were there, Mr. Mango. I was. He was. You were. Yes, I was there and your elocution was deplorable."

The audience at the hall, mainly white, had given Peter a standing ovation and then kept him busy for almost an hour answering questions.

"They ain't care how I say it, Mistuh Breed, but what I done."

"They ain't care, Mr. Mango?"

"They don't care." His voice was sullen.

"I done, Mr. Mango?"

"I has done."

"I have done, imbecile."

"If you don't stop calling me that I'm going to break your goddamn neck."

"Good. Your pronunciation was perfect for once. Messing up the verb 'to go' is too common, too niggerish. Gon. Gwan. Gwine." He crinkled his long, aristocratic nose. "Don't ever let me hear you swallow that participle again. Say it. Going to. Going to."

"I am going to break your goddamn neck."

Mr. Breed looked at him icily. "Your homework, Mr. Mango."

Peter turned over several handwritten pages and steeled himself for the diatribe which was forthcoming.

"Why so many slovenly ink spots? Why can't you spell a simple word like 'money'? Only a dumbbell would leave out the 'e.' Only an imbecile."

Carlotta Flowers had recommended the tutor to Peter. He had visited her his first week in Philadelphia and mentioned that he would like to brush up on his education now that he had a little spare time. She had recovered from her illness and was a little thinner than when he had seen her last in Beaufort but still quite beautiful to him.

"Peter Mango," she had exclaimed, smiling. "My dear man, what a lovely surprise."

She took him to seminars to hear visiting lecturers, first Lloyd Garrison, the fiery editor of *The Liberator*, and next Sojourner Truth, an electrifying gaunt woman who had been a slave.

"Does you . . . do you know Frederick Douglass?" Peter had asked Carlotta hopefully. She did, but he was not scheduled to speak in Philadelphia any time soon, to Peter's immense regret.

The abolitionists, delighted to meet him, invited Peter to address their assemblies and so did the colored churches. Every Sunday he attended Bethel A.M.E. Church and learned that they had been connected to Denmark Vesey's church in Charleston. The northern clergy accused of exporting insurrection had been from Philadelphia's Mother Bethel.

"Steal away," Peter sang along with the congregation. "I ain't got long to stay here . . ."

Carlotta also introduced him to black men who had been active with the Underground Railroad, traveling to the South time and again and escaping with bands of slaves. Peter developed a particular liking for Manuel Stone who had spent several months in jail for being in the vanguard of a mob storming a courthouse to free a runaway slave.

"As I recollect," Stone told him, "there was a young white man at my side by the name of Thomas Higginson. He spent some time in jail, too. He's now the commander of a colored regiment in South Carolina. You're from those parts, have you ever run across him?"

"Indeed I has . . . have." Peter was delighted at the coincidence. "Colonel Higginson is a grand fellow." He smilingly recalled how many times he had tried to join his regiment.

All of Peter's audiences, white and black, implored him to recount the abduction of the *Swanee* and his subsequent wartime experience. He in turn implored them to send funds and supplies to the Sea Islands for the relief of the contrabands who were still escaping to the Union side.

As it turned out, Turno had been right about Bite. He refused to report to the Philadelphia quartermaster to be assigned to a ship returning to Hilton Head. "I ain't going back," he had balked. "I is scared every minute the Sesesh gon get hold of me again. I is gon put some space between us." Peter could not talk him out of his resolve to get to Canada and they parted company for perhaps the last time.

"Have you ever read a book, Mr. Mango?"

"A bit of the Bible."

Julian Breed looked at him with unbridled disgust. "I have quite an extensive library and if you would . . ."

"I ain't interested."

"*Ain't.* Mr. Mango?"

"That's right, Mistuh Breed."

Peter was adamant. He had peeped at his teacher's books— Chaucer, Byron, Virgil—and had decided against them. His interest was newspapers, read voraciously: the Philadelphia *Bulletin* and *Press* and, whenever he came across one, *The New York Times* or the *Tribune*. He read aloud to his tutor the reports on the progress of the war at the various fronts, hunting for items about colored men, his pronunciation caustically corrected.

A headline about a Negro cavalry caught his attention one afternoon, and in his slow halting voice he read the article out loud. " 'The First and Second Regiments of Colored Cavalry under Colonel West made a dash across the Chickahominy River and two companies dismounted and charged into the camp of the Forty-sixth Virginia Cavalry killing thirty men and capturing thirty-five horses. The horses were immediately mounted by our troops who pursued the Rebels to within ten miles of Richmond.'

"Ain't . . . isn't that grand, Mr. Breed?"

"The word is 'cavalry,' Mr. Mango. The 'v' comes before the 'l.' We are not talking about Christ at Calvary. How many times must I tell you that?"

Desperately, Peter said, "That's from Horace Greeley's paper. He wrote 'bout me more than once."

"So I am aware."

Peter was deflated, having hoped that being called a courageous credit to his race by the prestigious editor would impress his teacher. He tried again.

"And I seen President Lincoln in the White House."

"You saw him, Mr. Mango."

"Yes I did. Which is more than you can say."

Mr. Breed raised his eyes heavenward for guidance. "Your friend the President is in serious trouble."

Such pessimism was not the tutor's alone but widespread this election year. The daily newspapers were full of it. The war was not proceeding well for the Union on the battlefield and criticism of Mr. Lincoln was rampant. The nation was war-weary. The Copperheads, Southern sympathizers, were screaming for peace and an end to Negro emancipation.

When Peter visited Carlotta one afternoon she showed him part of a letter Mr. Lincoln had written to his critics.

> . . . There are now in the service of the United States nearly two hundred thousand able-bodied colored men, most of them under arms, defending and acquiring Union territory. Abandon all the forts now garrisoned by black men, take two hundred thousand men from our side and put them in the battlefield or corn field against us, and we would be compelled to abandon the war in three weeks.
>
> . . . Freedom has given us two hundred thousand men, raised on southern soil. It will give us more yet. Just so much it has abstracted from the enemy. Let my enemies prove to the country that the destruction of slavery is not necessary to the restoration of the Union. I will abide the issue.

In his mind Peter saw Lincoln as he had been when they met in Washington. The long melancholy face, eyes sunk in dark wells, sad eyes that mirrored the nation's pain.

"It's a grand thing the President is saying." Never mind that Mr. Lincoln had once pushed colonization, which he no longer mentioned, and had been initially resistant to Negroes in the military. All that had changed.

Carlotta, also anxious about Mr. Lincoln's reelection, echoed Peter's tutor. "Our President is in trouble."

The Republican Party was in disarray, the radicals at odds with Mr. Lincoln's lenient amnesty program for the reconstructed southern states, particularly Louisiana where recently freed Negroes had been denied the ballot. Militant blacks, including Frederick Douglass, supported John Frémont for president on a platform of equal rights for Negroes.

"We're in a dilemma," Carlotta sighed. "Mr. Lincoln is too conservative for some people and too radical for others. Split the Republican vote and the Democrats will waltz into the White House."

Peter mentioned his worry about the election in a letter to Rain. She seemed to have recovered from her melancholia and with the help of the schoolmaster sent loving messages to him regularly. He also wrote to Chloe, using his newly learned grammar and penmanship, but received no reply which made him wonder if his letter had reached her.

The news became oppressive when Peter read a newspaper item about a sergeant in Jacksonville, Florida. One Alfred Turno. The newspaper reported that the sentence of the court-martial was to be carried out the following morning. It had come to this, Peter thought, horrified.

Jacksonville, Florida
October 1864

Alfred Turno stood motionless, a block of granite, a tic in his jaw the only indication of his distress. White soldiers filled his immediate range of vision. Beyond them a ring of black faces grimaced in anger and frustration. This event was for their benefit. Watch, listen, and learn. Death is a grim teacher.

Ironically, it was the success of their raid on Baldwin that had led to this moment. Sergeant Turno's company had been liberally praised by the brigadier general commanding the expedition. The troops under his command comprised three black regiments and an Ohio mounted infantry. The Baldwin raid had been a flank movement. To reach the enemy's rear they had sailed twenty-five miles up St. Johns River to Black Creek and then another four miles to an obscure landing in the woods. Due to a lack of steamers it had taken three days to reach this juncture.

Turno's column, in the advance unit under a major, was crossing a rickety floating bridge made of fence rails when hell came to visit. Sesesh cavalrymen, skirmishing on foot, attacked them from the rear.

"Advance," the major bellowed.

"Advance," Turno roared, turning his soldiers around. With a blood-curdling scream, they rushed their enemy, firing their weapons. "Remember Fort Pillow," a black corporal yelled into the astonished face of a Confederate soldier before shooting him dead. The massacre at Fort Pillow had become a war cry for black soldiers, making them fight more ferociously to avoid being captured. "Remember Fort Pillow." Sergeant Turno cracked open a gray-eyed man's skull with the butt of his gun, grunting, "That one's for Bryant. This one's for me." It was over in minutes, the counter-attack so fierce that the Rebel skirmishers turned and ran. Then a thunderous rumbling shook the ground. Galloping horses. The Ohio Mounted Squad was pursuing the enemy into the woods.

Several Rebels lay wounded or dead on the bridge. Twenty more were captured, discovering to their mortification that the majority of the enemy troops were colored. Union casualties were four wounded.

On their march to Baldwin, the Union troops built a bridge over the north branch of Black Creek, swollen by recent rains, and drove their wagon trains, artillery and caissons across it. They burned the trestle works on the railroads, stranding locomotives and trains, forcing the enemy to evacuate Baldwin and another camp in the still of the night. By the time the Union soldiers arrived, the area was abandoned except for a quantity of forage the Confederates had left behind in their precipitous flight. Horses. Wagons. Artillery. And a dozen Negroes. The able-bodied men were speedily inducted into the army.

The brigadier general, pleased with the raid on Baldwin, told his officers its results. They had broken up the rail transportation of blockade-run goods. The abundant supply of corn and cattle from the surrounding counties intended to feed the Confederate Army was now within their control. "As for our prisoners, we will try to exchange them only for colored men."

Sergeant Turno listened with a stony face. On a previous raid they had burned down three Sesesh plantations—whose owners were all in the military, a large grist mill, a storehouse and two bridges. That time they had brought out 119 Negroes, over a hundred bales of cotton and four mules.

For Sergeant Turno, drilling his men in camp, the combination was proving deadly—their success in freeing slaves, acquiring cotton, Sesesh prisoners and praise—all of it was choking him. The white soldiers in their brigade were paid almost twice as much as the Negroes were offered. And none of those white boys had a son that had been snatched back into slavery. Turno halted the drilling and addressed his squad, enumerating their grievances. They had been treated like trash long enough.

Like we ain't up to the mark of white soldiers what march along with us. But don't we do more fatigue duty? And fight the Sesesh good as them? Even more ferociously? Remember Fort Pillow. But the army say we is niggers. Insults our manhood. Let they families go hungry 'cause they cain't send no money home.

His squad grumbled in agreement, their black faces grim. They marched behind him to their commander's tent and laid down their arms, refused further duty until they received the same pay as white soldiers of equal rank. Warned of the consequences, Sergeant Turno refused to retrieve his arms and was arrested. At his court-martial he was found guilty of mutiny, mutinous conduct, conduct prejudicial to good order and military discipline, and was sentenced to death by execution.

Alfred Turno refused a blindfold. He wanted to see the faces of his executioners. Five white men raising their rifles. Why wasn't there a drum roll? Why wasn't a bugle blowing taps? A condemned man should at least hear his own funeral dirge. He took a last look at the greenness of the trees, at the blueness of the sky and knew what melody he longed to hear. "Bryant," he sang out loudly moments before a barrage of bullets hit him. "Bryant, Bryant, Bry——"

A few days after Alfred Turno was buried, Congress passed a bill equalizing the pay of Negro servicemen.

Philadelphia
November 1864

As the day of the election grew nearer even Abraham Lincoln despaired of winning. The nation he led was plainly war-weary, their faith in him and his army commander badly shaken. General Grant's campaign to defeat General Lee's army in the Virginia Wilderness not only failed but the casualties were staggering. Fifty thousand men returned home in pieces or in sacks. On other fronts the Confederates were victorious. And General Sherman's troops, although fighting fiercely, appeared to be stalled in their approach to Atlanta.

It had been a terrible year. An expedition into the interior of Florida had failed. At Fort Pillow in Louisiana, Negro soldiers and their white officers were massacred after the fort had surrendered to the Confederates. Reports were surfacing that the treatment of Union prisoners, particularly at Andersonville Prison in Georgia, was tantamount to murder, the jailer boasting that he had killed more Yankees than General Lee. The North was demoralized.

As a gesture of conciliation Mr. Lincoln had chosen for his running mate a southern Democrat, Andrew Johnson, the fiery Tennessee governor. A war patriot, he had made his mark by thundering that treason must be made odious, that the oligarchy of wealthy planters whose power had so degraded poor whites, as he himself had been, must end. He advocated breaking up the huge plantations, the base of planter power, and punishing the architects of the rebellion. The land should be sold to small farmers, black and white, and he promised to be a Moses leading the abused Negroes to the promised land.

At their convention the Democrats nominated General George McClellan for president, Abraham Lincoln's former army chief, fired twice for failing to vigorously prosecute the war. His platform declared the war a failure, called for peace and opposed the emancipation of the slaves. Copperheads, pacifists and plain folks weary of the hardships of war were flocking in droves to General McClellan's standard.

Depressed and apprehensive, Peter sought solace at the shipyard.

265

For once he did not berate the workmen but sat on a bench staring at the steamboat. If General McClellan was elected . . . it was too frightening to contemplate. It could all come to naught, their flight to freedom on the sturdy steamer. He could be returned to slavery. And his family. And all of the contrabands. Millions of them. But how could that happen? They would have to kill him.

The Democrats' platform was so chilling it forced the Republican Party to close ranks. Its radicals and malcontents raced back into the fold to work vigorously to reelect Mr. Lincoln. Frémont withdrew from the race. Frederick Douglass came in from the cold. And General William Tecumseh Sherman came through on the battlefield.

"Atlanta is ours," he wired the President and a jubilant Union. Other news of successful counterattacks in Virginia's Shenandoah Valley followed. Reinvigorated, its spirits raised, the North was now anxious to decisively defeat the enemy. Let us surge on to victory with Abraham Lincoln. In November he won reelection by a landslide.

Peter, deliriously happy, was given another present. The workmen finally finished overhauling the *Swanee*. A crew was assembled and he told his Philadelphia friends good-bye.

"I hope in the future you won't disgrace me," Julian Breed said primly in farewell.

"I cain't promise any such thing," Peter replied, "since I'm known to be an imbecile."

His teacher did not contradict him.

As the *Swanee* steamed down the Delaware River, Peter and his crew were infected with a new anxiety which was troubling the Union. General Sherman and his sixty thousand seasoned soldiers had cut their lines of communication and disappeared into the Deep South. In the absence of news to the contrary, rumors spread that the troops were starving in the woods, surrounded by the Sesesh, forced to surrender. Daily the North waited for word from their beleaguered army. They waited in vain.

22

On the March in Georgia
November 1864

General William Tecumseh Sherman's army, sixty thousand seasoned soldiers, grouped into a right and left wing composed of two corps each, the cavalry division separate. Twenty-five hundred white-topped wagons each pulled by a six-mule team. Six hundred ambulances with two horses each. Sixty-five heavy guns, the caissons and forges drawn by four teams of horses. A goodly supply of beef cattle and oxen on the hoof totaling thirty-five thousand animals, including mules and horses. A pioneer corps of two hundred able-bodied Negroes for each division, not soldiers but laborers promised ten dollars a month. The troops travel by four parallel roads converging at stated points, each soldier carrying forty pounds of ammunition. Trailing behind them is another vast army— black folks on foot, in oxcarts, astride swayback critters. An enterprising daddy rides on a blanket-covered mule. Four pockets are sewn on the blanket, two on each side, a small child stuck in each pouch. A wagon pulled by a lame horse is home to a dozen children. Their parents walk on either side, carrying pots and utensils and bundles of clothing, their own and a suit or dress their fleeing owners had left behind.

"Lazarus." A running boy is called, halted in his tracks by his mother's voice. "Don't get lost, chile. I ain't want to leave you behind."

This black horde, to General Sherman's dismay, attaches itself to him as his army departs from Atlanta. Under a flag of truce with the Confederate general, the city is evacuated, its residents sent farther south in order for Tecumseh Sherman to shorten his lines of defense and so that the poor people will not starve. Then everything considered of use to the enemy is destroyed. The engineer corps blows up the railroad bridge and telegraph wires, cutting off the Confederates' line of communication and the Yankees' as well. Mills and stores, factories and cotton gins, warehouses and the railroad depot are blow up. Ammunition exploding in an arsenal sets fire to several blocks. Overnight Atlanta becomes an inferno.

Ahead of General Sherman's army sprawls three hundred miles of hostile enemy territory to be conquered, dependent upon the Yankees' own resources, their supply lines broken. Behind them are the Union armies of the Cumberland, Tennessee and Ohio, also under Sherman's jurisdiction, who are expected to keep the Confederates off his tail while General Grant holds Lee's army at bay in Richmond.

General Sherman's troops leave Atlanta while it is still smoldering, their covered wagons spanning five miles of road. It is then that they start coming. The black horde. Brother. Sister. Put down that hoe and pick up you feet. Freedom is passing by. They cross the swamps and bayous, deserting massa's corn and cotton fields carrying little or nothing in their hands but the ache to be free. General Sherman, sitting erect on his black stallion, looking fierce with his slitted eyes and the lean face of a fox, counsels: "Stay put. Winning the war will bring you freedom. Don't slow down my army with your empty mouths." The blacks listen respectfully and keep on putting their feet in the road. Why wait? Freedom now.

Joyfully they lead the Yankee soldiers to massa's granaries and silos and smokehouses. Army trucks are filled with whatever the mills yield, sheaves of corn to feed the horses, sacks of clean rice to feed the men. The troops empty the cattle sheds, the smokehouses and cellars, unearthing barrels of flour and lard. "We will have fresh baked bread tonight," they crow, foraging for survival, ransacking deserted homes. Massa has fled so recently that his boots are still warm. "They fit," a grateful Yankee chuckles.

The soldiers then invade the slave quarters. Five turkey hens peck in the dirt in front of Vergie Owens's house. An unlit corncob pipe is in the old woman's mouth and her head is wrapped in a piece of burlap.

"Them's my turkeys," she tells the soldiers. She's a dairy woman

who was allowed to work on her own after completing her master's tasks.

A sergeant raises his pistol. Takes dead aim.

"Massa, you cain't shoot my hens."

He pulls the trigger.

The soldiers take Vergie's all. Twenty-two turkeys. Sixty fowls. Three hundred pounds of honey. Fifteen gallons of syrup. Fifty pounds of lard. And her blankets.

"You all is leaving me to starve?" she wails, not believing her eyes. "To freeze to death?"

"Join the others, auntie, marching behind us," a soldier suggests.

General Sherman discourages that. He wants only able-bodied men as scouts and pioneers and teamsters, and able-bodied women employed as servants and cooks. Some of the more comely ones become the favorites of officers who shower them with gifts while contributing to the growing population of mulattoes.

"I cain't go with you," Vergie wails. "Massa done hide my granchile somewhere 'cause she seed where he buried his silver and he scared she gon tell you Yankees. I got to stay here and pray that girl comes home. And you all is leaving me to starve?"

Farther down the road Willie Williams grins at the soldiers and tells them: "Massa try to frighten us. He say you Yankees gon put us in front of the battle and kill us if we don't fight. And throw our women and children in the Ocmulgee River. Massa say when the Yankees come, run hide in the woods. But he cain't put that over on us 'cause we knows a heap better. What for Yankees want to hurt black folks? Massa ain't no friend and hates the Yankees. So I is you all's best friend."

This best friend had hid an escaping Yankee soldier and just last week had helped two Rebels who were deserting to the Union side. He had fed them as they were being passed from black hand to black hand to safety.

The foragers commandeer Willie Williams's wagon, hitch it to his horse and make him load it. They relieve him of eight hundred pounds of bacon, fifteen stock hogs, seven head of cattle, twenty-one pounds of clean rice, twenty-five chickens, thirty ducks, his little hoard of money hidden in an earthen jar, and all of his clothes.

"Hey," he protests. "Them's my last pair of trousers."

"Nigger, you're wearing your last pair."

"You ain't leave me nothin to live on." Crying, Willie Williams follows his loaded wagon down the road.

And still they come. The black horde. Sailing down the Ogeechee in dugouts and canoes. Riding in donkey carts. Skirting the marshes on foot. Those who can't keep up the brutal trek of ten to twelve miles a day fall behind. Children are scattered. Lost. A father solves that problem by tying a rope around his five children and himself and two strays. Crossing a creek a passel of Negroes drown when one of Sherman's generals hauls up the pontoon bridge leaving them stranded.

And still the black horde comes. Negro scouts traveling with the advance guard fell trees and make corduroy roads. They construct rifle trenches and repair bridges the enemy has blown up. They lift cannons, caissons and stalled wagons out of the mud. They uproot railroad ties and twist them into knots around trees, destroying three hundred miles of Confederate track. When attacked by the Sesesh the scouts reach for their Springfield rifles and return the enemy's fire.

It is total warfare. Scorched earth warfare. In their march across the state of Georgia, Sherman's army destroys everything the Confederates can put to military use. Residences are spared unless they belong to high military officials who are considered traitors responsible for this bloody war. Savagely their property is burned to the ground. Houses. Mills. Barns.

Scorching the earth is practiced by the fleeing Confederates also.

Milledgeville. Governor Brown and the state officials flee, deserting the poorer citizens. Brown dismantles the governor's mansion, piles his loot into railway cars, leaving behind muskets and ammunition which General Sherman confiscates before blowing up the arsenal.

Sandersville. A Rebel brigade driven out by Yankee skirmishers sets fire to stacks of fodder in the field and a row of dwellings.

Fort McAllister. The Rebels mine it heavily with torpedoes. Sherman's troops assault and capture the fort.

Savannah. The Rebels blow up their ironclads and their navy yard before fleeing from the city.

General Sherman's army has marched from Atlanta to the sea, cutting the Confederacy in half and demolishing Georgia's railroad system. It took forty days. Sixty thousand seasoned soldiers. Thirty-five thousand animals. Two hundred black pioneers per division. And the vast horde trailing behind them has swelled to ten thousand black souls.

"Lazarus," a woman's voice cries out, agitated. *"Boy, where you be?"*

"I is right here, Mammy."

He had not been lost or left behind.

On Christmas eve General Sherman sends President Lincoln a wire. *"I beg to present you, as a Christmas gift, the city of Savannah, with one hundred and fifty guns and plenty of ammunition, also about twenty-five thousand bales of cotton."*

Beaufort
December 1864

The *Swanee* made the trip home from Philadelphia without incident. Simultaneously with the news of Savannah's capitulation, Peter arrived in Beaufort. He was too excited to wait for the sun to rise and reached home in the dead of night.

"Honeybunch, I is home," he cried, racing up the stairs.

He opened their bedroom door. Rain was standing there in her nightdress, looking tiny and shivering. Reverently, Peter gathered her in his arms. He wanted to laugh, he wanted to cry. He was home.

"Peter," she murmured against his cheek. "I ain't dreaming? It's you?" She pulled back to scrutinize him, to touch his face, his scraggly beard. They kissed, Peter lifting Rain up off the floor, holding her against him.

"It's been so long," she moaned, clinging to him, her upturned face rapturous.

Tonight, he knew, she would not desert him for her washtub. They made love and talked and made love again, the sweetness so incredible that his hunger could not be fed.

Abruptly Peter's leave was canceled. Every available boat was needed to transport General Sherman's troops from Savannah to Beaufort and from there to a secret battlefront which only he and General Grant knew. It had to be Charleston, Peter speculated along with everyone else. The war was finally drawing to a close.

That afternoon, Peter's last day in Beaufort, Rain was late coming home from work. Glory arrived from school alone. At five she had lost her chubby baby fat and was pretty like her mother, Peter thought, but also managed miraculously to resemble him. His sunshine child. He hugged her, squeezed her until she was giggling and wiggling in his arms.

"Mamma stopped at the colored hospital," she told him, "to leave some molasses."

The wounded were sent to Beaufort from the battlefields and the islanders were conscientious contributors of foodstuff. As the day waned, Peter became peevish. This was his last evening at home and his wife had disappeared. That woman was so peculiar.

Lily fed him and inquired, "What's Rain doing at the hospital so long?"

"How would I know?" he snapped and tramped upstairs to his bedroom.

A few minutes later Rain came home, raced up the steps and confronted Peter angrily, her chest heaving.

"Rain, where you been so long?"

"At the hospital. And walking." She spat the words at him like bullets. "I was at the hospital talking to Chloe."

Peter died. His brain refused to function, to order speech. The silence in the room was an admission of guilt that finally forced him to mumble "Chloe?" His raised eyebrows questioned whether he knew anyone so named.

Rain jogged his memory. "Chloe Harrison. That whore you been keeping company with right here under my nose."

Peter was stupefied. "What nonsense is you talking?" In his confusion his speech reverted to the familiar.

Agitated, Rain waved her hands in the air. "You cain't lie you way out of this."

"Please. What is you talking 'bout?"

Rain told him. She had gone to the hospital to leave a jug of molasses for the soldiers who dearly loved their sweetened water. "I gave it to this nurse and she is thanking me when this soldier hobbles into the waiting room on crutches. He done lost a leg but smiles when he sees her. 'Miss Chloe,' he says. 'Bless my eyes is that you?' He so happy to see her he keeps on babbling. 'Ain't this something,' he say. 'Ain't this nice. Here we is together again.

272

I hear that Captain Mango is home, too. I was his gunner.' Then the soldier winks at me. 'We were all in love with Miss Chloe on Folly Island,' he say, 'but it were Captain Mango what won out.' ' "

Peter felt a wild flicker of hope. "Is that what set you off, Rain? In a way of speaking we was all in love with Chloe 'cause she was so kind. But that don't mean . . ."

"You laid up with her," Rain yelled. "That hussy's face fell apart when I told her I is you wife. The man limped away, having done his mischief, and I ast her straight out and she ain't deny it. 'Yes,' she said. 'Yes,' like she had no shame."

Peter's mind was racing. What was Chloe doing here? And what exactly had she said, damn her. "Rain, listen." To what? his mind screamed. You gon tell her the truth? "Honeybunch, listen. I loves you like I ain't never loved another woman. You has got to believe me. I ain't gon lie and say it didn't happen but it was on account of the war. All that bloodshed and dying cuts a man down to the bone. Makes him study heself and wonder what life's all about. Who's the most precious person in it. If I didn't know it before I knew it then. It was you. Everywhere I went I asked God to keep me alive to get back to you. It were a terrible lonesomeness. So desolate. So when Chloe come along, she were just stepping in for you. I wasn't touching her but you. I wasn't calling her name but yours. 'Cause you is the only woman I does want. The only woman I does love. Chloe knew that. It made her sad but she knew it. Please believe me. It was the war. It took you beyond the reach of my arms and——"

"The war," Rain interrupted harshly, "ain't an excuse for everything."

"I'm just trying to explain . . ."

"You ain't the only one been in a war. I been in one since the day I was born. And my mamma and daddy, too. I is my daddy's chile, dark like him, but my brothers is as creamy as clabber."

Defiantly Rain stared at Peter who felt disaster settling in his bones. "I don't know what you is talking 'bout," he whispered.

She dragged her eyes away from his and striding to the window slammed the blinds shut. When she turned around her face was stony.

"Let me tell you what I is talkin 'bout 'cause I don't want you to die ignorant. Every time Massa Archer come to our shack, Mamma made Daddy and we chil'ren go out to the woodshed."

Peter fell into the chair before his legs collapsed. He didn't want to hear any more.

"Mamma was always after Massa to take we chil'ren out of the fields. Me and my brother Tonk went up to work in the Big House once but Missy seeing how much he looked like she own son, Raleigh, scream at Massa to get them mongrel niggers out of her house." Angrily, Rain looked at Peter who cringed.

In a calmer voice she continued, "So me and Tonk went back to the slave quarters and tried to keep out of sight. Mamma kept at Massa till he finally apprentice Tonk and my next brother to a printer in town. So they is gone and when Massa Archer drops by they is less of us to trot out to the woodshed with my daddy. We used to sit there, me and him, crying. He were a big man, so strong he could swing my mamma off she feet which he loved to do. It poked holes in me to see him cry like that."

Rain stopped talking and sat down on the bed. She stared at the worn green carpet as if it was grass, the wild grass in the woods bordering the slave quarters where she had lived.

Peter said, "Why you ain't tell me all this before? 'Bout you mulatto brothers?"

"There's more," Rain said coldly. "I was 'bout eleven years old when Massa come to the house one night. Me and Daddy was going out the door to the woodshed when Massa reach out and pat my behind. God, why he do that? My daddy give one terrible yell and knocking Massa down jump on top of him. He is choking Massa and Mamma screaming, 'Stop it.' She grabs the iron skillet and hits Daddy over the head, hollering, 'Kill him and you is a dead man, too.' Daddy knows he is already dead so he get up and run. Two hours later the bloodhounds catch him in the woods. They tear out his throat."

Tears were streaming down Rain's face. Peter could not bear to look at her. He studied his hands which were large and calloused. As large as her father's who had committed suicide by beating up his owner?

"We didn't see Massa for a long time after that. Almost a year. He took Missy to London and Raleigh went off to college. Come summer they both is home and Massa Archer in we shack again.

But Mamma ain't forgot Daddy. 'You promised me,' she tell Massa. 'Long ago you promised not to sell or beat my husband. Instead you killed him.'

"Massa say, 'He attacked me. I had to send the posse after him.'

"Mamma is staring at him like she cain't understand this man what done father three of her chil'ren. She say, 'I wants you to free all my chil'ren. You hear?'

"Massa ain't say nothing for a spell then he nods.

" 'Put it in writing,' Mamma say though she cain't read. Then she tell me to take my brothers out to the woodshed.

"The next day she warn me to keep out of Massa's sight. 'He promise me he ain't gon touch you but when you see him coming run. Hide in the hog pen. Wallow in the slop with the pigs so you be so nasty he don't want to touch you.'

"I didn't get a chance to hide in the pigpen. That very same night Raleigh come busting through we door, big and thick like he daddy. He look at Mamma. He look at me. He say, 'My father tells me there's some good pussy in this shack. Which one of you will it be?'

"Me and Mamma look at each other, scared. Then she tell me, 'Take you brothers out to the shed.'

"I hate her then 'cause she ain't fighting Raleigh like I craves to do. We coulda hit him over the head with the axe and bury him out in the woods. He was touching her 'fore we were halfway out the door. I sat in the shed hating him. Hating Mamma.

"The next night it were my turn. I was coming home from the fields where we'd been hoeing. I was a quarter hand. Our shack was a piece away from the others, Massa had seen to that. You had to cross a li'l old gully and that's where Raleigh grabbed me. I screamed, kicking and squirming, trying to get loose and him laughing till I bit his hand. He let me go then and socked me so hard I fell down. He dragged me into the brush, my face scraping along the ground. I was hollering so he banged my head against a rock and smother my mouth with one hand, the other one hitting me. 'Shut up,' he say, 'I is gon fuck you, dead or alive. Which way it gon be?'

"I try to shove him offa me but I is pinned to the ground. His fist knocks my head sideways. Blood runs down my nose, into my mouth. Then it come, the god-awful pain. An axe chopping wild inside of me. I bite his hand and scream and see the rock in his hand aimed at my head. I don't remember nothing more till it over and he gone. Blood's running down my leg. I cain't crawl 'cause it hurt too much. Finally, Mamma and some mens from the quarters find me. Carry me home. Mamma, she crying. One of the men he crying, too.

"We left alone again for a spell after that. Missy and Massa Archer gone to Virginia and Raleigh return to college. Me and Mamma babies born a week apart. Petunia come first, the midwife helping Mamma with the birthing. Then Mamma help me when my time come. Both of them babies pale as tallow. I hate it before Zee was born, a foreign thing growing big in me that I didn't want. But the baby herself, so scrawny and helpless, how can I help but love her? Me and Mamma name we babies after flowers 'cause people be so evil. I name mine Pansy but she so little I just called her Zee. Mamma say, 'I didn't want this to happen to you like it happen to me. I tried to keep them offa you. But never mind 'bout Raleigh. You is the mamma. Pansy's you chile.' We didn't know for sure who Petunia's daddy was but Mamma reckoned it was Raleigh, too, since Massa seemed only good for making boy chil'ren.

"I prayed that they would never return. Let they carriage tumble off the bridge. Let them drown. Let somebody shoot them. I didn't care how they died if only they didn't come back. But they did. We heard that Raleigh was 'bout to get married to some girl from Virginia. He come down to we shack one night, looked at the babies, smiled and left. I thanked God. It were over. Raleigh was moving to Virginia with his bride. But I thanked God too soon.

"I was alone in our shack when Massa Archer rode by on horseback one afternoon. He come inside and stood right in front of the door trapping me in there. There wasn't no window to jump through. No hole in the floor to scramble into.

"He say, 'Take off your clothes so I can see what you look like now that you is a woman grown.'

"I say, 'Mamma coming home directly.'

"He say, 'She's way down by the mill. I just left her there.'

" 'I ain't takin off nothing,' I say, wondering how I could get around him and into the pig trough.

"He snatches me. I is fighting him but it get me nothing but some hard knocks up beside my head. I is being bloodied again. Broken into again. When he finish with me and leave, I know what I has to do. I ain't a little bitty girl no more, but a woman grown. I is a mother.

"I march myself up to the Big House. It were all lit up and through the window I could see Missy sitting in the parlor reading. I walked right in through the garden door, my face bleeding, my clothes half torn off. She a tall woman with a long face, a Christian woman who goes to church every Sunday and lets us slaves sit in the gallery. Some masters said we didn't need religion but Missy said it was they duty to civilize the heathens.

"She jumped up when she see me. 'What's this?' she say.

" 'It's Rain,' I say, 'what has you son's baby and maybe Massa's too 'cause he done jump on me and my mamma. Keep them offa us, Missy, or I is gon throw we babies down the well and myself, too. We dead bodies gon poison the water. Poison the fields.'

"Missy throw back her head and gave one long piercing scream. I liked the sound of it and what it did do. Footsteps start up all over the place. Doors slam and folks came a-running. Black folks from the kitchen. The garden. The outhouse. Massa and Raleigh come crashing down the stairs. What a powerful scream. I would like to own it.

"Massa Archer see me and come to a dead stop. He is horrified but not as horrified as Missy. 'This girl is still a child,' she say, pointing a long finger at me. She slaps Massa's face, damns him for corrupting Raleigh who is coming at me snarling. 'You black bitch,' he said. Missy yell, 'Don't you dare touch her.' He stops, scared of his mamma who is calling them both dip-shit no-count scoundrels sleeping with the same nigger wenches and bringing that nastiness home to her.

" 'Sweetheart, Mother,' her menfolks plead. 'Calm youself down before you has a stroke.' Missy howls that she hates slavery. It's done turned them into a race of thieves and murderers. And she hates niggers, too. Try and civilize them and this is your reward.

" 'Mother dear. Sweetheart.' They circle round Missy, clucking like hens, trying to quiet her down. Cook runs to fetch the smelling salts and since nobody is paying me no nevermind I ease out the door. Missy done made it plain. She hates niggers. Especially Mamma and me.

"Next week her brother come down from Charleston. Missy done send for him. She tell him to clean out that brood in our cabin or she gon burn it to the ground herself. Our massa ain't say nothing but let us all be sold, scattered in different directions. Missy's brother buy me. Petunia and Zee sent to a nursery farm on James Island. My little brothers gone I don't know where. Tonk and Jamie snatched from the printer and sold. And Massa tear up our freedom papers. All I know 'bout Mamma is that my new owner told me later that she had died."

Rain walked to the window and stared out into the night. She did not know the details of her mother's death, that Elizabeth had been sold to a farmer and his wife who had a small spread but were unable to make her work. They sat her down before the cow. She would not milk it. They put her before the loom. She would not thread it. They hitched her to the plow. She would not pull it. They beat her, locked her in the barn for a week where the rats gnawed on her toes in the dark. But nothing prevailed. Disgusted, the farmer tried to sell her to a trader who refused to be tricked. "Take her to the asylum," he advised. "The wench is crazy." Insensitive to floggings, numb and dumb, the wench died.

Rain turned away from the window and exhausted, slumped down on the bed. Not knowing what else to do, Peter knelt beside her and reached for her hand. It was limp. Lifeless.

"I want to strangle somebody," he mumbled. The room offered up no sacrificial lamb in place of Archer and his son, Raleigh. Peter buried his head in Rain's lap. "I love you," he declared. "That's the only thing what matters." He looked up and touched her face gently. "But why you ain't tell me all this before?"

Rain answered wearily, "Same reason why you didn't tell me 'bout Chloe."

Peter stood up, the room suddenly crowded. Archer and Raleigh were camped on the rug. And Zee and Petunia. And Chloe. They were a brick wall that was looming up so high, Peter despaired of ever climbing over it. He stared at Rain, uncertain how to handle this terrible crisis. Did he know this woman he was married to at all? Who had lain beside him for years never revealing this secret until now?

Rain unbuttoned her dress and took it off. "It were my fault

Mamma had Petunia. She was tired of having babies. It was my turn."

"No," Peter protested. "You were still a child."

"I shoulda lived in that pigsty like she told me, then none of this would've happen. But I run to Missy like a dummy. Mamma never ran but did what she had to. I'm the one got us all sold. That's why she died. Her chil'ren all scattered. Her husband dead. All she went through for nothing 'cause she had a daughter what couldn't carry her own load."

"Stop it," Peter pleaded. "None of it was your fault."

"Then I broke my bargain with God. I told Him let Zee and Petunia stay close by so's I can see them and I'll never ask for nothing else. You can have the rest of my life. Then along you come, Peter, and I did want something else. You." Rain was wringing her hands as though she were wringing out laundry. "I was happy with you, Peter. You was so manly. Then the girls were gone. Sold. And I liked to have gone mad. But I had you. Then Glory and Peewee. So I told God, awright. It's a fair exchange. I'll keep what I have and let the girls go. But I got to hungering for them again. And ain't He punish me for that? He take away Peewee. And now you."

"I ain't taken," Peter yelled, standing over her. He grabbed Rain by the shoulders, forced her to look at him. "I never loved Chloe. Only you. And God ain't punishing you. Peewee died 'cause there was an epidemic. You has got to stop thinking . . ."

She pulled away from him. "It's done between us, Peter."

"No," he howled. "Never."

"I has got to leave you."

He shook his head. "I won't let you. Chloe . . ."

"She ain't in it," Rain stared past him. "I has got to go back to my bargain with God. There ain't gon be no peace otherwise. I cain't deny Zee no longer. God is punishing me."

Peter sighed. "Why you keep bringing God into it? And you didn't deny Zee. You told me 'bout her."

"But not that her daddy was white. You ain't gon forgive me for that."

Could he? Peter wondered. Was there mingled in his murderous rage at her owners anger toward her, too? "There ain't nothing to forgive," he insisted to her and to himself, "except that you didn't tell me sooner."

" 'Cause you is funny 'bout mulattoes," Rain reminded him.

He wanted to yell, You lied to me, said Zee's father was a black man, a slave. But because of his involvement with Chloe he didn't dare.

Rain took a deep breath and expelled it slowly. "Last week I went to see Maum Betty. She threw the bones and saw them. Two li'l sad-eye gals."

"I ain't gon let you go, Rain."

"Maum Betty seen them on a boat. And she told me I is got to——"

"Leave me?" Peter shouted furiously. "Is that what she said? I don't give a monkey's shit for all that voodoo."

Rain sucked her teeth. "Everybody's got they own voodoo. Some folks wears a cross to ward off evil spirits. Others drink wine and say it be Jesus's blood."

"Damn everybody else. It's Maum Betty's bones what's telling you to leave me."

"No, Peter. It's my own bones."

Wearily, they undressed and went to bed to argue for hours. Peter accused her of being spiteful, of punishing him for his infidelity. Rain insisted she was fulfilling her bargain with God. Peter cursed. He pleaded. They both wept.

Lily was not yet awake when Peter went to tell her good-bye early in the morning. He bent over her, noticing how much she had shriveled. She had always been a wiry woman with amazing strength in her hands but now she was spindly and flat. Her lips were parted, she was snoring gently.

Mamma. He felt like weeping. I ain't got you strength for lonesomeness and Rain wants to leave me. Hold on to her till I gets back. Pray the war ends and I be home soon. Don't let Rain go nowhere.

He walked around the bed and stared at Glory curled up in a knot sucking her thumb. Rain ain't gon take you from me, he vowed, his eyes filling with tears.

His bedroom was empty when Peter returned to it and for a

moment he panicked. He found Rain in the kitchen stirring a pot of grits with a wooden spoon.

"You got time for breakfast?"

"No. I has to leave right now."

Her eyes were puffed and swollen and she looked so forlorn Peter ached to hold her. Standing on shifting sand he desperately tried to find a toehold.

"Rain, I cain't live if you leave me. Please don't do nothing till I come back home. I'm going to look for Zee and Petunia. Everywhere I go, everybody I meet, I is gon ask them 'bout you chil'ren. If they live I'll find them."

"They ain't dead, Peter. Maum Betty seen them when she flung the bones."

Peter felt like flinging Maum Betty's bones into hell. "Promise me, baby cakes. Promise to wait till I comes back before you make any move."

Beneath his gaze Rain seemed to be hardly breathing. "Awright," she finally said. "I promise."

23

Savannah, Georgia
December 31, 1864

Looking like a gnome, Edwin Stanton, Secretary of War, sat at a long table between two aides, his long beard resting on his chest, his feet dangling inches above the floor. Peter was among the twenty Negroes sitting around the room facing Mr. Stanton. They were clergymen mainly, and an innkeeper, a tailor and several undertakers. They were Savannah's colored leaders except for Peter and a missionary from Pittsburgh. Most of them were former slaves.

The assembly was being held in an upstairs room of the spacious house General Sherman had chosen for his headquarters. He too was present, dressed in his battle fatigues, his unkempt beard adding to his rugged appearance. He was standing in front of a velvet-draped window, out of the limelight, allowing this to be Secretary Stanton's show.

Peter was surprised that Mr. Stanton remembered him and had sent a courier with a note inviting him to this meeting. It was a welcome respite, despondent as he was worrying that Rain might not keep her promise, that she and Glory would be gone by the time he returned home. Please God, he prayed, keep her there till I gets back. I'll do anything. Anything. Zee and Petunia were perhaps his only salvation. *If they live I'll find them.* Fear had wrenched that promise from him but the trail was cold. Already he had made inquiries, buttonholing field officers, captains, stewards, "Have you by any chance run across two little mulatto girls named Pansy and Petunia?" To date he had been stumbling around in a blind alley.

Edwin Stanton was also on a tour of inquiry in Savannah. He had already been in Beaufort visiting schools and plantations, talking directly to the former slaves, their superintendents and teachers. He concluded that the contrabands had made tremendous strides. They fought courageously as soldiers, worked industriously as laborers and learned rapidly as students.

And he agreed with the report of the Freedmen's Inquiry Commission founded to investigate how the Negroes' condition could be improved so they could protect themselves and be useful in prosecuting the war. The report recommended that the freedmen be taught self-reliance, receive regular wages to instill in them a sense of achievement, be settled on the abandoned plantations as workers, and be given every opportunity to buy their plots. Redistribution of the land was economically feasible for poor whites as well. A major drawback, the report noted, was the continued prejudice of Northerners against colored people, denounced by the commission as uncivilized and unpatriotic, giving aid and comfort to the enemy.

Shortly after Peter's arrival at the meeting, the Negroes chose as their spokesman a portly black man with gray side whiskers, Reverend Garrison Frazier, who had purchased his wife's freedom and his own twenty-five years ago. Systematically, the city fathers had threatened to close down his Baptist church, rumored to be a hotbed of insurrection. When introduced to Peter, he had clasped his hand warmly, making him feel welcome as a brother. "I understand," he said chuckling, "that the Sesesh wants you badly, dead or alive. It's an honor to have you here with us."

Mr. Stanton cleared his throat and formally began the meeting. "Thank you, gentlemen, for coming," he said, his voice gentler than Peter remembered. "I am desirous of making the best arrangements possible for the black refugees who have entered our Union lines. Their welfare is of the utmost importance not only to me but to the nation and so I thought to avail myself of your opinion regarding certain matters to guide me in my decisions."

Peter sat up straighter in his seat and glanced around at his companions. They had arrayed themselves in their Sunday best, black frock coats, striped trousers, their faces deadly sober. As Mr. Stanton posed his questions the aide at his side recorded the session verbatim.

Did the gentlemen understand the freedom given by the President's proclamation?

"Yes they did," Reverend Frazier responded, and the other men and Peter concurred. Freedom lifted them from under the yoke of bondage to where they could reap the fruit of their own labor, take care of themselves and assist the government in maintaining their freedom.

Squinting behind his spectacles, Mr. Stanton was surprised at their comprehension. Did they understand the enlistment of colored soldiers in the South by state agents?

The men nodded, they did indeed understand to their sorrow. Colored men were enlisted as substitutes, giving credit to the state. But for every black man enlisted by a state agent, a white man was left at home. And the bounties, promised by state agents, seldom reached the enlisted men who were often virtually kidnapped and even shot if they resisted. State agents should remain at home, Reverend Frazier concluded, and enlistments be made for the United States under the direction of General Sherman.

In answer to Mr. Stanton's query whether the slaves would fight for the Rebels if inducted into the Confederate Army, which was an ongoing rumor, the unanimous opinion was that they would desert to the Union at the first opportunity.

The secretary murmured, "I trust that your assumption is correct." It was a reasonable hope inasmuch as Confederate soldiers themselves were deserting to the Union by the thousands, entire companies crossing over into their lines. "Now please tell me," he said, "in what manner would you rather live, scattered among the whites or in colonies by yourselves?"

Peter looked at his comrades a trifle alarmed and read on their faces a similar concern. Was this a trick question? What exactly did Mr. Stanton have in mind? What did he intend to do with their homeless brethren?

"I would prefer it if we lived by ourselves," Reverend Frazier replied. "There is a prejudice against us in the South that will take years to get over. We can best take care of ourselves if we are placed on land that we can till until we're able to buy it. To assist the government, young men should enlist and serve wherever they are needed."

One by one the men were polled, all agreeing with Reverend Frazier except for the Northern missionary who stated he preferred to live among white people. Privately, Peter was of both persuasions. Surely there were benefits to be derived from mingling with others, a great deal to be learned. Still, it was a relief to get away from the constant pressure white folks exerted. If only they weren't so hateful . . .

"I agree with Reverend Frazier," he replied when asked for his opinion, "at least for now."

The inquiry continued. "One more question, men," the secretary finally said, pausing to look pointedly at William Tecumseh Sherman. "General, would you mind . . . ?"

It was not necessary to finish his sentence. General Sherman understood. Angrily, his face flushed, he strode out of the room. The manner of his departure did not disturb Edwin Stanton who had a reputation for being insensitive. He posed his last question.

"What is the feeling of the colored people toward General Sherman? How far do they regard his sentiments and actions as friendly to their rights and interest, or otherwise?"

Reverend Frazier smiled for the first time. "We feel inexpressible gratitude toward him, a man who should be honored for the faithful performance of his duty. Some of us called upon him immediately upon his arrival, and it is probable he did not meet the secretary with more courtesy than he did us. We have confidence in General Sherman. This is our opinion now, from our short acquaintance and intercourse with him."

This opinion was unanimous but Peter noticed that it did not sit well with Mr. Stanton who had endured a longer intercourse with the general. He thanked the Negroes for their comments and, bouncing down from his perch, left for General Sherman's study.

"Come in," Tecumseh barked as the diminutive Mr. Stanton entered the room.

"That was a very rewarding meeting," the secretary said innocently. "May I sit down?" Without waiting for an answer he almost disappeared into an overstuffed armchair. "Those Negroes were quite bright."

General Sherman towered over Mr. Stanton who, accustomed to being dwarfed, did not appear nonplussed.

"I find it exceedingly strange," the general said brusquely, "that you had to catechize my character with them."

He stood erect, his hand on his sword, a reminder that he had commanded a hundred thousand men in battle and had just led his army across three hundred miles of hostile territory to capture Savannah and liberate ten thousand slaves. Union generals were continually conducting slave raids into the interior, returning with hundreds of refugees, a thousand, even two thousand, but no one had equaled his feat in sheer numbers.

Mr. Stanton crossed his short legs. "There's no need for you to be huffy. The Negroes were quite warm in their praise of you." But, he explained, the sentiment in Washington had changed considerably from President Lincoln's initial plan not to interfere with slavery. The intent now was to cripple the South by depriving it of Negro manpower while providing an escape route for them to the Union side. He pulled a newspaper clipping from his pocket.

"This reporter suggests that you could have led fifty thousand Negroes to Savannah. But instead you drove them from your ranks and prevented their following by pulling up the bridges in your rear which caused the massacre of large numbers by the Confederate cavalry."

"My single purpose," General Sherman snapped, clearly incensed, "was to whip the traitors. To make them fear us and end this war, freeing all the slaves. Because I didn't want my army handicapped by ten or twenty thousand more Negroes I'm accused of being hostile toward them. Nothing could be further from the truth. Wherever I go they greet me with reverence and respect." He plucked the newspaper article from Stanton's hand and glanced at it briefly. "I've already investigated that incident of the pontoon bridge and accept General Davis's account of what happened."

"Yes, General Davis," Mr. Stanton repeated blandly. "I understand he's a Democrat and quite hostile to Negroes."

"That's ridiculous. He's an excellent soldier and bears colored people no ill-will. His route to Savannah followed the River Road requiring him to use his pontoon bridge day and night. His lead column often reached an impassable stream while soldiers in the rear were crossing over another one.

"That's what happened at Ebenezer Creek. The bridge was removed to be used further up while some of the camp followers were still asleep on the other side. They were set upon by a Confederate cavalry. In their fright some Negroes attempted to swim across the creek and drowned. It's rumored that others were killed by the enemy. It could have happened to any of my generals."

The secretary sighed. "The exigencies of war."

"Exactly. It's true we have no Negro soldiers. I prefer seasoned veterans to untried recruits. But the large Negro force we employed gave us admirable service."

Innocently the secretary asked, "You know about General Thomas's rout of the enemy at Nashville?"

General Sherman smiled. "We got the news piecemeal. His brilliant victory was necessary to mine at Savannah to make a complete whole. I compliment him."

Outwitted by General Sherman's advance into Georgia, the Confederates attempted to invade Tennessee and were soundly defeated by General Thomas, a defeat which ended Rebel aspirations in that state.

Mr. Stanton grinned wickedly. "There were several regiments of black soldiers with General Thomas who helped to whip the enemy. Raw recruits who fought courageously and with honor. Thank God they weren't consigned to fatigue duty."

General Sherman said icily, "I stand by my own principles, Mr. Secretary. They may be peculiar but they're mine."

In the days that followed the two men became less antagonistic. Together they visited the soldiers in their camps and journeyed to the edge of town to talk to the refugees huddled under makeshift tents. Then, under the direction of Secretary Stanton, General Sherman drafted Field Order 15 which was immediately published and put into effect.

The order reserved for exclusive Negro settlement the abandoned and confiscated lands of the Sea Islands. Possessory titles would be conferred upon the settlers who could claim up to forty acres per family. Able-bodied Negroes were encouraged to enlist as soldiers to contribute their share toward maintaining their own freedom and rights as citizens. The property rights of settlements now on the islands were not affected. Appointed to head the gigantic settlement plan was Brigadier General Rufus Saxton, trusted friend of the Negro.

January 1865

Peter transported two boatloads of Sherman's troops to Beaufort. In between he hurried home to make sure he still had a wife and child under his roof, frigid though Rain might be. She slept so distantly on the edge of their bed he was afraid she might fall off. Whenever he let his big toe drift across the mattress to touch hers she responded by jumping up and reverting again to her washtubs. Left hard and throbbing, Peter bitterly questioned his choice of women. Why was it that both Rain and Chloe had a passion for scrubbing dirty clothes?

He settled his anger on Chloe for placing herself in Rain's path like an errant bullet. Or had it been deliberate? What had possessed her to come to Beaufort? She could have refused a transfer or had she requested it? The thought unnerved him. He had considered going to the hospital at the offset to confront her but had been afraid Rain might find out and misconstrue his motives. But on this particular dreary day it presented at least a course of action.

The Contraband Hospital was on New Street, a former summer residence. The white clapboard house was built high up from the ground and had a double piazza which offered wounded soldiers some respite from the intolerable stench inside. But today was raw and wintry with a steady drizzle and the verandas were unoccupied.

Peter stepped inside the front door steeling himself, aware that medical equipment was so desperately needed that at St. Helena's Church, also converted into a hospital, tombstones in the cemetery had been uprooted and used for operating tables. Still, what greeted him was a shocking sight. The wounded population had exceeded all boundaries and bloody litters were everywhere. In the foyer. In the hallways. Patients resembling cadavers were shoved into corners on stinking, blood-caked blankets. Even the walls were smeared with blood. The walking wounded lurched about on improvised crutches, minus a leg here, an arm or two there.

"Hey," one of them called out, sticking his shrapnel-scarred face close to Peter's and leaning on crutches. Both of his legs were missing. "You got any tobacco?"

Peter shook his head. "Sorry, mate."

"Are you crazy?" the soldier screamed. "Why you come to a goddamn hospital with no goddamn tobacco?" Balancing his abbreviated body on one crutch, he waved the other one ominously at Peter as though about to brain him.

"Kill him," a gentle voice suggested from a corner.

"Shut up all that goddamn noise," someone else yelled, "or I'll shoot the pack of you like the mangy dogs you are."

A medic rushed by ignoring the fracas, his smock a bloody signature. Peter wondered if he had entered the lunatic asylum by mistake. But the threats were all verbal. The tobacco-hungry soldier lowered his crutch and, leaning forward, quietly sobbed.

Angrily Peter berated himself. Why had he come to a goddamn hospital without bringing tobacco? "What's your name, soldier? I'll send you a pouch of tobacco later today."

"Paul Cotter," the man whimpered, looking hopeful. "You promise?"

"Yes."

"On your mamma's grave?"

"She ain't dead yet."

The man began to blubber again, all hope gone.

Peter found his way to the office. The white man in charge reported impatiently that Chloe Harrison no longer worked there. She had abruptly quit a few days ago for parts unknown. The patients missed her. She had been a very competent aide.

En route home Peter felt dejected instead of relieved. Chloe had expected him to make an appearance. She had waited for days. No matter whether he went to upbraid her or to announce that his wife was leaving him, he should at least have shown up. Chloe had endured their final farewell alone.

It wasn't until the next day, following a sleepless night lying miserably next to Rain, that Peter remembered to send the soldier a packet of tobacco. And it was almost with relief that he set sail again reminding his wife, "Don't forget your promise. Wait for me."

Twenty transports a day docked at Beaufort's wharves spitting out General Sherman's hard-bitten veterans who swaggered about selling horses they didn't own to eager Negroes. The horses, army property, were confiscated and their befuddled buyers thrown in jail for receiving stolen property. "Dumb niggers." The soldiers grinned, pocketing from two to three hundred dollars for each critter sold. They spent the money like water, buying trinkets, watches, souvenirs, and when their funds ran out, appropriating whatever they fancied. "Uncle Sam will pay you for it later," they told the vexed shopkeepers. The marauding soldiers shot pigs and chickens, destroyed property and handled protestors roughly. They acted so barbarously that finally General Saxton declared Beaufort off limits to freedmen for their own protection.

In high spirits, the victorious army, almost as raggedy as the refugees and proudly wearing bullet-riddled hats, roared through the streets, singing and cracking jokes raucously. They had brought the treasonous slaveholding aristocracy of Georgia to its knees and were anxious now to oblige South Carolina, the architect of the infamy. At a safe distance, the colored folks looked at the high-jinxing soldiers with envious admiration and declared, "They is some jaunty sonsofbitches."

With a sigh of relief, Beaufort said good-bye to Sherman's troops who marched toward Pocotaligo, their destination known only to their commander and his chief, General Grant. The right wing feinted toward Charleston while other divisions seemed headed for Augusta, Georgia, all of it intended to confuse the enemy.

General Rufus Saxton plucked the *Swanee* out of the troop movement business. Initially, he was reluctant to be in charge of the mammoth task of settling on the Sherman lands upward of forty thousand freedmen who were still entering Union lines.

"I fear they will later be dispossessed," he told Secretary Stanton when they met in Beaufort, "and I do not want to be the instrument of raising their hopes falsely again."

He himself had promised that no man would be inducted into the military against his will, each would receive equal pay, and if the field hands preempted and worked the land they could buy it. But there had been a breach of faith and awful atrocities had occurred, boys of fourteen kidnapped into service and men with dependents shot down when they resisted. Yet despite all obstacles, the Sea Islanders, considered the most ignorant and backward of slaves, had made significant progress.

"Mr. Stanton, they have proven themselves capable of receiving the full rights of free men. And before I unwittingly mislead them again I would rather resign."

"They will not be dispossessed later," the secretary promised General Saxton. Congress was in the process of establishing a Freedmen's Bureau which would regulate titles to the Sherman lands. Negro family heads could preempt up to forty acres, rent them for three years, and buy them at any time within that period.

Reassured and elated, General Saxton and Reverend Ferdinand held mass meetings in Savannah and refugee camps to apprise the freedmen of their opportunity to become settlers. The Negroes listened. They asked pertinent questions. Much of the abandoned land had lain fallow for years and was in a terrible state of neglect. It would take time and money to restore it to fruitfulness.

"Suh, what guarantee we got that after improving the land it be ours? That it won't be taken away from us?"

The U.S. military would protect them in their rights, General Saxton replied, until they were able to protect themselves.

The Negroes were satisfied with his answer and on one exemplary day alone five thousand acres of Sherman land, as it was designated, were allocated.

General Saxton needed transports to move his human cargo to their new homes and requested several steamers including the *Swanee*.

Peter transported thousands of refugees that he found huddled in rags on the wharves of Savannah waiting to be picked up, their eyes yellow and feverish, the skin hanging from their bones. It was a bitter cold winter and the Negroes who had been traveling for two months in General Sherman's wake were plagued with dysentery and pellagra. The elderly, in particular, who had dared to believe they could withstand the hardships of the march, and the children too were grievously ill and dying in wholesale numbers.

Able-bodied men were speedily inducted into the army or the quartermaster's labor battalion. Women and children and the aged were dispersed to various plantations where they would harvest corn and potatoes and cultivate cotton, or to refugee camps which were filled to overflowing with destitute Georgians arriving at the rate of a hundred a day. The Negro residents welcomed the new-comers clucking, "It gon be awright. We doing fine here and you all is gon do fine also." The teachers dashed about with homeo-pathic salves and nostrums. The aid societies of the North, who had sent a shipload of food to the poor whites of Savannah, re-sponded to the crisis by quadrupling their commitment of clothing, medicine and cooking utensils to the freedmen and supporting a new crop of teachers. Wherever the Negroes settled on the coastal lands, the teachers pulled up stakes and accompanied them. They opened schools, for small children mainly, all other hands needed to quickly plant a crop and avoid starvation.

Peter slept wherever night found him, trying his best to return to Beaufort as often as possible while wondering why he insisted upon that torture. He slept on his side of the bed and Rain on her side, both of them wide awake and miserable.

At the time General Sherman granted the Sea Islands to the Negroes for settlement, all of that land was not under Union con-trol. But, a few weeks later, in South Carolina, it was, thanks to Negro troops. They advanced the Union line with their raids, free-ing the slaves who then defended their homes and freed others. As General Sherman's troops slashed and burned their way across South Carolina, plantation slaves deserted their masters and crossed over to the Union lines to further swell the refugee camps. Again, it was the Negro troops who helped to facilitate General Sherman's march. They kept open supply lines, disrupted Rebel saltworks and communication links. And they patrolled the Shell Road, the solitary avenue of land connected by a ferry between Beaufort and Charleston, preventing any advance by the enemy.

On and on the refugees came. From the lowlands. From the bayous and swamps. On they came to colonize the Sherman lands. The Northern press journeyed south to meet them. A reporter from

The New York Times was particularly impressed with a Negro minister who had led members of his flock from Savannah to a small island off Georgia. Carefully, they had selected and numbered their lots, laid out a village, put the numbers in a hat and drew them out, promising equal privileges to others who might join them. "It was Plymouth Colony repeating itself," the newsman joyfully reported.

The Edisto Negroes, who had fled from their island in camouflaged flatboats, were returning there with more style than when they had departed. Long a no-man's-land, Edisto was once again in Union hands and part of the Sherman land grant. A battalion of Negro soldiers, the 1st South Carolina, was being sent along to guard the refugees.

Brother Man admitted to Peter one afternoon, the big man's eyes twinkling, "I almost peed on myself when we left there. We came that close to being captured by the Sesesh."

The *Swanee* was at anchor at Beaufort's wharf and they were in Peter's cabin. Brother Man, sitting on the bunk, was looking around with nostalgia.

"Wish you were taking us back to Edisto, Peter. I has a soft spot for this here sassy steamboat."

"I'm sorry, too," Peter replied, "but we've been ordered to naval headquarters at Hilton Head. You all ready to move?"

"Been ready. Sister's done packed up our few belongings and is sitting on top of them itching to put her feet in the road."

Chuckling, Peter thought they had better hurry before their few belongings sank beneath her weight.

Absently Brother Man glanced out the porthole. "I cain't get over the beauty of Edisto. I already done staked out our forty acres. We got plenty of pecan trees and our north line is a little brook. The land's been lying fallow and is a mess but quick as spit I'll have it ploughed and growing me some corn."

"Things are working out just fine," Peter said, though his craggy face was sad. Fine for everybody but him. "Tell Sister soon's you all are settled I'm coming over to visit and eat me some pecan pie."

The following day Peter was at naval headquarters on Hilton Head. The harbor was one of the transfer points for the Georgia refugees. They crowded upon the wharves in desolate bunches plucked from the overcrowded refugee camps. They were an eyesore, sickly and bedraggled, one woman nursing at her breast a child who was already dead. Peter walked past them, looking for General Saxton's agent who would advise him how many of these mangy people he was to transport. The *Swanee* could carry a thousand and of late always had a full load.

"Lazarus?" a woman's voice called out. "Where you be?"

"Here, Mamma. Playing with Petunia and Zee."

The blood in Peter's veins froze. Carefully, so as not to stumble over his leaden feet, he turned around. His eyes darted quickly past an old man and a pregnant woman at the edge of the crowd. Lazarus, where you be?

Peter plunged into a sea of black faces which seemed to be merging, shutting him out. Lazarus, he silently hollered. And suddenly there they were. A pointy-face black boy and his playmates. Two girls as pale as tallow stared at Peter with Rain's burnished eyes.

24

Beaufort

February 1865

Please, Mamma," Glory wailed, "don't cry."

Upset by such bizarre behavior—Mamma on her knees in front
of two skinny, pale girls with bushy blond hair—Glory ran to her
father.

Absently Peter patted her head, his attention also riveted by the
spectacle of Rain. Not satisfied with kissing their cheeks and fingers
one by one, she had fallen to her knees to gather the girls into
her arms. He had not planned it as a surprise but had simply
opened the door and announced to Rain who was coming down
the stairs, "Here they be. Petunia and Zee. I found them."

Rain had frozen on the staircase, they all had, as though waiting
for God himself to set them in motion. Recovering first, Rain had
flown down the steps to pounce on the girls. Now she was doing
penance. On her knees.

"Thank you, sweet Jesus. Thank you."

Irritably Peter thought, it was me who found them. "Rain, stop
it. You're frightening the children."

They could have been twins, he decided, both of them yaller
and scrawny, their tangled thick hair framing their faces, colored
people's hair which gave them away. That and the dash of cinna-

mon in their skin. They seemed scared out of their wits by this strange man who had brought them to this house where an insane woman had fallen upon them like a vulture. She stood up, stepping back to give them breathing room, then leaned forward again, propelled by an inner urgency.

"Don't you remember me, Zee? I is you mamma. And Petunia, you is my li'l sister. When you all was on James Island I used to come every Sunday near 'bout to visit. You all would come a-running hollering, 'Rain is here. Rain. Rain.' The other chil'ren thought you was talking 'bout the weather." She laughed, a touch of hysteria in the sound. "You cain't have forgotten me."

Petunia, ten, stared at her, frowning with the effort to remember. "Rain?" she said, testing the word on her tongue. It had a familiar ring and she repeated it less tentatively. "Rain."

Zee opened her mouth but no speech came. Her auburn eyes filled with tears. "Mamma," she finally whispered.

Rain opened her arms and enveloped them in a wild embrace. "My babies. My darlings." All three of them were crying.

Glory pushed herself harder against Peter. He held her at arm's length. "It's all right, honey. Say hello to your kin." He pushed her forward.

It was painful for him to look at the girls and not remember . . . Your daddy raped my Rain. And your grandaddy, too.

"Glory," Rain said, acknowledging her at last. "Come here, chile." She held out a hand toward her.

"This here's my little girl, Glory. Honey, meet you sister, Zee. And my sister, Petunia." The children stared at each other glumly. "I tell you what, Glory. I is gon let Petunia be you sister, too. Ain't that lovely? You has got two big sisters to look after you."

Glory, uncertain about the loveliness of it all, stuck her thumb in her mouth and sucked hard. Her newfound kin were similarly mute.

"Peter." Rain turned toward him tremulous and melting. "How you find them? Tell me."

"On the wharf at Hilton Head."

He made it brief, promising to flesh out the details later when he had more time. The girls had lived on a plantation outside of Atlanta entrusted to the care of the cook. When their master fled from General Sherman's army taking only his family and coachman, the cook responded to the call of freedom and fell in behind the Yankee troops. In the confusion the girls were separated from her. A man named Simon found them sitting by the side of the road crying hysterically. To prevent his five children, the stray girls and his wife from getting lost he tied them all together.

Rain sucked in her breath, marveling at the wonder of it. "A man with five chil'ren of his own? God bless him and his wife. I gon tell them myself one day how happy they has made me. You know where they is?"

"Settling on Daufuskie Island. Rain, I have to go now." She stared at him disappointed. "But I'll be back tonight," he promised. The threat of hell and brimstone would not keep him away.

Shivering in bed, Peter pulled the blanket up to his nose. "There ain't much more to tell, Rain." He described Simon in detail. The heft of the man. His determination.

"A real sweetheart," she crooned. "There he were with five chil'ren of he own and still took care of mine."

"Yeh," Peter agreed, his teeth chattering. He had only one child. Could he manage to care for two more? Love them as though they were his own, half white though they be?

"You has got a chill." Rain placed her palm on his forehead. "And a fever. You got you feet wet?"

"I work on a boat, Rain. My feet are always wet."

"You forgot to wear you hip boots."

"No, I . . ."

"Lord, you is coming down with pneumonia." Nimbly, she hopped out of bed wearing one of the lacy nightgowns he had bought for her in Philadelphia. Peter stared at her tiny, delectable body outlined against the lace. It had given him hope when she had put it on.

"Rain, wait . . ."

She was gone.

Restless, entangled in the bedding, he heard her in the kitchen. Undoubtedly she was brewing up some sassafras root together with another poison or two.

In due time Rain returned with a steaming pewter cup. "Drink it down while it's hot," she commanded.

"It's scalding my tongue."

"Drink it."

He sipped the brew, hating it. "Baby love, come back to bed. You're all I need."

She slid in beside him, raising up on one elbow to supervise his drinking. When he finished Rain placed the cup on the floor and cuddled him in her arms.

"I is so sorry you feeling bad," she whispered, her breath tickling his ear.

The heat rose up like a brush fire in his groin. "Your herb tea done cured me."

Hungrily he kissed her. Busily his hands pulled off her flimsy nightgown and flung it to the floor. Tonight there would be no midnight trip to the washtubs.

In the days that followed, Peter came home several times, all of them disastrous. That first evening at supper, Zee asked him innocently, "Is you my daddy?"

"No," he yelled at his wife's daughter.

Rain's head jerked up. Her eyes raking over him uncovered the misery in his soul.

"No," he repeated his voice softer. "I is . . . I am . . . your Uncle Peter."

Silently, he cursed himself for being such a donkey's ass but he couldn't help it. The specters were there. Hovering over Zee and Petunia. Claiming them. Floating mists that rose up out of the girls' hair and encircled their heads like halos. Mists that bunched together to form faces. He could see their features in the wispy smoke. A droopy mustache. Long hair as pale as wheat. Lips that were a thin sneering line. "You their daddy?" the faces taunted. "Not hardly. You're a nigger and these gals are white. Half of them, that is. Our half. Ha, ha."

They were always there. Surrounding the two girls. A smoky essence dancing in and out of their hair. They tormented Peter. He howled. He cursed. He raised his fists threateningly. The children cowered away from him. Rain bit her lips, watching and waiting. Lily waited too, regarding her son fiercely until she could abide it no more.

"What's wrong with you?" she assailed him one evening when they were alone together in her room. "Why you holler at them chil'ren so? They'll be right nice soon's Rain fatten them up a bit and they stop acting like scared rabbits. But they cain't do nothing to suit you."

"Their white daddies keep bedeviling me, Mamma."

His mother looked at him with pity. She had grown closer to Rain since the truth had surfaced about the past, vindicating her oft-stated feeling that "something ain't right 'bout that gal." Now Lily sympathized with that "something." Why couldn't her stubborn son do likewise?

"I don't know what to say to you, Peter." She sounded tired. "White mens sell away they own flesh like pigs in a litter. What you has to remember is them girls ain't got no daddy but you."

Peter left his mother's room more miserable than when he had entered it.

25

Charleston
February 18, 1865

Charleston fell. The Confederates turned it into an incinerator before they galloped their horses over the Ashley River Bridge and then blew up the bridge.

General Sherman's secret destination had not been the cradle but the hand that rocked it. Columbia. The state capital. Under siege it collapsed and its mighty fall reached out to embrace Charleston. With their supply lines cut, the city and its harbor garrisons, including Fort Sumter, were ordered to retreat and destroy whatever they could not carry to keep it out of enemy hands.

The cotton was set to smoking in the public squares along with thousands of bushels of rice. Insanely, the huge Blakely cannon on South Battery when detonated flew up whole into the air then burst with a deafening roar, a huge chunk landing on a nearby rooftop. Three warships, exploded in their berths, ignited the wharves. The fire roared out of control and jumped to nearby rooftops.

"Dear God," the people shrieked, dashing out of their flaming homes, their clothes scorched and their children's hair on fire. Terrified black and white folks shouted at each other, "This way.

No! That street's in flames." Crying, cursing, they stumbled from fire to fire. In and out of bomb craters. Encircled. Endangered. There was no place to run to, no place to hide. From the Ashley River to the Cooper River Charleston was in flames.

Tongues of fire were leaping around the pier where two companies of the 54th Massachusetts landed. They had rowed in from the island where they had been stationed for months firing shells daily into the city. They were preceded to Charleston by companies of the 3rd and 4th South Carolina (renamed the 21st U.S. Colored Troops), the 3rd Rhode Island Artillery and the 52nd Pennsylvania. The Union colonel in charge of the city ordered that every able-bodied Negro resident and those who limped be impressed into battling the flames.

"Out the fires."

The command passed down the line.

"Man the pumps."

In the shadow of the auction block—which many a Negro soldier knew too intimately—they took up positions at the pumps. Bucket brigades were organized block by block as Negro firemen, wearing red britches and dragging their firefighting equipment, joined the soldiers. The city's white firemen, members of the militia, had fled with the military.

Choking on the smoke, their skin singed, Sandy and Pinch along with their squad dragged hoses in and out of bomb craters to spray the flames. They labored day and night, smudged and weary. More Yankee troops arrived to lend a hand and finally the last embers were stamped out.

Triumphantly, to the sound of drumbeats, the colored troops marched down Meeting Street behind the Stars and Stripes, as black people emerged from every nook and cranny, the old and the young, the able-bodied and retarded. White folks remained indoors, tense and anxious, wondering what the Yankees had in store for them. The Negro celebrants lined the sidewalks. Overflowed into the gutters. Waved their arms and wept for joy.

"Praise God we has lived to see this day," they caroled, "saved by our own black soldiers. Give God the glory. We is free at last."

March 14, 1865

The last passengers to disembark from the *Swanee* were the three men responsible for the trip to Charleston, General Saxton, Reverend Ferdinand and General Oliver Otis Howard, head of the Bureau for Refugees, Freedmen and Abandoned Lands. The Bureau was recently created to manage confiscated property throughout the South and to provide provisions to the destitute. General Howard was empowered to rent up to forty acres to freedmen and white refugees with an option to buy within three years. And to organize and manage schools.

Peter was conversing with the men as they were about to disembark and impatient to get them off his boat so he could be about his own business.

"Captain Mango," General Howard said in his gentle manner, "it has been my pleasure being on your steamer. I am in your debt for my safe arrival."

"You are welcome, suh," Peter replied, trying to keep his eyes from straying to the man's empty right sleeve. His arm had been lost in battle.

Peter was impressed by the slender young general who had the reputation of being a near saint, so piously religious that he allowed neither drink nor profanity to pass his lips. He had been one of General Sherman's commanders, and on the march to Savannah had restrained his soldiers from wanton pillaging, from absconding with the South's silverplate. Sympathetic to the Negro's cause, he had once stymied a woman slaveholder bearing a white flag who appeared at his camp to recover a runaway mother and child.

Reverend Ferdinand, bundled up in his black greatcoat, beamed a beatific smile at Peter. "When we labor in God's vineyards we are blessed with progress, Captain. This is a most rewarding day, isn't it?"

"Yes, Reverend," Peter replied, smiling back.

General Saxton informed him that they would be returning to Beaufort at seven o'clock tomorrow morning. Later today he and the minister were holding their second mass meeting at Zion Church, built and owned by Negroes, to encourage them to stake their claims on the Sherman lands. General Saxton was industriously sweeping them up, working harmoniously with General Howard.

When they finally departed, Peter dismissed his crew then stood alone at the prow, looking at the bombed-out city and feeling bruised by the sight. Ashore, he gingerly picked his way around bomb craters and made it to East Bay Street. The house where he and Rain had lived, the entire block, had been shelled and was a pile of shattered brick and debris. He stared at the rubble, fright clawing at the pit of his stomach. Had the folks moved out in time? And what would he find at St. Michael's Alley?

He had always imagined this day as being glorious, triumphant, but instead he felt wretched. Buildings were completely demolished or were shells, half blown away. Broken glass littered the caved-in sidewalks, and the earth was gouged with rubble-filled craters. The devastation found an echo in Peter's heart.

His life with Rain was in jeopardy. At home he didn't know from one moment to the next what nonsense might fall unbidden from his lips, hounded as he was by those smoky demons encircling Zee and Petunia. He had become a midnight crawler arriving home late at night and leaving before dawn in order to avoid acting like a madman with the girls, try as he did to be civil. In those midnight hours he and Rain made passionate love, forsaking all others in their frenzy, their greed, for who knew when this madness would end.

Peter hurried to Broad Street and St. Michael's Church. Yankee bombers had used its steeple to gauge their range and the Confederates had painted it black to decrease its visibility. Carefully Peter picked his way around the rubble, meeting people coming and going who were equally cautious. The buildings which remained standing in this area were almost a total wreck. Roofs caved in. Verandas collapsed. Broken pillars scattered everywhere. The mighty had fallen.

"Hello, Cap'n Mango," a Negro corporal said in passing. "You don't know me but I was on your boat many a day being ferried to Morris Island."

"It's nice to see you again," Peter replied, pleased when soldiers remembered him.

Colored troops on patrol duty were everywhere. They were the official guards, the keepers of the peace. There had been so much wholesale pilfering and looting by officers and their men that Charleston had been placed off limits to all regiments except the 21st U.S. Colored Troops, composed mainly of former slaves.

Peter turned down Church Street, skirting a fetid pool of water on which garbage was floating. At St. Michael's Alley he groaned out loud and shivered. Where Uncle Hiram's house had stood there was a bomb crater. His cottage had been shelled. Blown sky high. It had fallen back to earth in charred chunks and been sucked into a huge hole splattered with sooty bricks and shards of glass.

Uncle Hiram? Peter whispered. He waited horrified for an answer from the ruins, for charred lips to defy death and groan. But surely with firepower aimed at the church's steeple Uncle Hiram would have fled before his house became a graveyard. Who would know? Peter's mind raced. The Brotherhood. Gimpy, the glazier. If Gimpy was alive he would surely know something.

He was there. In the rear of the shop. Sitting in the shadows on a bench filing a piece of metal. Up front, a sheet of glass leaning against a wall mirrored the people and vehicles outside creating a kaleidoscope of movement and color. Gimpy opened the street door to stare at Peter, his mouth agape, his hair now snow white, his double chins tripled.

"My eyes ain't playing me false," he breathed, "it's really you?" He laughed from pure joy, all of his chins quivering, and pulled Peter inside.

The shadow in the rear of the shop stood up, dropping the piece of metal. Peter turned toward the sound. He caught his breath and forgot to exhale as the figure moved into the light. Then the space between them disappeared as both men rushed forward to embrace.

"Thank God," Peter exclaimed with a whoop of laughter, "you're alive."

Uncle Hiram was smothering him in a bear hug. "My boy. And so are you. Alive and kicking." He held Peter at arm's length. "Let me feast my eyes on you. Gimpy, look how this boy has grown into a man."

Peter laughed. "I thought I was a man the last time I saw you."

"You was, you was, but now you have grown more so since they put a price on your nappy head."

"And you haven't aged at all."

Uncle Hiram looked the same except every strand of his hair had upped and died. He was completely bald, his black head shiny.

"I'm sorry you didn't escape with us," Peter said.

Hiram shook his head, smiling. "I couldn't. But what's this?" He touched Peter's cap.

"They made me a captain. I have my own boat, the *Swanee*, and we transport anything that moves."

"A captain? Ain't that something." Gimpy covered his crotch with both hands. "This is too much excitement for an old man. I has to go pee." He disappeared into the back of the shop.

"I'm not surprised," Hiram said, gazing at Peter with pride. "You young men have acquitted yourselves nicely. Do you know that our black troops are the guards here?"

"So I noticed."

"And the gentry who fled are returning in droves."

"I noticed that also."

En route to the shop he had seen several houses bearing signs that the property was occupied by the owners who had taken the oath of allegiance. Poor whites had also been evident, shabby refugees displaced by the war. They were recipients of food rations, clothes and other necessities dispensed by the Refugees and Freedmen's Bureau.

Peter reported that his family was living in Beaufort with his mother and that his son had died, which dampened both his and Hiram's elation. "But how's our Brotherhood men, Uncle? What's happened to them?"

Hiram dropped down to a bench and Peter straddled a chair facing him.

"Most of our brothers who were slaves went off to war with their masters. Had to take care of them you know."

"Yeh. I was here when Amos left."

"A bullet got him at Manassas. And you remember Samuel, the ironmaker? When his master was killed in battle Sammy tried to come back here but another white man claimed he was his slave and made him stay. He finally managed to escape."

"Thank God for that." Peter groaned. "War is a misery, ain't it? I saw your bombed-out house and was afraid you might have been trapped in it."

"I was living upstairs with Gimpy when my house was hit. Been here for over a year ever since my wife Helen died."

"I'm sorry to hear she's passed," Peter said, feeling a momentary twinge. They had never gotten along well but still it was sad news. "Was she sick long?"

"For several months. You know that we had our problems."

Peter nodded. It had been no secret.

"I'm making no excuses for the shabby way I treated her, but toward the end when it was nip and tuck whether we'd come out of the war alive, we grew closer. Finally there was just Helen and me. No other women except the memory of one she never knew about."

"My mother?" Peter asked after a moment's hesitation.

Hiram seemed amused. "It took you a long time, boy, to figure that one out."

"Are you my daddy?" The question popped unbidden from Peter's mouth. Maybe . . . by some miracle . . .

Hiram moistened his lips. His amused look turned into a transfixed gaze as though he was trapped somewhere else in time. "It's my fault that I'm not." Regret was in his voice. "If you must know, I was a jackass not to have married your mother." He paused, and the words now seemed wrenched from him against his will. "It was because she was a slave."

Peter winced. "And you were free."

"And scared. You must understand that. I swore I'd kill her master if he ever whipped her. And that of course meant I would be committing suicide."

"You didn't love her enough," Peter said harshly, thinking about his mother's long, lonely years. "And why didn't you tell me this before?" The question had a familiar ring but he refused to acknowledge it.

"The time wasn't ripe."

"Why? Because I was a slave, too, like my mother? But now that I'm free like you——"

"Stop it, Peter. You have a right to be angry but it all happened many years ago. I regret the decision I made, if that's any consolation to you."

"It isn't."

Hiram shrugged. "I'm sorry. There's nothing more I can say."

His voice was bland, his attitude suggesting that in time he might be forgiven and if not, that was Peter's problem because he was through with it. The silence grew pervasive between them until Hiram cleared his throat and said, "So tell me, what's happened to your crew? I saw Stretch a little while back and——"

"What?" Peter jumped to his feet, his heart hammering. "He's here?"

"He was. In the jailhouse. Some of the white officers were exchanged but the Sesesh built a gallows in the courtyard for our men. Said they weren't soldiers but runaway slaves. Insurrectionists. And the penalty for that was hanging."

The skin on the back of Peter's neck crawled. "They didn't . . ."

"No. A lawyer argued their case in court, said they were soldiers and should be treated as such according to international law. Believe it or not he won the case. And for his pains white folks called him a nigger lover and he can't find work anymore. I understand that he's destitute. Anyhow, they didn't hang our men but transferred them to another prison camp in Georgia. Andersonville I believe it is."

"Stretch is alive." Peter laughed, exultant. "But how did you get to see him?"

Gimpy had returned to the room and said, "He was helping some officers escape."

"Who?" Peter asked. "Stretch?"

"No. Hiram."

"I was replacing the jail's wagon wheels in the yard where they exercised the white prisoners. Our men were kept up on the third floor and never brought down to the yard, but I saw Stretch more than once, yelling and waving at me from a window. Twice I managed to smuggle two white Yankees out of the prison in a wagon and took them to the waterfront. A Negro fisherman rowed them to a Union gunboat blockading the harbor. I was trying to figure out some way to get to our colored boys when the jailer became suspicious and got himself another wheelwright."

Peter's head was reeling. This was the Hiram he knew. Union boats periodically picked up refugees and escaped prisoners from

Charleston but he had never imagined that Hiram was involved. Peter started toward the door.

"I'm so glad you're safe, Uncle, and that Stretch wasn't killed at Fort Wagner. We were so worried . . ."

Hiram stood up, too. "Do you have to go?" he asked wistfully.

"I promised to put in an appearance at Zion Church."

Gimpy offered to drive Peter there in his wagon and Hiram accompanied them to the door.

"Tell your mother I'll visit her soon," he said. "Finally. After all these years."

Their eyes met and Peter smiled. It was a fleeting, tentative smile that promised forgiveness if not today, then tomorrow.

26

St. Helena
March, 1865

Peter found Cindy in the vegetable garden behind her shack dumping seeds into a furrow. She was wearing a shapeless dress knotted at the waist with a rope, its sleeves too short for her long arms, and a floppy man's hat perched on her head.

Seeing Peter she smiled. "What a nice surprise to look up and there you be."

When she invited him inside, he explained that his time was short but he had good news. Stretch had been seen in Charleston and was now in Andersonville Prison in Georgia.

"He's alive?" Cindy's long body swayed like a blade of grass in the wind. Then she threw back her head and shouted for all the world to hear, "Stretch is alive." She grabbed Peter and kissed him.

"Girl," he grinned, "get hold of yourself."

"I always said I would know it was ░░░░ad," Cindy exulted. "Now I can spend his money."

"What?" Peter wasn't sure he had heard her right.

"Massa Youngblood is selling and I gon be buying."

"Whoa!" Peter laughed. "Slow down."

"Oh, it's so grand. Stretch left me his prize money, what we didn't spend, saying to use it for myself. But I ain't touch nary a cent 'cause that would be admitting he were gone and I is holding onto that money for him. But now that I know he's alive I is gon buy this here place. Reverend Ferdinand say rush out to the Sherman lands but this here's my home. Mistuh Youngblood is selling it for five to ten dollars an acre. Ain't that a shame? Land he paid a dollar a acre for."

Peter was appalled. That was terrible, he declared, and had a few other unkind things to say about Dexter Youngblood.

"I was wondering how I could do it," Cindy said. "Now I knows. When Stretch come home we has our own li'l place to work like we please. Peter, I is so happy I could die."

Driving his buggy home, Peter contemplated the surprising nature of women. Damn if it wasn't natural, not touching that money. But not having dribbled it away Cindy could now put it to good use.

And hadn't his mother shocked him, too, the way she reacted to Helen's death? Mamma had been lying down in bed when he told her and she shot bolt upright. Her faded eyes seemed to brighten.

"I did it," she crooned, nodding to herself. "I swore I'd outlive that wench and I did."

Peter was shocked. Where was her remorse at the finality of death?

"I hope she didn't suffer too long," his mother said finally. Peter wanted to reveal that he knew about her and Hiram but didn't dare.

"You say Hiram is well?"

"Yes, ma'am. And promises to come visit you one day soon."

Lily's gap-toothed smile flashed and she, too, had that dazed look on her face as if she were someplace else at the moment.

"Wouldn't that be grand to see my old friend again."

The only woman who hadn't surprised Peter lately was Rain, firmly on the side of Zee when it came to a showdown. His first mistake last week was remaining home for supper one evening instead of returning to the *Swanee* and continuing to be a midnight prowler. It was the first time in weeks he'd been in the girls' company for more than a passing moment and the specters, lying in wait, ganged up on him, flying in and out of Zee's frizzy hair so that when she passed him a steaming bowl of gravy he missed it and the damn thing tumbled into his lap.

Holding his scalded crotch, he jumped to his feet and yelled at the gleeful demons, "Goddamnit, you did that on purpose."

Zee burst out crying, stuttering between her sobs, "N . . . no. I didn't." She was quite timid, more so than Petunia, a bony, mousey-looking child.

Rain hollered, "It were an accident. Why you cursing my chile?" She reached for Zee and cuddled the girl to her breast.

Lily inquired, "Son, is you going daft?"

And Glory, ever daddy's darling, glared at her half-sister evilly.

Peter retreated to his bedroom and unbuttoned his trousers to examine himself critically. No permanent harm seem to have been done but his crotch was still burning slightly. He was still holding himself when Rain came into the room a few minutes later.

"I'm sorry," he apologized. "I didn't mean to holler at Zee but . . ."

"Don't you ever goddamn my chile again," she ordered. Having delivered her ultimatum, Rain marched out of the room, not even caring, Peter thought, that his poor prick might have been scalded.

Remembering all this as he drove back to Beaufort from St. Helena, Peter concluded that he would never understand women.

April 14, 1865

The *Swanee* left before daylight, steaming up the inland waterways in order to rendezvous with the flotilla in Charleston. From Elliott's Cut she sailed into Wappoo Creek, the turns in the narrow channel not yet affording a view of the city, only cypress trees kneeling in the swamp against a backdrop of pine groves.

"My boat's going to sink," Peter had grumbled as the gangplank groaned under the milling hordes. He had contracted to carry a thousand freedmen but at least half that many again were sprawled about the main and passenger decks, hanging over the gunwales, trespassing into the fo'c'sle and some bold folks even peeping into the boiler room to wave at the firemen. The children, wide awake now that the sun had risen, ran under the crew's feet until a parental hand snatched them backward threatening to slap the pee out of them.

It was a breezy April day and everyone was in high spirits for the celebration at Fort Sumter. General Lee had surrendered to General Grant at Appomattox last Sunday and Confederate General Johnston was expected momentarily to surrender to Tecumseh Sherman. "Give God the glory," black folks proclaimed as they greeted one another and crowded at the rail for their first glimpse of the devastated city.

The *Swanee* was on time, Charleston harbor a scene of festive gaiety, the flotilla about to get underway. The vessels, overflowing with celebrants, were being led by a government schooner decorated with hundreds of multicolored flags stretching from the bow to the stern, from the foresails to the mizzenmast. Peter guided the *Swanee* into its place and half an hour later the lot of them set sail down the harbor, the air resounding with revelry, bands playing, people singing, cannons firing salutes.

There was a knock on the pilothouse door and before Peter could answer Brother Man pushed it open. "Thought I'd find you up here," he said smiling. "Ain't this a glorious day? I left Charleston a slave and return a plantation owner." He loved to so describe his forty-acre farm.

"You is addle-brained," Peter said, "but come in anyway. Where's Sister?"

"On the quarterdeck with July getting into everybody's business. Folks say the darndest things in front of her forgetting she ain't deaf. And Sister's savvy. Made me buy a mule 'stead of pulling the plow myself to save money." Brother Man chuckled, tickled with the state of affairs.

His mirth should have been contagious but Peter was feeling so lowdown the best he could manage was a weak smile. "July tell you he moving back to Charleston today? He came aboard loaded down with all his belongings."

"I is sorry to see him go," Brother Man said.

Peter was sorry, too. They had patched up their quarrel but he couldn't talk his friend out of leaving. July contended that he had never liked St. Helena. And he had lost his high regard for Dexter Youngblood who was returning to the North and selling his plantations to Negroes for a devilish profit. Looking stubborn, July had also revealed that he intended to look up his old girlfriend, Mariah, which surprised Peter. He had not realized his friend was still mooning over her.

"Maybe if July had come to Edisto with Sister and me he'd feel different about these islands," Brother Man said. "Peter, Edisto is the purtiest place and I'm gon be a rich man. Like you." He poked his friend in the ribs. "But hey, this old steamer's so crowded I ain't bumped into your family yet and I'm longing to see them."

Peter groaned inwardly. "They're not here."

At the last minute a rheumatic pain had crippled his mother and she took to her bed. And he had a terrible argument with Rain and spitefully she stayed at home to vex him. Equally stubborn he had refused to beg her to accompany him with the children.

"Both Rain and my mother are feeling poorly," he told his friend and changed the subject. "You planting cotton?"

"It's white folks what's crazy 'bout growing cotton. I look white to you?"

The door opened and July limped in. "We is almost there."

There was a solemn look on his face and Peter was suddenly glad that his mates were with him. With unspoken accord they stared at Fort Sumter looming up ahead. The last time they had sailed this close to it together, the dreadful possibility existed that its cannons might blast them into a watery grave.

Fort Sumter towered above them in disfigured glory. Its thick brick walls, pounded by smooth-bore shells and rifled 300-pounders, had melted beneath the iron impact. The second tier of casemates had collapsed onto the first tier, burying beneath piles of bricks the barracks where the soldiers had lived. Its parapets had been blasted into shapelessness and most of the portholes were closed.

"Jesus," Brother Man gasped, appalled. He was looking at an apparition, not an ominous fortress.

Quickly the flotilla discharged its passengers. A regiment of soldiers stood guard, white troops on one side and Negro troops on the other, bayonets gleaming on their muskets. They stood at attention as the passengers walked between them, the islanders laughing and waving, unable to contain their joy. Our black soldiers. So handsome. So correct.

Peter remained aboard until the passengers and crew had all disembarked. He discovered upon entering the fort that its devasta-

313

tion was even more vivid inside. Its grounds were littered with rubble and debris, with rotting planks and rusty wheels and the undefeated mud. As the brick walls had been shelled into collapse, the rubble formed a slope which had been shored up with thousands of sandbags rising in layers seven and eight deep. Heavy timbers, also piled high with sandbags, formed the roof of underground shelters which replaced the crumbled barracks. In these dank, dark holes soldiers and slaves had slept and eaten and defecated and gone berserk.

But now there was victory amid the ruins. In the center of the fort rose a new flagstaff and a gigantic platform carpeted with flowers. Four tall pillars festooned with ribbons formed a canopy.

On the platform General Saxton was surrounded by a bevy of military men. Henry Ward Beecher, the speaker of the day, was shaking hands with fellow abolitionists Lloyd Garrison and Dr. J. Leavitt. Clergymen were being greeted warmly by politicians as the military band played lustily. Seated on the platform in the space reserved for them were the teachers and superintendents, finally being recognized for their pioneer work with the contrabands. Miss Abigail was perched like a bird on the edge of her seat. A brand-new schoolhouse had recently been completed at her insistence and she had bought a house at the last tax sale, intending to settle in St. Helena and continue teaching. Her students had progressed remarkably under her tutelage and of all the volunteers she was the most trusted and beloved. The Negroes had withstood harsh tests, proving themselves worthy of citizenship, and the successful Project was being regarded as a guide in reconstructing the South.

Peter moved away from the front of the fort to the gorge where the parapets were totally destroyed. He could see in the harbor two buoys marking the spots where the *Cayenne* sank and the *Housatonic* had been blown up by the submarine. Beyond the buoys to the left was the muddy clump that was Morris Island. He was standing here finally on this sand pit which they had wrestled so long and so bloodily to possess.

The band stopped playing, the festivities were about to begin. He walked back to the edge of the crowd. On the platform an army chaplain was blessing the assembly and the flag, the same flag which had been lowered when the Confederates had fired on this fort and started the war. Rain should be here with me, Peter thought angrily. Why was she always so hardheaded?

Three sailors fastened the flag to the halyard with a floral wreath and then General Anderson stepped forward, his head uncovered, the breeze blowing his gray hair about his face. He had been in command when this flag had fallen. A hush fell upon the ten thousand spectators. They were in the presence of a manly general struggling not to cry.

"After four long long years," he said when he was finally in control, "I restore to its proper place this flag which floated here during peace before the first act of this cruel rebellion. I thank God who has so signally blessed us beyond measure. May all the nations bless and praise the name of the Lord, and proclaim glory to God in the highest, and on earth peace, goodwill toward men."

Peace on earth, Peter repeated silently and it struck him like a thunderbolt. Rain had never been at peace. She had always been on one battlefield or another and he was the donkey's ass at war with her now.

General Anderson grasped the halyard and pulled. The flag, pierced with shot, rose steadily and waved in the breeze. In one spontaneous motion the crowd jumped to its feet, shouting and waving. Their tumultuous merriment was joined by a thunderous hundred-gun salute from the cannons in the fort, the ships in the harbor and the surrounding forts. Smoke rose in billowing clouds. The band played madly. Joyous voices sang. "O say can you see by the dawn's early light . . ."

It was the beginning of a long day of festivities. The abolitionists proclaimed that the soil had drunk blood and was glutted. Millions were in mourning for the men slain in battle. Towns and villages had been razed. The wilderness had reclaimed fruitful fields. The sun had burned to darkness and the moon had turned to blood. But that night had ended and thankfully the people could rejoice and give thanks. No more war. No more accursed secession. No more slavery that had spawned them both.

The vessels sailed to Charleston for more abolitionist speeches at Zion Church, Negroes carrying Lloyd Garrison aloft on black shoulders. Then lavish dining and merrymaking.

Throughout it all Peter was distraught, aching as he was for Rain, regretting her absence and unable to shake his melancholy.

Later he would swear that his mood had been a premonition of disaster. He had felt most depressed at the selfsame time that a fanatic in Ford's Theatre in the nation's capital raised his pistol, took aim and fired. And the tallest tree in the nation fell.

The next morning at sunrise, with Secretary Stanton weeping at his bedside, Abraham Lincoln died.

The words wash in with the tide. We President is dead. Did you hear? In Beaufort the freedmen rush to their churches wailing. The Sesesh won't let us be. They is murdering our friends. No bells tolled you all come, but in panic the islanders hurry to their meeting places to hear the news that Easter Week. It travels by grapevine, leaps over rivers and mountains. Our President is dead.

In Washington, D.C., the procession is miles long following the casket to the Capitol. Thousands line the streets, gather on rooftops, climb trees, weep at the sight of the President's riderless horse trotting behind his coffin, his boots in the stirrups. Black and white soldiers march in front of their cannons. Military bands play dirges. Bells toll. Guns boom. Then the long train ride home to Springfield, Illinois, stopping en route for the soulsick to stare at the coffin and say good-bye to the hollow-faced man inside.

The Sea Islands are not on the road to Illinois so their good-byes are shouted to the wind. Good-bye, Massa Lincoln. God rest you soul, the best friend we Negroes ever had. Mercy Lord. The gov'ment is dead. We all gon be slaves again. No, Peter tells Rain, who is as confused as the others. The government goes on. The Sesesh cain't come back and claim us. That news takes hold but the wailing and gnashing of teeth continue for the dreadful loss of the Great Emancipator.

Lord have mercy on us poor black folks what's lost the best friend we ever had.

Good-bye, Massa Lincoln.

The last outpost of Confederate troops laid down its arms and the Rebel states prepared to reenter the Union. At the eleventh hour, recognizing belatedly the worth of black soldiers, the Confederates had tried to entice Negroes into their desertion-plagued army, promising freedom to any man who enlisted. But that did not work. The war was over.

27

Beaufort

August 1865

"How could the President do that?" Rain wailed. "We is gon lose we home."

She turned away from the stove where she was cooking collard greens to look at Peter seated at the table polishing his boots. He felt like slapping her because she didn't have any better sense than to say out loud what he also feared. Surely they had enough troubles without this confusion but still he had to vehemently contradict her.

"We ain't going to lose this house," he shouted, banging his boot on the table. "It ain't settled yet."

Rain's bottom lip trembled. "Stop hollering. Why every time you comes home, which ain't too often, you has to holler at somebody?"

The somebody she meant was Zee and Petunia, which pulled Peter up short. "I'm sorry," he mumbled, mentally kicked himself for being a donkey's ass.

It wasn't Rain's fault that an impostor was in the White House. No longer visible to the naked eye was the fiery unionist who had thundered that treason was odious. In Peter's mind President Johnson had become a skunk. Flattered by Southern aristocrats, who before the war had treated him with contempt and were now humble suppliants, the President was granting them amnesty and pardons in wholesale numbers.

Warmly the Old Guard—the elite planters, the generals and colonels of the Confederacy—embraced his reconstruction program. Wiping the blood off their hands they raised them to take the oath of allegiance, were pardoned, and restored to their former seats of power. South Carolina's provisional governor wistfully admitted that his people had a lingering hope that slavery could be restored one way or another. With that in mind the Old Guard met in state conventions to rewrite their constitutions. And President Johnson ordered the restitution of all property rights to them with the exception of slaves. Did that include the Sherman lands? And the town houses and plantations sold by the tax commissioners at the two auctions? Peter was not sure and at the moment neither was anyone else. Rumors were flying around like poisoned arrows and he didn't know what to believe.

During the past few months he had seldom been home because General Saxton was busily utilizing every vessel at his disposal to settle freedmen on the Sherman lands before the President's policy crystalized. By midsummer forty thousand freedmen had received possessory titles and were cultivating their little farms. And about seventeen thousand early settlers had already repaid their loans, understanding that clothing, food and fuel supplied to them had not been gifts but advances.

More acreage was being cultivated than ever before on the islands, the cotton and crops in excellent condition. It delighted Peter's eyes to see black farmers on little flatboats taking their produce and poultry to Charleston to sell. But was it all to end now in disaster?

Triumphantly waving their pardon papers, the planters were returning to the islands and putting in a claim for their land. The President graciously responded, decreeing that the thousands of unoccupied acres still held in reserve by the government be returned to their former owners. Reluctantly, General Saxton complied.

The returning planters, though, were experiencing some difficulties. House servants taken along when the planters left the islands, upon discovering that they were now free, promptly departed. Most field hands refused to work for their former masters, declaring they would rather roast in hell. Other hands demanded a share of the crop as payment, which the planters refused to consider.

The Edisto planters had also petitioned for the return of their property. Again President Johnson complied. But General Saxton delayed acting upon petitions concerning the Sherman lands which were being tilled by the settlers. He forwarded the petitions to General Howard, reminding him that the government had promised to protect the freedmen in their ownership. The two generals were both procrastinating, anxiously waiting for Congress to reconvene, hoping that the Radical Republicans would come to the aid of the besieged freedmen.

Rain refused to be mollified. The appearance on the streets of returned planters arrogantly expecting Negroes to step into the gutter to allow them to pass—which cloaked in their newfound dignity, they refused to do—heightened her fears.

And Peter, while trying not to reveal it, felt that he was sinking in quicksand, trapped on all sides. To add to his misery, Stretch had not been among the skeletons released from Andersonville Prison in Georgia, men who had lived in holes scraped out of the earth with their bare hands, their wounds maggot-infested, their clothes caked with mud and their own excrement. No long-legged galoot had emerged.

Peter came home early one afternoon while Rain and the children were still at school to discover Roland Caine striding up and down in his parlor. Both men paused in midstep to warily take each other's measure.

"Peter," Lily cried, obviously relieved to see him, "look who just came to visit. I told him you was away on a trip but would be back around two and Massa said he'd wait."

She had never looked so wrinkled and wizened to Peter, like a dried-up prune, as though their former master had sapped all of her strength. He was as stiffly erect and elegant as ever but a trifle thinner. The early winter in his face had turned to frost, his skin cracked and dry. He was carrying his heavy silver-handled cane which could knock a man's brains out, his commanding presence

319

dominating the room, sucking up the air, leaving Peter short of breath.

"Hello, suh," he said quietly. He had expected this confrontation, having heard that Roland Caine was back in town staying with a friend.

"I'm glad I didn't have to wait long to see you," Caine said as though they had parted company the day before yesterday and nothing significant had happened in between.

But his gaze was so intense Peter had the absurd notion he would be ordered at any moment to strip to the waist or open his mouth to have his teeth checked. He was still wearing his captain's hat and touched it now to reassure himself that it was firmly on his head. The gesture did not go unnoticed by Roland Caine.

"Captain Peter Mango," he said derisively. "Absalom told me you were in the pay of the Yankee swine."

"Yes," Peter said and added defiantly, "thank God for that."

Roland Caine grunted. "Well, we'll see whether you have God to thank or the devil."

Nervously Lily stepped forward, anxious to make Caine feel welcome. "How 'bout something to eat, Massa? They is some cold chicken and biscuits and . . ."

"I didn't come here, Lily, to eat cold chicken."

He did not deign to explain what he had come for but was looking around the room with a proprietary air. When the silence grew oppressive Peter stepped into the breach.

"How is Mistress Joanne? Is she here in Beaufort, too?"

Roland looked pointedly at Lily who was drooping. "No, she's at Rolling Acres where we lived out the war. It took her months to recover from the blow you dealt her, Lily. Such treachery. It was hard for her to believe you were such an ungrateful wench, deserting her when she needed you most. Her trusted friend."

Lily straightened up beneath the onslaught, its virulence reviving her. "Her friend, you say? Yes. But I was also her slave and that came first."

"A slave who was never horsewhipped," Caine said, his thin lips drawn in a tight line. "Perhaps that would have taught you some respect." He glared angrily at the woman who had been his nanny. "While you've been living here in comfort your mistress has endured untold hardship. After Jethro and Selena left . . ."

"They did," Peter gasped, delighted.

". . . disappeared in the middle of the night leaving your mistress sick and alone."

Roland Caine did not mention that Joanne had recovered nicely, to his surprise. Although complaining periodically about the unreliability of darkies, she had learned to adequately do her own cooking and housework. She even did his bookkeeping for the foodstuff he raised for the Rebel army, an enterprise which left him bankrupt. When the war ended the Confederates owed him thirty thousand dollars and he had on hand a like amount of their worthless scrip. They had earned his undying hostility as had the Yankees who had not only confiscated his property and freed his slaves but also became their teachers and advisers. But President Johnson, a true Southerner after all, was reversing that madness.

Peter, wondering when Roland Caine intended to get to the point, for clearly this was not a social call, suddenly remembered what Ellsworth had said. *My father will disown me, his disgraceful turncoat son.*

"Suh, tell me, please. How is young Master Ellsworth? I saw him when he was in the stockade and I wonder did——"

"He's dead." The words exploded from Caine like a bullet, its force causing him to shudder. "He was killed in the line of duty. In Columbia. By that butcher Tecumseh Sherman."

"Dear God," Lily moaned. Her legs wobbled and she stumbled to a chair.

Peter sighed. "I'm sorry to hear that." He felt a well of sadness. Poor Ellsworth had been exchanged after all but had not disgraced his father by defecting.

Attempting to be comforting, Peter murmured, "I know it ain't easy, suh, to bury your only chile."

"It will not have been in vain," Caine said tersely. "I refuse to let Ellsworth's death be meaningless." A muscle in his jaw twitched, his fierce gaze fixed on Peter. "Yesterday I saw Absalom and was kind enough to offer him a job as foreman at Caine's Landing. I expect the plantation to be back in my possession within a few days. I warned him he was going to lose his land, that it was going to be returned to its rightful owner. And if he wanted to consider my offer he should contact me at Mr. Lucas's house before I left for Rolling Acres." Roland's lips tightened. "Absalom told me straight away that he wasn't interested. He was working for himself and intended to stay that way come hell or high water. The bumbling idiot."

Lily struggled to her feet. "You is staying with Massa Luke? That terrible man? I saw him with my own eyes shoot Benjie dead."

"The nigra was deserting him. He deserved to die."

The silence in the room was deadly. Here were two more dastardly deserters, mother and son, being regarded with icy contempt by their former master. Peter put an arm out to steady Lily.

"Sit back down," he said gently. "Never mind. It's all right."

"No," Roland Caine bellowed, "it's not all right. When my plantation has been returned to me, and my house, which is now a bloody hospital, and this cottage, only then will it be all right. I came here to find out if you two had a shred of decency left, a shred of remorse, but like Absalom you've been corrupted by your Yankee handlers. Well take fair warning, before the ink dries on my deeds I'm throwing you black scoundrels off my property."

Finally, Peter thought, it was out in the open. He swept his hat off his head. "I paid cash on the barrelhead for this here house," he said, "and you're no longer welcome in it. Good day, suh."

"Start packing now, you black baboon," Roland Caine shouted. "I'll be back with force if necessary."

After he left, Lily moaned, "They ain't gon ever let we go. Once white folks own a slave they hangs on worse than a hound dog treeing a possum."

Edisto Island

Brother Man and Sister sat in a pew on the right-hand side in the first row. They were among the early arrivals, but soon the church was crowded with more than a thousand freedmen. They were raucous, there was nothing sanctified about the gathering as they faced General Oliver Otis Howard standing on the rostrum, his youthful face sad. On one side of him two planters were seated, and on the other side was the local Freedmen's Bureau agent, Mr. Shields, universally disliked by the Negro settlers.

President Johnson had sent General Howard a direct order to proceed to Edisto Island and try to effect a mutually satisfactory agreement between the settlers and their former owners. The planters were willing, the President noted, to care for the Negroes and use their labor. The church was stuffy, its stoves smoking as General Howard passed on this information to the settlers, loathing his task.

"I be damn," Brother Man said to Sister, a genuine look of surprise on his face. "After we has sweated to plant we crops, they is gon take the land away from us?"

That was the gist of the situation and the crowd roared "No" at the men on the rostrum.

A one-armed soldier stood up and, facing the one-armed general, said, "You aim to take our land who fought the Sesesh in bloody battle after battle and give it back to them?"

"It is the President's order," Howard replied, his voice pleading. "My friends, you are free to go wherever you please, we can praise God for that, and free to choose whoever you wish to work for. The planters on the mainland have already recovered their land and the President believes it only fair that Sea Island planters do likewise."

"No," the settlers groaned again.

A young man shouted from the balcony, "You is asking men what shot they masters on the battlefield to now ask them for bread and shelter for their wives and children?"

"Never," the Negroes roared.

Their voices were so strident, so angry, that General Howard, sweating in his uniform loaded down with braid, sought to calm them. "Let us sing a hymn," he suggested, "and let the words of God soothe our troubled brows."

A woman moaned, "How can we sing the Lord's song in a strange land?"

But they did sing for this was a funeral. Tears clogged in tight throats made their voices tremble.

> Nobody knows the trouble I've seen
> Nobody knows but Jesus . . .

Tears, too, were in General Howard's eyes. When the singing

ended he asked one of the planters to speak to the crowd, to assure them of his goodwill. The man stepped forward.

"I know some of you," he said, his manner conciliatory, and indeed there were several of his former slaves present. "And you know me as having been a fair-minded master." There were groans from several locations in the church contesting that assumption. The planter cleared his throat and took a new tack. "I have capital and you have labor, so let us join together." Mentioning that he had taken the oath of allegiance and had been pardoned by the President, he indicated his willingness to hire all his former bondsmen and pay them a fair wage. He was agreeable to continuing the schools and taking care of the indigent.

In reply an elderly black man stood up in the front row. Leaning on his cane he said clearly and succinctly: "I have listened to you and if you are sincere and honest you ought to set off one thousand acres of your land and give it to the children of the poor black people who have suffered under slavery."

"Amen," Brother Man shouted.

The crowd roared its approval and General Howard his disaffection. "We must develop a more Christian attitude," he protested. "We should forgive our enemies from the bottom of our hearts as I did though I lost my arm in battle."

"He also must have lost his mind," a woman murmured to Sister who nodded.

A committee was appointed by General Howard to work out a compromise—the two planters, the Freedmen's Bureau agent Mr. Shields, the one-armed soldier and another settler. They repaired to a small room to discuss the matter but reappeared a short time later to report an impasse.

"We will not sign work contracts," the soldier reported to the unanimous cheers of the congregation. "When a man comes to a river if he don't have a boat, he takes a log. If we cannot own the land we will rent it but won't ever again work for our former brutal masters."

The planters declared their refusal to rent and General Howard sided with them. In a loud voice he told the assembly that after the crop in the ground was harvested, the plantations on Edisto Island would be returned to the planters. The freedmen had a right to move but any who remained on their little farms would have to work for the rightful owners.

A voice from the balcony shouted, "We will protect our land with muskets if need be."

"I say amen to that again," Brother Man bellowed, standing up.

The whole church, it seemed, was instantly on its feet, shouting its indignation. Except Sister, who was huddled in her seat frightened, a speck of foam moistening the corners of her mouth.

Beaufort

It was a restless night for Peter, turning and tossing in bed next to Rain. Roland Caine's vindictiveness rankled. The man intended to put him and his family into the street and Peter didn't know which rumor to believe. Despite the President's leniency, Reverend Ferdinand was insisting that the town houses and plantations sold by the tax commissioners would not be affected. Maybe the reverend should tell that to Roland Caine, Peter thought, blinking at the shadows in the darkened room. He finally drifted into an uneasy sleep.

Zee was more than restless. In the spooky midnight a nightmare chased the child out of her alcove bed. In panic she raced down the hall pursued by the bogey man. Opening the bedroom door and whimpering for her mother, the girl scrambled into bed with her.

Peter, half asleep, knew it was Zee but the specters were with her. The gray-eyed men with wheat for hair were in his room. In his bed. Reaching for Rain.

"Get out," he yelled. Flailing out with his arms, boxing with shadows, Peter's fist knocked Zee to the floor.

Too frightened to cry—she'd been hit before—the child lay petrified in a shaft of moonlight. Just so had she been shoved into a slave coffle on James Island and ever since been passed from hand to hand. *Get out.* Stumbling to her feet she ran.

Rain jumped out of bed to follow her. "Zee, wait!"

Her cry brought Peter to his senses. They were gone. The demons and Zee and his wife. Trembling, he got out of bed and put on his clothes, taking his time because that's what he needed. Time to screw his head back on. Time to stop acting like a madman. He left off his boots which were for stomping and padded on bare feet down the hall to the alcove.

Rain was in bed with the girls, her arms around them both, Zee weeping on her mother's breast. Silently Rain looked at Peter then turned her head away.

"I was having a nightmare," he said. "Zee, I never meant to hit you. I'm sorry."

The girl squirmed closer to her mother whose arm tightened protectively around her. Peter wanted to crawl into bed with them and weep. He had never felt so miserable. So alone.

"Rain . . ."

She dove into silence. Her eyelids fluttered and closed, shutting out the unbearable sight of him.

Peter returned to their bedroom and avoided looking at himself in the mirror. He had socked Zee hard enough to scramble her poor brains. *If thy right hand offend thee cut it off.* He studied his calloused hands. If he cut off one of them would that satisfy Rain? Would she understand then how sorry he was? And forgive him? A stupid turd so blind he couldn't separate a haunt in his head from a skinny little girl.

A footfall made him whirl around. Rain was standing in the doorway in the lace nightgown he had bought for her in Philadelphia, her face drawn and weary.

"Peter," she said sadly, "we cain't go on this way."

"I know," he agreed. "But . . ."

"We is sneaking 'round like thieves in the night. You is scared to see the light of day in this house and I been favoring you 'cause I was scared, too. But I knew it had to end. You cain't stand them chil'ren. I knows it. They knows it and is scared to death of you. I seen how hard you been trying but we all is miserable and it ain't gon stop lessen I ends it."

"Rain, it was an accident. I didn't . . ."

"Like it's an accident you stays on you boat most of the time she's in port?"

He felt like an idiot. "There's always something to do on the *Swanee.* I have to order food for the crew and pay them their wages and . . ."

"Peter, I is gon leave you. There ain't no other way."

Dumbly he watched her cross the room and sit down in a chair, clasping her hands together to keep them from trembling. His heart stopped beating, its emptiness promising him eternal damnation.

"No," he whispered. "I won't let you go."

"You cain't stop me. It ain't in your hands. I broke my promise to God, first 'bout Zee and Petunia and they was taken from me. Then 'bout li'l Peewee and he died. And now all this."

With a bounding leap Peter was at Rain's side grabbing her shoulders. "We got to go through that again?" He felt like shaking her until her teeth fell out. "Zee and Petunia were taken because it was slavery time and we had no rights. Peewee died because there was an epidemic of smallpox. Hundreds of other folks died too. Why you have to make yourself responsible for everything?"

Rain pushed him away. "You also done changed. And that's my punishment, too. All them months you was with Chloe and now . . ."

"She meant nothing to me. I told you that."

". . . and now you hates my li'l girls."

Peter shook his head, denying the evidence. "Don't say that." Did he really hate them? Was he that accursed? "It's just that I cain't forget what they daddies did to you. But I is desperately trying to like those girls. All I need is a little more time."

"You have been trying, Peter. I know that but you cain't do it."

Tears welled up in Rain's eyes. She expected punishment, demanded it since that had been her lot, the price to pay for a moment's grace. As a child, as a woman, daring to love someone meant a hurricane was brewing to blow them away. It was a harsh lesson but she finally had to accept it as gospel. Give up the whole in order to keep a part and pray that God would turn His vengeful eye elsewhere. Peter was babbling about how he loved her but Rain wasn't listening.

"Hush," she said as though to a child, and put her finger across his lips. "It's the only way to get a little peace. I'll take the girls and . . ."

"No," he shouted. "You can take Zee and Petunia but Glory stays with me."

Rain jumped to her feet. Startling Peter with her ferocity, she beat him in the chest with her fists. "I'm not letting another chile be taken from me. Not by you. Not by anybody."

He grabbed her hands, imprisoned them. "You ain't the only one that's lost a child or have you forgotten? I didn't get to see Peewee alive because you didn't let me know he was dying."

Rain wrenched herself free. For a moment, too shocked to speak, her mouth worked soundlessly. "You is punishing me," she whispered. "I cain't believe you is . . ."

"I don't care what you believe," Peter yelled. "You're crazy like your mother. You can go but Glory stays and that's final."

In the morning Rain requested a carriage to move her belongings and those of the two children. She had dressed quickly upon arising as though being unclothed was to be vulnerable. Now decently covered she planted herself firmly in front of Peter, her auburn eyes defiant.

Her determination devastated him. Death could not have had a greater impact. His own death. Had he survived the war for this? Better to have been caught and hung by the Sesesh. Or gone down with the *Cayenne* to a seaman's grave. A god-awful misery bruised his heart, every beat against his rib cage flooding him with pain. Rain, baby. I cain't lose you. I cain't. But there was also guilt growling in his gut. He had added to the pain of this tiny woman he loved who had been so brutally manhandled.

"Rain. Forgive me. I didn't mean what I said about your mother. And I won't take Glory from you. I'll go if that's what you want and you stay here with the children." At least for as long as I have this house, he thought dully, wondering what other misfortunes lay in store for him.

Rain did not object. "When are you leaving?" she asked coldly.

Peter's mind reeled, groped in desperation for a way out. "Let me tell you the truth first," he begged. "I was too ashamed to mention it before, a grown man seeing spooks."

"Spooks? What you talking?"

"Your master and his son. They're here in this house bedeviling me."

Rain's eyes widened with interest. "They is dead?"

"They don't have to be dead to hound me. They're evil spirits. In this here house." He didn't admit they were really in his head whenever he looked at Zee and Petunia. Adamantly he insisted, "They're in these rooms. In the walls. It's them I be lashing out at, not your girls."

"Evil spirits?" Rain moistened her lips with the tip of her tongue as if to nourish the idea. "There's ways to loose evil spirits from a house, you know."

"Yeh?" Peter feigned innocence.

"Maum Betty's got a powerful cure. Goober dust."

"You know I don't cotton to Maum Betty," he protested but not too strongly.

Rain frowned. She had steeled herself to leave, and now spooks? "Maybe," she suggested, and paused to bite her bottom lip, "maybe we can try it. The goober dust."

She was so trusting it made Peter ache. "I don't know . . ."

"If it works . . ." She pulled up short, making no promises but the inference was clear.

"All right," he whispered, his heart racing. "Bring on your goober dust."

Maum Betty arrived, her head tied up in an old burlap bag with twigs sticking out of it. Fully six feet tall, she was a fierce-looking muscular woman who never smiled. Peter disliked her on sight and she wasn't fond of him either.

Generously Maum Betty spread her magic potion, a thin film of dust, over the front doorsill. With equal care she powdered the back door and all the thresholds in the house, mumbling incantations as her broad behind invaded every room, Peter and Rain following her as hushed as frightened children.

"Them evil spirits cain't survive here for long," Maum Betty said in parting, piercing Peter with *her* evil eye.

But his demons had been invited and remained in the coming days as Peter had known they would. He concealed this fact from Rain by biting his tongue, staying his hand.

"We has to give the potion a chance to work," he pleaded. "If it don't then I'll pack up and leave like I promised."

28

Edisto Island
October 1865

The word spread like fire in dry timber. *They done put they big feet on we land.*

The freedmen dropped their plows, jumped into their wagons or on the back of mules and hurried to the main road. Dried-out corn stalks stood waist high on either side of the road. Beyond a lane of trees, there were acres of cotton fields yet to be harvested, their bursting buds looking like a sea of snow-white foam. Here and there could be seen a cottage or little house a farmer had built himself.

Brother Man was resolute, his eyes steely and his lips clamped fiercely together. Riding in a neighbor's wagon, he was determined that white men would not rob him again. There were about fifty Negroes in the caravan spread out along the road.

"There they be," someone in the front shouted.

It was Mr. Shields, the Freedmen's Bureau agent, and five white men on horseback.

Brother Man shielded his eyes with a cupped hand and peered into a cloud of dust. The caravan halted, blocking the road as the party on horseback galloped up, Mr. Shields in the lead.

"You boys move out the road," he said, "and let these men through."

"Who they be?" a voice questioned.

Another Negro answered, "Planters, that's who." He had recognized his former master, who guided his horse forward.

"You know me, Hank," the planter called out. "Tell your friends to move. We've come peaceably to look at our property which is being returned to us."

"This is Sherman land the gov'ment sold to us," Brother Man hollered, standing up in the wagon. "By what right——"

Mr. Shields pulled out his pistol. "This is my right. Clear the road, I say."

At the sight of the gun, the incensed settlers jumped down from their wagons and swarmed forward. A shot rang out. A black man swayed and fell. Shouting ferociously, his comrades surged ahead brandishing hoes and pitchforks. Before this onslaught, the horsemen yanked their steeds around and in another cloud of dust galloped away.

"Damn Sesesh," a settler shouted. "Don't come back on our land."

"One of our men is shot," a voice announced.

The Negroes returned to their wagons. The big man lay on the ground where he had fallen, a bullet hole in his temple. He was quite dead. Brother Man.

Charleston
November 1865

Peter was selected as a delegate to the Freedmen's Convention in Charleston where Negroes were meeting from all parts of the state to protest the Black Codes. But he did not go. He had the time, the *Swanee* was temporarily idle, President Johnson having ordered General Saxton to cease settling Negroes on the confiscated lands. Peter had the time but decided not to journey too far from home, afraid Rain might not be there when he returned. The thought of it made him panicky.

He had cried bitter tears upon learning of Brother Man's death.

We have come to this? he asked God who was dry-eyed and did not reply. Why they kill Brother Man? When they gon let us be?

Hard on the heels of that tragedy came other devastating news. The Black Codes. With his eyes still wet Peter cursed the new state laws which intended to shove Negroes back into a semblance of slavery, to maintain them as a lowly paid labor force. The smoky demons surrounding Zee and Petunia were gleeful. "We've got your black ass," they taunted. Peter cursed them too, but silently, mindful that the goober dust was supposed to be working.

Outrages were escalating. There had been riots in Charleston and Savannah, mobs of whites attacking the former slaves. And closer to home, on Luke Lucas's plantation outside of Beaufort, a field hand who refused to contract for work or move had been hung. And a woman and her child beaten and dispossessed.

The Beaufort delegates to the Charleston convention had been selected at a mass meeting held at the Baptist church, the selfsame place where the first black soldiers had been recruited. "And this is our reward?" the Negro pastor, usually a mild-mannered man, had thundered. "These Black Codes spawned by the devil?" He was selected as a delegate along with Sergeant Prince Rivers, still in the uniform of the 1st South Carolina Regiment, and Peter.

Ever since President Lincoln's assassination freedmen had been meeting in assemblies all over the South—in Mississippi, in Georgia—to denounce the laws being speedily enacted to curb their climb toward equality. They demanded schools for their children, equal job opportunity, all the rights of citizens, and the ballot so they could protect their freedom. South Carolina had just enacted into law its Black Codes eliciting anguished howls from its Negro populace.

"You want to come with me, honeybunch?" Peter had asked Rain hopefully, with the intention of keeping an eye on her. She had looked so forlorn he yearned to kiss her but was not yet back in her good graces.

"I best stay here with the chil'ren," she had replied. "I reckon mostly menfolks will be there anyway."

Menfolks but not him, Peter decided. Leaving Rain at this particular moment was a chance he dare not take. An alternate replaced him as a delegate.

It was a decision that haunted Peter. Like fingering a rotten tooth to make sure the pain was still there, he went to the dock the day the delegation left for Charleston. Are you daft, nigger? he asked himself derisively, shivering in his pea jacket. Why are you standing on this stupid pier instead of being on your way to Charleston?

Disgusted with himself he went home to further worry his rotten tooth. In the parlor, after throwing a log in the fireplace, he picked up the newspaper which had in it a digest of the Black Codes. He sat on the settee for several minutes holding the paper and staring into the crackling flames.

"Peter?"

Rain had crept into the room so silently he had not heard her. Sitting down beside him she touched the newspaper. "This the one what got those awful laws in it?"

He nodded.

"You promised to read it to me."

He sighed. "I already told you what it says."

"Tell me again." She, too, had a rotten tooth.

"It says we're niggers, Rain, now and forever." Peter spoke slowly, looking down at the newspaper every now and again. "It says it's a crime for us to refuse to sign a work contract. Unemployed Negroes, the homeless, the disobedient, will be arrested as vagrants and hired out to farmers without pay. It says we cain't work on our own except as farmers or servants unless we get a special license and pay a special tax. Folks who quit their jobs without good reason will forfeit their wages.

"It says farm laborers have to work from sunup to sundown and cain't sell no produce without permission. Li'l chil'ren can be apprenticed out to work and learn a trade and be sent to school for six weeks a year if one is nearby. Runaway apprentices and servants will be returned to their bosses and flogged. Bosses can whip folks under eighteen. Adults can be whipped on a judge's say-so."

Peter picked up the newspaper and read directly from it. "Negroes cannot migrate into the state without paying a thousand-dollar bond and their good conduct guaranteed by a resident. Negroes cannot vote. Or join the forty-five militia regiments being organized to secure public order. Or keep a firearm. They can be arrested by any white person and if found guilty of a misdemeanor they will be flogged, confined to hard labor or sent out of the state. If found guilty of insurrection, homicide, housebreaking, assaulting a white woman, impersonating her husband for sexual purposes, stealing baled cotton, a mule or a horse, the penalty is capital punishment, death by hanging."

In disgust Peter flung the newspaper to the floor.

Rain sat quite still beside him, half of her face illumined by firelight, the other half in shadows. "White folks," she said, groaning. "One way or another they gon make us they slaves again."

Her words infuriated Peter. On top of everything else he had to live with the simple-minded? "Don't be a donkey's ass," he said coldly. "You sound too stupid."

"Who you calling stupid, Peter Mango?"

His voice rose. "Who's in this room with me?"

"You's the stupid one. You shoulda gone off to Charleston 'stead of staying home to yell at me."

"You're right about that," he yelled as Rain stood up and, with her head held high, marched out of the room.

Trying to control his rage, Peter quit the parlor, too, and stomped upstairs. He met Zee on the landing. She cowered at the sight of him, her eyes wide with fright, but not so the pale faces already entangled in her hair. They were laughing. Jeering. Hateful. Peter lunged forward to strangle them. With a muffled cry, Zee darted beneath his outstretched arm to scurry past him and fly down the stairs.

Peter stumbled into his bedroom and slammed the door. Trembling, he stood in front of the long gilded mirror. A wild-eyed man with thick bushy hair stared back at him.

You is going crazy.

I know.

You almost strangled Zee.

The enormity of it smashed into him like a blow. No, he whispered, reeling backward. I ain't gon let you all do this to me. Whoresons, where are you? Come out, damn you. Stop hiding in the girls' hair. Fight me like a man in the open. He wheeled around the room in a frenzy, looking for his demons. Come out, you diseased sons of a diseased mother. Where are you? He kicked open the closet door. Peered under the bed. Cursed until he was hoarse.

He trembled in his slave skin that he would shed if he could like a snake, shed his hide and let a new skin grow, black but free from the stigma of slavery. Dear God, he prayed, almighty God, help me. His eyes filled with tears. Help me, Lord. Do Jesus. He was weeping, hoarse gutteral cries shaking him.

His outburst ceased on a sob and he was empty. Mutely, Peter stared into the mirror at his craggy, wet face. He stood there for a long time drained and hollow. Then suddenly he saw it. In the mirror. A tendril of smoke. He watched it blossom, clouding his image. A bulbous nose appeared in the haze. Then two eyes. There they were in his mirror. The faces of two jeering white men.

Listen, Peter said fervently, slavery time is over. He smashed his fist into the mirror. Shards flew. A piece of glass embedded itself in the back of his hand. Blood oozed, dripped to the floor. Get out of my house, he yelled at the white images in the shattered mirror. The faces disintegrated into smoky tendrils. Then slowly, as if a soft wind was blowing, the haze drifted into nothingness.

Mesmerized, Peter stared into the mirror which now reflected only jagged pieces of himself. He had commanded the demons to go and they had departed. He took a deep breath and stepped into the void. Come back, he whispered. Nothing happened for a moment. He was about to panic when a puff of smoke appeared, the white faces in them no longer leering. Peter waved his bloody hand. "Be gone." The faces crumbled. Disappeared.

Once more he tried it, just to be sure, looking not in the mirror but at a blood spot on the floor. Let me see your plug-ugly faces again, he said, not unkindly since he was in control. There they were. In the bloodstain. Looking weepy. Go, Peter commanded, and this time they blinked out quickly like a doused light.

Peter was no longer trembling but breathing heavily when Rain burst into the room.

"Peter, I heard . . ." She stopped, staring at his bleeding hand and the splintered glass on the floor. She rushed forward and raised his hand to assess its damage.

"I . . . I . . . stumbled," he replied, still dazed.

"And crashed into the mirror? Dear God, you is bleeding like a stuck pig."

Peter submitted to his wife's ministrations, sitting down meekly as she washed his wound in a basin of water, then doused it with some of her ill-smelling herbs before bandaging up his hand, all the while mumbling that he had smashed to bits the prettiest mirror she'd ever had. Fact is she never had a piece of a mirror before, much less such a large one.

"There now," she said, patting the bandage. "I hope it don't hurt too much."

"No, it don't hurt at all."

Actually, he was feeling blissful. Whatever had trapped him in the power of those white devils was no longer beyond his control. But how could he tell Rain what he barely understood but felt in his bones?

"Honeybunch," he lied, looking at her with his impish smile, "it was your goober dust."

"What?"

"Maum Betty's goober dust has done it. Rid this house of them white demons."

Rain's eyes lit up like candles. "Peter," she whispered as though afraid to speak out loud. "You is sure? You is gon stop hollering at Zee and Petunia, scaring them so? You is sure you can like them?" There was yearning in her voice but she was looking at him soberly without guile. It was clear that she would leave him otherwise.

"I'm certain." Peter understood his life depended upon it.

He stared at Rain overwhelmed with tenderness. He had been a madman to hurt her so. Well, no brutes, including himself, would ever abuse her again. His feeling of bliss expanded, a sweetness coursing through him like the aftermath of lovemaking.

"Baby cakes," he said, his good hand cradling the side of her face, "do you know how much I love you?"

Rain smiled. Nodding, she turned her head and kissed the inside of his palm.

29

Charleston

January 1868

Glory and the girls wanted to accompany them to the dock but Rain said, "No, stay home with you grandmother," craving this time alone with Peter. So they all hugged and kissed him goodbye and in the confusion his carpetbag was almost left behind.

It was Zee who called out, "Uncle Peter. Your bag."

She was smiling, no longer flat-chested at fourteen nor frightened of him, which had not happened overnight. Everyone understood that Glory was her father's favorite, but he had managed to be fair to Zee and Petunia and by now he liked them. Whenever Peter glanced in their direction and even thought he saw smoky demons he would look at the jagged scar on his hand and murmur, "Slavery time is over."

"You gon miss you boat," his mother said.

Lily had reached a fragile old age and had paused there, a little forgetful but far from senile. She preferred to forget that Hiram had died from a heart attack and occasionally would wonder aloud when was he coming to visit her as promised. Peter had been in Charleston at the time and tearfully had held the dying man in his arms.

Peter hugged his mother again. "Don't you be worrying now, you hear? I'll be back home soon's this business is over."

He helped Rain climb onto the coachman's seat and sprinted up beside her. The children waved at him.

"Good-bye, Daddy."

"Good-bye, Uncle Peter."

Peter picked up the reins. The mare knew the way to the dock and would be there too soon for Rain, who had replaced her head wrap with a flowered hat and was tightly clutching Peter's arm. She had visions, not unreasonably, of hooded horsemen shooting him down.

Terror was stalking the Southland masked in white sheets, raggedy poor whites riding with the likes of former Confederate general Nathan Forrest, now the Imperial Wizard of the Ku Klux Klan. And there were the unmasked terrorists, the Regulators. The Knights of the White Camellia. The police. The white militias. All told, more than a thousand Negroes and their political allies had been murdered during the past year. The governor was loath to use the force at his command, the black militias, fearful, he stated, that it might cause a race riot. The Negro regiments had been honorably discharged except for about eighty-five thousand who remained in the military to assist the government in maintaining order. Reports indicated that Negro soldiers returning home in the South were being brutally treated.

Sitting next to Peter Rain shivered, her bottom lip drooping. "How come it's always you what has to go?" She did not want him out of her sight.

"Because I'm an imbecile," he replied and chuckled, thinking about his Philadelphia schoolteacher.

"Yes, you is," Rain agreed, "but how come it's always you what . . ."

Peter squeezed her hand. "That's the selfsame thing you asked me when I became a registrar."

And indeed it was, Rain wondering why he was always raising his head up above the crowd inviting a sharpshooter to take dead aim.

After President Johnson fired General Saxton in '66 for being too sympathetic to Negroes, Peter was released from service and became a registrar of voters and a political organizer. With General Saxton out of the way, the militia brutally moved in on the settlers on the Sherman lands, tore up their deeds and demanded that they work for their former masters or move. Prodded at gunpoint whole villages packed up their children and put their feet in the road again. But the town houses and plantations sold by the tax commissioners were exempt and not returned to the planters. Peter, secure in the butcherman's cottage, did not again see Roland Caine, now living with his wife at Rolling Acres.

Sister was less fortunate than Peter. Uprooted from Edisto, she moved in with Cindy. The two women worked well together although Sister never fully recovered from Brother Man's death and Cindy still clung to the notion that somewhere Stretch was alive. At times Peter felt impatient with her. You had to bury the dead, not carry their corpse around but then again, maybe she was right to keep on hoping. Cindy insisted, "If I thought he were dead I could grieve but I ain't got that feeling."

Her farm was prospering as were those of most of the other settlers on St. Helena, which was now practically an all-black island. Most of the Northerners who had bought plantations at the tax sales sold their property to the freedmen and returned home. Miss Abigail remained, still beloved, her school expanded and thriving.

July was thriving, too. Upon his return to Charleston he had joined those folks roaming about the city who were looking for their kin sold away during slavery or lost during the war, and he had been rewarded. He found Mariah in a refugee camp, looking like a haunt but overjoyed at seeing him. They were married now and living over his carpentry shop. Recently he sent a little statuette of Peter to him. It was a remarkable likeness, his features carved into the wood, his eyes, his nose, his bushy head of hair.

As a political organizer Peter was part of a group of men conducting their campaigns from cotton field to cotton field, meeting in churches and barns. Republicans from the North, white and black, came down to lend their expertise to home-grown leaders. Peter traveled about the countryside with them corralling both Negroes and whites into the Republicans' Loyalty Clubs, realizing that the night riders were trying not only to terrify Negroes and prevent them from politicking but also to keep poor whites from joining them. Terror succeeded with the fainthearted, inasmuch as being tortured or hung on a cottonwood tree was a terrible price to pay.

Others refused to be intimidated. "The planters never cared a hoot about us," a white farmer told Peter upon joining the Loyalty Club. "They called us white niggers. Took the best fertile land and left the harsh scrub for us. I ain't never had no love for them."

There were also planters who were experiencing a change of heart, Dr. Agnew Travis among them. The Negroes, including Lily, had demolished his Beaufort home the night the two Rebel forts fell. Dr. Travis had left town a secessionist but returned full of abolitionist fever, railing against the Black Codes and the criminals executing them. He joined the Negroes who were demanding one-man one-vote, the right to ride on any conveyance, travel on any steamboat and educate their children in any schoolhouse. The political clubs proliferated in the black belt and Piedmont areas.

The planters, taking due note, modified their tactics. "We are your friends," they told their former slaves, "and know what's best for you better than the damn Yankees we wish to replace in your affection." The planters invited the freedmen to barbecues and picnics, provided sumptuous food and drink and politicians on the stump promising the moon in exchange for their votes. The Negroes ate the barbecue and when given the vote by Congress went to the polls and voted the straight Republican ticket.

The steamer was in its slip and folks were boarding it when Peter's carriage reached the dock. Rain, sounding pathetic, said, "You can still find someone to go in you place."

"I cain't," he said gently, understanding her fears, which he shared. But no threat of danger could deter him. Too much was at stake.

The elite planters, returned to their state legislatures by President Johnson, had enraged the Radical Republicans by sending to Congress from their Confederacy its vice-president, four generals, five colonels, six cabinet members and fifty-eight legislators. The South thus returned to Congress stronger than when it had left. Then only three fifths of black people had been counted to determine representation but now that they were free all were counted. The Southerners flexed their muscle, threatening to revise the tariff, disestablish the national banks, repudiate the national debt and hamper the new corporate enterprises with strict regulations. Their interests threatened, Northern industry rushed to embrace the Radicals' program. Congress wrested Reconstruction from President Johnson and came to within one vote of impeaching him. They nullified the Black Codes and dismissed the South's state legislators.

State conventions were now being held throughout the South to write democratic constitutions by delegates chosen by the new electorate—a coalition of loyalist and poor whites, Northern emigrés, supposedly reformed slaveholders and black men. Peter had been elected as one of Beaufort's delegates, along with Dr. Travis.

"We are going to write a grand constitution," he told Rain who was regarding him glumly. He understood that Negroes who had attended the Charleston Freedmen's Convention were also delegates now—a school principal who had been educated abroad, an A.M.E. minister, and an army major. Peter felt awed at being selected to serve with them.

At the moment Rain didn't care that they would debate and hammer out an egalitarian constitution that would increase rights for women, give the state a divorce law and free public schools, a homestead act to primarily protect poor whites and manhood suffrage without property qualifications. Segregation on public transportation and facilities would be outlawed. And for the first time the political arena would be opened to poor whites and Negroes.

Peter vaulted to the ground then lifted Rain down from the carriage. Her cheeks were wet.

"Baby cakes, it was more dangerous when we escaped on the *Swanee*. You didn't cry then."

"No," she said, and dabbed at her eyes with the back of her hand. "And I ain't crying now."

Resolutely, Rain settled the flowered hat more firmly on her head and swallowed her last sniffle.

Peter sighed. Everything they had lived through, their escape on the *Swanee* and all that had happened since, had led to this. It was necessary for him to go to Columbia to ensure their freedom. He understood that but did Rain?

"I have to go," he said.

"I know," Rain agreed. She touched his cheek with her finger-tips. "But I ain't gon stand for no foolishness so don't go and get youself shot."

"I promise," Peter said, his lips curved in a half-smile. "No bullet holes."

They kissed, then Rain let him go, consoling herself that he was a man who always kept his promise.

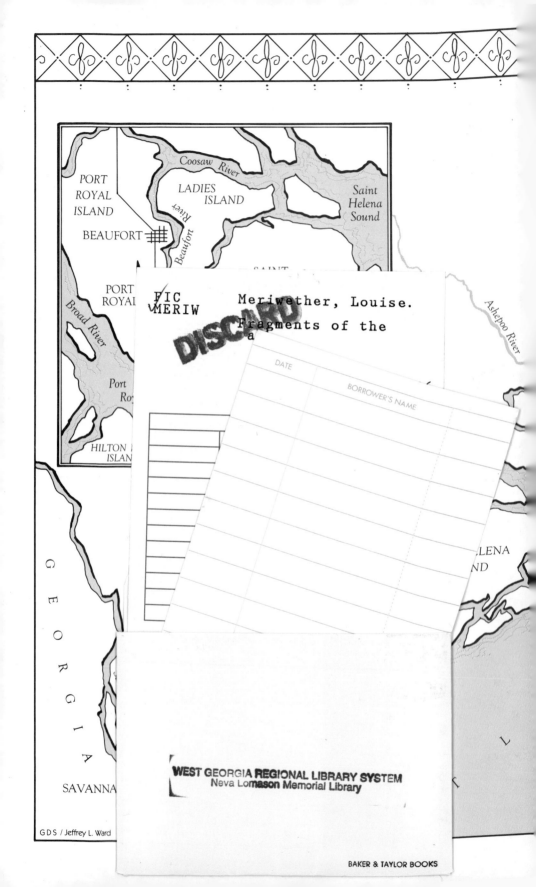

PORT
ROYAL
ISLAND

Coosaw River

LADIES
ISLAND

Saint
Helena
Sound

BEAUFORT

Beaufort River

SAINT

PORT
ROYAL

Broad River

Port
Ro

Ashepoo River

HILTON
ISLAND

LENA
ND

G
E
O
R
G
I
A

SAVANNA

GDS / Jeffrey L. Ward